PRAI
THE SE.

"If you like your detectives hard-boiled but with a redeeming soft center then step forward Xavier Priest, your newest PI hero. In *The Seminarian*, Hart Hanson has sent his gloriously unforgettable characters into a wondrously twisty-turny mystery that the reader will never want to end. More please!"
—Stephen Fry

"*The Seminarian* is a fast-paced crime thriller with smart, snarky characters and a deep affection for Venice Beach culture. Hanson has hit his stride on this one, I hope we see more of Xavier Priestly and the gang. Highly recommended."
—Christopher Moore, *New York Times* bestselling author of *Lamb, Noir,* and *Razzmatazz*

"Fast-paced, witty, and ebullient, *The Seminarian* is a thoroughly satisfying mystery with a thoughtful heart. It's a joy to spend time with Xavier Priestly and his crew."
—Meg Gardiner, #1 *New York Times* bestselling author

"A study in contrasts, this book is by turns bloody, gritty, and violent, heartwarming, thought-provoking, and laugh-out-loud funny. An unusual, inventive, unforgettable read that will appeal to mystery aficionados looking for something different."
—*Booklist* (starred review)

THE
SEMINARIAN

BOOKS BY
HART HANSON

The Seminarian
The Driver

THE SEMINARIAN

HART HANSON

BLACK STONE

PUBLISHING

Printed in the United States of America
Originally published in hardcover by Blackstone Publishing in 2024

First paperback edition: 2024
ISBN 979-8-212-63139-6
Fiction / Mystery & Detective / Hard-Boiled

Version 1

Blackstone Publishing
31 Mistletoe Rd.
Ashland, OR 97520

www.BlackstonePublishing.com

For my sons: Hartwick and Joe . . .
If the odds of any particular, unique human being born are
one in four hundred trillion, then what are the odds of ending up with two excellent sons like you?

1

Jutting a quarter of a mile into the Pacific Ocean, the Venice Pier was less gritty than the beach. Cool breezes eddied under a crystal blue sky, seagulls crying and hovering. Two sea lions bobbed between the pylons. The sound of wind and waves, of portable speakers playing Mexican music, electronica, and rap, the roar of gigantic airliners taking off from LAX a few miles to the south, the thump of helicopters—all of these drowned out the cacophony of crowd noise, buskers, and barkers from the Venice Boardwalk.

Xavier Priestly leaned over the fish-gut and seagull-poop-stained wooden railing of the Venice Pier, squinting through polarized Ray-Bans into the blue-green depths of the Pacific Ocean. Priest's fishing buddy, Yorben Ybarra, slouched in a red, white, and blue striped lawn chair in his usual spot, on the other side of an illustrated sign warning that if you ate what you caught, you'd get cancer. Roughly the size of a single axle U-Haul, Yorben parted his glossy black hair down the middle and slicked it back with what looked to Priest like a combo of spittle and Vaseline.

Priest muttered an incantation.

"What are you even mumbling now and whatnot?" Yorben asked.

"I didn't think you could hear me," Priest said.

"I got better hearing than average," Yorben said. "What did you say?"

"Nothing. Psalm 8:9."

"Bible magic isn't nothing," Yorben said. "Bible magic's the good stuff."

"The Pope gets his robes all up in a knot if you call it magic," Priest said.

"Tell me what you said."

Priest relented. "'The birds of the air, and the fishes of the sea, that pass through the paths of the sea.'"

"I want fish of the sea, not birds of the air. Once I caught a seagull through the beak who snagged my bait. It wasn't good," Yorben said.

"You're concentrating on the wrong part of the verse," Priest said.

"That part that says, 'that pass through the paths of the sea.' Like, what? Whales? Walruses and poisonous snakes and whatnot? I don't want to catch any of those neither."

"Yorben, this conversation we're having is why I didn't want you to hear me."

Yorben tilted a bottle of wholesale Chinese cooking brandy into his mouth and sucked until the plastic bottle collapsed. He shook the bottle to make sure it was empty and tossed it into a garbage can ten feet away. His lips moved—*Three points!* He reached into the Los Angeles Kings backpack hooked over his chair and produced a second, identical bottle. He bought the stuff wholesale from a guy on Navy Street who imported it illegally from Malaysia.

Yorben Ybarra was one of those guys who always knew a guy.

Although they'd only ever spent time together on this pier, Priest had always enjoyed Yorben's company. Priest liked to think that fishing revealed people's true nature. Were they patient? Were their interests varied? Were they open to trying new things? New thoughts? Did they fish for food or fun or competition with themselves or others? Were they open to people, or tightly screwed into their narrow worldview?

One of Yorben's best qualities was that he talked the kind of shit that in no way demanded a response. Yorben pontificated on fishing, women, politics, religion, and baseball. He put a lot of heart into describing the movies and TV shows he watched when he couldn't sleep. And apparently, Yorben never slept. Even when Priest had seen the movie or TV show, he didn't recognize Yorben's recaps, which made them all the more entertaining. He found Yorben to be a delightful combination of diverting and relaxing.

"Y'ever think that while you're up here praying to your People-God to catch fish and whatnot, them fishes down there are praying to their Fish-God to not get caught?"

"There's no such thing as either a Fish-God or a People-God."

"You don't know."

"People don't need to know things to believe them. That's the major curse upon this world."

"Too bad we can't use bullshit for bait," Yorben said, "because you got a endless supply of that."

What Yorben Ybarra wanted with all his heart was to catch a shark. There was approximately zero chance of that happening, though, because Yorben baited his line with expired discount Vigo's Canned Mussels, thus ensuring that the only fish he could hope to catch was shovelnose, which Priest considered a flattering name for an uggo bottom-feeding fish that was also, according to the warning sign, mega-carcinogenic.

Priest fished for halibut with a homemade lure he had pains-takingly fashioned to resemble a live anchovy. Yorben said the lure looked like Priest had banged a tin can between two stones.

Priest was aware that Yorben's backpack also contained a hu-mongous, battered Ruger .357 with a duct-taped grip that looked like it would explode in his face if he pulled the trigger. Yorben kept the gun close because, although he himself was as pure as the driven snow, a significant portion of the Ybarra clan were proud criminals, and this had what Yorben called *ramifications*.

"Dirty Princess approaching, nine o'clock," Yorben said.

"Dirty Princess" was what Yorben called Dusty Queen—but only behind her back, because Yorben wasn't suicidal.

Dusty stood out from the usual Venice Pier joggers, tourists, gangbangers, skaters, surfers, fishers, and freaks. She wore black stretchy jeans, black tactical boots, a black leather jacket, black gloves, and a black Cordura backpack. Her forearm was thrust through a black, full-face matte black Shoei helmet. Dusty was a martial-arts enthusiast who hired herself out as a house-sitter and personal bodyguard between stunt gigs for TV and movies. Tattooed, shredded, slim, and graceful, Dusty Queen looked like a Finn crossed with a Korean crossed with a Pict crossed with a Carthaginian crossed with a Martian. When people asked where she was from, Dusty replied, "Southern California." If pressed harder, she said, "Alhambra," always in a discouraging tone.

Because her stunt-performer job meant wearing wigs and helmets and hats, Dusty had always buzzed her hair short and dyed it either inky black or fiery orange. But today her head shone like a platinum halo. And she sported a new tattoo, a baby owl perched on her wrist. As far as Priest was concerned, both the owl and the halo were bad signs.

"I need to hire you," Dusty told Priest, before he could make fun of her hair. "Officially."

Xavier Priestly worked as a licensed freelance legal investigator, contracting himself out to big-shot lawyers at big-shot law firms. Smaller practices also engaged him when they thought it was worth Priest's minimum rate of one thousand dollars a day. Even the LA district attorney's office used Priest from time to time, to look into things that the police could not.

In his mid-thirties, Priest had built himself a solid reputation as an investigator who was also an asset in the courtroom, unfazed by theatrics or prosecutorial bullying, willing and able to get beneath the opposing counsel's skin without alienating the jury.

"Officially? What's that mean?" Priest asked.

"I want to pay," Dusty said.

"Oh, c'mon!" Priest said—because how many times had Dusty Queen pulled his ass out of flaming shitpits? A dozen? More? Priest and Dusty had never even considered being more than friends, but over the years, they'd become the kind of friends who'd do anything for each other. Priest knew that, and he knew that Dusty knew that. He felt a trickle of apprehension in his guts.

"Totally professional," Dusty said. "If it makes you feel better, extend me a friends-and-family discount, but I need client privilege."

"Privilege?" Priest asked. "You don't trust me without client privilege?"

"I trust you totally," Dusty said. "But I don't want to feel guilty if you perjure yourself for me without the easy protection of client privilege."

"Why do you need client privilege?"

"Shouldn't I only tell you that after I've got it?"

"Tell me and I'll let you know if you need it."

"I can't find Nikki."

"Nikki's missing?"

"I can't find her. So yes, missing to me," Dusty said.

"Who's Nikki now?" Yorben asked.

"Gimme a dollar," Priest told Dusty.

"Smallest I've got is a twenty."

As Priest took Dusty's twenty-dollar bill, his line *zzzinged* and his rod bent. He handed it to Yorben and walked off with Dusty, pleased that he hadn't had to explain who Nikki was, because his tone—which Priest could not always control—would have hurt Dusty's feelings, and while Priest didn't mind insulting ninety-nine-point-nine percent of humanity, Dusty was not ninety-nine-point-nine percent of humanity.

Sometimes he wondered whether Dusty Queen was even mortal.

2

Priest lived in a funky, old adobe building on the Venice Board-walk, a five-minute walk north of the Venice Pier. Dusty left her Moto Guzzi in Priest's garage so that they could drive together in Priest's bad-ass new second-hand matte-black Chrysler 300. Heading east on Venice Boulevard, Priest opened the window and fluttered his hand in the slipstream, warm even in what passed for February in Southern California.

"I preferred the Porsche," Dusty said.

Priest's standing policy was to change automobiles a min-imum of twice a year, more if one of his investigations broke tempestuous. Changing vehicles was a proven method of reduc-ing profile and visibility, advisable for the type of investigator who tended to piss people off by sending them to jail or cost-ing them millions of dollars. All fine and true, but it was also true that Xavier Priestly jumped at any excuse to get himself a new car. He'd drive into the CarMax near LAX, leave one, pick up another, and run through the paperwork with hardly more than a thumbs-up from the finance department.

"Where are we headed?" Dusty asked.

"Gimme a minute."

"To what? Run through your breathing exercises? Does that mean you're irked?"

Priest was irked most of the time. He countered it by utilizing breathing and mindfulness exercises in his ongoing effort to live in the *carpe diem* moment. Irritation—Priest had learned from his therapy-enthusiast sister—was repressed shame and guilt. Misguided regrets. Anxiety about things that hadn't happened yet.

Priest was also a fan of Secular Prayer, despite not believing that God—or any other Supreme Being or Beings—was watching from the nethers or the farthers. Formulating his thoughts and asking for strength and favors from an indifferent universe helped Priest to crystallize his desired outcomes. Bonus: it forced him to humble himself in the face of an infinitude of entropy and chaos.

"Are you irked because this is about Nikki?" Dusty asked.

"Can I have ten fucking seconds, please?"

A little over a month ago, Dusty had taken a gig as a bodyguard for an expensive escort named Nikki Celeste. When one of Nikki's clients devolved into a stalker, Dusty confronted the stalker outside Nikki's apartment and—catastrophically for the creep—discovered that he was carrying duct tape and a spritzer bottle of liquid Rohypnol. To discourage said stalker, Dusty broke all four of his major extremities and a half-dozen of his minor extremities, and it turned out that Dusty's enthusiasm was due to feelings she'd developed for Nikki.

Ridiculous, childish, foolish romantic feelings. For an escort.

"Was Nikki on the job when she went missing?" Priest asked.

"Yes . . . What's with the groan?"

"Which hotel?" Priest asked.

"Peninsula . . . Priest, I can see you literally biting your tongue."

"That's so I don't groan again."

"I haven't had sex in a month," Dusty said.

"Since we're sharing, same here."

"Unlike you, it's the longest I've gone without sex since I was fourteen."

"Why?"

"We started young in Alhambra."

"Why are you not currently having sex?" Priest clarified.

"Nikki and I haven't slept together yet because I refuse to pay for sex and Nikki refuses to have sex for free . . . Your knuckles are turning white."

Priest relaxed his grip on the steering wheel. "I get you not having sex with Nikki, even if it's stupid," he said. "What I don't get is why you're not having sex with anyone else."

"It's called fidelity."

"Fidelity means you'd be having sex with Nikki and no one else. What you're being is *celibate*."

"They teach you that distinction in priest school?"

"The Catholic Church is run by super-weird perverted old men," Priest said. "Of course, they have opinions about every possible iteration and nuance of sexual activity."

"*Emotional* fidelity then. Is that a thing?"

"I suppose," Priest said, knowing it was absolutely a thing.

He knew that Dusty was extremely successful with a ratio of sexual partners that favored women approximately four-to-one, and he had to admit that denying herself in order to prove her love to an escort was both impressive and rank bullshit.

"Being in a pure and chaste relationship is good for me," Dusty said.

"A pure and chaste relationship? With a *hooker*?"

"The heart wants what it wants," Dusty said, turning the air vent toward her face and leaning in, sweating from anxiety. Because Dusty was not by nature an anxious person, Priest felt a pang of guilt. To his surprise, the guilt stood alone; it did not elicit irritation. It simply replaced it.

"We'll find Nikki," he said.

"Thank you. My skills are all about keeping people from disappearing. Yours are in finding them after people like me fail."

"Did you talk to Nikki's pimp?"

"Priest . . ."

"Excuse me. Did you talk to Parris?"

"Yes."

"Did Parris tell you not to involve the police?"

"Yes."

"So, you came straight to me?"

"No."

"No?"

"I went straight to the police," Dusty said.

"Even though Parris told you not to?"

"Sometimes, I don't do what people tell me to do. Guess what?"

"The cops did not give a shit."

"Not even a micro-shit," Dusty said.

"Tell me what you know."

"Nine p.m. last night, Nikki meets a client at the Peninsula Hotel. Ten a.m. this morning, me and Nik are supposed to grab breakfast at Cora's. Nikki doesn't show. Noon, I go to the Peninsula and talk to the hotel manager, who, by the way—"

"Also did not give a micro-shit?"

Dusty rolled her head around. Priest heard her vertebrae pop. One of Dusty's favorite forms of exercise was to run along the bottom of the Santa Monica Bay cradling a jeweler's anvil she'd painted yellow and dropped off the end of the Venice Pier.

She skipped rope using marine chain.

She walked up and down flights of stairs on her hands, sometimes clapping between steps.

"You're grinding your teeth," Dusty said. "Maybe you should just say what you've got to say before you pop an embolism."

"Nikki is a prostitute. You're a dumb-ass, love-struck enabler. You're not even getting any, and she's got you wrapped around her finger."

"*Getting any*? What are you, sixteen?"

"Nikki sells sex, Dusty. She's the one who makes it a commodity, not me."

"Six months from now, Nikki's outta the game."

"She promised you that, huh?"

"Yes, Priest, Nikki promised me that. You want to slow down? You're doing sixty in a forty zone. Do your breathing exercises. I won't interrupt."

"Do you even know Nikki's real name? Or do you believe her parents wrote *Nikki-with-two-k's Celeste* on her birth certificate?"

"We agreed that Nikki will share her birth name with me when she's out of the game," Dusty said.

"Like a blank slate? New beginning? Nikki quits hooking, and you'll be like two college girls finding true love for the first time?"

"Don't say it like you got a mouth full of shit."

Priest grunted, which he intended as a scoff, but which Dusty took as acquiescence, once again allowing guilt to nudge irritation out of the way.

"You know anything about the client?"

"Parris said he's a first-timer. She got a credit card, but guess what?"

"Parris told you there was no use telling you the name on the card because it was reported stolen," Priest said.

"Why'd you say it like that?"

"Like what?"

"Putting so much stress on the phrase 'Parris told you.'"

"Parris is lying. She's still charging Nikki's hourly rate to the client's card, and she's not going to raise any red flags as long as the charges aren't declined. Like law enforcement, Parris knows that Nikki will eventually turn up. Like everyone else, Parris does not give a micro-shit."

"You give a micro-shit," Dusty said.

"No, I do not."

"You're here."

"I'm here because twenty bucks is exactly what it costs for me to pretend to give a micro-shit. You get a description?"

"Of the client?"

"Yes, the client. I know what Nikki looks like."

"Mid-forties. Fit. Shiny suit. Sweepy hair. Chunky gold rings with onyx. Chunky gold watch. Chunky cuff links with obsidian."

"That's more info than we'll get out of the hotel manager. Where's Nikki live?"

"Near UCLA," Dusty said.

At Venice and Sepulveda, Priest turned left and headed north to Westwood.

A savvy escort's apartment was located wherever it would bolster her or his legend. In Los Angeles, the most popular legend was Struggling Actor. Struggling Models did all right, too, but that was more of a New York appetite. Broad-shouldered Chicago dispensed with the cover story altogether—escorts are escorts and that's sexy. Why pretend otherwise?

Ideally, the fuckpad vibed iconic. Hollywood, the beach, Beverly Hills, or the Hollywood Hills—never North Hollywood—and preferably featuring a nighttime view of the grid or the Hollywood sign or the Capitol Records building.

A loft downtown, steps away from Grand Central Market and Angels Flight.

A love-nest on the sand in Malibu.

Parris Ferrer had urged Nikki Celeste away from Struggling-Actress-Who-Only-Works-Rarely-As-An-Escort-To-Pay-For-Acting-Lessons and toward Struggling-Artist-Who-Only-Works-Rarely-As-An-Escort-To-Pay-For-Her-Post-Graduate-Degree-In-Fine-Art.

Nikki Celeste lived on the top floor of a converted mansion on a hill, a few blocks west of the UCLA campus, not far from fraternity row.

Priest preferred to approach his investigations in a deductive manner, pushing back to gather as much of the big picture as he could before picking out granular details. Context before pretext. The opposite of what they'd taught him in seminary, where all investigations—worldly and spiritual—were predicated upon the indisputable fact of a Holy Plan that makes sense of the universe, even if we are not equipped to see it with mortal eyes. Priest parked at a tennis court at the bottom of the hill. They walked a few blocks up to Nikki's building, an androgynous, black-clad biker and a big-nosed beach-bum in Keen sandals, burnt-orange cargo shorts, and a dark navy *Hecho en Venice* T-shirt. A sundowner breeze wafted toward them from Beverly Hills, bearing the scent of night-blooming jasmine. They climbed six stone steps to the vestibule of Nikki's three-story building.

Three doorbells.

Apartment A featured a label with a full name.

Apartments B and C showed only initials.

G.S.D. in Apartment B.

N.C. in Apartment C. Written in green ink by the same hand as Apartment B.

"You got a key?" Priest asked.

Dusty shook her head. Of course, she didn't have a key! A working escort couldn't risk her lovelorn former bodyguard popping in unannounced.

"You ever even been inside?" Priest asked.

"We meet other places. You want me to jimmy the lock?"

Priest indicated the Apartment B doorbell. "Is G.S.D. another of Parris's hookers?"

"You know what century it is, right, Priest? You know you should respect sex workers, not shame 'em? What do you care what people do for a living?"

"You're right. I'm sorry," Priest said. "I was raised Catholic. It bent me in a judgmental direction. Jesus got a boner for Mary Magdalene, so why shouldn't you?"

"Jesus pings queer . . . Don't give me that look. Who are you? The Pope? Yes, G.S.D. works for Parris. Giselle Santa Domingo. Her legend is that she's getting her doctorate in philosophy. Her clients are mostly designers, architects, and movie directors."

"That's a very specific clientele."

"Clients who prefer striking features to orthodox beauty," Dusty said.

"Just come out and say she's freaky looking."

"Giselle does stand out from the crowd," Dusty said.

"Ring the bell. Tell Giselle Placido Domingo that you need to get into Nikki's place. Try to sound worried."

"I am worried, Priest. My stomach's in an acid knot."

Dusty rang the bell and identified herself as "Nikki's friend Dusty Queen." The door buzzed. They climbed a flight of wooden stairs to the second floor. A tall, skinny woman wearing UCLA sweats leaned over the banister. She had curly orange hair and a freckled Grecian-statue nose that extended flush from her forehead down her extremely long face to just above her lips. She looked like an ancient coin come to life. If Priest had seen Giselle Santa Domingo walking the campus, he'd have assumed she was an astrophysicist or a med-student specializing in thoracic surgery. Or a philosopher. The woman looked brainy. Parris Ferrer knew her business.

Dusty introduced Priest and explained that they needed to get into Nikki's apartment.

"Does Parris know you're here?" Giselle asked.

"Not from us," Priest said.

Giselle led them up to Nikki's door on the third-floor landing. A blue ceramic plaque with yellow lettering was screwed onto the door: *No Soliciting.* When Priest turned to Dusty to crack hilarious, she shook her head.

Giselle handed Dusty the key and walked away, fluttering her fingers over her shoulder.

"Ms. Santa Domingo?" Priest asked.

She turned to face him from one step down, which put them eye to eye, even though Priest stood five-foot-eleven-and-three-quarters.

"Are you worried about Nikki?" Priest asked.

Giselle laughed and descended the stairs like an orange sunset.

"What the hell was that?" Dusty asked.

"She knows that. Nikki took off with the client of her own free will, which means she's probably not dead. Be happy."

"If Nikki left of her own free will, she would've told me."

Priest grunted. Again, Dusty generously decided to accept it as an apology.

Nikki's place was decorated exactly the way a client would expect an art history major's apartment to be decorated: tasteful, sharp-edged, minimalist wood-and-glass Scandinavian furniture. The only verve and color in the place derived from the art. Priest looked at the signatures—more than half the pieces were signed "Callie Vaughan."

Priest indicated one of them—a golden pointillist doughnut encircling what was either a sheaf of wheat or a hank of hair. "The client is supposed to think the escort Nikki Celeste's real name is Callie Vaughan, am I right?"

"Yes," Dusty said. "Some of the clients buy her paintings."

"Added bonus," Priest said, "a secondary revenue stream activated when Nikki recommends young, up-and-coming artists and/or galleries to her clients, from which Parris Ferrer receives a generous finder's fee."

"You see the worst in everybody and everything."

"It's my job," Priest said. "Same way your job is to set yourself on fire and get shot off buildings."

"That's make-believe. You see the worst for real."

The place was designed to massage the egos, groins, and wallets of high-rolling, high-paying clients who got off on the extra libidinous spark derived from feeling that they had somehow—through dint of personality and raw animal magnetism—breached the impenetrable emotional armor of a jaded professional sex worker, touching her authentic heart and soul, learning her real name, sleeping in her bed, waking and cooking breakfast together. In her home. A personal encounter. Something real.

Parris charged double for that.

"This is a nice place," Dusty said. "Why the groaning again?"

Like one of Nikki's clients, Dusty was caught up in the reverie that she and Nikki would someday live here together—that bed was *their* bed, that kitchen table was *their* table, where the two of them would sit drinking lattes on Sunday mornings, watching students walk down the hill toward the campus.

At least Dusty hadn't been fooled into thinking that Callie Vaughan was Nikki's real name.

Priest squashed the impulse to smack Dusty on the back of her stupid, lovesick head.

Dusty noticed. "Within me is a peacefulness that cannot be disturbed."

Priest and Dusty had first met at a "Mindfulness Through Sailing" course in Marina Del Rey. They'd bonded over their mutual disdain for mantras and affirmations and Dusty's amusement that Priest couldn't tie a proper knot. They still repeated the mantras to each other from time to time.

"I breathe in calm," Priest responded. "I breathe out joy."

The Barska biometric wall safe in Nikki's closet was ajar and empty. On the bed sat the dove-gray Tumi roll-along bag she took to meet her clients. Typically, it would hold a change of clothes, lingerie, sex toys, recreational drugs, poppers, erectile dysfunction pills and creams, massage oils, and porn. Currently, it contained only a phone and a padded manila envelope labeled *Parris*.

"Are we going to open that?" Dusty asked.

"Let's get Parris to do it," Priest said.

3

Thirty-five minutes later, Priest and Dusty sat across from Parris Ferrer at her usual booth at the House of Pies in Los Feliz. Parris tapped the keyboard of her garish, top-of-the-line seventeen-inch Alienware gaming laptop. At her elbow languished a slice of half-eaten Boston cream pie and a lipsticked cup of cold black coffee.

Parris had filled the vacuum left when celebrity madame Heidi Fleiss crashed and burned in the mid-1990s. Parris had learned from Fleiss's mistakes, embracing the internet and all the dodges and tricks it afforded what was—in the strict legal sense—a legitimate and lawful online matchmaking service. As a member of Parris's defense team, Priest had been engaged to search for evidence of criminal wrongdoing in Parris Ferrer's business. He had come up with nothing probative. Neither had the district attorney. Parris not only walked but received an out-of-court settlement after suing the LAPD for an invalid arrest warrant.

"Writing a short story, Parris?" Priest asked, when he could wait no longer. "Maybe a first-person essay on tax evasion in the sex-worker trade for *The New Yorker*?"

"Fuck a duck, Priest," Parris said. "You come to my place of business without an appointment, you wait your turn. And do not even think of touching my Boston cream pie."

Priest pulled his finger back.

Parris Ferrer possessed a gift for discerning weakness and vulnerability in other human beings—her stocks in trade. Parris told people that she was born and bred in Fort Worth, but her whisper of an accent sounded more like Oklahoma than Texas. In her mid-fifties, toned and formidable despite a steady diet of black coffee and pie, Parris wore her chestnut hair ironing-board straight. Her tawny eyes bulged slightly—maybe some kind of thyroid issue there. She favored animal-print clothing: ostrich, leopard, snake, crocodile, and her favorite, tiger. Which she wore today.

"How'd you get into Nikki's apartment?" Parris asked.

"I'm a highly skilled investigator. Dusty is a security expert in tip-top physical shape. How do you think we got in?"

"Did you like Giselle?" Parris asked. "She's totally your type. Smarter than you. More successful than you. Out of your league."

Giselle Santa Domingo had covered her ass, calling ahead to warn her boss.

"I'm not crazy about her choice of career," Priest said.

"Catholic bullshit," Dusty said. "Remember?"

"Does the fact that Giselle's a sex worker lessen her value as a human being?" Parris asked.

"We were discussing my *league*," Priest said, "not the intrinsic value of human beings."

"Leagues are exactly a measure of the intrinsic value of a human being," Parris said.

She slapped shut her laptop, opened Nikki's Tumi, extracted the padded envelope, and dumped the contents onto her computer lid.

Four pairs of earrings.

Five rings: two diamond, one ruby, one emerald, one sapphire.

A couple bracelets.

A string of pearls.

Parris took a bite of her pie and said, "Huh."

She scooped the jewelry back into the envelope, tossed the envelope into the Tumi, and extracted Nikki's phone.

"What's that? Some kind of burner?" Priest said.

"Silent Circle Blackphone," Dusty said.

Parris tapped what felt like a half-dozen separate access codes into it with her short, blunt, alternating orange-and-black fingernails, and the phone came to life.

"Verified boot sequence. Triple password protection. Auto-delete feature in case of theft," Dusty said.

"Perfect for illegal doings," Priest said. "Contacts. Calendar. Locations. Client predilections and perversions. Voicemails. Credit/debit situations."

"As you yourself proved beyond a reasonable doubt in an actual court of criminal law—thank you—my matchmaking enterprise is one hundred percent legal," Parris said. "Anything Nikki chooses to do above and beyond that is literally her own affair."

"From which you extract a sixty-percent cut."

"Deep breaths," Dusty told Priest. "Flies and vinegar and honey . . ."

Parris tossed Nikki's Blackphone back into the Tumi. "I'm going to have to do a fuck-ton of make-goods and substitutions for Nikki's regulars."

"Not to mention finding another Callie Vaughan to sell off those paintings," Priest said.

"Maximizing income streams is the key to financial stability," Parris said. "But yes, it is a grievous pain unto my ass."

"The travails of living off the avails," Priest said.

"I suppose you never paid for it?"

"Look at me and you'll see a man who could never be lonely."

"All I see is a humongous nose attached to a guy who is unwilling to pay a premium for the best life has to offer," Parris said.

"What about Nikki?" Dusty asked.

"Nikki ran off with a client," Parris said. "It happens. Maybe she's getting married, or believes she fell in love. Copious amounts of cocaine will do that to a person. Interferes with higher judgment."

"Nikki doesn't do drugs," Dusty said.

"Nikki does whatever the client tells her to do," Parris said.

Dusty looked down, face burning, jaws clenched. Later tonight, she would swim off her excess adrenaline, slicing through the ocean a mile offshore between the Venice Pier and the Santa Monica pier and back again, alone in the dark, daring sharks in a gray Farmer John wetsuit and yellow-tinted goggles, floating on her back when she needed to rest, her face up to the universe, her ass aimed squarely back at planet Earth.

"Relax," Parris said. "Nikki will get bored or piss the client off, or he'll turn out to be a creep." She zipped up Nikki's Tumi like it was a body bag. "Then she'll come back."

"Told you," Priest said to Dusty.

"What if the client's already a creep?" Dusty asked. "What if he fell in love with her—like that stalker—and she said no but he took her anyway?"

"Girls like Nikki are not what you call rare birds," Parris said. "Throw a rock in any acting class in the Valley and you hit three Nikki Celestes."

"Tell that to her stalker," Dusty said.

"I would," Parris said, "except he's vanished off the surface of the earth."

"Good riddance," Dusty said.

"We're done here," Priest said to Dusty. "Wanna get some pie to go?"

"Priest, you get lonely, you give me a call," Parris said. "I'll extend you the employee discount. Giselle thinks you're cute."

Out in the House of Pies parking lot, Priest's phone pinged—a message from Yorben: *THANK U!!!* Attached was a photo of Yorben holding a five-foot common thresher shark like a child soldier cradling an AK-47.

"What's that?" Dusty asked.

"Yorben caught a shark on my rod," Priest said. "Things are looking up."

4

Before he even opened his eyes, Priest knew something major had happened.

Earthquake?

Tsunami?

End of the World?

When he managed to open one eye, he saw the silhouette of a hefty man looming over him. He opened the second eye. The man was a young forty-something or a stressed-out thirty-something. Black. Wearing an inexpensive but clean brown suit. Salesman? Middle manager?

The odd thing was that the man had only one eye. Hazel. Set immediately above his nose.

Then things got more confusing.

The sound of hazel was drowned out by the *ah-OO-ga!* emanating from the man's orange tie. Priest tasted tin in the cool sheet caressing the bottom of his left foot.

"What the hell?" he asked—but if he made any noise, he couldn't hear it.

The man in the brown suit leaned forward. He smelled of

L'Occitane After-Shave Balm. A swirly mixture of purple and yellow.

The man's lips moved.

Priest smelled Altoids—bright white, with a sound like fine sandpaper on glass.

The man's single eyebrow arched. His mouth made sounds like a doorbell.

A question?

Priest's nose and eyes and tongue and skin were all working, but they weren't working properly.

What the *hell*?

Priest tried speaking again. "Where am I?"

This time he heard himself, but from a very great distance. And not through his ears, but from approximately where his spine met his skull.

His tunnel vision widened.

Hospital.

Something had happened . . . But it hadn't happened to the whole world . . . It had only happened to him . . . Xavier Priestly . . .

Yes, that was his name.

Xavier Priestly.

Behind the man in the brown suit, a female uniformed LAPD officer guarded the door. Eavesdropping. Keen. Ready to help.

Cyclops was her superior.

In plainclothes.

Detective Cyclops.

Oh, boy . . .

The uniform stepped backward, into a brassy fog.

Priest focused on the detective. His single hazel eye separated into two, quite small, eyes.

He leaned in close.

His lips moved.

His eyebrows squeaked and pumped.

He was asking Priest another question.

Priest organized his thoughts:

He was himself, Xavier Priestly.

In a hospital.

Being questioned by a detective.

Priest wiggled his toes. The resulting sensation smelled like chili.

The detective moved his lips. Priest saw pearly puffs of air and heard something. Not words, but vibrations with interrogative vibes.

"What?" Priest tried.

He heard that. Far away and muffled, but he heard it through his ears. Still, the sound of his voice was pink.

"Did you see who attacked you?" the detective asked.

Priest sucked in a deep breath, and the world coalesced into something more organized and corporeal. The universe reasserted itself, standing at wobbly attention. It existed, and Priest existed within it, still at a remove, but at least, he was in and of the real world again.

"I am Detective Garnet Diodato, LAPD."

Behind Detective Diodato, a hefty, tattooed Hispanic guy wearing thick glasses on a glittering chain filled the doorway. "The doctor said not to push too hard," he said.

A nurse.

An expanding cold black ball burned in Priest's chest. He clenched his fists, scrunched his eyes shut, and breathed again, striving to find his calm center.

He heard Diodato's voice: "And . . . he's out again."

Priest took that as kindly permission.

"Priest? Can you hear me? Can you open your eyes? It's Baz. If you can hear me, try to open your eyes . . ."

Priest opened his eyes.

It was like trying to lift bricks with his eyelashes. His reward was Baz Amberson's concerned and intelligent face, bright with relief, smiling. She wore skull earrings with zirconium eyeballs and smelled like coffee and lavender.

"Hey," Baz said.

Baz Amberson was a short woman with an outsized aura, a criminal defense lawyer in her late thirties who—aside from hating on her calves—was otherwise confident in her physical appearance. An opinion that both Priest and Dusty shared. Baz had been married to another lawyer for five years. She'd divorced him three years ago and a year later started dating a sheriff's deputy who'd briefly played center field for the Dodgers. That relationship was doomed because Baz didn't want to get married again and didn't want children, while the deputy was looking to settle down, move to Antelope Valley, and start a family of ballplayers. Antelope Valley was Cop Land. As a Black defense lawyer, Baz felt she wouldn't fit in.

"How are you feeling?" said Detective Diodato from the other side of the bed.

Diodato wore a dark blue suit, which most likely meant that this was a whole different day, but it was the exact same cut as the brown suit from . . . yesterday?

"Two-for-one-week at Men's Wearhouse," Priest said.

Diodato turned to the uniformed cop at the door. "Victim is a haberdasher. Could be an important clue. Possible somebody attacked the victim for criticizing his apparel."

The uniformed cop scribbled in her notebook.

"That was a joke, Officer Alison," Diodato said. "A *quip*. You don't have to write down my witticisms."

"Detective says write something down, I write it down," said Officer Alison.

A go-getter.

Priest cleared his throat. The tattooed nurse appeared and spooned an ice flake into his mouth. Priest closed his eyes, just for a moment.

———

Priest opened his eyes.

Night.

Another doctor looking down at her iPad . . .

. . . up at Priest . . .

. . . down at the iPad . . .

Slow motion. Priest could almost read the words reflected backward in her glasses, which were smudged with fingerprints. She wore a name tag: DR. NGO.

"Kidney function is returning," Dr. Ngo said. "That's good."

Who was she talking to?

Priest shut his eyes.

———

Priest opened his eyes.

Morning.

Massive headache.

Gritty eyes.

Dick hurt.

What the hell?

He slid sideways into the world, like a drunk slipping out of his chair. His hand went exploring. His junk was there, but there was a hose sticking out of it. He fought the urge to yank it out, because what if it was a Foley catheter? There'd be a balloon in-flated in his bladder. Yank all you want, that sucker was staying put.

Dusty's face loomed over him. "Endurance is resilience crossed with determination," she said.

"Rock. Paper. Scissors" was the best response he could come up with.

"Oh, boy," Dusty said. "Pudding?"

"Pudding? Is that my name?"

"Please tell me you're trying to be funny."

"Why'd you call me Pudding?"

"I *offered* you pudding," Dusty said. "You haven't eaten anything in four days."

"What the hell?" Priest asked.

"You got stun-gunned," Dusty said. "Upper spine. Back of the neck. Again on the sternum. Syringe in the carotid. Another in the ass. The needle broke off."

"Someone injected me? With what?"

"They won't say. What do you remember?"

Priest shook his head. Maybe he felt the stun-gun burn on the back of his neck. His upper back. His chest.

"Does shaking your head mean you have no memory?" Dusty asked.

"I don't think so."

"That's an ambiguous answer."

"I don't remember. What do you know?" Priest asked.

"The cops advised us not to tell you anything," Dusty said. "They want you to remember on your own. I probably shouldn't have said anything about not eating."

Priest reached up, felt a dressing on the right side of his neck. He pressed on it. Not painful. Just sore.

Dusty turned toward the door and said, "Cadence? He's awake."

Officer Cadence Alison. Go-getter. Taker of notes. Recorder of detective quips.

If Dusty weren't infatuated with Nikki Celeste, she would most definitely have asked Officer Alison out already.

Dusty rolled optimistic.

"I promised Baz I'd call as soon as you woke up," Dusty told Priest.

Into her phone, Officer Cadence Alison said, "Mr. Priestly is awake."

"Is your name actually Cadence?" Priestly asked. "Are you from a military family? Does anyone call you Cady? Seems like they mixed up your first and last name."

"He thinks he's funny," Dusty told Officer Alison.

"Does Detective Diodato have one gigantic eye?" Priest asked.

"They said you might have lingering side-effects from whatever drug cocktail was pumped into you," Dusty said.

"My doctor's eyeglasses are filthy. Unsanitary. I want this catheter out. My dick hurts. My nurse has gang tattoos."

"Simmer down there, Priest," Dusty said, "Harmony and peace surround me."

"With every breath, I let peace into my body," Priest said, shutting his eyes.

———

Priest opened his eyes.

Dusty was gone. Baz stood over him. When he reached out to take her hand, she flinched.

Irritated with himself, Priest said, "Sorry."

"My bad," Baz said.

Baz had grown up with a drunken, physically abusive father.

She must have been in and out of the emergency room twenty times before she was twelve years old. When she was fourteen, her father put her into a three-week coma after poor little Baz had dropped a six-pack of beer while lugging groceries up the stairs.

Hospitals triggered Baz. It was an amazing display of friendship for her to visit him here. To sit with him.

Baz took Priest's hand. She knuckled his fingers into a tight, resistant ball.

"Look at the two of us," she said. "Couple of nutjobs."

5

Detective Diodato wore a black sports coat with gray pants. His orange tie was back, incandescent and festive, like something he had been forced to wear on a dare or because a beloved child had given it to him as a birthday present.

Priest felt himself withdrawing from anti-anxiety meds. He hated anti-anxiety drugs. They made him anxious. He was having an even harder time than usual behaving like a civil human being. He had thought he was doing pretty well, until he answered one of Diodato's questions, "For fuck's sake, I told you, I don't remember."

Detective Diodato grimaced at Baz. "You're positive this guy isn't just your garden-variety asshole?"

"Uh-huh. He has an incredibly high IQ," Baz said, as though Priest wasn't there.

"Not an *incredibly* high IQ," Priest said. "Middle genius. You want *incredibly* high, drop by the Jet Propulsion Lab at Caltech. I only look smart compared to normal people, who are mostly idiots."

"Smart doesn't make for non-assholes any more than dumb makes for saints," Diodato said to Baz.

"Only one in two hundred people are as smart as Xavier Priestly," Baz said.

"One in two hundred and thirty-four," Priest said.

"He notices everything—"

"Not everything. Only what's pertinent."

Even patient and understanding Baz sighed in frustration.

"I get it. Your lawyer filled me in," Diodato told Priest. "You got a bad reaction to meds. You can't help yourself from being a dick."

Priest did a breathing exercise that Dusty used to calm herself before major stunts:

Breathe in, count of five . . .

Hold, count of seven . . .

Breathe out, count of nine.

Priest still felt like smacking Detective Diodato in his stupid patient face, so he switched to a faster-acting but less effective *five-in-five-hold-five-out* pattern. He tightened and released random muscles, anything to gain control, and the cold black ball in his chest eased. Dusty's structured breathing was working, unhitching his runaway vagus nerve from his wonky autonomic response system.

"Try me again," Priest suggested.

"Do you remember being brought to the hospital?" Diodato asked.

Diodato's eyes sat so close together that it probably distracted people, made him a comic figure, vulnerable and approachable, but slap a pair of sunglasses on the guy, and he became intimidating, a hundred ninety-two pounds of muscle crammed into a five-foot-eight frame.

"No," Priest answered.

"Do you remember yesterday?"

"I cannot answer with certitude."

"Can you remember, say, five days ago?"

"I don't know how much time has passed," Priest said.

"Since when?" Diodato asked.

"The Big Bang."

"What's your best guess?"

"Thirteen-point-eight billion years?"

Diodato looked at Baz.

Baz sighed. "Priest, I know you're confused. You hate anyone seeing you confused, so you confuse everyone. But could you please not do that now and instead help this man do his job?"

Baz was right. Which made Priest angry. Which made him sad.

"Please repeat the question?" Priest said.

"How long do you think you've been in the hospital?"

"You wore a brown suit. Then a blue suit. Then today, the black sports coat. So, minimum of three days. I remember telling you my name. I remember Baz being here. Then Dusty. Then the kidney doctor. I don't know in what order anything happened. I hallucinated. Or maybe dreamed. Dusty called me 'Pudding.'"

"Let's start with your last clear memory," Diodato said.

"It was a Tuesday. In February."

"Time of day?"

"Evening."

"That was five days ago," Baz said.

"I'd rather Mr. Priestly came to things in his own time," Diodato said.

"Why?" Priest asked.

"If we put him on the stand, the defense won't be able to suggest that we manipulated his recollections in any way," Diodato said.

"Smart," Baz said. She was probably salting that strategy away to use in court against some poor cop down the road.

"Tell me what you can about that Tuesday."

"I worked at my computer until about three in the afternoon. I did some fishing on the pier," Priest said.

"Santa Monica Pier?"

"Venice Pier," Priest said. "Fishing for halibut."

Priest told Diodato about Yorben, Dusty, Nikki, and Parris.

Priest told him about Dusty's reluctance to accept Parris Ferrer's insistence that Nikki had run off with a client and would come back when, inevitably, it went sour. About Dusty's insistence that she was the one Nikki loved.

"Do you remember your response to that?" Diodato asked.

"My response was, 'I'm going to earn every cent of the twenty bucks I got paid to find Nikki Celeste,'" Priest said. "But I can't remember if I said it out loud or just thought it."

"Ms. Queen driving off on her Moto Guzzi, that's the last thing you remember? . . . Are you nodding, or do you suffer from temporomandibular joint disorder?"

"Priest is the king of odd gestures," Baz said.

Diodato scribbled in his notebook. One of those guys who used a pencil, who licked the tip of his pencil before he wrote—which might mean that Diodato had a mentor who had done the same. Somebody worth emulating. Somebody who pointed out the value of being able to erase notes in a police notebook because police notebooks were discoverable in a trial.

"The doctors say that you will regain your memory, over time, starting with sense impressions," Diodato said. "Write them down as they occur to you."

"What about this situation with the missing escort?" Baz asked.

"Forget it," Priest said.

"Definitely a viable avenue of investigation," Diodato said. "Has Mr. Priestly been investigating anything for you or anyone else that might prompt someone to want to kill him?"

"Last three months, he's worked only for me, conducting computer searches in a mundane corporate forensic accounting investigation."

"Nothing with gangs? Organized crime?"

"No," Baz said.

"Don't tell her too much, Detective," Priest said. "For all you know, she put a hit on me."

"Did you?" Diodato asked Baz. "Because I certainly understand the temptation. I might even look the other way."

"No," Baz said.

"Could this have anything to do with your father?" Diodato asked Priest.

"He's been in prison for over a decade."

Priest's old man, Oliver Priestly, was incarcerated in a federal penitentiary in Sheridan, Oregon, serving a thirty-year sentence for felony homicide of a Medford cop killed by one of his father's accomplices during a bank robbery.

"There are rumors that your father hid millions of dollars' worth of gems stolen from safety deposit boxes."

"The FBI concluded that the existence and value of those gems were exaggerated for an insurance claim," Priest said.

"Your father's treasure doesn't have to be real for somebody to get the idea that his son might know where it's hidden."

"Why kill me without asking about the treasure?"

"We can't be certain that killing you was the intended outcome."

"Maybe an abduct-and-torture-for-information scenario?" Baz suggested.

"My father told me there's no treasure. I believe him," Priest said.

Diodato penciled something into his book. "Just because you don't believe the treasure is real doesn't mean other people agree with you. Your old man's kind of a folk hero up there in Oregon. They wrote songs about him being an outlaw genius."

"Outlaw geniuses don't end up serving thirty years in a federal penitentiary."

"How long ago were you a seminarian?" Diodato asked.

"I left the seminary shortly after my father was imprisoned," Priest said.

"Any connection between the two events?"

"No."

"You mind I ask why you quit?"

"I couldn't imagine a career as Father Priestly, then Monseigneur Priestly, Bishop Priestly, Archbishop Priestly, Cardinal Priestly, Pope Priestly the First, and, God willing, Saint Priestly."

"I bet you used that joke a few times, and I understand it's a very personal question that you might prefer to avoid. But the questions people want to avoid are the most useful in an investigation."

"I quit studying to be a priest because the Roman Catholic Church, God, and I all came to the conclusion that the priesthood was not for me," Priest said.

"Can you think of anyone who might want to kill you for that?"

"Besides Jesus?"

"Yes, Mr. Priestly. Besides Jesus."

"What has any of this got to do with me getting attacked?" Priest asked.

"Religious fanatics are one of your main types of fanatics. Religion. Sports. K-Pop," Diodato said, enumerating them on his fingers.

"Nobody in the world cares whether I became a priest or not. Besides, ten years later?"

"What about child sexual abuse?"

"Are you asking, did I abuse any altar boys who grew up and want me dead?"

"Not necessarily you, Mr. Priestly. But is there any situation, misconstrued even, where maybe someone holds you responsible for a cover-up, or even just silence? Something that might also explain why you left seminary so abruptly?"

Diodato had already checked with St. John's.

As though they knew anything.

"I didn't abuse any kids," Priest said. "I don't know anybody who abused any kids. I have met people who were sexually abused as children. None by any priests that I knew."

"You attended St. John's Seminary in Camarillo?"

"Yes."

"Did you know anyone at St. John's who was homosexual?"

"Three of my fellow seminarians who admitted it. Maybe another three or four who didn't. Theologically speaking, it doesn't matter."

"Because sexual orientation is irrelevant to Holy Orders," Diodato said, "on account of the vow of celibacy?"

"Exactly."

"Are you homosexual?" Diodato asked.

"The nature and order of your questions are getting pretty close to conflating pedophilia and homosexuality," Baz said.

"Not my intention," Diodato said.

"I'm not gay," Priest said. "Also, not a pedophile."

"I understand if you feel defensive on behalf of the Roman Catholic Church," Diodato said.

"The church deserves every bit of shit it catches," Priest said.

"Is that the reason you left?"

Everybody who found out that Priest had been to seminary wanted to know why he gave up on becoming a Roman Catholic priest.

"Celibacy was not an option," Priest said. It was an explanation that worked on ninety percent of men, gay or straight, and it had the added advantage of being true.

"You quit seminary in your mid-twenties," Diodato said. "Did something happen to make you rethink celibacy?"

Priest's sex life had unfolded in a normal way. As an adolescent, he'd lost his virginity after half of his friends and before the other half. He'd only deviated from the norm when he stopped having sex for two years in the prime of his life. Upon leaving St. John's Seminary, Priest had rejoined the majority of heterosexual males in the fat part of the sexual bell curve.

"I met someone around that time," Priest said.

Diodato waited for an explanation, which Priest did not provide.

"Did anything aside from the issues of celibacy and/or romance lead to your decision to quit the seminary?"

"Are you a religious man, Detective Diodato?"

Priest hit a nerve with that bland question. Diodato hesitated before readopting the grave mien of the weary working detective. "I got an Italian father, Southern Baptist mother. I'm a hybrid in every sense of the word."

There was no way this guy hadn't considered the clergy himself, at least as a boy. Being a cop was Diodato's alternate way of serving humanity. Maybe he was questioning his faith, after years of investigating violent crimes and murders, after seeing what humans did to each other every day in Los Angeles, California. The City of Fallen Angels.

"Do you believe Jesus left his grave?" Priest asked. "I can see the answer is no, because what reasonable adult believes that?"

"Have you ever been married?" Diodato asked.

"No."

"You're currently single?"

"If I've never been married, how could I not currently be single?"

"I mean, are you currently in a relationship?"

"I broke up with someone about a month ago."

"She the killing type?"

"No way," Baz said.

"The breakup was mutual. No hard feelings," Priest said.

The tattooed nurse appeared in the doorway. "Ahem!"

Diodato raised a hand in assent. "I'm going to keep an officer at your door as a precaution. Please let me know when you remember anything about the attack, no matter how trivial."

"Do you think it was a hit?" Priest asked.

"At this juncture, it behooves us to keep an open mind," Diodato said.

He nodded and tight-smiled at Baz on his way out.

"You weren't exactly coming in hot with the lawyer blocks," Priest said to her when Diodato was out of earshot.

"I've always wanted to ask you about your father's buried treasure," Baz said. "And did you get a load of the man's shoulders? They are the perfect height for slow dancing."

———

The next day, during his first attempt at walking unassisted, heading toward the vending machines for a Kit Kat, Priest experienced a rapid series of strobe-like impressions:

His burglar alarm sounding.

His own bare feet walking down the stairs, toward Speedway.

Speedway, empty in the middle of the night.

His garage door open.

His car. Trunk open.

A lack of noise—the burglar alarm stopping.

A swish sound.
A shock.
Falling.
A face.
A beautiful face.
Bright blue shoulder-length hair.
Sunglasses.
Falling.
Darkness.
Nothing.
Nothing.

Priest pushed his rolling IV pole over to where Officer Cadence Alison sat in the corridor outside his room. Dutifully, she wrote down the list of images in the order Priest dictated. Like Diodato, she licked her pencil. Officer Alison probably thought Detective Diodato was a pretty good detective. A role model.

"Mr. Priestly, once you achieve a bowel movement, the doctor says you can go home," the tattooed nurse shouted from behind his station.

"Bring me a large cup of black coffee and three doughnuts," Priest said, "and I'll be out of your hair in forty-five minutes."

The nurse took Priest literally. An hour and a half later, he was in an Uber with Dusty, waving goodbye to Officer Cadence Alison, and rubbing the itchy burn on the back of his neck, where somebody wearing a blue wig had tased him before stuffing him into the trunk of his own car.

"Eech," Priest said.

"I woke up from a coma once," Dusty said. "I knew I was back in real life, but I felt all slippery and unbalanced."

"I'm lagging," Priest said. "I'm unsynchronized."

"If it's any consolation," Dusty said, "you always seem like that to me."

The Uber dropped them on Speedway behind Priest's place.

"Stay behind me," Dusty said, pushing the door open and heading into the courtyard of his building.

"Are you my bodyguard now?"

"I've always been your bodyguard," Dusty said, coming back and pulling him along behind her.

"You worried Blue Wig will come back to finish what she started?" Priest asked.

"Prepare for the worst, hope for the best," Dusty said. "That's my motto."

"I thought your motto was, 'If you can't see the bright side, polish the dull side.'"

"That's not a motto; it's cleaning instructions," Dusty said.

She led Priest upstairs and made him wait on the landing as she entered his apartment to make sure it was empty.

"Wouldn't I know if somebody wanted me dead?" Priest asked, entering his apartment. "Like a general vibe I'd pick up?"

Priest sat on his couch while Dusty fetched him a glass of water.

"Of course, you would," she said, "because you're a famous psychic."

"All I'm saying is that if somebody hired Blue Wig to kill me, it's for a reason I don't know about. Something I'm not even aware of."

"Because you're a famous psychic."

"Can I borrow a gun?"

"Only if you're considering suicide," Dusty said. "If anyone knocks on the door, ask who it is before you open up."

"Nobody ever knocks on my door."

"Exactly," Dust said.

———

"Well, you do drive people crazy, X," Priest's father said.

They were speaking by phone because Oliver Priestly's entire cell block had lost video privileges after some sort of violent brouhaha about yams in the prison cafeteria.

"Nobody's ever wanted to actually kill me before," Priest said.

He was trying to judge the rhythm of their conversation so that he could chew his granola when his father spoke. It was only polite. His father loved granola, and the version they provided in federal prison was what his father called *non-delicious*.

"Don't underestimate yourself, X," Oliver said. "I'm sure plenty of people have wanted to kill you. They just haven't had the means or opportunity. If you didn't recognize your attacker, then she was probably contracted. Ergo, you're looking for somebody with easy access to contract killers."

"Say, like my old man in prison?"

"See? Now even I want to kill you."

"My father is joking," Priest said. Prisoner conversations were routinely monitored by the California Department of Corrections.

Oliver Priestly lived in a world where violent acts and lethal threats were not only mundane; they were considered entertainment. What he craved in his communications with his son was news of normal, mundane, everyday life on the outside. Chance encounters on the boardwalk. Yorben fishing. Baz's latest case. Dusty's bodyguard gigs. It wasn't until they were about to hang up that Priest circled back to the subject of the attack.

"Heads up, Dad," he said. "The cops might get in touch with you."

"Me? Do they think I put out a hit on you?"

"The legend of Ollie Priestly's buried treasure," Priest said.

"It's things like this that make me regret choosing a life of crime," Oliver said.

"I'd've thought maybe your biggest regret would be losing everything and getting locked up for the rest of your life," Priest said.

"Depends on the day," Oliver said. "Are you alone?"

"Yes," Priest said. "Why?"

"Where's Dusty?"

"She's up on the roof with her night-vision monocular, looking for killers. Why?"

"I'm wondering if your attack might be connected to the missing escort," Oliver said. "Maybe the smart thing to do is take it like some kind of warning."

"You mean . . . stop looking for Nikki?"

"Yeah. The smart thing, maybe, is what I'm saying."

"I can't do that."

"Why not?"

"Dusty might be crazy to fall for an escort, Dad, but I still gotta help her."

"Why?"

"Why?"

"I mean, what's the exact nature of the relationship between you two?"

"Dad, do you only help people you sleep with?"

"Mostly," his father said.

"Dusty is eighty-percent lesbian, and I'm one hundred percent not a woman," Priest said. "And before you get all argumentative, neither of us is locked away in prison with a limited selection of partners."

"What's that you're chomping on?" his father asked. "Is it granola? What do they put in it these days? Some nature of dried berries?"

Which signaled the end of their conversation.

6

When the police impounded Priest's Chrysler 300 because it was a crime scene, Detective Diodato had warned Baz that they'd probably hang onto it for a while.

"How long?" Priest asked Baz.

"Detective Diodato's advice is to pretend you'll never get it back," Baz said. "Then it's a nice surprise if it happens."

Priest didn't care. It was an excuse to get a new car! In light of someone maybe still wanting to kill him, Dusty didn't want him wandering around a car lot, so Priest checked the LAX CarMax website, found a silver 2014 Jaguar XFR that made his neck prickle, printed up the details, and sent Dusty to pick it up with instructions for *exactly* what to say to Lena in Finance.

Instead, Dusty brought him a brown 2014 Jeep Grand Cherokee Summit.

"Understandable mistake," Priest said, kicking the Jeep. "The two vehicles are nearly identical."

"I'll explain," Dusty said, "when you stop kicking the car."

"Some things shouldn't be called Summit. This bucket is one of those things."

"The Jaguar is beautiful," Dusty said. "It really pops. It's the opposite of invisible. Guess what's one of the best things to be when you're being hunted?"

"Invisible?"

"There you go."

"*Invisible* and *ugly* aren't the same thing," Priest said. "A strip mine is visible from outer space."

"And like a strip mine," Dusty said, "the Jeep provides a good field of vision so I can see what's going on around us in the kill zone."

The Grand Cherokee's interior was also brown.

"It's a Jeep-sized turd," Priest said. "I can actually smell it."

Dusty went upstairs to put her stuff in the guest room while Priest answered a few questions from his tenant, Beck Moe, the Flat Earther who rented out the ground floor of Priest's building. Beck slept in a back room, rented out bicycles, electric scooters, and roller skates from the front, and got his meals at a discount from vendors along the boardwalk. Priest explained the incident in his garage, framing it as an assault when he caught someone trying to steal his car.

"Methhead, I bet," Beck said. A dedicated pothead, Beck hated methheads.

On Priest's second day hiding in his apartment, Baz parallel parked in front of Priest's garage, trailed by Diodato in his unmarked Charger. Dusty let them in. Priest threw open the skinny French doors that opened onto a foot-deep balcony overlooking the Venice Beach paddle-ball courts. From time to time, passersby had been known to toss detritus from the boardwalk into Priest's living room, but the cost paid off in fresh air.

While Dusty prepared one of her horrible, healthy green smoothies in the kitchen, Diodato, Baz, and Priest conversed in the living room. Now that Priest was having memories of his own, Diodato felt comfortable parsing out a bit more information.

At approximately six o'clock in the morning—

"*Exactly* six o'clock in the morning," Dusty said.

Dusty had arrived to see if Priest felt like riding his bicycle to keep her company during her run to Manhattan Beach and back. She had found Priest's garage door open and, visible beneath the back bumper, a single flip-flop and the red aluminum Easton Typhoon baseball bat that Priest kept under his bed in case of intruders. Peering into the car through the driver-side window, Dusty saw Priest's keys in the ignition. Finding the car door unlocked, she had fetched the keys, opened the trunk, and found Priest unconscious, wearing only tattered boxer-briefs featuring a cartoon sloth hanging upside down from the crotch.

"I took one look and knew beyond all doubt you were dead," Dusty said from the kitchen. "Luckily, I was wrong."

"What made you open the trunk?" Priest asked her.

"The flip-flop," Dusty said. Her tone indicated *Duh!*

"You're positive it was a woman who attacked you?" Diodato asked Priest.

Priest said that, if it wasn't a woman, it was a very fetching young man. Why?

"She had to be quite strong to pick you up off the floor and stuff you into the trunk," Diodato said.

"I could do it," Dusty said.

"Is that a confession?" Diodato asked.

"Is it?" Dusty asked Baz.

"No. What it is, is an example of why, when you talk to the police, you don't make jokes."

"I wasn't joking," Dusty said. "I'm just saying I'm a woman, and I could pick Priest up off the floor and stuff him into a trunk."

"Did I have any marks on me from falling?" Priest asked. "Scrape marks or dirt from being dragged?"

"No," Diodato and Dusty said in unison—which probably meant that Blue Wig had tasered Priest and tumbled him into the open trunk before he hit the ground. While he was splayed in the trunk of his car, she'd injected him in the neck and ass.

"One of many possible scenarios," Diodato said. "But what if more than one person was involved?"

How did Blue Wig get to Priest's place without an accomplice? How did she get away? There's no way she was foolish enough to use a taxi or a ride-sharing app, which probably indicated that Diodato hadn't found any evidence that she had.

"That's why she wore the blue wig," Priest said. "Take it off, meld in with the morning walkers, cyclists, and joggers heading toward Santa Monica along the beach or boardwalk."

"Meld?" Diodato asked.

"It's the Venice Boardwalk," Priest said.

"Getting away might have been Plan B. Maybe she expected to drive away in Priest's car," Baz said.

"Keys were in the ignition," Dusty said.

"Where do you usually keep your keys?" Diodato asked.

"I'd rather not say," Priest said.

"You think I'm going to steal your car?"

"He leaves them in the ignition," Dusty said. "He doesn't want you to think he's an idiot."

"It doesn't seem prudent," Diodato said.

"It wouldn't be if it weren't for the kill switch," Dusty said.

"I told you," Priest said to Baz.

"Told her what?" Diodato asked.

"I told Baz that someday the kill switch would come in handy."

"You bought a car with a kill switch?"

"I installed it myself. I install a kill switch in all my vehicles."

"Why?"

"I like keeping my keys in the ignition, but I hate people stealing my stuff."

Dusty delivered smoothies to the table.

"I will not drink that," Priest told Diodato. "I advise you against it, too."

Diodato looked at Baz, who sipped her smoothie and raised the glass to Dusty. Diodato slugged back the green goo. "It's not bad," he said. "Why drive off with your body?"

"No body, no murder," Baz said. "No murder, no homicide investigation. Priest would become just another missing person, and we all know how actively those are investigated."

"Amen," Dusty said, obviously thinking about Nikki.

"What about a kidnapping scenario?" Diodato asked.

"I'm not rich," Priest said. "What's the ransom?"

"First, maybe a way to pressure your father to give up his treasure—"

"There's no treasure."

"His *alleged* treasure. Or what if the killer wanted to get you out of the way? Stop you from doing something? Something at work, maybe? You've been out of commission for over a week. Maybe it's 'mission accomplished', and that'll be the end of it."

Diodato asked Priest and Baz for a summary of all the work Priest was supposed to have done between the day he was attacked and, say, a month into the future.

"Without violating client privilege," Baz said.

"It seems like there should be an argument that, if a client is trying to kill a member of his or her legal team, client privilege is waived."

"For *that* client," Baz said. "But not for all my other clients."

Priest and Dusty exchanged looks. Somehow the cop and

the lawyer were freighting all this client-privilege blather with pheromones and other sexy vibes.

"Who knows about the kill switch on your car?" Diodato asked.

Baz.

Dusty.

His ex, Tina.

That was it.

Diodato said he'd ask Tina whether she had mentioned the kill switch to anyone else.

"Say hi for me," Dusty said.

Diodato asked Dusty if she'd mentioned the kill switch to anyone else. When Dusty shook her head, Diodato told her to think about it, it was important, because anyone who knew about the kill switch could probably be removed from the list of people who might possibly have contracted someone to murder or kidnap Priest.

"For example, Nikki Celeste?" Diodato proposed.

"I've never mentioned the kill switch to Nikki," Dusty said.

Baz said she hadn't told anyone either.

Forensic analysis of the piece of hypodermic needle that broke off in Priest's ass was a dead end—no pun intended. They were waiting for toxicology tests now: Priest's urine, blood, and hair.

"The needle will be too ubiquitous to trace," Priest said. "A brand favored by diabetics and junkies."

Diodato sucked air through his teeth. "And now I'm afraid I have to ask a few questions with regard to Ms. Queen," Diodato said.

"Here we go," Dusty said.

"It's a pretty murky world you navigate, Ms. Queen," Diodato said. "Let's say, for example, you bust somebody's legs. Or put someone in a coma. And that person has a good friend. It would be a symmetrical response for that good friend to hurt your good friend. Get my drift?"

"I wish every time somebody got mad at me, they took it out on Priest," Dusty said. "As for Nikki's stalker, the police did not charge me with assault. I got my ass chewed for being rougher than I had to be, but your people agreed it was a legal response to a threat against the person I was hired to protect."

"The stalker has since gone missing," Diodato said.

"Absolutely nothing to do with me," Dusty said.

"There's two kinds of missing," Priest said. "One is where a person flees to a jurisdiction without fussy banking regulations or extradition charges."

"This feels like the other kind of missing," Diodato said.

Priest agreed. He'd spent a couple days trying to chase down Nikki's stalker and found no evidence that he'd fled willingly. Meaning he'd probably been dissolved by sulfuric acid or fed to pigs.

"Maybe the stalker had friends," Diodato said. "Or contacts in low places. We'll be looking into it."

"You mind if I ask a couple questions?" Priest asked.

"Not if you don't mind me not answering," Diodato said. "I will be withholding certain pieces of evidence as standard police procedure, even from you."

Priest tried anyway . . .

Had the car been dusted for prints?

Yes.

Had Diodato spoken to Parris Ferrer?

Yes.

"I still don't think there's any connection between Nikki going missing and what happened to me," Priest said.

"How can you be so certain?" Diodato asked.

"Dusty hired me in the late afternoon. We visited Parris that same evening. You want me to believe Parris could set up a contract killing in the time it took us to get home?"

When he said it out loud, it didn't sound as impossible as it had in his head. For all he knew, Parris Ferrer had assassins on speed dial.

"On the subject of Nikki Celeste," Baz said to Diodato, "do you have any objections to Mr. Priest continuing to look for her?"

"Not as long as I'm kept in the loop."

"Well, that's too bad," said Baz.

"What?" Diodato asked.

"I was hoping you'd tell Priest to back off," Baz said. "If there is a connection to Nikki, maybe Priest backs off, nobody tries to kill him again. Message received."

"I suspect everybody in this room knows that Mr. Priestly is going to continue to look for Nikki Celeste no matter what I say," Diodato said.

"The two cases are not connected," Priest said.

Priest and Baz walked Diodato down to his car.

"Will Dusty Queen be requiring legal counsel?" Baz asked Diodato.

"Dusty Queen is or has been a person of interest in a number of open assault cases," Diodato said.

"That's a non-answer," Baz said.

"Dusty works in personal security," Priest said. "Part of the job is smacking people."

"It seems to be her favorite part of the job," Diodato said.

"Were any of the people who got assaulted good people who didn't deserve assaulting?" Priest asked.

"Your friend has taken part in exactly the kind of nefarious undertakings that boomerang ugly. For her. And maybe for her friends. If I were you, Mr. Priestly, I'd take your lawyer's advice and book a vacation."

"Did I suggest he take a vacation?" Baz asked.

"If you didn't, you should," Diodato said, pheromones leaping around like static electricity again.

"Not only do I not need to hide from Dusty," Priest said, "but Dusty is the main reason I don't have to hide from anyone."

"For a guy who lost his faith, you got a lot of faith," Diodato said.

He gave Priest his card and honked twice as he drove south on Speedway toward Venice Boulevard.

"Well," Baz said, "that could have gone worse."

"Baz, as my lawyer, do you mind not crushing on the detective investigating my attempted murder?"

"I appreciate that he's doing a thorough job," Baz said.

"Just to impress you," Priest said.

"That's sweet."

"If Diodato's so good, why is he wasting time looking at Dusty?"

"First, he's doing his job. And second . . ."

"Yeah? And second?"

"I thought my dramatic pause conveyed my message better than words," Baz said.

"Oh, c'mon! It's Dusty!"

"You see Dusty differently than most people do," Baz said. "If I didn't know better, I'd think you were one of those couples destined to stay married for decades and then die within a couple of days of each other."

"Oh, c'mon! Dusty prefers women, and I'm not one of those people who's gonna pine away for someone who's unattainable."

"I'll give you that," Baz said. "You turned your back on God in a hot flash."

And with that, she drove away, double-tooting the horn.

Dusty ensured that Priest was safely ensconced in his apartment before heading out for her evening swim. Priest told her that he was in for the night, but he was lying. He left a note taped to the refrigerator door and drove off in the Rolling Brown Turd.

———

Parris Ferrer wore an ocelot-patterned pantsuit with a matching diamond and ruby pendant. Black lipstick. Blue eyeshadow. She looked like a scary feline clown, taking miniscule bites from a slice of Bayou Goo pie and iced coffee. Priest had an unobstructed view of the pendant because Parris had thrown her head back like a baying hound, irritated that Priest had sidled up to her regular booth in the House of Pies.

"Parris?" Priest said. "Any thoughts?"

"You want to know if I know anything about a beautiful hit woman?"

"Or man."

"Good for you, Priest, yes. Very woke. Let's go gender-neutral—a beautiful *hitter* who wears a blue wig and stabs targets in the neck with hypodermic needles filled with mystery drugs?"

"I wouldn't fixate on the granular aspect of the blue wig, Parris," Priest said. "I should've said someone who wears disguises and drugs their victim."

"Was the drug supposed to kill the victim?" Parris asked. "Because look at you, all not dead."

"If you are sending a message to Dusty to back off on looking for Nikki, could you give me the message verbally, instead of fatally?"

Moving like the jungle cat she emulated, Parris jammed

her hand down Priest's shirt and raised his arms. Her acrylic tiger nails scribbled across his chest, into his armpits, and into the small of his back. She reached down the crack of his ass. Her nails flicked at the undercarriage of his scrotum. Then she shoved her hand down his front and poked around for a wire between his dick and balls.

"I'm worried you aren't totally convinced," Priest said. "You barely went knuckle deep up my ass."

Parris indicated that Priest could sit, dug a porta-pack of sanitizing gel out of her purse, and rubbed her hands together like a super villain.

"As I already told your detective, the attempt on your life has nothing to do with me. I do not care if you look for Nikki."

"You lie to detectives all the time."

"No, Priest, I do not. You know why? Because I avoid them," she said. "And they tend to avoid me ever since—thanks to you—I successfully sued the LAPD."

"I told Detective Diodato that the timeline was too short for you to have taken out a hit on me."

"Well, there you go, then."

"Unless I underestimated you?"

"I told you what happened to Nikki. And you know what, Priest? You think the same thing. So do the cops. So fuck-the-get-out-of-here-off."

"Do you mind if I order a slice of blueberry pie?"

"Now I *am* thinking of taking a contract out on you," Parris said.

"Excellent. How exactly would you go about that?"

"I'd hire Dusty Queen."

"Why does everyone keep pointing at Dusty?"

"When Nikki had her stalker, I approached a well-respected mainstream security firm with a solid reputation. I told them

I'd prefer to forego increased personal security, ignored police warnings, useless restraining orders—all that useless bullshit—in favor of the only direct action that works on stalkers."

"Broken bones and comas?" Priest asked.

"The security firm advised me to hire Dusty Queen."

"Which security firm?"

"Security Outcomes . . . Yeah, yeah, I know you hate Fiso."

Cody Fiso owned and managed Security Outcomes, the go-to executive protection and private investigation destination for CEOs, studios, celebrities, and other high net-worth individuals.

"What exactly did Fiso say?" Priest asked.

"Fiso waved his big Samoan hands in my face and told me that, if I wanted that kind of quasi-legal action taken, I should approach someone else. And that someone else was Dusty Queen. And you know what?"

"Dusty put the stalker in a coma," Priest said.

"Money well-spent."

"And when he woke up from the coma, he vanished."

"I wouldn't know anything about that," Parris said. "Dusty Queen disappeared the psycho on her own initiative."

"Dusty didn't do that."

"What burns me," Parris said, "is that, if a studio or celebrity asked Fiso to kick a stalker's ass, he'd do it. But Nikki's not a celebrity. She's just an art student struggling to put herself through university."

"Nikki is not an art student, Parris. She's a sex worker. If you start believing your own lies, you'll lose all connection with the real world."

"Hey, brains-for-shit, perception *is* the real world."

"I don't suppose you'd tell me Nikki's real name in case she ran home to Mom and Dad?"

"As far as I'm concerned, her name is Nikki Celeste. Why are you working so hard to find Nikki when she doesn't want to be found?"

"Dusty thinks Nikki wants to be found," Priest said.

"One of these days, Dusty Queen is gonna kill somebody for money," Parris said, "if she hasn't already, and you'll be telling all the high-priced lawyers you work for that you barely knew the woman. Now fuck yourself gone, Priest. Fuck yourself off into the wide, wild world."

———

Instead of fucking himself off into the wide, wild world, Priest went to visit his sister Olive and her husband Martin Prince at their tall, narrow, book-infested house in the Hollywood Hills.

Olive Priestly was ten years older than her little brother, and Martin Prince was twelve years older than Olive. Olive and Martin increasingly looked and sounded like each other. They both wore their hair shoulder-length, with bangs. Olive wore bowler hats. Martin favored fedoras. Olive was three inches taller than Martin, and Martin's ass was three times wider than Olive's. Their nimble imaginations had made them semi-famous and semi-rich, and their neighborhood's touch of old Hollywood appealed to Olive and Martin. Screenwriting partners, spouses, and enthusiastic potheads, Priestly & Prince made a ton of money taking other people's stories and running with them, deepening the lies and fiction. How many times had the two of them stayed home on Oscar night and toasted each other with champagne when some other writer collected an award for their work?

Priestly & Prince were apt to leap to wild, unfounded conclusions that—when Priest was stuck on a case—he used to shake up his brainbox. Olive and Martin forced him to look at things from another point of view and motivated him to think deductively rather than inductively. As far as Priest was concerned, his older sister and her even older husband were human Magic 8 Balls. Clustering, mind-mapping Voodoo Chiles.

To appreciate the view of the famous grid of LA properly, Olive and Martin were obliged to climb up onto their roof. Which is where the three of them sat, on cushions, drinking bottled Belgian beer, smoking weed, and eating cheese and sandwich meats off *Reservation Dogs* TV trays.

"You're the only person to have seen Blue Wig and live," Martin said.

"This isn't a movie," Priest said.

"It's called spit-balling, honeybunch," Olive said. "And the point of spit-balling is not to throw-up obstacles, but to establish conceptual momentum."

Both Olive and Martin were convinced that the attempted hit on Priest—or the warning—had to do with Nikki Celeste.

"I'm interested in the art angle," Martin said.

"Parris Ferrer buys art," Olive added. "Nikki sells that art under a fake name, at a significant profit. We call that a 'motive.'"

"Figure a ten-times mark-up?" Martin said, waggling his hand. "The original artist finds out, demands a cut—"

"Where are you getting these numbers?" Priest asked. "Plus, wouldn't the rogue artist take his or her art back after dealing with Nikki?"

"Not right away," Olive said. "It would reveal the motive too soon."

"In real life," Priest said, "it doesn't matter when the motive is revealed."

"The artist likes the prices Nikki is getting, kidnaps Nikki in an effort to coerce her—"

"Moving on," Priest said.

His mobile buzzed. It was Dusty, wondering where he was. Priest texted her for the sixth time that he was fine and coming home soon, not to worry. In return, she texted some personal questions that only Priest could answer, her way of confirming that Blue Wig wasn't holding a gun to his head or using his dead fingers or gouged-out retinas to unlock his phone.

To Priest's disgust, Olive and Martin could not be dissuaded from the notion that Dusty was involved. They commenced listing what made her Priest's likely secret nemesis:

Dusty was violent and strange, with a dark past.

She regularly consorted with criminals.

She was a criminal.

She was a fitness fanatic.

She trained as a martial artist.

Her sexual proclivities were mysterious.

"Blue Wig is not Dusty," Priest said.

"Anything else we can do to help?" Olive asked.

"Anything *else*? Are you suggesting that you've already helped?"

Olive and Martin followed Priest down off the roof. While Martin checked under Priest's car for a bomb, Olive gave her brother a stamped metal stencil the size of a dog tag, in which various geometrical shapes had been cut.

"What's this for?" Priest asked.

"Laser-cut titanium," Olive said.

Priest pointed out that what something was made of did not convey its function, and Olive explained to Priest that recent scientific advances proved that certain geometric shapes have the power to affect space, time, and gravity on a quantum level.

"Invisible yet profound," Olive said.

"You're high," Priest said.

"Exactly what they do depends upon the electromagnetism generated by the person holding the shape," Martin said.

"Science!" Olive shouted, extending her arms toward Heaven.

"Just saying 'quantum' doesn't make it science," Priest said. "You'd love my tenant. He's a Flat Earth nut."

Olive grabbed Priest's cheeks and told him he didn't have to believe in the power of geometric shapes. Titanium weighed practically nothing.

"Think of it as a good luck charm," she said.

"In the movie," Martin said, "the assassin's bullet would miraculously strike it, instead of piercing your heart."

Priest relented. It was easier just to take the stupid thing than argue with a couple of stoners who thought life was a movie.

7

Priest considered the Hinano Café to be the best bar in the world. Hinano also served the best burger in the world. Priest ordered a cheeseburger with Swiss and chili on an egg bun and a mug of draft, Dusty a veggie burger on sesame and iced tea.

Dusty was taking her time getting over her resentment that Priest hadn't taken her along to act as a bodyguard when he went to see Parris. Buying Dusty lunch at Hinano might not help, but it could not hurt. He demolished his cheeseburger in three bites, ordering another between bites two and three.

"Somebody's enjoying life to the fullest after a recent brush with death," Dusty said.

Priest always ate like a prisoner. In seminary, an instructor had accused him of gluttony—one of the seven deadly sins.

Priest gulped his draft and decided it was time to tell Dusty that everybody suspected she had either orchestrated the hit or was tangentially involved.

"Everybody?"

"Pretty much."

"Even Baz?"

Priest decided that, while Dusty could swallow a ton of shit, if any of that shit came from Baz, it might be too much to bear. "Baz knows better."

"And you?" Dusty asked.

"I know better, too. You want another veggie burger? A stupid question, because nobody anytime anywhere has ever wanted another veggie burger."

"I get it if you won't help me find Nikki," Dusty said. "That's why you went to see Parris, right? To tell her you're off the case, just in case she's the one who hired Blue Wig. I get it. I understand. Gimme my twenty bucks back. No harm, no foul."

"That *is* why I went to Parris," Priest said. "But I came away even more convinced that the attack on me and Nikki going missing are not connected. Correlation is not causation."

Dusty Queen wasn't someone who smiled with her mouth. You had to look very carefully at the way she minimally squinched her eyes.

"Thank you," she said, squinching.

Priest explained that his first step in finding Nikki would be identifying her client.

"How?" Dusty asked.

"Genius investigator stuff," Priest said. "Leave it to me."

"You're taking me with you, right? . . . Don't waggle your head like it was an actual question. You need a bodyguard. As I'm sure everybody has pointed out to you, if you need somebody leaned on, that's my thing, not yours."

"I need to talk to Giselle without you in the room."

"Like you had to talk to Parris without me in the room?"

"Yes, Dusty. Sometimes people are more truthful when you aren't there all coiled up and ready to strike."

"Or you want to ask questions that might hurt my feelings?"

"You have feelings?"

"You drive. I'll ride shotgun. Literally."

Priest wasn't sure whether Dusty was using "literally" literally, and he was too chicken to ask.

8

When Priest pulled up in front of Nikki's place in Westwood, Dusty said, "Anything bad happens, scream. There's always a chance I get there in time to avenge your death."

"What do you want?" Giselle Santa Domingo called down, leaning over her banister, the question all sexy and escort-like.

"I have a few more questions, if you don't mind," Priest said.

"Like what?"

"Like did Nikki leave a computer in her place that I can take a look at?"

"Yup," Giselle said. "Not that it will help you find her."

Giselle let Priest into Nikki Celeste's top-floor apartment. Nikki's desk was in front of a window, looking out over the back of the house, Palos Verdes Peninsula rising above the flatlands to the south. The laptop was in the bottom drawer of the desk.

Priest stuck it into his bag.

"What is that supposed to be?" Giselle asked, tapping Priest's bag with the tip of her toe.

"My briefcase," Priest said.

The bag was Priest's inheritance from his father the bank robber. A black, stained, over-sized cracked leather satchel with mismatched handles and a retractable shoulder strap that unspooled from a hidden compartment. Priest thought the design was brilliant.

"Why don't you get a backpack? Like a normal person?"

Priest shared his theory about backpacks: only children, hikers, soldiers, adventurers, and photographers should wear them. Messenger bags sat awkwardly on his hip. His father's briefcase—which Oliver Priestly had used to tote around his robbery plans and stacks of cash—was perfect. For some magical reason, it didn't bump when Priest trotted. It was big enough to hold a laptop and books and binders and all the rest of his stuff.

"If you insist upon carrying a briefcase, it should be *brief*. It's right there in the name," Giselle said. "I hope you don't think you're taking Nikki's laptop with you."

"I think I thought I was?"

"You can look at it for as long as you want. At my place. Where I can watch you. You can't take it."

"Why?"

"In case Parris comes looking for it."

"I'm pretty sure you could take Parris in a fair fight."

"Don't be ridiculous. Parris doesn't fight fair."

"Mind if I take a few photos?" Priest asked.

He took Giselle's shrug for assent and—thinking of his sister and her husband's art-theft theory—took a quick photographic inventory of Nikki's art, including the signed "Callie Vaughan" originals, before following Giselle down one flight of stairs and into her apartment. He declined a beer. She gave him a fizzy water with lime, slumped back on her couch, and placed her long legs on the glass-topped coffee table, across from Priest. He didn't mention the cocaine residue near her heel. Giselle didn't appear to be high, but she looked so relaxed she might be working overtime *not* to appear high.

"Why do you say I won't find anything helpful on this laptop?"

"Because that's not Nikki's personal laptop. It's her work laptop."

"What's the difference?"

"You let your client see the laptop, right? You even use it together. The last thing the client wants to see is that you snooped on him and his wife and kids on vacation in the Turks and Caicos."

"That's totally what I was hoping to find."

"That's why you research your client on your phone."

"You mind if I take a look anyway?"

"You mind if I sit here and watch?"

That suggestive tone again. Giselle knew her job. Priest opened Nikki's computer. It wanted a password.

"I have no idea," Giselle said.

Priest tried variations of the name *Dusty Queen*, knowing that Nikki did not possess that kind of romantic heart. Next, he tried Nikki's bogus artist name: *Callie Vaughan*.

"Yeah, okay, I get it." Giselle said. "Try her full name."

Priest typed *Calliope*, hoping to make Giselle laugh because he assumed Callie was actually short for Caroline or Calista. He tried not to look shocked when it worked.

"You're good," Giselle said.

Priest went straight to Nikki's recent browser history:

Scenic route to Ojai

Best tapas Ojai

Baby owl

He clicked on the baby owl search, hit "Images," and up popped a GIF of two baby owls perched on a branch while a third scrambled for purchase before dropping out of sight.

"Is this a secret entrance to some kind of escort portal?" Priest asked.

"A what?"

"A place on the dark web where discerning clients can shop for fringe sexual offerings?"

"No. It's a video of a baby owl falling off a branch."

"Why?"

"Law of transitive cuteness," Giselle said.

"What?"

"Nikki tells clients she likes all animals with big eyes, but especially owls," Giselle said. "Client tells her she has huge eyes. Law of transitive cuteness."

Dusty's most recent tattoo was a baby owl.

"But Nikki doesn't really like owls?"

"Nikki prefers hard and shiny to fuzzy and cute."

"What else does she like?"

"What do you mean?"

"Does Nikki like girls? When she's off the clock?" Priest asked.

"Off the cock?"

"I'm asking what's her sexual preference?"

"Nikki's a pro," Giselle shrugged. "When it comes to sexual preferences, we tend to cultivate a go-with-the-flow attitude."

"Go with the flow of *cash*, am I right?" Priest said.

"Judgy," Giselle purred.

Priest ignored the purr but didn't not hope that she would purr again. Which she did.

"Will knowing Nikki's off-duty sexual orientation help you find her? Or are you asking because you're worried that Dusty is going to have her heart broken? Because that is most definitely what's going to happen."

No feline purr there. Just chilly reptilian facts.

"What I'm trying to figure out is, if Nikki ran off with a client, was it for love or money?" Priest asked.

"Love of money," Giselle said.

He scrolled back through Nikki's search history:

Best walking shoes for pronation

Best tapas Santa Barbara

Best tapas Santa Ynez Valley

Best tapas Montecito

"Nikki really loves tapas," Priest said.

"She really doesn't."

"Then this search is bullshit?"

"I told you. This is her work laptop. She sat with the client and looked at these things together. Believe me, her client pronates and loves tapas."

Giselle licked her finger, leaned forward, wiped up the coke dust, and sucked it off her finger. When Priest left, she'd either dip back into her supply or head out to find more.

Miniature golf Los Olivos

Spa Chumash Casino

"None of this looks like fun to me," Priest said.

"It's not fun. It's work."

He indicated another GIF of an owl looking up as a hand appeared in the frame and placed a yellow hat on its head. The owl then looked straight into the camera.

"Cute," Giselle said.

"Did Nikki say anything to you about this latest client?" Priest asked.

"Sexual taste-wise?"

"Something that might help me identify him?"

"Like, moles or scars?"

"I don't need to identify his dead body," Priest said. "I need to find out who he is."

"Me 'n Nik have pretty much been ships in the night the last few weeks. I was in Singapore. Bora Bora. Tahiti. A couple other private archipelagos along the way. On a yacht."

"Also not fun? Because work?"

"Definitely work. Definitely tons of fun."

The fun didn't make it to her voice.

Slightly coked up, Giselle rattled on for a minute about how Priest should relax. That Nikki would be back in a few days. Couple of weeks at the most. Was he thirsty? Would he like to party a little before he went home today?

Next on the laptop search history: *Ulysse Nardin Classico 31mm*

"Any idea what this is?" Priest asked.

Giselle shrugged. "Some kind of wine?"

"Wine doesn't usually come in calibers, does it?"

Maybe an exotic caliber of cartridge?

Film?

A camera lens?

What else was measured in millimeters?

Priest hit "Images."

Up popped a fancy vintage watch.

"Ah, smart girl," Giselle said. "Nikki was fishing for her client to buy her a watch. She doesn't have to share gifts with Parris."

Priest clicked back to "All" and saw a link that was dimmed—a link that Nikki had clicked on. He clicked the link and found himself looking at a listing for a Ulysse Nardin at Gepner's Watch Shop on Pico Boulevard in the Pico-Robertson neighborhood.

Listed as sold for fifteen thousand dollars.

"Oooh, nice," Giselle said.

Priest sent the link to his phone.

"You ever have any clients who wanted you to wear a blue wig?" he asked.

"Is that what you like?"

"What if I did?"

Giselle crossed to a mirror. She pushed and it clicked open, revealing a walk-in cupboard full of sex toys. She pulled out a platinum white wig, a long sea-green mermaid wig, and a Gorgon wig made up of startlingly realistic rubber snakes.

That one she put on.

It was undeniably sexy. Priest's groin shifted. Giselle sensed it and smiled. What would be so wrong with an afternoon of cocaine and Medusa sex? After all, Priest had recently escaped death. Like Dusty said, he should be living life to the hilt.

But Dusty was waiting downstairs. What would she think? If anyone understood falling for an escort, it would be her. That thought settled Priest down. When it came to falling for escorts, it was important that Priest keep to the high road. He refocused on the problem at hand.

"What's the attraction?" Priest asked, circling his index finger over Giselle's snaky head as though they didn't both know he was obviously attracted.

"The wig thing? It's a fetish. Cartoon characters. They got a Japanese word for that, but I forget it."

"Manga? Anime?"

"Maybe. I forget."

"Where would you get a blue wig?" Priest asked.

"Wacky wigs are not hard to find. They aren't expensive because they aren't made of real hair. The idea is for the client to know it's not real. You're supposed to look like a cartoon. See?"

She tilted her head. The snakes twisted and writhed. One looked like it kissed her on the lips. Priest got it. He totally got it.

"Yeah, but where, specifically, would you buy one?"

"Off the internet. Amazon. Target. Costume supply."

Giselle reached up to remove the snake-wig. Her T-shirt lifted to reveal her midriff. Priest saw bruises and discolorations.

"Thanks for your time," he said.

Giselle clicked the wig safely back behind her spotless mirror.

"I'm telling you, Nikki'll come back. Don't forget your hideous mortician's bag from Russia or whatever."

"Is there any chance that Nikki went home?"

"Home?"

"Back where she came from."

"No way."

"Do you know where she came from?"

"Someplace dry. Someplace horrible," Giselle said. "Do you want to know where I'm from? I'll give you a hint. Not from here. Someplace wet. I wouldn't go back, either."

"Why?"

"I hated it."

"I mean Nikki."

"She hated where she came from, too."

"Say Nikki woke up one day and decided she was done with it all. The escort life. The fake name. The fake identity. And she decided to go home . . ."

"Home?"

"I'm looking everywhere Nikki might have gone," Priest said. "Can you give me a hint?"

"Like I said. Dry."

"Do you know Nikki's actual, real name? The one on her birth certificate?"

"Nikki doesn't know the name on my birth certificate."

"Does Parris?"

"If she does, she won't tell you. Or she'll lie."

"Would Parris tell you?" Priest asked.

"Nikki's real name? Not a chance!" Giselle laughed. "Plus, she knows I'd never ask for myself. You know why? Because in this game, who you were before doesn't matter."

"Thank you," Priest said.

"For what? Anyone asks, I told you to go to hell."

Priest collected Dusty from the shadows alongside the house. He told her about Giselle's bruises and the trip to Bora Bora. Maybe Nikki was there. Maybe she'd return in a few days or weeks. Bruised and lashed. Maybe Nikki would do as she'd promised: leave the sex trade, settle down with her androgynous stunt performer with a penchant for breaking the bones of stalkers and other bad men.

"Nikki loves me," Dusty said, "and I love her."

"You've never even had sex," Priest said.

"You only think that's weird because you're a man."

"Thank you," Priest said.

"Don't even. You know it's not a compliment."

When Priest returned home, as Dusty did her calisthenics on the roof, he sat at his computer and downloaded the photos he'd taken of Nikki's fuck-pad, entering them one by one into Google Image, Yandex, and a few more specialized and expensive image-retrieval search applications. One, particularly designed to help art investigators look for stolen paintings and forgeries, utilized artificial intelligence. Another, for paparazzi, was most often used to find plagiarized photos.

Priest requested a range of results, from exact matches to images that might be rendered by the same artist.

Then, he went to bed.

9

Baz reserved a conference room in a Century City high-rise. With a view of downtown LA in the middle distance, Priest and Baz drank coffee, ate Oreo cookies from two-packs, and sifted through their recent cases for anything that might inspire somebody with a grudge to go to the trouble of killing Priest.

Four hours later, they had a small pile of cases—won and lost—that could have generated thoughts of revenge from aggrieved parties.

"We've done a lot together. We make a good team," Baz said. "Would you ever consider taking a full-time position as this firm's lead investigator?"

"And give up my freedom?" Priest asked.

"You're supposed to ask about the benefits," Baz said, "which are amaze-balls."

"Do you think my briefcase looks like it came from a communist country?" Priest asked.

Baz laughed and clapped her hands, very un-lawyerlike. "There's a reason I, sometimes, ask you not to bring it to court. On the upside, it tells jurors that you are efficient, that you put function before form, that you have a certain retro-nobility, and that whatever you pull out of it is the truth, gotten through diligent hard work, insight, and honor."

"What's the downside?"

"It's revolting," Baz said.

"Revolting?"

"It calls your overall judgment into question . . . Don't mouth-fart me! You asked for my input."

———

The next morning, Priest exited his bathroom, clad only in a towel, to find Dusty already fully dressed, drinking coffee, and staring down at the paddle-ball courts. He inhaled the odors of coffee, the ocean, sunscreen, the ubiquitous smell of harsh weed, and loved it all.

"What's doing today?" Dusty asked.

"Security Outcomes," Priest said.

"Cody Fiso? Seriously?"

"Don't make a big deal," Priest said.

"You said you'd never speak to him again."

"I said I'd never *work* for him again. The way I see it, if Fiso does me a favor, it's like he's working for me. I'm fine with that."

"Maybe eat some breakfast first," Dusty suggested, "so you have something to throw up."

Myths and legends swirled like dust devils around Cody Fiso, starting with the fiction that he stood seven feet tall when he was actually only six-foot-nine. In cowboy boots. In bare feet, Fiso was six-six max. Legend had it that he weighed three hundred pounds. Reality: two-seventy, most of it muscle, the rest made up of compressed manic energy, a chunky Rolex, and a gold neck chain that looked like a bicycle lock. He'd worked in federal law enforcement, which could have been either a false-hood or God's own truth; not even an investigator as adept as Xavier Priestly had been unable to uncover any meaningful insight into Cody Fiso's past beyond him being the eldest of four Samoan sons. There was either no more information to be had or else Fiso had worked for an organization secretive and paranoid enough to expend the energy and resources to keep it a secret: CIA, FBI, NSA, Secret Service, federal marshals, a super-secret private mercenary organization, or all the above.

Fiso had subcontracted Priest as a private investigator three times. Each time Priest had discovered things that Fiso had not wanted discovered. Each time Fiso had done his best to apply boundaries to Priest's investigations. Priest had not only crossed those boundaries, he'd painted them orange and set them on fire. What normal human being was able to avoid looking exactly where he was told not to look? As Priest had informed Fiso, he—Priest—was demonstrably a normal human being.

What Priest knew for certain was that a stick-up-the-ass streak of dedication to duty ran deep in Cody Fiso. Beyond his size, there was nothing rebellious or unorthodox about the man. Fiso believed in an orderly universe and had no qualms about imposing order on any chaos that broke out in his general vicinity, whether it was any of his business or not. Fiso was one of those irritating people who told other people to calm down, dampen their furnaces, cool their jets, pump the brakes. Fiso believed in hierarchy, in Dante's Nine Circles of Hell, in submitting to the rightful authority of those above him and exerting his God-given authority over those beneath him. These fundamental qualities brought Cody Fiso into direct conflict with Xavier Priestly, a godless man who rebuked all authority. Who rejected the doctrine of the Divine Right of Kings. Who thrived in confusion. A disruptor who acted as an agent of chaos to reveal the truth. Xavier Priestly and Cody Fiso clashed on an ancient, metaphysical level—Archangel Michael versus Lucifer—a level that Fiso believed was real and Priest assuredly did not.

Fiso called Priest "The Seminarian" because it annoyed him. Fiso and Priest annoyed the fuck out of each other.

Fiso's company, Security Outcomes, provided bodyguards, private investigators, hackers, counter-surveillance experts, undercover moles, industrial espionage and counter-espionage agents to anyone who could pay his fees.

Priest drove east on Venice Boulevard to Culver City and the offices of Security Outcomes, a maze of secure, interconnected buildings between Higuera Street and Ballona Creek. Whenever Fiso needed to expand his operations, he bought out his neighbors and added to his real-estate portfolio.

Dusty sipped an espresso in the atrium as a young man with two prosthetic legs showed Priest to Fiso's outer office. Priest heard Fiso's voice shouting at him to enter the inner office. That was a first. He usually met Priest in a conference room.

"Always good to see the Seminarian," Fiso said.

Fiso's outer office may have looked like the future, but his inner office looked like a suburban dad's 1980s man cave: gigantic steel roll-top desk; wooden stereo credenza with antique bowling pins arranged on top, begging to be knocked over; glass-topped conference table with bamboo legs bound in cast iron; and a well-worn custom Big-'n-Tall black leather La-Z-Boy recliner. Overdone overkill. Like Fiso himself.

Priest felt a jolt of nostalgia for his own father's man-cave in his childhood home on Canby Street in Portland, Oregon. Oliver Priestly had spent a lot of time down in the basement, supposedly trying hobby after hobby in a vain quest to find something that interested him as much as selling cars. It was years before Priest realized that his father was down there planning heists of banks, armored cars, and Indian casinos.

"What did you do?" Priest asked Fiso. "Recreate your father's home office?"

"I loved my old man," Fiso said. "He died of a heart attack when I was twenty-five. My brothers got his cars and motorcycles. I inherited all this stuff. My father was a great and good man. This helps me keep his memories close."

Priest disliked Fiso on a visceral level but admired his unwillingness to be embarrassed or self-conscious about his emotions, opinions, or tastes. The man was an open book. Priest preferred closed books. Priest's job was to open closed books, and he was good at it. Open books like Fiso made Priest feel unnecessary and irrelevant.

"Please, sit," Fiso said.

Aside from Fiso's father's stainless-steel battleship of a roll-top, a plexiglass stand-up desk stood at about the height of a refrigerator, facing the picture window that looked out over a concrete sluiceway known to Google maps as Ballona Creek. Legend had it that Fiso had been standing at that desk when the creek overflowed its banks after a rainstorm miles upstream in the San Gabriel Mountains. Fiso had seen a foolish, hypothermic boy being swept downstream, clinging to a Boogie Board, and run out, plunged into the filthy torrent, and dragged the kid to safety through the foaming brown maelstrom.

Cody Fiso: hero and legend.

Opposite the picture window, the entire wall was taken up by a dozen flat-screen televisions playing the major news channels, a stock market feed, live security-cam footage at a storage unit, and a nature show featuring jellyfish.

"How's your father?" Fiso asked, sitting down so that Priest would sit and, once he did, shooting back up to his feet.

"In prison until Doomsday," Priest said. "Thanks for asking."

"Any developments on the McGinn disappearance?"

"I gave up on that years ago."

"I don't want to call a former seminarian a liar," Fiso said, "but I don't mind saying I think you are lying."

The mystery of Charlie McGinn's disappearance had been the Great White Whale of private investigators for decades. McGinn had played bass in a one-hit psychedelic rock band back in the seventies, but being a rock star and audio-recording genius had been McGinn's side gig. He also held a doctorate in physics from Stanford and had worked on a DARPA-level secret weapons development at the Point Mugu Naval Base in Oxnard, California. On October 17, 1978, Dr. Charles McGinn, rock god, set off from his home in Topanga Canyon in a perfectly restored 1936 Lancia Astura Pinin Farina Cabriolet, either to report to his super-secret weapons job (according to redacted documents released in 2015 by the United States Navy) or to pick up a rewound P-Style pickup from his guitar tech in Encino (according to his wife).

McGinn hadn't arrived at either destination. He and his Lancia had vanished. Even before the internet, conspiracy theories blossomed. McGinn was covered in three episodes of *America's Most Wanted*. With the rise of online communities, message boards dedicated to the mystery of Charlie McGinn had proliferated internationally.

Finding Charlie McGinn became an obsession for thousands of armchair investigators, conspiracy theorists, retired cops, and amateur sleuths. Professional investigators knew that solving the mystery would not only make them legends but also ensure international plaudits.

Highly paid speaking tours.

Highly paid talking-head punditry on cable news.

Highly paid podcasts.

There were hundreds of theories about how and why Charlie McGinn had vanished, none of which had been proven:

He'd defected to Russia with secret weapons plans.

He'd been murdered by a jealous Jaco Pastorius.

He'd been abducted by China / North Korea / East Germany / Alpha Centauri.

He'd been scooped up by the CIA and was now working on time travel and multiverse dimensionality at a secret base in Alaska, or inside an active Hawaiian volcano, under the ice in Antarctica, or in a classified Illuminati base on the dark side of the moon.

Priest had first heard of McGinn's disappearance while in seminary, but he'd really become interested when pursuing his degree in criminology at Mount Saint Mary's. In a course taught by a retired LAPD homicide detective, Charlie McGinn had been held up as an example of what happens when too much information shifted the information/noise ratio so radically that the truth was no longer discernible.

"Asking the public for help in an investigation is a desperate, last-ditch measure," the ex-detective had lectured, "because the public is stupid, paranoid, venal, forgetful, duplicitous, suggestible, excitable, and flighty. Write that down."

The lecture had reminded Priest of one Jesuit in seminary who taught that the Bible was so crammed with revelation and metaphor that untrained laymen would only be overwhelmed. Priests, the Jesuit had taught, were the only experts who could be trusted.

Preferably, Jesuit priests.

Meaning: *Suck on it, Protestants.*

"How about you?" Priest asked. "Still looking for McGinn?"

"Yes," Fiso said, "and I will find him. And when I do, you will owe me a hundred thousand dollars."

Priest and Fiso had an outstanding bet about who would find McGinn. Priest thought the bet was for ten thousand dollars. Fiso thought it was for a hundred thousand.

"I don't want to waste your time here, Fiso," Priest said,

because Fiso was wasting *his* time. "The scenario I provided you ring any bells?"

"Female. Late twenties, early thirties," Fiso said. "Wears a blue wig . . . Are you nodding or shaking your head? Those gestures convey opposite meanings. You know what works better? Words."

Fiso demanded verbal responses. Non-verbal responses were ambiguous, and Cody Fiso hated ambiguity above all else. He recorded every conversation.

"Female," Priest said. "Blue wig. Hypodermic in the neck."

"Ouch."

"I don't remember if it hurt. I don't remember anything."

"Side effect of the drug?"

"So I'm told."

"You got any reason to doubt what you were told?"

"Of course."

"Priest, you are what people call a misanthrope."

Was Fiso mocking him from behind that gigantic slab of a face? Priest couldn't tell for certain, and that irritated him. No way he could do his breathing exercises without Fiso noticing, so he tried to slow down his heart rate through willpower alone. It did not work.

"I don't see any other reason you'd lose your memory of the event," Fiso said. "No head trauma. No significant loss of blood. Your heart didn't stop, so no oxygen deprivation. Did law enforcement identify the drug?"

"They won't tell me."

"Had to be rapid-acting. But not so fast that you didn't have time to fight back, bust off a piece of the needle in your ass."

Fiso had provided that last detail to let Priest know that he had a source in the LAPD. It was a detail that had not been released. Still, Priest felt the tiniest surge of pride that Cody Fiso thought the broken needle was a result of Priest fighting back and not simply a case of clumsy ass-injection.

"Like I said, I don't want to waste your time or my own," Priest said. "Parris Ferrer told me that you had some knowledge of quasi-legal operators who might cross the line from time to time. I wondered if any of them wore wigs and drugged people."

"Tiger-lady-pimp Parris Ferrer told you I knew where to find a *hitter*?"

"She said you advised her to hire Dusty Queen when she, Parris, wanted a stalker roughed up."

"Untrue," Fiso said. "I advised Parris Ferrer to deal with the stalker through legal channels. My exact words were, 'I am not Dusty Queen.' If Parris took it as a recommendation, that's on her."

"Pretend for ten seconds that I'm Parris Ferrer," Priest said. "I come to you and say I need someone made dead, preferably by a young woman in a blue wig with a hypodermic needle full of mystery amnesia drugs. After you advise me not to break the law—because you're an ethical straight shooter—who do you tell me you aren't?"

"The person I would tell you I am not," Fiso said, "is Dusty Queen in a blue wig."

"Try again," Priest said.

"You're a professional investigator. I'm sure you've registered that Blue Wig's modus operandi is to make her targets disappear."

Priest knew exactly where Fiso was going. Patterns were everything. If people did things only once, they'd be a lot harder to catch.

"The stalker that Dusty Queen put in the hospital disappeared hours after he was released," Fiso continued.

Priest stood up. "Dusty is not Blue Wig. Sorry for you wasting my time."

"I might dimly recall something," Fiso said, staring out at Ballona Creek.

"What's with the dramatic pause?" Priest asked. "Are you looking for me to slip you a hundred bucks, like a bartender I'm pumping for info? If so, tell me, because I don't actually know how payoffs work. Can't you just bill me?"

"I'm thinking," Fiso said. "It's a thing I do sometimes before I speak."

"Seriously. I'm not the kind of shadowy investigator with his finger on the pulse of the codes of the street. Should I be offering you a *thousand* dollars? Slip it to you when we shake hands? Leave it on your desk while you stare out the window hoping a drowning kid needs saving?"

"I saw a surveillance tape of a guy maybe getting jabbed in the neck in the parking lot of the Alkali."

"What's the Alkali?"

"Busted casino off Highway 95. One of those scrubby desert towns halfway between Vegas and Reno," Fiso said.

"What do you mean *maybe* got jabbed?"

"It was substandard footage, badly lit, edge of the frame, in the dark. A shadow maybe jabs a guy, maybe in the neck. There's no blood, so not a knife. Maybe an ice pick. Maybe a slap. But maybe a hypodermic."

"Did the guy survive?"

"Who knows? He falls out of frame. It remains an open missing-persons file. Nevada State Police found his burned-out car a year later near a railway siding on the Utah border."

"Similar *modus operandi*. Jab the target in the neck, cart off the body in his own vehicle," Priest said.

"You are applying a ton of cha-cha to my meager observation," Fiso said. "All I saw was a pixelated shadow and another pixelated shadow at the edge of a frame."

"When was this?" Priest asked.

"Fifteen months ago."

"You remember the target's name?"

"Jack Stallion."

"Oh, c'mon! *Jack Stallion . . .*"

"Big-shot music producer. It's his legal name."

"Why'd the Nevada State Police show you the tape?"

"What?"

"What part did you play in the investigation?" Priest asked. "After Jack Stallion went missing, why'd the staties show you the tape?"

"It wasn't the state police. The Alkali showed it to me."

"The casino? Why?"

"They were looking to hire me in case they were sued for not providing appropriate security precautions in the parking lot for their customers. I turned down the assignment."

"Maybe you could just answer more fully," Priest said, "instead of forcing me to ask 'why' after everything you say."

"I turned down the assignment because the Alkali Casino did not provide appropriate security precautions in the parking lot for their customers, and they couldn't pay me enough to say, under oath, that they did."

"Out of curiosity, how much would have been enough?"

"You got any relevant questions?" Fiso asked.

"No," Priest said, adding, "I owe you."

"Don't think I won't collect."

Approaching the shit-brown Jeep Cherokee in the Security Outcomes parking lot, Priest squinted at Dusty and imagined her in a blue wig. Not an iota of a jolt of recognition. Then he felt guilty for even entertaining the notion. Then he felt irritation at himself for feeling guilty.

They were driving beneath the 10 freeway on Washington Boulevard before Dusty asked, "Anything?"

"Enough that I owe Cody fucking Fiso a favor."

"Home?"

"Not yet," Priest said. "I want to stop at Gepner's Watch Shop on Pico to make some inquiries."

"Can't you do it by phone?"

"No," Priest said, crawling into the back seat.

"Is this about Blue Wig or Nikki?"

"Twenty bucks is twenty bucks," Priest said, digging through his duffle bag. "Even if I do think you are wasting your time looking for Nikki when she'll come crawling back any day now."

Priest found his priest disguise and crawled into the back of the Cherokee to pull it on. The disguise had worked well for Priest in several investigatory situations that didn't require him to take the stand. While misrepresenting oneself in the course of an investigation wasn't illegal, it tended to look bad to judges, juries, and the opposing attorneys.

Dusty parked across the street from Gepner's and told Priest she'd stay with the Cherokee, reasoning that, if Blue Wig were smart enough to lay in wait inside the watch store, then Priest had no chance of survival anyway. She assured him that, if she saw any suspicious woman between the ages of fifteen and fifty enter the store while he was in there, she'd follow, taser blazing. Priest suspected she was packing heat more lethal than a taser, but he'd long ago decided that a "Don't Ask, Don't Tell" policy was best when it came to Dusty Queen. She tended to answer his questions truthfully, and sometimes plausible deniability was preferable to knowledge.

Outside the watch shop, Priest nodded at the near-comatose security guard, an armed and scowling man who hid his extreme boredom behind a terse nod of his own. Priest noted the patch on the guard's shoulder: SECURITY OUTCOMES. A foot soldier in Cody Fiso's expanding imperial army. Fiso would not condone the scowl.

Priest entered Gepner's and stopped dead, framed in the doorway. He pulled his best Man-of-God-in-the-Temple-of-Commerce face. It wasn't difficult. Banks of glass counters displayed thousands of glittering watches. Priest allowed himself to gape because it seemed in character for a humble parish priest, and it worked like a charm. A brisk young saleswoman wearing a rose-gold Chai pendant approached. Her name tag identified her as Alma.

Over the next few minutes, Priest allowed Alma to draw an awkward and embarrassing story out of him. It involved a young parishioner who had allowed herself to be dazzled by an older man with money. The older, wealthy man bought her a Ulysse Nardin Classico 31 mm. watch here at Gepner's. The young parishioner had recently come to confession suffering extreme guilt.

"I advised her, spiritually, that a gift isn't really a gift when it comes encumbered by, um, reciprocal obligations of a sinful nature," Priest said, screwing his face into the expression of a naive priest who nonetheless considers himself an expert on sin, especially in the form of transactional sex.

"My parishioner would like to return the watch to the man who gave it to her," he said. "Not as penance. This is something she wants to do for herself. But the, uh, gentleman in question, never provided her his full name, just a . . . a . . . a pet name? If she can't find the man to return the watch, she'll give it to charity."

"Or, Father, Gepner's will buy the Classico back at the full purchase price," Alma said. "Tell your parishioner to speak with me directly."

Alma was aching to meet the young woman in question.

Priest pressed Alma for the name of the gentleman who'd bought the watch, insisting that as much as the parish would appreciate fifteen thousand dollars, his conscience-stricken parishioner was looking for a symbolic way to regain her self-respect, and it was his spiritual duty to help her. Alma resisted, in the name of discretion. Priest wondered if they could find a compromise in which Alma called the gentleman and ask if he'd do the right thing and agree to meet with his parishioner so that she could return the watch.

Priest waited, giving Alma time to imagine calling a customer and providing him with the phone number of a priest who wanted to arrange a meeting with a dismayed young woman to return the expensive watch given in payment for sexual favors.

In the end, Alma decided to write the old perv's name on a Post-it.

Priest handed Dusty the Post-it as he climbed behind the wheel of the Grand Cherokee. He yanked the collar from his neck and started the engine.

"Stephen T. Tedeschi," Dusty read off the back of the card. "That our guy?"

"He's *a* guy," Priest said. "It remains to be seen if he's *our* guy."

Dusty squinched her eyes at Priest in her closest approximation of a smile.

"Where do you want to buy me lunch?" he asked. "Versailles?"

"Better to use a drive-through," Dusty said, in bodyguard mode.

There were worse things in the world than In-N-Out for lunch while not getting murdered.

Safely home later—Dusty made Priest promise that he would stay inside with the door locked until she finished her night swim—Priest sat down for some internet sleuthing on watch buyer Stephen T. Tedeschi.

It took Priest about three minutes to find him. Tedeschi worked as a commercial real estate mini-mogul in Silicon Valley.

Google Images provided his smiling face on a shuttle-bench ad: *Call Steve T for your commercial real estate needs. The T stands for Timely!*

Tedeschi's Yelp reviews were good. More than one satisfied client said the T stood for "Terrific." Stephen T. Tedeschi didn't maintain a Facebook page, but his wife Erica Tedeschi did, and she referred to her "best friend and soul mate, Stephen" in her profile. In a short video—finishing a five-kilometer Turkey Trot in a eucalyptus grove in Moss's Landing, California—Stephen matched the description that the manager of the Peninsula had provided to Dusty: fifties, fit. Another photo showed Stephen finishing the Sea 2 Sky triathlon in Vancouver, British Columbia. Another, finishing the Malibu Iron Man behind the actor who'd played Urkel. Other photos showed Stephen T. exerting himself near Hilo on the Big Island of Hawaii, and in Sedona, Arizona.

Erica Tedeschi, a pleasant-faced woman nowhere near as fit as her husband, had also posted photos of Stephen with the family. In one, Stephen and Erica kissed while their teenage kids—Steve Jr. and Brooklyn—made gagging faces in the background.

Priest felt bad for the kids. Stephen T. Tedeschi was nowhere near as terrific as his family thought.

10

Back from her swim, Dusty said she wanted to check in on her house-sitting assignment, a luxury condo on the beach at the southern end of the Marina Del Rey Peninsula. What she really did was cover her newly luminescent platinum hair with a wool cap and withdraw like a moray eel into the cave of darkness that was Venice Beach at night with a couple cans of Red Bull, Mexican internet Ritalin, and her battered ATN Gen 3 night-vision binoculars. What Priest didn't yet know was that Dusty had also installed a spy camera—with a feed she could monitor on her phone—on the roof of the multi-story apartment on 20th and Speedway for wide-angle surveillance over the back of Priest's building.

Less than an hour after Priest's online investigation into the life and times of Mr. Stephen T. Tedeschi, he heard a string of boy-voiced profanities from the Venice Boardwalk immediately in front of his building. Not rare. Skateboarders were masters of profanity, and like squid, skaters were mostly social animals who traveled in packs. A lone curse was an oddity.

Priest heard a slap and a yelp, followed by another burst of cursing pitched at a frequency that would make dogs bark.

Priest opened the skinny windows that looked out over the boardwalk. "What's going on down there?"

Dusty emerged from the shadows between the paddle-ball courts, gripping a boy's ear. He was maybe twelve.

"I asked you to please not silhouette yourself," Dusty said. "You're a target."

The kid wore a red hoodie, a camo backpack, stretchy black pants with lots and lots of angled zippers, and a red T-shirt emblazoned with *When They Go Low, We Get High!* He tried to roundhouse Dusty.

Mistake.

In a blurry, back-and-forth, one-handed motion, she knocked his fist away and slapped his left cheek. The kid was shocked into silence for a long five-count.

"I dare you to try that again," Dusty said.

"Don't do it, kid," Priest advised.

But the kid accepted Dusty's challenge and swung at her again. So she slapped him again, harder this time. She shifted her hold from his ear to his backpack to keep him on his feet, supporting him like he was a four-foot-nine, fall-down-drunk skydiver.

"The smart move is complete capitulation," Priest told the kid.

"Priest, please go inside," Dusty said.

The kid looked up at Priest for the first time. He had a prominent nose and a tiny, thin-lipped mouth with a slightly receding chin that—despite his lolling head—looked determined rather than weak. Unfocused, his eyes were green and oversized, his close-cropped hair almost black, his face pale. He resembled an under-sized, under-aged vampire Marine. The kid tried to kick Dusty. Exasperated, she reached down behind him and yanked his boxers up midway over his backpack. He made a noise like a mewling cat.

"Jesus, Dusty," Priest said, wincing.

"Let us in before somebody calls the cops."

Priest didn't see anyone closer than the basketball courts to the north and the Pier to the south, certainly not anyone who'd call the police, but he made his way down to the steel security gate on the boardwalk. When he swung it open, the kid shouted, "Help!" Dusty snicked him in the throat, reducing his shouts to a gurgle.

"If you're going to kill the kid, just do it," Priest said. "Or maybe just let him go before we fully commit to kidnapping?"

"He had this in his backpack," Dusty said, reaching behind her and pulling out a small engraved, silver, pearl-handled semi-automatic pistol.

"What's that? A toy?"

"Nope," Dusty said. "Twenty-five caliber Baby Browning. It'd sting pretty bad if he shot you in the guts. If he shot you in the head, it'd totally scramble your basic math skills."

The kid batted at Dusty again. He was brave, but not a fast learner.

"We should call the cops," Priest said. "Let them handle it."

"There are photos of you on his phone, coming and going, *today*. Photos of the building. Front gate. Side door. The garage."

"Why are you spying on me?" Priest asked the kid.

"Fuck you . . . you fucking . . . faggot," the boy said, struggling to form words through his spasming larynx.

Would a killer hire a little kid to keep an eye on her victim? Of course. This was Los Angeles. Why not?

"Bring him in," Priest said. "I'll call Diodato."

Give the boy some credit, he was quick. He shucked off the backpack and turned to face them in the dim light of the courtyard, dukes up, weight balanced on the balls of his feet. He reminded Priest of a cornered meerkat. Not scary, but capable of startling you.

"Good body position," Dusty said. "Chin down. Eyes up. But your legs are spread too wide."

"Fuck you," the kid said, adjusting his stance.

Instinctively responds to coaching, Priest noted.

"Right foot pointing where he wants to hit, so he's a south-paw," Dusty said. "You're left-handed, aren't you, Priest?"

"Only for some things," Priest said.

"Like punching?"

Dusty was poking Priest. Why?

"What's your name?" Priest asked the boy.

"Fuck you, fucker."

"Nice to meet you, Fuck You Fucker," Priest said. "It suits you."

The kid's cheeks were red, either from humiliation or being slapped or both. But his eyes were dry. A normal kid would be weeping by now, wouldn't he?

Dusty removed the magazine from the Baby Browning.

"Leave that alone," the kid said. "It's mine."

"Six-shot magazine," Dusty told Priest. "Two cartridges missing."

"Did you shoot two people?" Priest asked. "Or one person twice?"

When Priest moved, the kid's eyes flicked. He adjusted his feet.

Dusty dug into her own backpack and produced a blue wig.

"What the hell?" Priest said.

"Make him try it on," Dusty said.

"Fuck you, pervert!" the kid said.

"Dusty, he's not her. Blue Wig was at least six inches taller."

"Make him try it on. Be sure."

"Fuckin' freaks," the kid said.

Dusty wore her most stubborn face. The boy was going to put on that wig one way or another. Priest took the wig and plopped it on the kid's head. He shook it off immediately, without dropping his dukes.

"Voila! Not him," Priest said. "I'm absolutely positive. Satisfied?"

Dusty nodded and put the wig back in her backpack.

"Let me go," the boy said, "or I'll tell the cops you offered me ten bucks to suck my dick."

"Ten bucks is all you charge?" Dusty asked. "You suffer from low self-esteem on account of your big nose and shitty personality?"

"I'm calling Diodato," Priest said. "We can't abduct a kid off the beach, even when he's armed."

Dusty emptied the kid's backpack. A few T-shirts, rolled-up khakis, two pairs of black skater shorts, boxer-briefs. *Terminator*-style Under Armour sunglasses. Top-of-the-line Android. Biker's wallet with an American flag and a chain. Pouch of Bugler rolling tobacco. Zig-Zag rolling papers. An Altoids tin with two expertly rolled joints in it. Good weed. Better weed than you'd expect even a precocious sixth-grader to score at middle school, even if it was stale.

"Don't touch my shit," the kid said.

"Six hundred bucks in the wallet," Dusty said. "All in fifties. Credit card."

"Is the name on the card Fuck You Fucker?" Priest asked.

Dusty angled the credit card in the low light. "Anthony Orange."

Orange?

"Orange?" Priest asked.

"O-R-A-N-G-E," Dusty said. "Like the fruit."

"So Fuck You Fucker is just a nickname, right?" Priest asked the kid, stalling for time. Pulling up memories, doing math.

Orange.

The kid lunged at Dusty again. Priest had never seen anybody move faster than Dusty, and this boy wasn't going to be the first. He jabbed at Dusty's solar plexus. Dusty toe-flicked him in the groin with what appeared to be negligible force. The boy dropped and turtled on the brick floor of the courtyard.

"Dusty!"

"I'm doing him a favor. He's gotta learn."

Priest lifted the kid by his waistband and let him dangle: "Breathe in through your nose, out through your mouth."

The boy did what he was told.

Priest set him back on his feet.

Dusty plucked another card from the kid's wallet. "Tarquin X. Orange."

"Tarquin? Like the last king of Rome?"

"Fuck you," the boy grunted.

Dusty read the card. "Titanium Boxing Gym. Las Vegas, Nevada." She turned to the boy. "What division? Ninety pounds?"

"Fuck you."

"Looks like you wrote 'Pow-Pow' on here. That the nickname you fight under?"

"That's right," the kid said.

"Cool. How old are you?"

"None of your business," the kid said.

"He's twelve," Priest said. Then, to the boy, "What's the X stand for?"

"It stands for fuck you," Tarquin said. Then, to Dusty, "What are you? Tranny? Some kind of oriental dyke?"

Dusty tilted toward him. The boy stepped back, accepting the harsh reality that he was outclassed.

"The word 'oriental' is not acceptable in the context you used it," Priest said. "Nor is 'faggot,' in any context. Or 'tranny.' Or 'dyke.'"

Dusty flapped an envelope she had from the backpack to get Priest's attention. Written on the front, in red felt pen, was a single word.

Quinn.

The boy horked and spat as Dusty pulled a letter from the envelope and read it to herself silently.

Dusty glanced up at Priest and raised her eyebrows.

"What?" Priest asked.

"Meet your son."

Priest extended his hand for the letter.

"It's up to Pow-Pow to show you," Dusty said, folding the paper into the envelope and stuffing it into the backpack.

"You think I'm your father?" Priest asked.

"No," the boy said.

"Okay, well, here's your choice. Either come inside of your own volition and under your own steam, or we call the police and let them deal with you."

"I'll come inside," the boy said, "if the Terminator promises not to hit me again."

"I worked on one of those movies," Dusty said.

Priest led the way upstairs.

"What a shithole," the boy said.

"You want something to drink?"

"Beer," the kid said.

"I got grapefruit juice."

The boy grunted and dug into his backpack for his roll-your-own fixings. He rolled a cigarette one-handed—nonchalant, like a cowboy—lit it up with a match and blew a jet of smoke through his nose.

"If you're going to smoke, we're heading up to the roof," Priest said, irritated by the kid's adroitness. Who the hell was he emulating?

Up on the roof deck, Tarquin X. "Pow-Pow" Orange shoved the cigarette into the corner of his mouth, folded his arms across his chest, and watched Dusty plug in the patio lanterns, providing Priest with his first opportunity to take a good look at the boy. Tom Ford hoodie. Japanese Vans. Rip Curl skate backpack. Top-of-the-line Samsung phone. Somebody was providing the boy with more than the bare necessities. Probably the guy on the credit card, Anthony Orange.

"That gun belong to your mother?"

"No. It's my gun."

Much clearer than Priest's memory of the Baby Browning was the image of a young woman who'd threatened him with it thirteen years ago: early twenties, naked except for a pair of silver-sequined cowboy boots, twirling the tiny pistol on her index finger, threatening to shoot Priest if he didn't "commence with round three within the next thirty seconds." Priest—also then in his early twenties—had found the boots and the gun disturbingly alluring, or alluringly disturbing. Maybe Tarquin X. Orange was the result, sitting here today on Priest's roof deck, smoking under the patio lanterns, picking tobacco off his tongue. A tough little nugget. Maybe Priest should call the boy *Round Three*.

"Is your mother's name Rachel?"

"It was."

"What happened?"

The boy didn't answer, just jetted smoke out his nostrils and hunched.

"Did Rachel *die*?"

A short, angry nod. Even after almost thirteen years, Priest felt a stab in his heart and in his gut.

"When?"

"While ago."

"I'm sorry to hear that. Really sorry. What happened?"

"Fuck you is what happened."

"I'd appreciate it if you told me. Please."

"Car accident."

"I am truly sorry to hear that," Priest said.

"Ninety people die in car accidents every day," the boy said. "That's the average. A hundred and sixteen died on the day my mom got killed."

He'd looked it up. A child's effort to make sense of an indifferent universe.

"What's Anthony Orange to you?" Priest asked. "Uncle? Grandfather?"

The kid nodded.

"Which?"

"Grandfather."

"He know where you are?"

"Don't worry about it."

"How long have you been away?" Dusty asked.

"Couple days."

"How long before he gets worried?"

"Couple days."

The kid hadn't answered "Fuck you" to a series of personal questions. Progress was being made.

"Where does your grandfather think you are?"

"Boxing camp in La Quinta. I'm not lying to him; there's a boxing camp. I'm just not telling him the truth that I didn't go."

The kid was flagging in front of their eyes. The adrenaline Dusty had whipped up in the boy by slapping him around was subsiding fast.

"Tomorrow we'll figure out what happens next. Dusty is going to hang on to your gun. No smoking in the house."

"I'm taking the weed," Dusty said.

"It's mine," the kid said.

"You want to fight me for it?"

"You two together or what?" the boy asked.

"Or what," Dusty said.

"Which one of you's supposed to be the man?"

"Definitely your son," Dusty told Priest. "He thinks he's funny."

"You know what? Gimme back all my shit," the boy said. "I'm taking off."

"Taking off where?" Dusty asked.

"Fuck you is where."

"It's dangerous for a kid to be out there alone this time of night," Priest said.

"You said I could leave if I want."

"We said your choices were stay or we call the police," Priest said.

"I'll move my stuff out of the guest room," Dusty told Priest. "He can have that."

"If I take off before the cops get here, you'll keep my gun and weed, right?" the kid asked.

"And your wallet," Dusty said. "And all your money."

A flash of relief on the kid's face. He needed a reason to stay that didn't make him look like he'd capitulated, and Dusty had them.

Dusty put the wallet, the gun, and the Altoids tin into her backpack. "Pow-Pow, you did the right thing coming here."

"How do you know?" the kid asked.

"I read the letter," Dusty said. And then, to Priest, "Get me that sleeping bag I bought for you. I'll sleep on the roof."

"I'll sleep on the couch; you take my room," Priest said.

"Don't be ridiculous," Dusty said.

Priest gave her the sleeping bag. It was still in the packaging.

"Good luck," she said, heading up for the roof.

"Thanks," Priest said.

"I was talking to Pow-Pow," she called back.

Priest scrambled two eggs for the boy. He ate them so fast Priest went ahead and scrambled three more, adding a couple slices of sourdough toast with peanut butter and hash browns. The boy drank an entire carton of orange juice while Priest re-made the guest bed with fresh sheets.

"The door locks, if that makes you feel better. There's the bathroom. Towels under the sink. You got a toothbrush? . . . No? . . . What kind of kid has a gun but no toothbrush? You'll find a new toothbrush in the medicine cabinet."

After the boy shut and loudly locked the door, Priest sat down at his computer with a bowl of pistachios and entered "Anthony Orange + Las Vegas" into the search engine. Up came a LinkedIn page and a bunch of local news stories about mall openings and real-estate purchases, mostly auctions and fore-closures. In the accompanying photos, Anthony Orange looked old-school Vegas with his slicked-back Grecian Formula hair and shiny suits. Flashy.

Priest accessed a private database maintained for subscrib-ers, mostly private investigators and corporate security types. Anthony Orange, sixty-nine years old. Small business owner in Vegas. Rented out space to auto repair shops. Weight-loss clin-ics. Acupuncture. Nails. Hair salons. Mostly located in strip malls. Orange owned and operated an air-conditioning sales and installation company. Dozens of appearances in small-claims court and the landlord-tenant division, mostly as a defendant but three times as a plaintiff in disputes over the rightful own-ership of a condominium. Two of those he won, the last he lost.

Two assault convictions.

Receiving stolen property.

Money laundering.

Illegal gambling.

The arrests and convictions were all in the distant past, the latest a half-century ago. Anthony Orange was either reformed, smart, or lucky.

After years of investigations into litigants' private financial lives, Priest surmised that, at first glance, Anthony Orange might not be what you'd call an outright criminal, but neither was he one hundred percent on the up and up.

Priest thought about Orange's daughter, the naked girl with the gun and the shiny cowboy boots. He typed "Rachel Orange" into his search engine.

Local Vegas media reported that, twelve days ago, Rachel had died in a car accident. A male companion, the driver, had also been killed, 7:45 in the morning, at the intersection of Desert Inn Road and Durango Drive, when the speeding drunk driver of a Nissan Armada—also killed—struck the median and collided head-on with a brand new Ford Puma registered to Rachel Orange. Rachel's funeral was three days ago.

The boy must have come straight to LA after the service.

Her obituary read: *Rachel Lillian Orange, 36, of Las Vegas, was tragically taken from us all too soon, leaving behind her loving father, local businessman and entrepreneur Anthony Orange, and her beloved son Tarquin. Before her untimely and tragic death, Rachel worked as a well-known and popular event planner in Las Vegas.*

It went on to say that Rachel had survived the deadliest mass shooting in modern history on October 1, 2017, during which she'd risked her own life to help others and had later organized fund-raising events to help pay for the funeral expenses of local victims. During COVID, Rachel had organized virtual events for furloughed restaurant staff, even while her own party-planning business was wiped out, obliging her to move in with her father, Anthony Orange. In recent months, Rachel had made significant steps toward re-establishing her business. The obituary went on to say where she'd gone to high school. Priest hadn't known that she ran track, although he did remember sudden, spontaneous footraces every time they came upon an empty corridor. Rachel had won those races every time, even when she had to kick off her shoes to fly past Priest, barefoot, flinging him the finger over her shoulder.

No mention of a husband. No indication of who Tarquin's father might be.

————

Priest startled awake when Dusty let herself in the next morning, bearing a bagful of Zelda's cinnamon mini-doughnuts and three cups of coffee. He was in his reading chair, printouts in his lap.

"You brought coffee for the kid? He's twelve!" Priest said.

"I thought he might want coffee with his morning cigarette. If he's still here."

"You see a kid with a big nose and broken legs in the alley?"

"No."

"Then he's still here. Probably exhausted from mouthing off and getting kicked in the nuts."

"You been looking into his life?"

"Some. But most of this is what I've dug up on Stephen T. Tedeschi, real estate broker, up in Palo Alto."

Researching the boy had left Priest thinking about Rachel, and thinking about Rachel made sleep impossible, so Priest concentrated on finding Nikki.

"Stanford grad, huh?" Dusty said, reading Priest's notes.

Priest knew Dusty was thinking about how she had never finished high school. That the extent of her education was a GED.

That she'd been raised in foster care. That she had no family. That she made a living as a stunt performer and personal trainer and bodyguard. That she'd never be rich. That she didn't have her own home because she preferred to house-sit, mansion to mansion, a virtual squatter, making sure rich people didn't get robbed while they were at their holiday homes or on a shoot in Australia or Prague. Between house-sitting gigs, if Dusty needed a place to crash for a few days or a couple of weeks, she found herself a temporary fling, or took a movie job out of town, or crashed at Priest's place in the very room where Tarquin Xavier Orange currently slept.

Dusty was comparing herself to Stephen T. Tedeschi and finding herself wanting.

"No way this guy leaves his wife and family for an escort," Priest said, figuring that, if he irritated Dusty, she might stop second-guessing her life choices for a minute. "He'll get tired of her and send her home."

"What are you going to do about your son?" Dusty asked.

"I can't just assume he's mine."

"I'll rephrase. What are you going to do about the boy who is obviously your son?"

"Who knows who else slept with his mother? Her obituary says she was a very popular figure."

"Spit in a tube all you want, Priest, but save yourself a hundred bucks and look in the mirror. That boy's nose came straight off your face. Poor little bastard."

"He's kind of an asshole," Priest said.

"Weren't you an asshole when you were twelve?"

At age twelve, Xavier Priestly had been an altar boy in thought, word, and deed. Compared to Tarquin Orange, Priest had been a saint. He sure as hell wasn't packing heat, rolling his own cigarettes, or crossing state lines carrying a backpack stuffed with guns, drugs, and hundred-dollar bills.

"I recommend you head up to Palo Alto," Priest said. "See about Stephen T. Tedeschi and Nikki."

Dusty looked at him, blew out her cheeks, and squinted. She was thinking about Blue Wig, out there in the dark with a syringe full of poison, eyeballing the back of Priest's neck.

"I'll be careful while you're gone," Priest said.

"What about Pow-Pow?"

"He's an asshole, but I doubt he's a professional contract killer."

"I mean, you can't leave him exposed to, like, danger."

"So now you think I should send him home?"

"No. That is not at all what I think."

As a kid, Dusty had been gotten rid of on more than one occasion. She was sensitive on the subject.

"I'm getting mixed messages," Priest said.

"I'm not transmitting mixed messages. You're just up your own ass."

"What do you want to happen?" Priest asked.

"All three of us should go," Dusty said.

"To Palo Alto?"

"Yes."

"Take the boy?"

"That's why I specified all three of us," Dusty said.

"I don't think that's legal."

"It's only illegal if we transport him over state lines."

"You get that off a movie you worked on? Or one you watched?"

"I asked Baz."

"It's not just a legal issue, Dusty. What are my responsibilities? Shouldn't I tell the boy's grandfather that he's here? What if the kid doesn't want to come with us? Which I guarantee he will not."

"How's about you call him by his name?"

"Tarquin?"

"I agree, stupid name," Dusty said. "But it's better than 'the boy' or 'the kid.' Call him 'Pow-Pow.'" Maybe then he might want to go somewhere with you."

"I guess *Fuck You Fucker* is out of the question?"

"Tell me about his mother," Dusty said.

"Like what?"

"Do you even remember her?"

"Oh, yeah."

"Was it okay for seminarians to play hooky, go to Vegas, and get women pregnant?"

"As long as we did it between vespers and the Adoration of the Blessed Sacrament."

"Maybe that joke works if you're a seminary student?"

"No," Priest admitted. "Not even then."

II

Rachel Orange had been the seventh woman with whom Priest engaged in any kind of sexual activity. The first was Kaylee Cronauer, tenth grade, who had performed an abortive bonfire hand job at a beach party on Netarts Bay, abortive by virtue of Kaylee's hand cramping up at a crucial juncture because she'd been shucking mussels all afternoon.

Rachel Orange was the fourth woman Priest had enjoyed sexual intercourse with. The first was Sandy Westfall—his girlfriend, eleventh grade—whom Priest dumped a few days later so he could ask Jezelle Morgan to the Spring Fling, in the hope that Jezelle would become the second girl to have intercourse with him. Which she was, but then—adding yet more shame to that of how shabbily he'd treated Sandy Westfall—Priest had puked up Purple Jesus Punch while kissing Jezelle post-coitally. Jezelle told her friends that they had barely even made out, and the widely repeated purple-puke story had ensured that Priest's high school sex life was over.

Unwillingly, if deservedly, chaste—an incel—Priest had been sexually stranded, horny, lonely, and furious until the summer following his high-school graduation. He took a custodial job at the community center, where he met Mary Innarone, his first true, serious love. Mary was a college girl interning as the program director at the community center. She had used Priest to get over *her* first true, serious love, a fully adult assistant port engineer. After a long, passionate, intensely emotional summer, the assistant port engineer begged Mary Innarone to marry him, and, to Priest's dismay, she agreed. He consoled himself by hiking six hundred miles of the Pacific Crest Trail, from the California state line to the Canadian border. He blamed his romantic woes on his karma and Oregon. He couldn't flee his karma, but he sure as hell could get out of Oregon, so he moved to California to go to college at Mount St. Mary's University in Los Angeles, where he met his next love, Leslie Sala. Leslie was a grad student with whom Priest fell deeply in love for a glorious eight months, after which Leslie followed her thesis adviser to Steinbeis-Hochschule University in Berlin.

Twenty years old, twice rejected, twice heart-broken, Priest had transferred from Mount St. Mary's University to St. John's Seminary in Camarillo and begun the three years of celibacy expected of seminarians.

During his third year, seminarian Xavier Priestly began suffering doubts about his calling. His fellow seminarians—all except the fanatics and the mentally ill—endured similar doubts. One of Priest's exacerbating problems was that his fellow seminarians creeped him out. The lone exception was a short, stocky Pole with the fun-to-say name Leszek Dudek. Dudek insisted that celibacy was neither required nor advisable for seminarians until the very moment that the Sacred Sacrament of Holy Orders was officially bestowed by the Holy Ghost, marking the moment when they ceased to be seminarians and became priests.

"You and me are engaged to Jesus but not yet married,"

Dudek had explained. "Is totally okay to fuck until the actual vows."

Although Dudek was unable to provide any corroborating theological writings—aside from vague admonitions to reread St. Augustine's *Confessions*—it had been his considered opinion that seminarians were free to live life without ecclesiastical restriction. Meanwhile, Dudek had been seeing a woman who was totally fine with his intended future as a Catholic priest because she was married to a tractor mechanic down the road in Oxnard.

"He is unable to satisfy her, due to blood-pressure medication," Priest remembered Dudek saying. "So, everybody is fine. Everybody is happy. The Lord God wants happiness for all His children."

In a flash of insight, Priest had realized that he did not believe the Lord God wanted all His children to be happy, because, if the Lord God genuinely wanted His children to be happy, He'd have created the world in a whole different happy mode, instead of the pain-generating machine He'd landed upon. Like St. Matthew's Foolish Builder, seminarian Xavier Priestly had built his religious convictions upon sand. When he confided in Dudek, Dudek advised him to get himself a girlfriend, get drunk, play the lottery, and have a little non-mortal-sinful fun.

"Get those devil shits out of your blood," Dudek had urged him.

Dudek left the seminary two months later, having decided to dedicate his life to social work in the developing world, starting with Haiti.

"Take my stuff," he said, shaking Priest's hand and pointing to his ecumenical gear, including his heavily annotated Polish bible.

"Do you still believe in God?" Priest asked.

"You bet!" Dudek said. "Why not? Who do you think told me my calling changed from telling people how to have a relationship with God so they can be happy in the next world to helping people find a little joy in this world?"

Without Dudek, Priest had felt stranded among his fellow seminarian creepazoids, striving hourly to reignite his belief in the brotherhood of those called to dedicate their lives to the Glorification of God, which involved praying together, singing insipid hymns, baking bread, and weirdly competitive three-on-three basketball games. One Friday night, Priest missed a three-pointer and juxtaposed the name of the Lord with a graphic reference to the structural limitations of the human anus. A fellow seminarian had consoled him, "Don't worry about it. We are still men, after all."

Priest had asked himself, "What exactly is a man?" He had asked so hard that he suspected he might have voiced the question out loud. Days later, Priest's father was arrested for bank robbery and felony homicide. Priest's mother, Sharon, had pried a power of attorney from his incarcerated father, sold his father's stake in the chain of car dealerships he owned with Uncle Larry for three million bucks, and gifted Priest and his sister Olive a million dollars each "for tax reasons."

Sharon Priestly and Neil, the man who became her second husband, spent the remaining million on a boat and set sail around the world even before Oliver Priest was found guilty and sentenced to twenty years in federal prison for bank robbery, with an additional thirty for felony homicide. That was more than twelve years ago. She and Neil were still out there, riding the wind. Olive was convinced that their mother had become a stereotypical yachting drunk, but Priest decided that maybe Mom only got drunk to Skype with them.

After his million-dollar windfall, Priest had asked himself if he wanted to donate the money to the Holy Roman Catholic Church. His immediate, visceral response was *nope.*

He sent some to Dudek in Haiti but kept the rest. If that money was a test from God, then Priest had failed harder than the invasion of Iraq.

As advised by the *Seminarian Handbook*, Priest confided his doubts to his confessor, Father Clement, omitting any mention of his million-dollar windfall. A perpetually dyspeptic chain-smoking Capuchin, Father Clement quoted Cicero: *"Can earthly things seem important to him who is acquainted with the whole of eternity and the magnitude of the universe?"*

Priest had irritated Father Clement when he asked why a Roman Catholic priest needed to quote a pagan on questions of faith. Surely the Catholics could come up with something better? Father Clement suggested that Priest retreat to a retreat, read St. Ignatius, and pray for guidance. He had offered to set Priest up at the New Camaldoli Hermitage in Big Sur—run by Benedictines—or the Villa Maria del Mar in Santa Cruz—run by Sisters of the Holy Names of Jesus and Mary. Priest felt that even one more day of bread-baking, peace, tranquility, and reflection might shove him into a life of crime, like his father before him, so instead he followed the sage advice of his lusty friend Dudek and decided to indulge in his own personal unofficial Rumspringa.

Vegas, baby!

His first night in town, Priest won a quarter of a million dollars playing Deuce-to-Seven Single Draw in Bobby's Room at the Bellagio. That garnered him an invitation to a shadier private game with a hundred-grand buy-in in a suite at the South Point. During a break in that game, Priest met Rachel Orange, who had been hired by the organizers to provide food, drink, and interstitial entertainment that, to Priest's surprise, consisted, not of strippers and lap-dancers, but a magician, two comics, a mind-reading act, and a contortionist.

Rachel was ebullient and pale with jet-black curly hair. She was sparky, talkative, kinetic, and swivel-hipped. Priest wondered if she was the girlfriend of somebody dangerous, but no, Rachel was single and pursuing what she called the "dues paying" portion of a career as a freelance events organizer and talent booker. She worked private parties and obscure gambling rooms to build a rep around town. As the contortionist entertained the other card players, Priest listened to Rachel talk about her ambition to become the main talent booker for one of the big, corporate casinos like Caesars or Mandalay Bay or her personal Everest, the MGM Grand.

"I have an eagle eye for talent," she had informed Priest. Somehow it came off as factual and not boastful.

Twenty-four hours into the game, Rachel had to leave to deal with a crisis when the drummer in Wonderwall—the Oasis cover band she'd booked for a private party at the Tuscany—had gone missing with one of the guest's American Express Black cards and a Ziploc bag of pharmaceutical-grade cocaine.

Would Priest care to accompany her? Or was he committed to seeing through his winning streak?

Priest had cashed in his chips. Using Jesuit logic—and motivated by a desire to impress Rachel—Priest needed less than an hour to find the drummer holed up with a sous-chef from Treasure Island, the two of them watching porn and working their way through the big bag of coke in a room at a blinking neon mess of a hot-sheet motel in Meadows Village.

As far as Rachel was concerned, Priest had saved her career. "If it weren't for you, I'd have to go back to being a cocktail waitress." She bit Priest's earlobe, reached into his shirt, and tweaked his nipple. "You should be a private detective."

Chastity was no longer an option.

Three hours later, inspired by the drummer and the

sous-chef, Priest and Rachel Orange were mostly drunk in Priest's hotel bed, gathering their wits after making love in the shower. Rachel announced that she'd decided to take a few days off so that they could kill the rest of the week together, spending his poker winnings and having sex.

"Wow," Dusty said. "Somewhere in there you must have conceived Pow-Pow."

"We don't know that for sure yet," Priest said.

"Rachel went back to work. I went back to St. John's," Priest said. "But only to collect my stuff. I transferred from seminary back to Mount Saint Mary's University, got a degree in criminology, and became a legal investigator."

"Do you think that she didn't tell you she got pregnant because she still thought you were going to become a Man of God?"

Priest explained that a year and a half after he and Rachel had hooked up in Vegas—a year and a half of comparing every woman he met to Rachel Orange—he had returned to Vegas to look Rachel up. He texted her, and to his surprise and delight, Rachel remembered him and suggested that they meet at Lou's Diner on South Decatur.

When they met, Rachel was pushing a stroller. With a baby boy in it. She didn't even tell Priest the kid's name, much less that he was the father.

"What would you have done if she'd told you?" Dusty asked.

"Something more and better than absolutely nothing."

Rachel had told Priest she was with someone.

They were going to get married.

Nice to see you again, though. Good luck with everything.

"So I came back to LA and spent my inheritance on the down payment for this place."

"Did she know about your inheritance?"

"Yes."

"And she didn't make a grab for any of it?"

"Nope."

"And you had no idea he was your kid?"

"I'm pretty sure she suggested that the kid belonged to whoever she was going to marry," Priest said. "If I'd known the baby was mine, I'd have given my inheritance money to Rachel." It was free money. It's not like he had earned it.

He'd gone to see Rachel with the vague, crazy hope that maybe there was something more to be explored between them. He figured he hadn't made much of an impression on her.

"Well, we know that isn't true," Dusty said.

"Do we?"

"You'll see when you read the letter," Dusty said, "which Tarquin will show you when he feels like it."

"What if he doesn't?"

"Your job is to make him feel like showing it to you."

"Okay. How?" Priest asked.

"Your job is to figure that out."

"Seems like I have all the jobs."

"Think of it as a test. You're good at tests."

"Not when I don't know what's being tested," Priest said.

"Duh! Tarquin is testing to see if you get to be his father," Dusty said.

Would Priest have chosen Oliver Priestly to be his own father? Would he have chosen Sharon Priestly to be his mother? Who could be a good parent with role models like Oliver and Sharon? Olive, a beneficiary of intense therapy, insisted that the emotional baggage her brother Priest wouldn't put down was the reason that all his relationships turned out to be just friends or friends-with-benefits.

"Rachel was great," Priest said.

"You knew her for one week, during which she took your

second virginity and turned you against God," Dusty said. "Cognitive dissonance. You *have* to think she was great."

"Rachel wasn't the reason I quit seminary."

"I'd love to hear all that someday," Dusty said. "But it seems like maybe we've got more pressing concerns."

"Like surprise offspring and blue-wigged contract killers?" Priest said, wondering if the two were connected.

Both the boy and Blue Wig had connections to Nevada. But Nevada was a big state. And it was in no way certain that Blue Wig was Cody Fiso's parking-lot maybe-hitter. Or whether Fiso's hitter was a woman. Or whether Fiso's hitter used a hypodermic needle. Or whether there had even been a hit.

"What?" Dusty asked.

"I gotta wonder if Blue Wig and the boy are connected."

"Does that mean you've stopped wondering if she might be me?"

"I never thought it was you, not even for a second."

The toilet in the guest bathroom flushed.

The boy sneezed and said, "Fuck!" The shower went on, and Priest heard the squeak of feet as the boy stepped into the tub.

"What kind of psycho tells his own sneeze to fuck off?" Priest asked.

"Cut the kid some slack," Dusty said. "His mother just died."

"I'm not the one who pantsed him and kicked him in the nuts," Priest said.

12

Priest introduced the kid to Yorben out on the pier.

"What're you fishing for?" the kid asked.

"Shark."

"Fuck off!"

"You fuck off!" Yorben said, extending his bag of mini-doughnuts. "Take three."

The boy took two.

Yorben snickered, pointed at Priest, and said, "Contrary. Like his old man. 'Nobody tells me how many doughnuts to take!'"

"My Pops says I got my stubbornness from him," the kid said, exhaling cinnamon dust and crumbs.

"Stubbornness and contrariness aren't the same thing," Yorben said. "You surf?"

"He's from Vegas," Priest said. "Not a lot of waves."

"Looks easy," the kid said. "If you can skate, you can surf."

The kid reached for more doughnuts. Yorben told Priest, "Get him his own. Show him the skatepark and whatnot."

Yorben liked the kid; Priest found that heartening.

Twenty minutes later, Priest and the kid sat on a low concrete wall across the bike path from the skatepark, each with a bag of doughnuts.

"You skate?" Priest asked.

"Better than them."

That could not possibly be true.

"I'm still hungry," the boy said when the bag was empty.

Priest took him back to Zelda's for breakfast burritos to go, then headed across the sand, past the skate park, toward the Venice Breakwater where the beach curved toward the car-sized boulders that made up the breakwater. A half-dozen round, concrete fixtures stuck out of the sand like the vertebrae of a beached sea monster, extending from a much-graffitied concrete box, either a relic from Venice's gilded age or a sewer pipe junction. Photographers liked to stand on that box and get shots of surfers with the Venice Pier in the background, three-quarters of a mile to the south. Priest sat on the concrete box and opened the burrito bag, what he hoped was a clear invitation for the kid to sit with him. The kid didn't. He took his burrito and sat on one of the sea monster vertebrae a dozen yards away.

Wouldn't the best thing for everybody be to call up the boy's grandfather? Tell Anthony Orange to come fetch this little asshole and take him back to Vegas?

Suddenly, the boy was standing in front of Priest, mouth full, asking who had kicked Priest's ass in his own garage. Priest told the kid the same cover story he'd told Flat-Earth Beck, and anyone else who asked—he'd been assaulted by someone in a blue wig when he interrupted her in the act of stealing his car.

"You got your ass kicked by a *girl*?"

"So did you," Priest said. The kid's face scrunched up like a fist. "But I've seen Dusty Queen take down plenty of full-grown men. Even guys who saw her coming."

The boy's face unscrunched. "Dusty says you're helping her find someone who's missing."

Priest said only the bare minimum about Dusty and Nikki. He referred to Nikki as Dusty's girlfriend and left out that she was an escort. Nikki had disappeared with some guy, Dusty was worried, and she'd asked Priest for help.

"If she's a dyke, why'd she run off with a guy?"

"Are you trying to be a dick? Or are you just ignorant and don't know any better?"

"If she's a *lesbian*, why'd she run off with a guy?"

"People aren't always one thing," Priest said.

"Did you ever get married?"

"No."

"How come?" the boy asked.

"Maybe I'm gay, too."

"Are you?"

"No," Priest said.

"You have girlfriends?" the boy asked.

"I've had a few."

"Why didn't you marry any of them?"

"It didn't work out that way," Priest said.

Maybe the kid was hoping Priest never married because he had never gotten over Rachel. Maybe there was some truth to that. That's what Priest decided to tell the boy if he asked, but thankfully the kid's hormonal boy-brain skipped back to the more lascivious topic of Dusty and Nikki.

"Maybe Dusty's girlfriend isn't full-on lesbo," the boy said. "She still craves dick."

Where'd he get "lesbo"?

Where'd he get "craves dick"?

"We don't know if or why Nikki ran off with this guy. Dusty is worried that maybe he took Nikki against her will."

"Did she call the police?"

"Of course."

"So?"

"So, they don't think it's urgent," Priest said.

"But Dusty does?"

"She does," Priest said. "That's why she came to me."

"I don't get it," the kid said.

"I'm a legal investigator."

"Yeah, that's in the letter," the boy said. "You wear disguises? Shit like that?"

"I wouldn't call them disguises."

"So, yes."

The boy was interested. Priest shrugged. He didn't like the feeling of wanting to impress a child, even one that might be his.

"How long will it take you to find him?"

"I might've found him already," Priest said.

"Where?"

"Palo Alto."

"Where's that?"

"You ever hear of Silicon Valley?"

"Like, San Francisco?"

"That's right."

"You found him?"

"I found somebody who might be him," Priest said.

"If you're so good, why can't you find whoever attacked you?"

"That's official police business. They told me not to interfere."

"You gonna do whatever the police tell you to do?"

"They could take away my investigator's license."

"Cops are easy to fool. Cops are dumb as fuck."

"Who told you that?"

"Everybody knows," the kid said.

Priest told the boy that police, in general, were not dumb as fuck. Dumb fucks could be found in any group of human beings, even cops, but it didn't mean cops as a group were dumb fucks.

"Agree to disagree," the boy said.

"How'd you find me?" Priest asked.

"The letter."

"How did you get here from Vegas?"

"Greyhound."

"Don't you have to be sixteen to buy a ticket? Show ID?"

"Dude!" the kid said, "There's lots of ways to get people at the bus station to buy your ticket. Offer them five bucks. Show 'em your dick. Don't you know anything?"

"There's lots of ways to do everything," Priest said. "I wanted to know your way."

"My way was five bucks," the boy said, rolling a cigarette.

"You shouldn't smoke," Priest said. "Two things boxers need. Good legs. Good lungs."

"I want my bush, too."

"I don't know what 'bush' is."

"My weed. I want it back."

"Like Dusty said, you shouldn't be smoking that stuff at your age."

"What do you care?"

Good question. Who was Priest to this kid? A sperm donor. And even that hadn't been subjected to any kind of proof. Every time he and Rachel Orange had had sex, he'd worn a condom. But there'd been more than one drunken Tilt-A-Whirl in that carnival of lust. There was that unexpected skinny-dip romp . . . naked in the pool . . . where would Priest have gotten a condom? Maybe he should sniff the kid, see if he smelled like chlorine.

When it came to the conjugating of the conjugals between Xavier Priestly and Rachel Orange, there was no doubt who was the enthusiastic rookie and who was the sexual sophisticate.

Rachel was fun, experienced, and game for anything. Priest had never gotten the impression that he'd taken her to exciting new erotic frontiers. But he'd made up for it with ardor, fervor, and a nagging feeling that he had some catching up to do.

"Do you want to come with us?" he asked the kid.

"Where?"

"To Palo Alto. To check into this guy who might know where Dusty's friend is."

"Why?"

"You got something else to do?" Priest asked.

"Fuck, yeah."

"So, no?"

"I just said yes," the kid said.

"To coming with us to Palo Alto?"

"No! Fuck. I mean yeah, I got something else to do."

"Yo!"

Priest turned to see Detective Garnet Diodato laboring across the sand toward them. Diodato wore a brown suit, and it was obvious that he'd worn the jacket more than the pants. He balanced a coffee from Menotti's and a wrapped breakfast sandwich.

"Good morning," Priest said, suddenly glad that the boy had ditched his *When They Go Low, We Get High!* T-shirt in favor of one featuring The Hulk.

"It's against the law to smoke under the age of twenty-one," Diodato told the boy.

"What are you? Some kind of cop?"

"He's a police detective," Priest said.

"You don't think I'm twenty-one?"

"I don't think you're thirteen."

"I got a note from my mommy," the boy said, dragging on the cigarette and jetting it out his nose at Diodato.

Diodato turned to Priest. "You believe this kid?"

"He's a pistol," Priest said.

"If you want to spend the day with Child Services, I'm more than happy to oblige," Diodato told the boy, putting his sandwich and coffee down like he was ready to spring into action.

The boy pinched out his cigarette, shoved the butt into his pocket, and strutted off across the sand.

"You better be on your way to school," Diodato called after him.

Priest held his breath, expecting the kid to flip Diodato the finger over his shoulder. But he just kept walking, didn't even look.

"Neighborhood kid?" Diodato asked Priest.

"New face," Priest said.

"You see him hanging around, give me a call," Diodato said. "Kid that young on his own'll get eaten alive." He sipped his coffee. "How you feeling? Hundred percent?"

"I'll be a hundred percent when you tell me you caught Blue Wig."

"Is that what you call her? I call her that, too. No, I haven't caught her yet."

"Hey!"

Priest and Diodato turned to see Baz approaching across the sand, shoes in one hand, a coffee in the other.

"Good morning, Ms. Amberson," Diodato said. Priest's eyes immediately stung from the pheromones jumping between them. "I was just about to bring your client up to date on the investigation."

"Good morning, Detective," Baz said. "I got here just in time."

"Ms. Amberson and I sifted through all your legal investigations for the last few years."

"Together?" Priest asked.

"In order to avoid any potential client-privilege conflicts," Baz said.

"And?"

"We found some billable hours that hadn't been logged," Baz said. Baz and Diodato laughed and twinkled at each other. A cop laughing at lawyer humor. The delicate fabric of the universe was in danger of rupture.

"There's a couple I want to run by you, see if you agree on my take," Diodato said.

"Like who?"

"Darius Clay," Baz said.

Darius Clay was a talent agent who'd been sued for malfeasance by a group of clients and engaged Baz to defend him. Priest had discovered evidence that Clay had, indeed, done what his clients accused him of doing: adding surcharges and cash penalties to their contracts, which he then invoked and pocketed himself. In the process, Priest had discovered that Clay was also hiding income from his ex-wife and two children. Priest had informed Baz, and Baz had advised a furious Clay to make it right with his ex-wife before he lost his malfeasance case in court.

"I'm getting fucked over by my own lawyer. I'm gonna have you disbarred," Clay had threatened. "You're fired."

Clay had proceeded with another lawyer and lost the lawsuit. Then not only did Clay's ex-wife sue him, but the district attorney decided to pursue criminal charges.

Darius Clay decided that Xavier Priestly had leaked the details and had sworn one day to get his revenge.

"Did you? Leak details?" Diodato asked.

"No," Priest said, "that would be a clear violation of client privilege."

"If I even suspected that," Baz said, "my firm would never have hired Priest again."

"Honestly," Priest said, "in the real world, there are few

threats less threatening than a threat made by an angry Hollywood agent."

"Kimberly Fry," Diodato said.

Kimberly Fry was a Los Angeles County school board official who had collected life insurance after her fiancé died of kidney failure. Working on behalf of the insurance company, Baz had hired Priest, who discovered that Ms. Fry—who was having an affair with her yoga instructor—had ordered two gallons of extra-strength antifreeze online. Antifreeze of a strength which was not needed in Southern California unless you intended to poison your fiancée for insurance money.

The insurance company alerted the district attorney, who decided to open a homicide investigation. Kimberly Fry beat the murder rap but—in a move of epic hubris—circled back to sue the insurance company for her fiancée's life insurance. But while the standard for a homicide is "beyond a reasonable doubt," the standard for a civil suit is "a preponderance of evidence." The jury decided that the preponderance of evidence implicated Kimberly Fry in the poisoning of her fiancée, which prompted her fiancée's family to countersue for his wrongful death. They won.

"Kimberly Fry is not Blue Wig," Priest said. "She's a dwarf."

"Dwarves can hire contract killers," Baz said.

But they all agreed that it didn't scan.

"Six years of legal investigations, and only two people want me dead?" Priest asked.

"I also had your father interviewed," Diodato said.

That interview would have been conducted by either a Portland homicide detective or an investigator from the Oregon State Criminal Investigation Division.

"Your father says nobody has approached him about his non-existent buried treasure in several years," Diodato explained. "No one has made any threats against the well-being or safety of his children. He says that, if such a treasure existed, he'd give it up instantly if it ensured your safety."

"That's big of him."

"You don't believe that to be true?"

"I'd like to think it's true," Priest said.

"But you can't be sure?" Diodato asked.

"The whole time I thought my father was a car salesman, it turned out he was a bank robber, so, yeah—trust issues."

"You mind I ask how often you see your father?"

"Face-to-face, a couple times a year," Priest said. "On the phone or video link, once a week."

"The warden at Sheridan is going to transfer your father to another detention facility in case somebody hired Blue Wig from inside, intending to pressure your father."

What might be a stupid rumor outside prison walls took on the guise of hard fact behind them.

Poor Dad, Priest thought, *having to make a new life in a new place, re-establish himself and his bona-fides, face a new group of assholes.*

"Maybe he'll enjoy the change of scenery," Priest said, thinking that one concrete wall couldn't look all that different from another concrete wall.

"Once your father is relocated, he might reveal something to us that he couldn't in Sheridan."

"I'll leave word for him to call me."

"You'll let me know if he tells you anything he didn't feel he could share with law enforcement?"

Priest nodded.

Poor Dad.

"Do you have anything to tell Detective Diodato?" Baz asked.

"Like what?"

"Like have you made any progress in finding Dusty's missing friend?" Baz prompted.

"Oh, yeah, right. I'm heading up to the Bay Area tomorrow morning to chase down a lead."

"You found the guy Nikki Celeste ran off with?" Diodato asked.

"That's what I need to find out."

"Can I get his name?"

"I'll leave the name with Baz in case anything goes wrong, but otherwise, my client doesn't want to involve the police."

Diodato shrugged. Turnaround was fair play; he'd asked Priest to let him know if the search for Nikki Celeste led to any information related to Blue Wig's attack. So far, no.

"Getting out of town is a good idea," Diodato said. "The fewer people that know where you're headed, the better. Any other developments?"

Like a twelve-year-old son I didn't know existed showing up, armed and dangerous, smoking roll-your-owns and mouthing off to cops?

"Nothing comes to mind," Priest said.

"Enjoy your road trip," Diodato said. "Be safe."

He left, a stolid presence moving across the blowing sand. Baz turned to Priest, who was waggling his eyebrows at her.

"What?" she asked.

"Nothing," Priest said.

"That man is conducting a vigorous investigation into the assault on you."

"Does that vigor pique your romantic interest?" Priest asked.

"I have a weakness for competence, yeah," Baz said. "Why else would I like you?"

She patted his cheek and left, stretching her stride to walk in Diodato's footsteps.

13

Priest's father Skyped from prison at five o'clock that afternoon, while Dusty and the boy played hoops near the handball courts.

"I was questioned by two cops," Oliver Priestly said.

"Sorry you got dragged into this," Priest said.

"Sorry I couldn't help."

Priest thought it was funny that his father was apologizing for *not* being the source of the attempted hit on him.

"Are you okay, X?" Oliver asked. He had called Priest "X" or "X-Man" since he was a kid. Priest didn't mind X. He hated X-Man. "Any lingering after-effects from the attack? PTSD? Anything like that?"

"Nothing like that, Dad. I'm fine. How about you?"

"They're moving me," Oliver said. "Seven years, Federal Correctional Institution - Sheridan has been my home. No idea where they're sending me. I'll let you know."

"Sorry," Priest said.

"I never said it was a good home. What's new with you?"

"It turns out you might have a grandson," Priest said.

There was a brief silence before Oliver laughed. Priest told

him the shortest possible version of the Rachel story, ending
with the boy living with his grandfather in Vegas.

Oliver grunted. "What's he like?"

"The boy or the grandfather?"

"My grandson."

"If he's your grandson, your grandson's a dick."

"The kid left-handed?" his father asked.

"What's that got to do with anything?"

"I'm left-handed," Oliver said. "You're left-handed. It's a
family tradition. What are you going to do?"

"You got any advice?"

"About what?"

"Fatherhood?"

"Don't rob banks," his father said.

"I'm pretty sure that's not funny, Dad."

"Did I ever tell you how proud of you I am?" Oliver asked.

Priest found that he couldn't answer.

"You had the courage to leave your seminary for a more
adventurous life," his father said. "Maybe if I'd had that kind
of courage—left the comfort and boredom of that fucking car
dealership—I wouldn't have ended up trying to steal some kind
of excitement out of life."

"And your family?" Priest asked.

"There's a lot of kinds of prisons," Oliver said. "You had
the courage to leave yours is what I'm saying. And I'm proud
of you for it."

Priest slammed his laptop shut.

It wasn't the worst conversation they'd ever had.

14

At breakfast the next day, the kid—mouth jammed with peanut butter toast—informed Priest that he'd decided to adjust his busy schedule and go to Palo Alto after all.

"What about your grandfather?" Priest asked.

"What about him?"

"I think it's time to give him a call."

"Pops'll come right away and get me," the kid said. "If that's what you want, go ahead and call him."

Priest glanced at Dusty and remembered what she'd said: the boy was testing him. Priest had no idea how to pass the test, but he was pretty sure that calling Anthony Orange to come and take the kid home would be a sure-fire fail.

"He's not worried?" Priest asked the boy.

"I called Pops this morning, told him the camp was going great. That I knocked a kid out."

"Remind me never to trust anything you say," Dusty said.

"What a shitty car," the boy said when he saw the Cherokee. "The outside is the color of dogshit, and the inside is the color of people shit."

The boy claimed that he'd get sick if he sat in the back seat, especially if he looked at his phone. Priest advised him not to look at his phone. Dusty said she'd prefer to sit in the backseat because, if she sat in the front, they'd look like a family, and that made her want to puke.

The boy went still. Thinking of his mother, probably. Dusty was right; Rachel Orange's death was still an open wound. Of course.

"Dude," the kid said, pointing at Priest's briefcase. "Get a backpack, why dontcha? Is all your shit ass-ugly?"

"It belonged to his father," Dusty said. "Priest is attached to it. Tell Pow-Pow your fascinating backpack theory, Priest."

"The only adults who should carry backpacks are soldiers," Priest said.

"Or bodyguards," Dusty said. Her backpack was black ballistic nylon with so many ties and pockets and reinforcements that it looked like a semi-sentient battle robot.

"Why do you even got your father's briefcase? Is he dead?" the boy asked. "Is it like your inheritance?"

It occurred to Priest how much the little shit would love to hear that his paternal grandfather was in prison for armed robbery and would never get out, thanks to statutory homicide.

"My father retired to a walled estate in Oregon," Priest said. "He doesn't need his briefcase anymore, so he gave it to me."

Priest drove, the boy in the passenger seat, Dusty in the back. The boy stuck his earbuds in, but he was only pretending to listen to music while he eavesdropped on Priest and Dusty. Dusty was hoping to confront Stephen Tedeschi today. Priest figured that Tedeschi would either not be home—who takes an escort home?—or would deny knowing Nikki. If that happened, Dusty was likely to drag the guy into the nearest dark place and go to work on him. What was Priest supposed to do

then? Take the kid for ice cream? What if Tedeschi had Nikki
ensconced in a nearby hotel while he dealt with the frayed end
of his marriage? What would Dusty do then? Plead with Nikki
to come to her senses?

Dusty thought Priest was overthinking: "If he's home, we'll
ask him where Nikki is. If he's not home, we'll ask his wife
where he is. If she doesn't know, or won't tell us, we'll tell her
that wherever her husband is, he's with an escort."

"Your girlfriend is an escort?" the boy asked. "Like, a call
girl?"

"A sex worker," Dusty said. "It's just a job."

"Pop said he'll hire me up a super-hot high-class call girl for
my sixteenth birthday."

"It's nice to know that there are still old-fashioned gentle-
men out there who know that it pays to wait until the time is
right," Priest said.

"Dude," the boy said, "I'm not waiting for *nothing*."

Priest was about to ask the kid what his mother had felt
about Pops' "special birthday surprise" when he felt Dusty's knee
on his back through the driver's seat.

"You want this Nikki babe," the boy said to Dusty. "*And*
this guy wants her. She must be, like, super good at sex."

"Don't anybody look," Dusty said. "There's a red Altima
following us . . . Pow-Pow! I said *don't* look. 'Don't' is a con-
traction of 'do not.' You should have learned that by grade six.
Or did you get left back?"

"I'm not stupid. If you didn't want anyone to look, you
shouldn't have said anything," the boy said.

"There's no alternate route through these mountains," Priest
said. "Could totally be a coincidence."

"Sure," Dusty said.

"What do you want me to do?" Priest asked.

"Why are you asking her?" the boy asked.

"I believe in expertise," Priest said, irritated that every conversation with this kid was freighted with a life lesson. "When it comes to personal security, Dusty is a pro."

"I thought you were a stuntman?"

"Risk assessment is risk assessment," Dusty said.

"Want me to pull over for gas?" Priest asked.

"If she's been following us since we left your place, then she'll know we got gas in San Fernando," Dusty said. "We gas up again too soon, she'll know we're onto her."

"We could send the kid in to pee. You get pee shy?" Priest asked. "Can you piss under pressure? . . . Showing me your middle finger is not an answer."

"After we come down from the Grapevine, the 5 splits off to the right from the 99. Take the 99," Dusty said, "then make like you suddenly remembered it's the 5 you want and cut across. See if the Altima follows."

The kid bounced on his seat, galvanized. "If you got attacked because you caught somebody trying to steal your car, then why are they trying to steal your car again, even though it's a different totally shitty car?"

"We don't really know why Priest was attacked," Dusty said. "We just tell everyone it was a car theft." And then, to Priest, "Take the Maricopa Highway exit."

"What if she already knows where we're headed?"

"The only way she could know where we're going is if one of us told her," Dusty said.

"Or Diodato. Or Baz. Or the kid."

"The kid is one of us."

"I don't even know what you are talking about," the boy said.

Priest exited the 99 at the Maricopa Highway.

"I'm going to look," the boy said. "I'll point at something, okay?" Nobody disagreed, so the kid pointed at a truck and said, "Oooh, look at the big shiny truck!" as though Blue Wig might read his lips through tinted glass from two hundred yards.

"When we're back on the 5, she'll be paranoid," Dusty said. "Set your cruise control for seventy-five and relax. We'll give her an hour, maybe two, to decide that we didn't make her. No more turning around for sneak peeks, Pow-Pow."

"Then what? Confront her?" Priest asked.

"If I was alone, I'd kill her," Dusty said.

"What?" the boy said. *Delighted.* He might be a sociopath. Or just a twelve-year-old boy. What did Priest know?

"She's kidding," Priest said.

"No, I'm not," Dusty said. "There's no way to prove she's the woman who stabbed you in the neck with a syringe. It's your word against hers, and your word is all drugged-up and confused. The police will have no choice but to let her go. All things considered, it'd be better to kill her."

"No, Dusty. If we get her, we hand her over to law enforcement. Especially with the kid here."

"Fuck that," the boy said. "If she tried to kill you, you should kill her back. Those are the rules."

Rules?

"Too many witnesses," Priest said. "Dusty would have to kill all of them, too."

"Including *us*?" the boy asked. "You and me? We're the witnesses."

"Priest," Dusty said, "I'm starting to think Pow-Pow isn't a complete dumbass." She squinched her eyes, and the kid laughed again.

Couple of sociopaths, Priest thought. *My son and my best friend.*

"We don't know for sure she planned to kill me," Priest said.

"Even if it's okay to murder a murderer—which it is not—it's not okay to murder a kidnapper. We kidnap a kidnapper."

"First time I ever heard eye-for-an-eye sound merciful," Dusty said. "You learn that in seminary?"

"What's seminary?" the boy asked. "Something to do with semen?"

"It's a kind of college," Priest said.

"It's priest school," Dusty said.

"Priest school? You went to *priest* school? Like to be a *priest*?"

"Your father was studying to be a priest when he met your mother," Dusty said.

"You were going to be a priest, then you met my mother and decided not to be a priest anymore?"

"It wasn't that simple," Priest said.

"I thought priests can't have sex."

"I wasn't a priest yet."

"Lucky for you, Pow-Pow, or you wouldn't exist," Dusty said.

"So, what happened? You flunk out of priest school?" the kid asked.

"I didn't flunk out."

"You get kicked out for having sex with Mom?"

"No!"

Why did Priest feel the impulse to justify himself to this boy?

"Then why?" the kid asked.

"You wouldn't understand."

"I'm smart," the boy said, stung. "Fuck you."

"Okay, take it easy."

"People don't know how smart I am."

"Fine," Priest said. "Here's my smart answer. I realized that everyone else felt the presence of God. Or thought they did. But not me. I wanted to, but I didn't. Some actually said God talked to them."

"The crazy ones," the boy said.

"The lucky ones," Priest said.

"I get that," the boy said. "People won't talk to you, fuck 'em."

"Even if that Altima is following us," Priest said to Dusty, "it might not be Blue Wig."

"Run through alternatives for me," Dusty said. Serious. Not sarcastic.

Priest listed possibilities: What if Cody Fiso had taken an interest in that old case in Nevada and was following Priest to see what kicked loose? What if Diodato had managed to persuade his superiors that Priest needed protection? What if Baz had persuaded her law firm to keep an eye on their star investigator?

"Conceited or what?" the boy said.

"Priest is literally their star investigator," Dusty said.

Priest kept another few options to himself: What if his convict father, alerted to his son's problems by whoever questioned him at FCI Sheridan, persuaded somebody on the outside to take an interest? What if Anthony Orange was keeping tabs on his grandson? What if Dusty was Blue Wig and set up this whole shenanigan to prove that she wasn't?

"In three or four hours," Dusty said, "depending on traffic, we're going to take 152 West to Palo Alto. It runs through a state park. Whatever we decide to do, that's where we'll do it."

"State parks are full of dead bodies," the boy said.

"What?"

"Dead bodies in shallow graves. That's what I heard."

Priest pulled between two trucks and stayed there until the Altima passed. The driver was an Asian man with some kind of giant sheepdog in the back seat, slobbering on the windows.

"False alarm," Dusty said.

"Fuck," the boy said.

"No, not 'fuck,'" Priest said. "It's a good thing."

Once they got to Highway 152, they drove on land every bit as flat as the Great Plains, although Priest knew the Diablo Range—a fancy name for what was really a bunch of hills—were up ahead, behind what looked like clouds. The sun lowered, shining directly into Priest's face, squeaking in below the sunshade. Even wearing sunglasses, he squinted. Dusty also wore sunglasses—mirrored, of course—which made her look impassive and dangerous in the rearview mirror. The kid stared out the passenger window, his back to Priest, watching the flatlands roil and fold into a series of hills, up toward the Pacheco Pass, veering north along the San Luis Reservoir, then southwest again.

The Pacheco Pass Highway was the main route between Interstate 5 and Silicon Valley, but at this time of day, the traffic was light. As the hills grew steeper and more purple, California buckwheat and honey mesquite appeared in the ditches and berms along the road, stunted cottonwoods clustered in the hollows, and ancient gnarled blue oaks climbed the hills over chaparral and grass. The road grew windier and steeper as they climbed. The areas between the hills became rocky ravines. The oak trees swarmed up the sides of the hills until only the very tops were treeless. Another turn and the hills were covered with oak, interspersed with ash and alder, the world folding in on itself as the sun descended. It was starting to get dark as they ascended a long rise, the road curving and cresting, a delight to drive.

There was a truck behind them for a while, but it turned left off the highway toward a cavernous, open-ended Quonset hut full of heavy equipment.

They reached the crest of Pacheco Pass and started down the other side.

"I have to take a piss for real," the kid said.

The berm on their right dwindled and ended, marked by a huge old valley oak and an abrupt turnout.

Priest pulled over. A cloud of dust drifted out over the highway. The boy threw open his door and trotted behind the oak, just out of the headlight beams.

"I'll drive for a while," Dusty said.

Priest was stepping around the Grand Cherokee when a big sedan—an Altima—pulled off the highway, skidded to a stop, slammed into reverse, and accelerated into the back of the Grand Cherokee. The Cherokee's airbags blew, and the collision pushed it ten feet forward, knocking Priest into the trunk of the oak hard enough that he dislocated his shoulder. He landed sitting, his legs splayed between the front wheels of the Cherokee, his face a foot from the grill. The boy hurried from behind the tree.

"Run!" Priest yelled at the boy.

The Altima pulled forward twenty feet, then jammed back into reverse and accelerated again toward the Cherokee. Priest tried to pull himself out of the way with his good arm, but there was no time. His head was going to split like a melon against the oak tree.

His last thought was that he'd been right about there being no God, but otherwise, he'd gotten just about everything wrong.

Which is when Dusty appeared between the Cherokee and the Altima.

She fired twice at the Altima, causing it to swerve just enough to miss the Cherokee. Priest found himself staring up into the driver's window of the Altima. Even without the blue wig, he knew it was Blue Wig, looking at him almost pleasantly as she put the Altima in a forward gear and accelerated toward Dusty, who was now standing between the Altima and the highway. Priest knew she would not survive the collision.

Wrong.

Dusty moved like a toreador, rolling off the hood into a crouched firing position on the passenger side of the Altima, firing twice and then three more times in rapid succession.

The Altima sped away onto the darkening highway.

When she was sure the Altima was gone, Dusty returned to Priest.

"Fucking stupid fucker," she said. "Fuckwad fuck."

Dusty didn't tend to swear. She was either really irritated with him or relieved that he was alive. Or both.

"The boy," Priest grunted.

"Seriously, Priest," Dusty said. "Don't you think it's time you called him by his name?"

She trotted over to the Grand Cherokee as Priest pulled himself up against the oak using his good arm. He sat against the tree to steady his vertigo. He heard the boy's—Tarquin's—voice.

"Fine. I'm fine. That was awesome."

"Fucking stupid fucker," Dusty said, trotting back to Priest.

"I'm sorry," Priest pleaded. "Stop swearing at me."

"I'm not swearing at you, you stupid fucking fucker."

Dusty grabbed Priest's right arm by the wrist, flipped him to the ground, put her foot in his armpit, and yanked his shoulder back into place.

Priest passed out.

———

Tarquin resolved into an urgent blurry image, leaning over Priest, bleeding from his mouth, asking, "Can you even hear me?"

Tarquin held up three fingers and waved them in Priest's face but didn't ask Priest how many he saw, which was the whole point of the exercise.

Dumbass delinquent.

"Are you okay?" Priest asked. "You got blood all over your chin and shirt."

"I bit my cheek."

"How long was I out?" Priest asked.

"Maybe ten seconds is all," Tarquin said. "Your eyes didn't even shut the whole way."

Behind Tarquin, a big Silverado pulled over and disgorged four working guys. Two Hispanics, one white, one Black—the boss. All wearing orange vests. The boss spoke into a mobile. Other cars pulled over along the shoulder.

This was turning into a thing.

"Where's Dusty?" Priest asked.

"She said she was never here. She said first thing is to make sure you understand that."

"I understand. Do you?"

The kid spat blood. It dribbled down his chin. He wasn't as cool a cucumber as he wanted Priest to think. "Yeah. There's more."

"Go," Priest said.

"Dusty said tell you she got her."

"How does she know?"

"She said tell you to shut up and listen if you asked any questions," Tarquin said.

"Go."

Tarquin closed his eyes, straining to repeat what Dusty had told him as accurately as possible. "She said there was just me and you in the car. I had to pee. We pulled over and got hit-and-runned. We didn't see nothing. You got knocked down. Nobody shot at anybody because the bullets are illegal. You're my long-lost biological father. We're still getting acquainted. The cops might check up on that." Tarquin opened his eyes. "Now you can ask questions."

"The cops are going to call your grandfather. Does he know about me?"

"Yeah, he knows."

"What will he do when he finds out you're with me and not at boxing camp?" Priest asked.

"He'll go agro. But he'll tell the cops everything is fine."

"You gonna be able to lie to the police?" Priest asked.

"I can lie."

Thinking of the kid and Diodato on the beach, Priest said, "I know you can lie. What I don't know is if you can lie and look innocent. It's a whole other talent."

Tarquin spat blood. His lip quivered, and his eyes filled with tears. He flinched and rocked.

"Jesus, kid, relax," Priest said. "I'm sorry."

"Sucker," Tarquin said, without changing his crybaby face.

The delinquent little asshole could definitely lie and look innocent.

The road construction crew from the Silverado gathered around. The boss waved his phone and shouted that the cops would be here in five minutes, the ambulance even sooner, fresh from another accident up the road.

Priest hoped that accident up the road wasn't Blue Wig in the ditch with an illegal bullet in her head and the Grand Cherokee's paint all over her back bumper.

"You breathing okay, man? You bleeding?" one of the road crew asked. Then, without listening, to his co-workers, "I don't see no blood."

"Could be internal? Don't move him."

Priest didn't feel like he was bleeding inside. His shoulder ached. And his hip. "I'm okay," he said. "I got knocked down is all."

Sirens.

In case Dusty was looking down on them from up on the hill or across the highway, Priest lifted his arm and gave a thumbs up. The road crew clapped.

"This is a bad stretch of road," the crew boss told Tarquin. "Lots of people die along here."

The ambulance arrived. Then the California Highway Patrol in an Expedition, followed by a CHP Charger. An older male trooper and his partner asked Priest and Tarquin questions while two more took photos of Priest's Grand Cherokee.

"You check out fine," the EMT told Priest. "But anything hurts enough you need pain killers, get your ass into emergency or your doctor, get MRIs, all that stuff. Okay?"

A tow truck had arrived and was hooking up the Grand Cherokee.

"Yeah," Priest said. "Is my son . . . is Tarquin . . . okay?"

Weird to say that out loud . . .

"He bit his cheek. No need for stitches. Ice water will help. But he won't be playing trumpet anytime soon."

"Thank you."

"Dangerous piece of road."

A CHP officer reminded Priest to grab whatever he needed from the Grand Cherokee before it got towed, which gave Priest a chance to see if there was any sign of Dusty in there. Nothing. Her backpack was gone.

The EMTs offered to drive Priest and the boy to Hazel Hawkins Memorial Hospital in Hollister but warned Priest it would cost a ton of money. Did he have good health insurance? Yes, Priest had good insurance, but he didn't want to go to the hospital. The oldest CHP officer talked to the boy. Tarquin played his role to the hilt, tearing up about his mother dying recently and coming to spend some time with his biological father, even patting Priest on the shoulder, which, to Priest's complete shock, made his own throat close up. Another cop called Anthony Orange and nodded, which reassured Priest that Tarquin had been right: the old man wasn't going to make any trouble with law enforcement. When Tarquin reached for the phone, the cop said, "Your grandfather says he'll talk to you later."

Another CHP trooper who looked like a teenager introduced herself as Officer Harb and offered to drive Priest and his son to a hotel in Hollister on her way back to the station in Gilroy.

"Thank you," Priest said.

On the way, in the back seat, the boy fell asleep. Or pretended to.

"Hell of a thing," Harb said. "Boy loses his mother. He's lucky to have you."

"Not so lucky today," Priest said.

"Losing a mother at his age," Harb said, "it makes a deep impression. I worked with Child Services for two years before moving to highway patrol. Kids without parents can lose their way real easy. They take all their sublimated anger at being abandoned and turn it on themselves, and then it explodes. Like a black hole, sucks everyone around them in."

Priest managed to resist telling her that black holes don't explode. Instead, he said, "I'm new at this dad stuff. I'll take any professional advice you got."

"Love him is all," Harb said. "Show you care. Therapy works for some kids."

Grateful for the darkness, Priest wondered what exactly to do with his face, and then said, "He smokes."

"Dope or cigarettes?"

"Both."

"How do you know?"

"He doesn't bother to hide it."

"Really?"

"He rolls his own cigarettes right in front of me."

"Twelve years old?"

"He thinks he's some kind of tough little cowboy," Priest said.

"I know it's tricky because you haven't been his primary caregiver, and he'll resent you interfering, but my advice is tell him no. At least that forces him to misbehave behind your back."

"Behind my back is good?"

"Going behind your back reinforces that what he's doing is wrong, and he'll know you care enough to try to stop him."

"I'll talk to his grandfather."

"He a good guy, the grandfather?"

"I don't know," Priest said.

Priest's initial investigation had indicated that Anthony Orange wasn't a particularly good guy. But there was no way to tell if, beyond that, Anthony Orange was a bad guy.

Officer Harb dropped them off at the Best Western in Hollister, Tarquin wearing his backpack, Priest lugging his father's briefcase with the arm that hadn't been dislocated. Priest gave Harb his business card.

"I owe you," Priest said.

"Thank you, Mr. Priestly," she said. "Good luck to you both." And then, to the kid, "Don't smoke."

Priest worried that Tarquin might tell Harb to fuck off and mind her own business, but he looked sheepish and stared at his feet. Psychopathic little shit. Priest waved as Harb drove away. Before they went inside, while Priest dialed Dusty's mobile, Tarquin rolled himself a cigarette.

"She's right. You shouldn't smoke," Priest said.

"It helps me relax."

Dusty had either turned off her mobile, was stranded somewhere out in the boonies without service, or didn't want her phone betraying her location if an investigation were launched.

While the boy smoked outside, Priest booked a room with two queen beds. He texted Dusty where they were. He wondered where she was, and then wondered if he should rent a car and drive back out along the highway to look for her.

Nah. Dusty would find them.

In the room, Priest and the kid took turns showering. Priest watched a bruise the size of a dinner plate rise on his chest, which the boy found amusing. Tarquin threw away his blood-soaked Hulk T-shirt and put on a red one with *WTF* across the chest and beneath that, *Work-Train-Fight!* They got dinner in the hotel restaurant, sitting at a four top in case Dusty showed up. Club sandwich for Priest. Tarquin ordered a burger but had trouble chewing with his torn-up cheek. Without consulting the boy, Priest ordered macaroni and cheese, ice water, and a chocolate shake. Tarquin ate it all without complaint.

Priest thought about Officer Harb: *Show you care.* He wasn't certain he did care, but he was willing to fake it.

"How was your mother's memorial?" Priest asked.

"What?"

"Did people come? Did she have a lot of friends?"

"Tons of people came," Tarquin said. "Pops has friends, too."

"Any of your boxing buddies come? Your coach?"

The kid sucked on his milkshake and glared.

Priest was doing something wrong. Which made it even worse that Dusty didn't show up to rescue them. Eleven o'clock at night, back in the room, Priest watched the energy drain out of the boy like beer from a bottle. Apparently, kids came without low-battery warnings; they just stopped dead.

Priest let Tarquin control the remote and bit back his irritation when the kid never landed anywhere for more than ten seconds—until he found a cartoon.

"What's that?"

"*Rick and Morty*," Tarquin said. "Genius."

The boy watched the TV, slack-jawed, eyes flat, chuckling

from his throat like a death-rattle. In repose, did they always look like zombies? Or was Tarquin traumatized and exhausted from the events of the day?

Should Priest engage him further?

Should they discuss the moralities and ramifications of everything that had happened?

By the time he decided that might be the right thing to do, Tarquin was asleep, wrapped tightly around himself, smaller, dumber-looking, and uglier than when he was awake.

———

Seven o'clock the next morning, Priest showered again, poked at his bruises, tried in vain to raise his right arm over his head, then roused the boy. They headed down to the hotel restaurant for breakfast.

Dusty sat at a table near the window, drinking coffee and eating a fruit cup and yogurt.

"Nice lip," she said to Tarquin. "Nice eye," she told Priest.

"How worried are we?" Priest asked Dusty.

"About Blue Wig? Not very. I got her."

"You're certain?"

"Not a direct hit, because those bullets would have put her down. But I saw blood, probably from shattering glass."

"Then let's rent a car and go see about Nikki," Priest said.

"Thank you," Dusty said.

Priest called Stephen T. Tedeschi using the phone number from the bus-stop bench, portraying himself as an app creator flush with a recent influx of Chinese venture capital and in need of commercial space. Tedeschi agreed to meet Priest in his real-estate office on Alma Street in downtown Palo Alto.

Through Tedeschi's picture window, Priest saw Dusty and

the boy sitting on a bench near the bike path, sipping milk-shakes and discussing God knows what.

Accustomed to tech entrepreneurs, Tedeschi didn't even blink at Priest's black eye or his thermal camo long-sleeved T-shirt and hiking pants. Priest revealed an enhanced version of the truth—he was a legal investigator for a major Los Angeles law firm—and added a non-subtle threat of blackmail: "I will tell your wife that you're paying an escort."

Stephen T. Tedeschi cradled his head in his hands and insisted that his older brother, William T. Tedeschi, must be Nikki Celeste's client.

"Billy's got my American Express Platinum," he said. To prove it, he produced photos of himself and his brother standing in front of Tedeschi Brothers Real Estate with their arms crossed, looking tough, like a couple of personal injury lawyers. They looked a lot alike . . . except that Bad Boy Billy looked like a lot more fun.

"Billy and I started this business together," Tedeschi said. "I was commercial. Billy was residential." He confided that Billy had gotten caught up in a rent scam, then an insurance scam, then a mortgage scam. Every time, Stephen had bailed Billy out.

"Expensive," Priest said.

"It's not Billy's fault. It's the cocaine."

"It's Billy's fault he snorts the cocaine," Priest said. "Lucky for you, coke dealers don't accept American Express."

"I figured that's why Billy bought the fancy watch," Tedeschi said. "To pawn for coke cash."

"He bought the watch for the escort," Priest said. "Her name is Nikki Celeste. She's also quite expensive."

"You don't have to tell me," Tedeschi said. "I'm the one paying for her."

Priest informed him that Nikki Celeste thought his coked-up

brother was a successful commercial real-estate whiz named Stephen T. Tedeschi who'd fallen in love with her and was promising to take her away from her sordid life as a sex worker.

"What can I do?" Tedeschi asked.

"Cancel the card," Priest said.

Tedeschi declared that he couldn't possibly leave his poor, addicted, coke-head brother high and dry: "Billy might do something stupid."

Priest shoved the insistent parable of the Prodigal Son out of his heart and concentrated on his own selfish objective: find Nikki for Dusty.

"Can I take a look at your latest credit-card statement?" Priest asked.

Tedeschi pulled up the statement on his computer.

Parris Ferrer was charging him five grand a day for Nikki's services. Give her credit: Parris knew exactly how to walk the razor's edge of maximum recoupment without triggering buyer's remorse.

Priest informed Tedeschi that there was nothing preventing the escort's business manager—who was not a nice person—from continuing to charge the card five thousand dollars a day even if Billy ditched the escort, which for all anyone knew, might have been a week ago.

"That's thirty-five grand straight out of your pocket, and for what?" Priest asked.

"Why does a big Los Angeles law firm care about any of this?" Tedeschi asked.

"I'm not at liberty to tell you that. What I can tell you is that I'm just the first of several investigators who will be knocking on your door. The next guy will be FBI."

"Fuck me," Tedeschi said. He'd finally seen the light. "I'll cancel the card."

15

Back at Priest's place in Venice—Tarquin holed up in his room, doing whatever kids do on their phones—Priest sipped beer with Dusty up on the roof.

Dusty was suffering the existential angst that all disappointed clients suffer after an investigatory setback. No matter how much Priest told her that they'd made headway, Dusty just sighed and grunted. She blamed herself for how very nearly Blue Wig had succeeded in killing Priest.

"I am here. I am now," Priest said.

"I don't feel like trading affirmations today," Dusty said.

"When you don't want to is when you're supposed to," Priest said. "I'd appreciate it if you quit blaming yourself."

"I'd appreciate it if I hadn't fucked up so completely."

"Mathematically speaking, you balanced the equation."

"You figure? How?"

"By shooting her," Priest said.

"That does cheer me up."

"We can't tell Baz about Blue Wig trying to kill us, or you shooting her," Priest said. "Same with Diodato."

"I get Diodato—but we tell Baz everything. We totally trust Baz."

"Nothing to do with trust," Priest said. "Baz is a lawyer. An officer of the court. Even just admitting that I filed a false incident report with the California Highway Patrol would place her in an ethical conflict. Add in that you shot someone with an unregistered weapon using illegal ammunition, which is attempted murder. It's not fair to put any of that on her."

"*Attempted* murder," Dusty said. "Rub it in, why dontcha, that I didn't succeed."

Priest raised his right hand and placed his left over his heart. "I swear I will never reveal that you failed in your earnest attempt to commit murder. I'm going for groceries. What do you want for dinner?"

When Priest returned from Ralphs, he found Dusty and Tarquin sitting at the kitchen table. They watched Priest restock the refrigerator. When he was done, Dusty stood up and said, "I'm going out."

"I got ice cream," Priest said.

Tarquin was hell on juice and ice cream.

Dusty didn't answer. She patted Tarquin on the back with her left hand and squeezed his neck with her right hand. Dusty was abandoning the kid, but she was also providing moral support. For what?

Priest saw the envelope propped against the salt and pepper shakers, placed deliberately so that Priest could see *Quinn* written on the front in bold, red felt pen, the letters traced by thinner, black ink. Priest pictured Rachel leaning over her own kitchen table late at night, laboring over the letter and its contents, tongue stuck in the corner of her mouth, worried because her difficult son was out somewhere making her life more difficult.

Priest took a seat across the table and waited. For the first time, he saw Rachel in their son's face.

"Well?" Tarquin said.

"Well, what? . . . You stick your middle finger up in my face one more time, I'm going to snap it off."

"Why do you gotta be so fucking weird? Open the fucking envelope!"

Priest extracted a three-page letter written on pale blue paper.

Folded into thirds.

Black ink.

A newspaper clipping fluttered onto the tabletop. Priest opened the clipping to reveal a photo of himself, striding in front of the Grand Park fountain in downtown LA, snapped by a *Times* photographer a block north of the Criminal Justice Center on Temple Street. He was dressed in what Baz called his court costume—a well-made conservative gray suit—glancing up at the photographer with irritation. Priest looked unpleasant and intense. Olive had said the photo made him look like exactly the kind of man you would not want rooting around for incriminating evidence in your secret life.

The headline over the photograph read "Investigator Puts City Councilman Behind Bars." The story explained that a city councilman had sued a local school board member for slander, libel, and defamation after the school board member accused him of accepting bribes. The school board member had hired Baz to defend her; Baz had hired Priest. Priest had uncovered evidence of bribery, kickbacks, extortion, and money laundering, which allowed Baz to put on what she called a "spirited" defense of her client, spirited enough to garner the attention of the press, which garnered the attention of the FBI, LAPD, and the Sheriff's Commercial Crimes Division.

"I don't see how some dude who's not a cop puts people in jail," Tarquin said.

"I didn't put anyone in jail," Priest said. "A prosecutor, judge, and jury did that."

"The paper says 'investigator'—that's you—put the city councilman behind bars. It says it right there. It's the headline."

Priest heard the boy, but he was busy appreciating that Rachel Orange had kept tabs on him. The article was four years old, and the clipping had been cut from an actual newspaper, not printed up later from an online digital archive.

He suppressed the urge to smell the writing paper because it might look weird to the kid.

"You want me to read the letter?" Priest asked.

"If you want."

Either Tarquin wanted Priest to read the letter with all his heart, or Dusty had forced this whole father/son moment on them both, and now Tarquin was having regrets.

The letter was dated three months prior. Christmas Eve. Rachel had numbered each page in the upper right-hand corner and circled the numbers many, many times, pressing into the paper, which probably meant that she'd labored over this letter. That it was important to her.

The salutation was standard: *Dear Quinn*—

But the first line was not: *My beautiful, perfect son who I love more than anything.* Meaning that Rachel had probably found "Dear Quinn" inadequate.

"You are one slow fucking reader," Tarquin said.

"I'm a careful reader," Priest said.

Rachel wrote that she'd composed the letter because, after her own mother died, she'd spent the rest of her life wishing and hoping that her mother had left a note or message of any kind. She'd searched for weeks after her mother's funeral. She even accused her father—Pops, Anthony Orange—of keeping it from her. And since Rachel and Tarquin hadn't gotten along very well lately, had barely spoken since their big fight at Thanksgiving, she wanted to make sure that, if something happened to her, he would know that she knew he loved her. All the arguments they'd had were normal, arguments that any single mother and her high-spirited growing-up-fast son would have.

The arguments were meaningless, she wrote. Quinn should forget they ever happened. Because when two people cared enough to argue as much as they did, it meant they loved each other, even if they didn't agree about a lot of things.

Quinn was the most important thing in her life, she wrote, and she was incredibly proud of him. He was her only child, and there was nothing in the world more powerful than that. She was convinced, beyond the shadow of a doubt, that their bond was more powerful than any other mother-and-child bond, the strongest bond of love in the whole world.

In history.

In the universe.

Priest was aware of the boy's eyes on his face, trying to guess where Priest was in the letter, gauging Priest's response to his mother's words.

"She really loved you," Priest said.

"I don't need you to tell me."

Rachel wrote that she'd always intended to tell Tarquin about his biological father when he turned eighteen. That was still her plan. If life went the way she hoped, Tarquin would never even see this letter.

His father was a man named Xavier Priestly.

That's why I gave you the middle name you've hated since you first heard it. Ha-ha!

Rachel wrote Priest's address in purple. She also provided

the address of Baz's law firm, because he seemed to work for them a lot. She had included the news clipping to make Priest real to the boy. She wanted him to see his father's face, and his own face reflected in the scowling man in the photo. In real life, she wrote, Xavier Priestly's face was kinder than it looked in the photograph. He was a good man. He was incredibly smart. *So now you know where you got both your brains and your nose. Ha-ha!*

Rachel wanted Tarquin to know that Xavier Priestly had showed up a year and a half after they'd first met—when Tarquin was between crawling and walking—and that she'd sent his father away without telling him that they'd had a child together because, by that time, she and Quinn were living with someone else. Someone she was engaged to.

But the engagement was a lie, and the man she was engaged to was not a good man. She'd never even say his name again, much less write it down, because he'd broken Quinn's arm when he was three years old. Rachel had kicked the man out, and the two of them—Rachel and Tarquin—had been alone together ever since. Except for Pops. Because it turned out good men were scarce. And she couldn't very well go chasing after Xavier Priestly after all that time.

"I wish she had," Priest said. "Chased me down."

"Right," Tarquin said.

"You remember getting your arm broken?" Priest asked, realizing that he was thinking about finding this man, tracking him down, and breaking *his* arm.

"It was my wrist that got broke. Not my arm," Tarquin said.

"This guy who broke your *wrist*, you remember his name?"

"It was like, Elton?"

"Like Elton John?"

"I don't know who that is."

"You know why they didn't get married?" Priest asked.

"He never got a divorce from his first wife?"

"Did he have a job?"

"Like a fireman or something," Tarquin said. "Whaddayou care?"

"Is Elton his first name or last?"

"Why? You think he's my real father?" Tarquin said.

"No," Priest said, "your mother wouldn't lie about a thing like that."

Priest read aloud: "*If anything happens to me, I want you to find Xavier Priestly and tell him who you are. If he says he doesn't remember me, you show him my photo.*"

"I can read," the boy said. "It's not like you have to read it to me. I can read."

Tarquin had claimed he could read too many times.

He bristled whenever his intelligence was questioned. That was probably why Rachel had taken the time to praise his intelligence, encouraging him from beyond the grave because too many people told him he was stupid. Because he had reading issues.

Priest read silently.

That's why I wrote this letter. I know you won't like it, and you're pretty firm about not doing things you don't want to do, but I'm asking you to PLEASE go see Xavier Priestly. I need you to have someone in your life who is blood-related, who is family, besides your grandfather.

If I'm gone, I need you to be influenced by more than one kind of man.

Anthony Orange was a different kind of man from Xavier Priestly, in a way that mattered to Rachel Orange.

Maybe Xavier Priestly won't want anything to do with you, and if so, I'm wrong about him, but at least we tried. It doesn't have anything to do with who you are. It has to do with him. But I don't think I'm wrong.

"Your mother wasn't wrong," Priest said.

The rest of the letter reiterated how much Rachel hoped Tarquin would never see the letter. How much she wanted to watch her son grow into a man, watch him fall in love, and live the big life she knew he was destined to live. How happy she would be, shortly after his eighteenth birthday, when she'd burn the letter and the two of them would take a trip to Los Angeles, together, to meet Xavier Priestly.

Priest folded the letter back into thirds. He tucked the newspaper clipping inside and slipped it all back into the envelope, tucked the flap, and shoved the envelope across the table to the boy.

Then he stalled because he was convinced that whatever he said next would carry undue influence.

"I remember your mother," Priest told Tarquin. "I remember her very well. Still, I'd love to see a recent photograph."

"I already decided that, if you didn't remember her, I wouldn't show you the letter or her photo. Fuck you, you don't remember her."

"I remember her. Your mother wasn't a person you forget."

Tarquin must have heard the truth in Priest's voice. He showed Priest a photo of Rachel on his phone.

She looked older than she should have. Tired.

She'd been a single mother who worked. A single mother raising a difficult child in a difficult place under difficult circumstances while Priest blithely lived his unencumbered life, investigating people, fishing off the pier, hanging out with Dusty, sleeping with a series of women who eventually expected more and moved on to more constant men.

"I did what Mom asked," the boy said. "I came here. I talked to you. I showed you her letter. So now I can go home."

"Is that what you want to do?" Priest asked.

"I got a life."

What could Priest say to that? It was true. They all had lives. Everybody had lives. Except Rachel Orange. Only living people had lives, and this kid was most definitely alive.

"My name is Tarquin Orange, not Tarquin Priestly," the boy said.

"Names don't matter much," Priest said.

The boy's chin jutted.

Priest had fucked up. No matter how Priest meant it, the boy had taken it another way, and it wasn't good.

"I don't even want Xavier for my middle name," Tarquin said. "But I'm stuck with it."

The kid was talking himself into being angrier. It had gone sour. Priest had just let Rachel down, and he had no idea what to do about it. He wished he could have five minutes with Baz, or Dusty, even Olive. They'd all know what to say.

"Do you want to go back home?" Priest asked.

"Fuck yeah! And I want my gun. And my bush."

"Why do you think your mother wrote the letter?"

"The fuck do I know?" Tarquin said. "In case I need bone marrow or something!"

"Is your grandfather old?"

"Yeah, Pops is fucking old!" Tarquin said. "He's my grand-father. Grandfathers are fucking old!"

"I mean, is he dying? Because it seems like your mom was afraid you'd be alone. Can he take care of you? He's got all his marbles? That kind of thing?"

"Pops is the smartest guy you ever met. We get along great. Better than me and Mom. I'm like him. Not like you."

"Did your Pops give you this letter?"

"What?"

"I assume your mother left this letter with your grandfather to give to you in case something happened to her."

"Yeah," Tarquin said. "Pops gave it to me."

The kid was a good liar. A prodigious, accomplished, and deceitful false witness of biblical proportion. But he was lying now, and Priest knew it.

He should have felt relief that Tarquin wanted to go back to his life in Las Vegas with his grandfather. He should have felt unburdened. Back in his twenties, like millions of young men, Priest had enjoyed a hot week with an enthusiastic and thrilling woman. When she found out she was pregnant, she didn't track him down. When she had a baby boy, she didn't let him know. When he'd tried to reconnect with her a year and a half later, he'd been sent away. Despite their time together—and the way Priest felt about Rachel—she hadn't felt enough about him or thought enough of him to involve him in supporting their child.

Priest remembered Rachel standing in the parking lot of Lou's Diner on Decatur in Vegas, bending over a stroller, smiling up at him but very definitely—and very gently—tossing him back into the ocean like a too-small fish.

He'd replayed that memory hundreds of times, and every time a shard of black ice twisted in his gut. Now, like his mother before him, a full decade before, Tarquin Orange was throwing Priest back.

Priest liked living alone in his place over the Venice Boardwalk. He liked solving his little mysteries. He liked being a serial monogamist who hooked up with interesting women before or after they'd experienced true love. And when those interesting women moved on—which they invariably did—Priest was always good with it. He always understood. *No hard feelings! No regrets! See you around!*

Priest decided the best way forward was to take the same

approach with this boy, his son. No regrets. Priest would start a bank account for Tarquin, for his education. Rachel had been impressed that Priest went to college. Priest would make a good education possible for her son. That was probably the main reason she wanted Tarquin to meet Priest anyway, and Priest would provide that. He would turn his guest room into Tarquin's room and make sure Tarquin knew he was welcome.

Weekends.

Vacations.

Tarquin could find work along the boardwalk in the summers. Attend junior lifeguard camp. Have a familiar place to call home when his grandfather eventually died.

That's what Rachel Orange had wanted for her son.

Options.

It was obvious that Tarquin loved his grandfather. They were birds of a feather.

"I'll drive you," Priest said.

The relief in the boy's face was instant and dramatic. "Don't worry about it," he said.

"Me and your grandfather should meet," Priest said.

"Pops might want to come here and pick me up. He loves road trips. He loves driving."

"Whatever works best for you."

"The sooner the better works best," Tarquin said.

He headed up toward the roof, patting his back pocket for his tobacco.

Priest took the opportunity to call Anthony Orange and introduce himself.

"My friend, you are one goddamn lucky sonofabitch that I didn't tell the cops you kidnapped my kid," Orange said. "You had enough of him yet? He's got school. Not to mention the boxing camp in La Quinta he was supposed to be at, which

I'm going to sue the hell out of for not informing me he didn't show up."

Priest told Orange that the boy had shown him the letter.

"That fucking letter. Tell you what, I wasn't going to show it to Tarquin until he was older. What he did was go digging through my shit. Tarquin in the house, what you need is a plutonium safe."

Priest decided not to point out that even a small safe made of plutonium would kill everyone in Nevada and Southern California.

"I'm sorry about Rachel," Priest said.

"You hardly knew her."

"What I knew I liked."

"Enough to knock her up, anyway."

Given that his daughter had only been dead a few weeks, Priest had to admire the old man's mettle. No wonder his twelve-year-old grandson liked him.

"Put me on with the little fuck," Orange said.

Priest shouted up to Tarquin to come down and talk to his grandfather. Priest had no idea the boy could move so fast, although after a "Hi, Pops," he just grunted "Yeah" and "Okay" four or five times, then tossed the phone back to Priest.

Priest and Orange planned to meet the next day for a handover and lunch at a restaurant in Palm Springs.

"Melvyn's," Orange said. "Old school. You know the place."

Priest did not know the place, but a cliched image of an old-school Palm Springs restaurant popped into his head, so maybe that's what Orange meant. Baz loaned Priest her BMW. Dusty insisted on coming. Priest couldn't persuade her that Blue Wig was probably taking a few days off from killing after being shot in the face.

"I'll sit in the back seat. I won't go into the restaurant, unless I hear screaming or see a woman in a wig."

"It's Palm Springs," Priest said. "I'd be surprised if you didn't see all kinds of people in wigs."

Dusty advised Priest to confiscate Rachel's Baby Browning until Tarquin was old enough to get it back legally. "He can come back and claim it on his eighteenth birthday," she said.

"Handguns aren't legal until you're twenty-one."

"Whatever. Make it a now-you-are-a-man moment."

"Fuck that," Tarquin said. "It's my inheritance. And I want my bush."

"What's that?" Dusty asked. "Pubic hair?"

"It's what he calls weed," Priest said.

"I flushed your bush," Dusty said.

Tarquin stomped up to the roof.

"You should hang onto him," Dusty told Priest.

"Like a stray dog?"

"Yup. Best outcome for everyone."

"You're serious?"

"He's your child."

"What makes you such an expert?" Priest asked. "I've never heard you say one word about your father."

"That's *exactly* what makes me an expert," Dusty said. "You think having a bank robber for a father is the worst that can happen to a person? Because it isn't."

"I have no legal claim. Vegas is his home. We haven't even confirmed that I'm his father."

"Look at his nose. Look in the mirror. Then look at his nose again. Paternity confirmed."

Priest told Dusty about his plan to set up an education fund, to make the guest room Tarquin's room, available any time, no advance notice required.

"I'll give him his own key," Priest said.

Dusty squinted at the ceiling and shook her head. "I guess we'll see if he leaves anything in that room."

"What?"

"Boys mark their territories. If he doesn't leave something behind, it means he's never coming back."

"I don't know what you want me to do, Dusty. Kidnap him?"

"Tell him you want him to stay."

"I did."

"Really?"

"More or less," Priest said.

"Less more or more more?"

"I made it crystal clear."

"How?" Dusty asked. "By telling him it's up to him?"

"It is up to him."

"But you didn't come right out and tell him that you want him to live with you here?"

"I told him he's welcome any time," Priest insisted. "Don't *growl*. In case you forgot, there's still a hit out on me. It would be irresponsible of me to . . . What? You're just walking away?"

———

During the entire drive from Venice to Palm Springs, Dusty didn't speak to Priest. When they found Melvyn's Restaurant, she refused to leave the car, except to hug Tarquin and whisper something in his ear.

Sitting across the booth from Anthony Orange, Priest extended a red pleather drawstring bag that had once held a Sherlock Holmes magnifying glass that his sister Olive had given him for Christmas twenty-five years ago. Orange looked inside, barked in recognition, and slapped Tarquin on the back of the head.

"Nogoodnik," he said to Tarquin. The boy grinned and shrugged. Orange pushed the drawstring bag to Tarquin and said, "Do me a favor. Put it in your rucksack."

"Rucksack? What's a rucksack, Pops? Nobody says rucksack."

"What's that? Nobody? I'm nobody now? Is that it?"

Priest watched as Tarquin took the pleather bag containing Rachel's pistol from his grandfather, taunted Priest by waggling it in his face, and tucked it into his backpack.

"He also had an Altoid box," Priest said, "with a couple of joints inside."

"That was his mother's," Orange said. Then, to Tarquin, "She would not have liked you knowing she got high." Then to Priest, "It wasn't often. Rachel didn't drink. Everybody's got their own ways of taking the edge off." Then to Tarquin, "What'd I tell you about alcohol?"

"Liquor is brown."

"What else?"

"If it's clear, it's queer," the kid said.

"Case in point," Orange said, pointing at Priest's ice-water and mugging while Tarquin laughed. The two of them vibrated on their own retro wavelength.

Tarquin ordered a milkshake, the old man an Irish coffee. Priest ordered a latte. He could discern no indication that the boy and his grandfather had any problems or issues. They adored each other. Tarquin constantly popped his grandfather in the shoulder. Orange responded by gently twisting Tarquin's ear and nose. The Orange family body language marked Priest as a third wheel. An outsider. When Tarquin mentioned that Priest had been attacked and hospitalized by a woman who later tried to run him over with her car, the old man laughed.

"Exactly how many women have you knocked up and

then vamoosed from?" he asked Priest. Without waiting for an answer, he turned to Tarquin and demanded, "What'd I tell you about crazy women?"

The kid jutted out his lower jaw, cast his eyes around, and knocked on the table with his knuckles—a perfect imitation of his grandfather. "Avoid them crazy bitches even when they're super-hot. *Especially* when they're super-hot. God don't give out favors with two hands."

"Wise ass," Orange said, delighted by Tarquin's impersonation. "There's your proof sitting right across from us, drinking his crappuccino. Some crazy chick running him over."

"I wasn't involved with her in any way," Priest said.

"Of course, not," Orange said, winking and jutting his finger at the ceiling. "She's just some homicidal maniac who fixated on you for no reason." He turned to Tarquin. "Here is wisdom I am passing on to you from the depths of my considerable experience. Don't let nobody lead you down the garden path by your salami."

The old man and the boy belonged together. Tarquin hardly took his eyes off his grandfather, sneaking peeks to see what Orange thought of Priest and vice-versa. When Priest repeated how sorry he was about Rachel's death, the old man's hand fell on the nape of Tarquin's neck. The boy leaned his head back against the old man's arm.

Priest was definitely doing the right thing, returning the boy to his grandfather.

Orange stood, indicating that it was time for him and Tarquin to head home to Vegas.

Priest gave each of them his card. "Call anytime."

"Yeah, thanks," Orange said, conveying with his tone that he'd never do any such thing. As far as Anthony Orange was concerned, Xavier Priestly was some random college kid who'd knocked up his daughter during a visit to Vegas. Orange never asked whether Priest had a family of his own. Whether he'd ever married. He didn't ask him anything. "Shake hands with Mr. Priestly," he told Tarquin.

Tarquin shook Priest's hand. "Dusty said she wants to come and watch me fight some time," Tarquin said. "Tell her I'll text her."

"Will do," Priest said.

Tarquin measured Priest for a moment, then looked away. Too late, Priest realized he should have said, *Watch you fight? Count me in! I can hardly wait!* "Pow-Pow Orange!" he said—too late.

"Ha!" said Orange. "That's what the little shit wants everyone to call him, but nobody does." Then, to Tarquin, "What did I tell you?"

"You don't get to pick your own nickname," Tarquin said, knocking on the table, jutting his chin, pointing at the ceiling.

From his seat at the restaurant window, Priest watched them cross the parking lot together and get into a black Buick Regal. Tarquin never even glanced back, but Orange did. No smile on his face. Just an appraising look as though he was thinking, *Is that all there was to this bullshit?*

When Priest raised his hand in farewell, the old man nodded and waved him off, like he was accepting a gesture of surrender.

Priest nursed his coffee, hoping Dusty would get out of the car, come into the restaurant, slip into the seat vacated by Old Man Orange, order some lunch, and demand what he was going to do next to track down Nikki Celeste.

Dusty stayed in the car.

Driving back to LA, Priest told her everything that had happened. She grunted a couple of times and then pretended to sleep the rest of the way back. When they pulled up to Priest's place, she immediately got out of the car, striding off without even warning him to be careful.

Unlocking his front door, Priest felt ill-tempered, vengeful, and combative.

He wanted to strike out.

He got the opportunity when he went through the results of his reverse-image art search. Using a VPN, he sent anonymous emails to all the artists that Parris—with Nikki's help—had ripped off. He informed them that their work had been misrepresented and that Parris owed them money. He gave them contact numbers and email addresses for the FBI Art Squad.

But he doubted that justice would ever be done.

The following day, it was Baz's turn to tell Priest how wrong he was to deliver Tarquin back to his grandfather.

"I guess Dusty called you," Priest said. "Got you all fired up."

"That's correct," Baz said. "And I didn't believe her when she said that you gave him the option of staying or going."

"What's wrong with that?" Priest asked.

"You didn't think that's maybe too much reality to dump on a twelve-year-old boy who just lost his mother?"

"Words don't matter, Baz," Priest said. "You know what matters? Actions. *Deeds*. People should be judged on what they do, not what they say."

"People—especially children—need to hear things that other people tell them using words," Baz said. "Kids are like juries. They don't see actions. If they do, they aren't good at interpreting their meaning. Kids make pictures in their heads while listening to words. Saying the right words *is* the action."

Priest was smart enough not to point out that neither of the two women kicking his ass on the subject of offspring were mothers. Out of the three of them, he was the only one who was the *de facto* parent of an actual child. He argued that having a hit out on him meant that he couldn't take Tarquin in.

"That shouldn't stop you from letting him know that you want him," Baz said.

"I didn't want to pressure the boy. I didn't want to make anything heavier than it had to be."

"Some things are heavy, Priest. Some shit is heavy shit. A person's gotta strain a little to lift it."

"I'm getting mixed messages from you on how much of a burden to put on a child," Priest said.

After Baz left, Priest remembered what Dusty had said about boys marking their territories. He searched Tarquin's room and found Rachel's letter and the newspaper clipping in the waste can. Unsure what to make of that, he smoothed the letter, folded it, and slid it into one of the many secret interior pockets of his father's horrible briefcase.

16

Priest rented a silver Hyundai Elantra and drove to Cody Fiso's office in Culver City, Dusty sullenly riding shotgun.

"It's been a week since Stephen T. Tedeschi shut down his credit card," Priest said. "By now Nikki's realizing she hooked up with the wrong Tedeschi."

"And?"

"And she'll ditch the guy."

"Huh."

"Anyone ever tell you that you can make 'Huh' sound like 'Die, motherfucker'?" Priest asked.

"Simplicity. Compassion. Patience," Dusty said.

"Peace. Forgiveness. Kindness," Priest responded.

"What if Tedeschi kidnapped Nikki against her will?" Dusty asked. "What if she's in a lot worse danger than a credit card getting declined?"

"Billy T. Tedeschi is a loser cokehead, not a killer . . . Let me finish before you pretend to fall asleep again! The main thing is for you to understand that the moment you handed me that twenty dollars, I was obligated by the rules and standards of the

Guild of Investigators to provide you your money's worth, no matter how misguided your quest to find Nikki."

"Am I up to twenty bucks' worth yet?" Dusty asked. "I feel like the answer is no. Tell Fiso hello from me."

———

"Another visit from the seminarian," Fiso said. "What now?"

To his credit, anvil-like chin resting on his boulder-like fist, Fiso listened as Priest filled him in on the confrontation with Blue Wig at the side of the highway on the Pacheco Pass, leaving out extraneous details like Dusty Queen and Tarquin.

When Priest finished, Fiso asked, "And what do you require from me?"

"I need the emergency rooms and urgent-care clinics in Central California and Nevada canvassed to see if anyone matching Blue Wig's probable injuries came in to get stitched up."

"Injuries consistent with superficial bullet wounds and/or shattered automobile glass fragments to the face and neck?" Fiso asked.

"Yes."

"And you expect me to believe that you fired the gun?" Fiso asked.

"I'd appreciate it," Priest said.

"And you can't ask the homicide detective investigating the attack on you to do this because . . ."

"The gun discharging the bullets was unregistered."

"And the ammo?"

"Grievously illegal."

"Dusty Queen fired that weapon. Admit it."

Priest said nothing. Fiso said nothing.

The silence stretched for quite a while, until Fiso said,

"Priest, if you're going to insult me by asking for my help while lying to my face, then get out of here and leave me alone."

"If it was Dusty who did the shooting, then you'd have to agree that she can't be both the person trying to kill me and the person trying to kill the person trying to kill me," Priest said.

"Just because I lack the imagination to figure out what Dusty Queen might be up to doesn't prove she isn't up to something."

"Oh, c'mon!"

"Was Dusty with you or was she not?" Fiso asked. "Tell me the truth or go away."

"Fine," Priest said.

"Thank you. It seems awful coincidental that Blue Wig knew where you were going."

"Obviously, she tailed us," Priest said.

"And the person who almost got you killed by deciding you were not being tailed was . . ."

"Fiso, what kind of tortuous Rube Goldberg genius super-villain plan would that entail?"

"Again, just because I lack the imagination . . ."

"Oh, c'mon! Dusty is an open book."

"Written in a language nobody but you can read."

"Dusty would never put the kid in danger," Priest said.

"What kid?"

Fuck!

Priest wanted a favor, and Fiso possessed a highly sensitive internal bullshit detector, so Priest provided a succinct and honest account of Tarquin's loss of his mother, his sudden appearance on Priest's doorstep, and why he was with them when Blue Wig attacked.

"Wow," Fiso said.

"Don't worry about the boy. He is not a factor," Priest said.

"Your *son* is not a factor?"

"In life and the universe, the boy's a factor," Priest said. "But as it pertains to this case, no, he's not."

"Does the boy have a name?" Fiso asked.

"Tarquin Orange."

"Where is Tarquin Orange now?"

"At home, in Vegas, with his maternal grandfather, Anthony Orange."

"I suppose that's the prudent choice," Fiso said.

"Thank you," Priest said. "Will you help me or not?"

"By . . ."

"By canvassing emergency rooms and urgent-care centers in Central California and Nevada."

"That falls well within the scope of your own investigatory abilities," Fiso said.

Priest white-knuckled the tubular aluminum arms of Fiso's father's chair. Why did people have to question everything? Why did people have to understand everything? Why did they always require context and explanation?

"The most any hospital can ethically provide a civilian investigator is a *yes* or *no* predicated upon whether a person suffering that general type of injury was treated, and they don't even have to do that," Priest said.

"You must pretend to be law enforcement all the time."

Priest agreed that he was not above misrepresenting himself as a cop, but "My lawyer advised me that, while the police are investigating an attempt on my life, it might be best to avoid breaking the law."

"You have no other options?"

Fiso was taking the opportunity to glean insights into Priest's investigatory processes—did Priest have any nifty little tricks and hacks that Fiso hadn't considered? Priest gave up his most obvious option: he could always press his sister and brother-in-law, the famous screenwriters, to call hospitals and say they were researching a movie starring their good friend Leo, Ryan, Other Ryan, Chris, Other Chris, Other Chris, Australian Chris, or Gerard. Two minutes of Googling would show that Olive and Martin had done movies with all those stars, plus others including Brad, George, and Russell.

"Why not do that?" Fiso asked.

"Because it would take weeks for Olive and Martin to build up enough trust with their sources to persuade them to impart actual privileged medical secrets."

"What do you expect me to do?" Fiso asked.

"Half your investigators are former or moonlighting cops. Get one of them to call around."

"I could do that," Fiso said.

"I'm not asking for a favor," Priest said.

"It seems like you are."

"I'm not."

"You intend to pay me?"

"I'm looking to barter," Priest said.

He dug into his briefcase, removed a binder, and placed it on the coffee table between them. Fiso's eyebrows, the breadth of window-washing brushes, shot up into his volleyball-sized forehead.

"Wow. Three-ring binder. Made of aluminum," Fiso said. "Fancy and super important."

"It's a completed investigation file."

"Into what?"

"Read it."

"Why should I read it when you can just tell me?"

"Because you won't believe me."

"Try me."

"Trust me."

"I'm not going to read this whole binder while you watch."

How did everything with Fiso turn into a dick-measuring contest?

"Peruse the title page," Priest said.

"Is it the location of your father's buried treasure? You don't need a fancy binder to persuade me. Simple set of GPS coordinates would do the job."

"I'll leave the binder with you," Priest said, standing. "If you think the contents constitute fair exchange, then it's yours, and I owe you nothing more in return. If not, as a matter of professional courtesy, I trust you will not act upon or divulge to others the information therein."

"How many of the dozens of favors I've done for you is this binder supposed to cover?"

"All of them," Priest said. "And you will still owe me."

"This binder is that good?"

"Yes."

"Get the fuck outta here," Fiso said, not as an exclamation of disbelief but as an instruction. "Unless . . . Is this Charlie McGinn?"

"If you'd just read the file—"

"No way you give up Charlie McGinn," Fiso said. "That's a hundred grand just for our bet. There'll be a TV series or movie. Play it right, finding Charlie McGinn is worth millions to the right guy."

"You're the right guy," Priest said.

"Why not just provide me GPS coordinates?"

"Read the file," Priest said.

Matthew 4:8, Satan's third temptation of Christ on the mountain: *All these things I will give you . . .*

"I don't need to read the file," Fiso said. "If you tell me you found Charlie McGinn, then you found Charlie McGinn. You're full of shit, but you're not a liar."

They shook on it. Like Satan and the Son of God on the Mount of Temptation, Cody Fiso and the seminarian had each other by the balls.

17

Unable to hide away in his apartment any longer, Priest decided that what he needed was some fishing. He sauntered out onto the pier, waving at the Bubble Guy and the Live Karaoke Guy, who were doing their respective things for the tourists. Despite the warmth in the air, and the visibility of Catalina Island way out on the horizon, the water looked choppy and gray.

Priest found Yorben at his usual spot.

"Is what I heard true?" Yorben asked him.

"I'm guessing no," Priest said.

"Beck said you got stuck in the neck with a syringe by a tweaker trying to steal your car."

"I don't know for sure that it was a tweaker," Priest said.

"I don't like the sounds of that," Yorben said. "I got a needle phobia and whatnot."

Priest gave Yorben the broad outlines of the truth, tossed in sending Tarquin back to live with his grandfather in Vegas, and the fact that both Baz and Dusty were mad at him for it.

"My opinion, them women are being way too hard on you,"

Yorben said, "which women cannot help doing, especially when the man is not married. Like you."

"Are *you* married?"

"Not currently. But I've been married three times. All I know is, when I'm not married, I get criticized ten times more than when I am married."

"*Three* women married you?"

Flipping through the digital photos of the shark he'd caught on Priest's line, Yorben said, "You did the right thing. You're not set up to be anyone's daddy. He barely knows you. All that boy was doing was fulfilling his mother's dying wish. Like a chore. If he wanted more outta you, he'd've stuck around."

"That's what I thought," Priest said, distressed, because that was exactly what he thought.

"How's it going finding Dusty's girlfriend?"

Priest told Yorben as much about Nikki and the Tedeschi brothers as he could without violating Dusty's confidence.

"Dusty Queen falls for an escort," Yorben said. "That's gotta be the stupidest thing I ever heard. Dusty should know better. You know what lies in that direction?"

"Heartbreak?"

"Heartbreak and sorrow and whatnot."

Priest said he expected Nikki to show up any second now that her golden goose had stopped producing eggs stolen from his twin brother..

"How long ago the john's credit card get shut down?"

"Week," Priest said. "I don't think they're called 'johns' anymore."

Yorben's lips moved. He waggled his head back and forth. Some mighty big arithmetic happening there. The Fundamental Theorem of Calculus. The Euler-Lagrange equations. The Fibonacci sequence.

"What?" Priest asked when Yorben's head stopped moving.

"No way the john and the escort are still hanging out," Yorben said.

"How do you know?"

"Sure, maybe, if the guy's holding the call girl prisoner in a buried shipping container in the desert or his crawlspace or some such perversity. But no way a call girl falls in love. Not with Dusty. Not with the client. Why? Because call girls do not know true love. For them, all human feelings are transactional and whatnot."

"What makes you such an expert?" Priest asked.

"Pimps and hoes in the family. Cousin level and beyond."

"You think Nikki's shackled to the wall in an underground sex dungeon?"

"Maybe. Or dead."

"I hope not," Priest said. But hearing Yorben say it out loud made it seem that much more plausible.

"Most likely, the call girl takes off on the guy thirty seconds after his card gets declined for the third time. Sooner, if they're out of coke. And guess where she goes?"

"Home?"

"Home is where she goes."

"If Nikki came home, she didn't tell Dusty," Priest said.

"Y'ever think maybe the sex hooker—"

"Sex *worker*, Yorben. Worker. With a *w*."

"—sex *worker* took off with the guy to get away from Dusty?"

"Why's everybody trying to blame Dusty for everything that goes wrong?"

"How come you trust her blind?"

"What?"

"Blind trust. Like, without a doubt, you trust Dusty Queen?"

"Yes," Priest said.

"How come?"

The faith Priest had in Dusty Queen was like the faith his fellow seminarians had in Jesus Christ. There was no rational reason behind it. It just *was*. But unlike his fellow seminarians, Priest saw no reason why other people should share that faith.

"Follow my reasoning if you can," Yorben said.

"I'll try."

"Dusty Queen falls in love with the sex hooker, right? Maybe it's okay for a while, maybe it's good. But Dusty, she is in there for the long haul. Dusty is scary and intense. The sex hooker wants to move on, right? Nothing personal, it's just . . . life's too short for bullshit like love and whatnot."

"Life's too short for bullshit like love?"

"You gotta think like a sex hooker," Yorben said.

"Maybe just call her Nikki?"

"One thing hustlers of all natures—call 'em what you want—hustlers know obsession and whatnot. They manipulate clients' feelings, especially a big spender. A mark. Fun times, money flows. But Dusty Queen ain't no kind of mark. And she's not paying."

Fuck.

Everything Yorben said about Dusty and Nikki made sense.

Fuck.

Priest texted Giselle: *Nikki back?*

No response.

Maybe she was with a client.

Priest texted: *Silence means yes?*

———

There'd still been no response from Giselle by eleven that night.

Midnight came and went.

Tossing and turning, Priest wished he was having sex.

He texted his ex, Tina: *U up?*

She texted him back: *LOL.*

Priest practiced his calming breathing exercises: *in for five heartbeats . . . hold for seven heartbeats . . . out for nine heartbeats . . .*

Foolproof, guaranteed stuff, especially since, when done right, in a state of mindfulness, the heart also slowed down.

Breathe in for five heartbeats . . .

Had he done right by Tarquin?

Yes.

Hold for seven . . .

Had he done the right thing bartering his self-respect and independence by turning over to Cody Fiso the results of his search into the Holy Grail of Charlie McGinn?

Yes.

Breathe out for nine . . .

Was he doing right by Dusty?

Silence.

Was he dragging his ass looking for Nikki because he disapproved of Dusty's being besotted by an escort?

Because he thought Dusty was doomed to get her heart broken?

Because he didn't know if it would be better or worse for her if he found Nikki and brought her back?

Did a true friend do what his friend wanted? Or what his friend *needed*?

Was Priest's religious training pushing him to act like an actual priest by deciding what was best for another person whether she liked it or not?

Silence.

Silence.

Silence.

This was just like praying. It was one of the reasons Priest no longer had faith in a Supreme Being. If there was a beneficent Godhead out there, then every so often He or She or They or It should bounce back Light or Thought or a Celestial Sound or some other assurance from beyond the void.

What if silence *was* the bounce?

Silence.

Priest's phone PLINKED. He was disappointed when it wasn't Tina texting with a change of heart. It was from Parris Ferrer: *cum c me*

Priest texted: *Is Nikki back?*

Parris texted: *CUM C ME!!* followed by three emojis of a smiling turd.

Priest texted: *why?*

Parris texted: *2 discuss ART motherfucker.*

Priest texted: *On my way,* adding a heart emoji.

Dusty sat at Priest's kitchen table, eating the kid's disgusting sugary cereal.

"Did you move back into my guest room?" Priest asked. "You think I'm in danger again?"

"Blue Wig might have had time enough to recover from her injuries," Dusty said. "You going somewhere?"

"How's a piece of pie sound?" Priest asked.

"We're going to see Parris?"

"I am," Priest said. "You're going to wait in the car."

"Then why ask me if I want pie?"

"I'll get yours to go."

Priest drove.

"Why are we going to see Parris?" Dusty asked.

"She texted me that she wants to talk."

"Did she say what about?"

"She implied that it had something to do with the art that Nikki sold under false pretenses."

"The 'Callie Vaughan' stuff?" Dusty asked.

"I was in a bad mood," Priest said. "So I ratted Parris out to all the artists I could identify."

"How does that help find Nikki?" Dusty asked.

"That's what I'm on my way to find out."

"Why can't I come in with you?"

"You know what? This is the last time I ever let a client act as my bodyguard," Priest said.

"*Let?*"

"It's exhausting explaining everything you're going to do, then doing everything you said you'd do, unless you decide not to do what you said you'd do, and instead do something else—after explaining what that is—and then performing a post-mortem on everything you've done or not done."

"Are you telling me to mind my own business?" Dusty asked. "When all of this is totally my own business?"

"Thank you for understanding."

Three blocks west of the House of Pies, the traffic on Franklin bunched. Directed by Google Maps, cars in front of them U-turned or cut away into alleys and side streets.

It took twenty minutes to draw up parallel to the House of Pies parking lot. Flashing lights. First responders. Uniformed cops outside, holding back the looky-loos. Detectives inside, interviewing possible witnesses. EMTs and more detectives clustered near a black Mercedes G-Wagon parked three spots from the entrance.

"That's Parris's Mercedes," Priest said.

"Lots of celebrities drive those G-Wagons," Dusty said.

Crime-scene techs finished erecting a tent around the G-Wagon. ABC 7, NBC 4, and Fox 11 news helicopters held station high overhead. An LAPD helicopter circled beneath. Whatever happened here had happened within the last hour.

Two uniformed cops on Franklin waved them forward. Priest took a right on Vermont and pulled into the United States Post Office parking lot. A six-foot white cinderblock wall separated them from the patio area at the House of Pies.

"What do you think?" Dusty asked.

"I think we're not getting any news from Parris tonight," Priest said.

The rental car's engine ticked as it cooled.

"We might as well go home," Priest said.

An unmarked Crown Vic pulled into the post office parking lot. Detective Garnet Diodato got out, touched his toes, twisted back and forth from his waist, slapped his face, straightened his jacket, and moved toward Vermont Street.

"Twenty bucks says he doesn't see us," Priest said.

As though he'd heard Priest, Diodato looked directly at them. He squinted, put his hands on his hips, and shook his head. Priest handed Dusty the same twenty-dollar bill she'd paid him to find Nikki.

Here on in, Priest was working for free.

18

Priest and Baz sat beside each other on red resin chairs, alone in an interview room in the Hollywood Police Station. Priest wrinkled his nose at the smell of flop-sweat and cleaning products, stale coffee, fear, and resignation.

"Detective Vidal comes to us from on high," Baz said, for the second time.

"Got it," Priest said.

"Listen to me, Priest. Detective Vidal is from Robbery-Homicide. Do not underestimate her. Don't be funny."

"Got it."

"Rampant paranoia would not be an overreaction in this situation," Baz said. "Red alert . . . Don't flap your lips at me! Repeat what I just said."

"Red alert," Priest said. "Danger, Will Robinson."

"I don't know who that is," Baz said. "No, don't tell me. I don't care as long as Will Robinson did what his lawyer advised."

Detective Diodato opened the door and then stood aside to let a tall, stooped woman in her fifties precede him into the room. She had short, spiky brown hair and a jaw like Abraham

Lincoln's, and she wore black Rockport referee shoes and the same kind of horn-rimmed glasses favored by nuns.

"Welcome to the Hollywood Police Station," she said, sitting down across from Priest. "I'm Detective Rhonda Vidal." She placed her elbows on the table and leaned toward Priest. Her glasses were trifocal, which indicated to Priest that Vidal was the kind of cop who looked closely at things but did not forsake the big picture. "Mr. Priestly, if I'm satisfied with your answers to the questions I'm about to ask, you will go home tonight. If not, you will be transported downtown for further questioning."

"My client is here of his own free will at two-thirty in the morning," Baz said before Priest could accuse Vidal of blackmail. "He has every intention of cooperating fully."

"Detective Diodato has provided me with a rundown of his perceptions of your interactions with, and relationship to, Parris Ferrer," Vidal told Priest. "He's also warned me that, when you're stressed, you can be impolite. He says I shouldn't take it personally, that it's a psychological condition."

"We appreciate your understanding," Baz said.

"I informed Detective Diodato that I'm familiar with that psychological condition. It's called *Douchebag Syndrome*. If you are rude to me, I will respond by politely taking you into custody, and I will politely keep you in custody until you learn your manners."

"Best behavior," Baz advised Priest.

"Where's Dusty Queen?" Priest asked.

"Best behavior means letting other people ask the questions," Baz said.

"Ms. Queen is next door," Detective Vidal said. "We're going to interview her after we interview you."

"I am also representing Dusty," Baz reminded Priest. "So the quicker we get through this, the quicker I can get to her."

Baz wanted Priest to shut up and let her do the talking.

"You have any problem with that, Mr. Priestly?" Vidal asked.

"With what?"

"Sharing a lawyer with Ms. Queen?"

"Why would I have a problem with that?"

"In the interest of moving things along, I'm going to take that as a no," Vidal said. "But from now on, please don't answer my questions with a question."

Diodato crossed his arms and peered into his Styrofoam cup, his set-together-too-close eyes measuring how much coffee he had left. Priest found it reassuring that, with barely an inch of coffee in there, Diodato figured he had enough to see him through the rest of Priest's interview.

"Obviously, we're here because somebody killed Parris Ferrer," Priest said.

"Priest," Baz said.

"I'd like to ask you a few questions before confirming why I'm asking them," Vidal said. "You know, the traditional process, in which I'm the interviewer and you are the interviewee."

"As an experienced legal investigator, my client totally understands," Baz said. "He simply forgot himself in the moment."

That was for Priest, not Vidal.

"Furthermore . . ." Priest said.

"Agh, with a 'furthermore' now," Diodato muttered.

". . . Parris was killed with a needle to the neck."

Vidal tilted her head, adjusting from the long view to the short through her nun's glasses.

"My client has no first-hand knowledge of whether or not a homicide took place," Baz said. "If a homicide did take place, he is unaware of who the murder victim is and/or the means by which that person lost his or her life."

Baz was using her full-on lawyer voice. *Red alert, Will Robinson! Red alert!*

Diodato drained his coffee and lifted it toward the mirror. He no longer thought he'd be out of here in a few easy minutes.

"Needle to the neck is a very specific detail," Vidal said, adjusting her trifocals.

The glasses were a tell. Vidal smelled blood in the water. Did Baz know that? Of course, she did. Baz had trained Priest to look for lawyer tells in the first place.

"My client is guessing," Baz said.

"I'm not guessing," Priest corrected her. "I'm surmising."

"My client—who will forthwith stop talking except to answer direct questions—is an astute investigator, despite being a rude show-off. His statements are based on acute observation, not personal knowledge. I hope you will consider not immediately arresting him—which he totally deserves and would serve him right—and instead provide him the opportunity to tell you why he thinks he knows what he thinks he knows, and what observations he made to draw the inferences he's drawing, because I'm sure he understands that these are exactly the kind of details that, currently, only the police and the murderer know."

"Why do you think it was Parris Ferrer who was murdered tonight?" Vidal asked. "And why do you think Blue Wig did it?"

Baz indicated that it was Priest's turn, so Priest described how, as he and Dusty had driven by the House of Pies, they'd seen a flurry of police, forensic, and EMT activity around Parris Ferrer's distinctive Mercedes G-Wagon.

"Distinctive how?"

"The upholstery is leopard," Priest explained. "Her vanity license plate says *GRRRRRR*. It's her regular parking spot."

He told the detectives that, because the EMT activity was *not* urgent, then whoever was in the Mercedes G-Wagon was either healthy or dead. And because the police activity *was* urgent, he knew that the victim inside Parris Ferrer's Mercedes was *not* healthy.

"Therefore," Priest concluded, "Parris was either the victim or—less likely—the murderer."

"Why less likely?" Vidal asked.

"If Parris were the murderer, you wouldn't be checking so hard to see if I am the murderer. And you wouldn't still be holding Dusty Queen next door."

"Go on," Vidal said.

Priest had pulled into the post office parking lot just moments ahead of Detective Diodato. The most likely reason that Diodato—a violent crimes detective based in the LAPD's Pacific Division—was arriving at a homicide scene in the Hollywood Division was because he had been summoned, so the murder must, in some way, resemble a murder or assault case he was currently working on. Upon seeing Priest and Dusty, Diodato had immediately taken them into custody and separated them, which suggested that the active case in question was Priest's own case. Not to mention that—and Priest clarified that he was making an educated guess here—Parris Ferrer was probably on Diodato's list of prime suspects in the attack on Priest.

An attack that featured a needle in the neck.

Priest pointed to his neck where Blue Wig had injected him.

"Why were you at the House of Pies?" Vidal asked.

"Don't say a word about wanting a slice of pie," Diodato warned.

"Parris sent me a text, asking to see me," Priest said. "I can show you, if you want."

"Let me see that first," Baz said.

Baz looked at the text exchange on Priest's phone and then handed it to Vidal, who showed it to Diodato.

"You believe him?" Vidal asked Diodato.

"Yeah," Diodato said. But he wasn't enthusiastic.

"Why would Ms. Ferrer want to talk to you about art?" Vidal asked. "I assume that's some kind of code."

"Not a code," Priest said. "I exposed one of her money-making schemes to certain injured parties."

"What I want you to do," Baz told Priest, "is proceed very slowly and be ready to stop talking at any moment."

Priest explained about the art on Nikki Celeste's wall. How it was bought. How the signatures were replaced. How Nikki sold the art at inflated prices, under the name "Callie Vaughan," which her customers believed to be her real name.

And how—in a fit of pique—he had ratted Parris out to the victimized artists.

"If Parris was killed by a needle to the neck, then Blue Wig did it," Priest said. "If Parris died in some other way, it could be one of these artists."

"Will you give us a list of these artists?" Vidal asked.

"If Baz says 'yes,'" Priest says.

"Yes," Baz said.

It took forty-five minutes for Detective Vidal to reorder and re-ask her questions. Some revolved around the attack on Priest in his garage. Some concerned his search for Nikki Celeste, including his recent trip north. Priest omitted Blue Wig's attempt to crush him to death with her car on the Pacheco Pass, and Dusty's subsequent illegal efforts to shoot Blue Wig to death. He did mention the hit-and-run because, if the police computer spat up the California Highway Patrol report, Priest would have a hard time explaining why he'd left it out.

On Baz's recommendation, Priest provided Vidal and Diodato with the identities of both Tedeschi brothers, mostly to buy a little time. He had to think of a way to use Baz to send the message to Dusty that she, too, should leave out

the Blue Wig perturbation when Vidal questioned her. All
that occurred to Priest was Proverbs 10:19: *When words are
many, transgression is not lacking, but whoever restrains his lips
is prudent.* Which was way too general. Not to mention, it
would tip off Baz that Priest and Dusty were conspiring behind
her back. He'd have to trust in Dusty's natural prudence and
cowboy-level taciturnity.

A uniformed cop brought in a cup of coffee for Diodato
and a laser-printed copy of the CHP hit-and-run report from
the Pacheco Pass. The report would feature Tarquin Orange.
Priest now had to worry about whether Vidal would interview
Tarquin. Priest felt confident that the boy would stick to the
fake story and lie to police.

Confusing. Was that pride he felt? Or shame?

"You have a *son*?" Diodato asked. He turned the file around
on the table and placed his index finger on Tarquin Orange's
name.

"I had no idea the boy existed before he showed up on my
doorstep a couple days before I decided to take him along to
speak to Stephen T. Tedeschi in Palo Alto."

"Not the kid on the beach?" Diodato asked.

"That's him," Priest said.

"Father of the year," Diodato said. "Letting a kid that age
smoke. Letting him mouth off to a police detective. Skipping
school. Taking him on a road trip when there's a murderer after
you. What kind of father are you?"

"Don't worry. Tarquin is back in Las Vegas with his legal
guardian. His grandfather," Priest said.

"Dusty Queen didn't accompany you to Palo Alto?"

"She met up with us the next day."

"I didn't know the two of you went anywhere without the
other."

"Dusty was giving me some alone-time with the boy."

"Being a private investigator is not a bring-your-kid-to-work kind of job," Diodato said.

"I'm new at the father stuff. I messed up."

To Priest's relief—which he hoped was not obvious to either Baz or Diodato—Detective Vidal remained focused on the investigation into Nikki Celeste's disappearance and what it might have to do with Parris Ferrer's murder.

The good brother.

The bad brother.

The credit card.

The watch.

Priest could tell from Detective Vidal's terse nods that his story scanned for her. The search for Nikki Celeste was the most apparent link between Blue Wig's attack on Priest in his garage and Parris Ferrer's subsequent murder.

Priest hoped to keep Cody Fiso out of it completely. One reason was courtesy between private investigators who sometimes strayed into legal gray areas. The second was that the giant knob might cast shade on Dusty. Priest decided that being a liar on the wrong side of the law during a homicide investigation was a wretched state of existence.

"How are we doing?" Baz asked, a lawyerly way of asking whether Priest was liable to be released any time soon.

Tense silence. When Priest inhaled to speak, Baz clamped his knee.

He exhaled and waited.

"I'm going to let Mr. Priestly go home," Vidal said.

"Thank you, Detective," Baz said. "Of course, my client will make himself available if you have any follow-up questions."

"What about Dusty?" Priest asked.

"We're holding her," Vidal said.

"Dusty didn't do anything I didn't do," Priest said.

"Priest!" Baz said.

"You were not carrying"—Vidal referred to her note-book—"a hidden throwing knife in your shoe, brass knuckles, a ballistic knife, a shuriken, or a knife disguised as an air gauge. All of which are illegal in the state of California. We're holding Ms. Queen on those weapons charges."

"How long was Parris dead before you found her?" Priest asked. "Because Dusty was with me."

"How about you tell us how long Dusty was with you before we help you provide her an alibi?" Vidal asked.

"Stand up, Priest," Baz said. She had switched to being Dusty's lawyer and was worried that, if Priest provided Dusty an alibi, it might clash with whatever alibi Dusty provided for herself. "We're leaving, if everybody is good with that."

Ten minutes later, Priest stood on the curb outside the Hollywood Station, wondering what to do next. His rental car had been towed from the post office parking lot. He didn't know how long Baz would be tied up with Dusty. The eastern sky was getting light. A breeze in the palm trees carried the smell of sage and garbage, fried food, car exhaust. Classic Hollywood. Hearing a door open, Priest turned to see Diodato escorting Baz. They shook hands, very professional, before Diodato went back into the building. Baz walked toward Priest.

"Breakfast?" she asked.

"What about Dusty?"

"They're booking her on those weapons charges. Then they'll transfer her to Lynwood. I might be able to arrange bail, but Vidal will put up a fight, so not worth it . . . Don't snort at me. Detective Vidal's hard-assery is mostly your fault."

"Me? Why?"

"Priest, I know you think that irritating people is a way to get at the truth, but sometimes the truth is that you are just irritating."

"When can you get Dusty out?"

"The opportunity will not present itself until late this afternoon. I intend to use that time to get some food and sleep. Now, do you want to get some breakfast with me? Or do you want to go straight home to your apartment and lock yourself inside until I tell you that you can come out?"

Priest considered asking Baz if there were any legal reasons he couldn't continue to look for Nikki Celeste now that Nikki was undoubtedly a person of interest in Parris Ferrer's homicide. But since neither Vidal nor Diodato had specifically ordered Priest to back off his search for Nikki, he decided not to raise the question.

"Priest? I'm serious. I need you to lay low."

"For how long?"

"Until I say come out. A few days. A week. Do you hear me?"

"I hear you," Priest said.

"One of the several messages you should have gotten in the last five hours is that Blue Wig is still out in the world killing people," Baz said.

"If it was Parris who contracted the hit on me, I'm probably safe now," Priest said. "Maybe Parris refused to pay Blue Wig, so Blue Wig killed her. Maybe I'm completely out of the woods."

"What could possibly go wrong leaping to that conclusion?" Baz said.

"I could eat breakfast," Priest said.

"NORMS or Du-Pars?"

Only two options. Baz was freshly out of fucks to give when it came to letting Priest have a say in anything.

19

Three o'clock the next morning, Priest's eyes grated open.

His gut clenched like a baby's fist.

He ran through his breathing exercises. He wondered what Tina was doing and listened to the surf pound and tried in vain to synchronize it with the pounding in his head.

He got out of bed, got dressed, gathered two fishing rods, left his apartment, and clambered over the wall separating his place from the multi-unit apartment building next door. He scuttled around the front of that building to the far side, hoisted himself over a chin-high cinderblock wall onto the next property, and eased through a steel mesh maintenance gate onto the deserted boardwalk. He walked north along the boardwalk for a couple of blocks, nonchalantly but with purpose, then followed a pedestrian walkway to Speedway and tucked himself between a garbage bin and a heavily graffitied dumpster reeking of turned ketchup. From there he watched to see whether anyone had followed him.

Ten minutes later—nothing and nobody.

Priest headed back across the boardwalk, between the

basketball courts behind the Muscle Beach outdoor gym, and headed toward the ocean, past the handball enclosures, over a graffitied wall, over the bike path, and across the sand down to the ocean's edge. He sat on the sand, his back to the surf, partly to check again whether anyone had followed him and partly because, ever since he'd been jabbed in the neck with a mystery amnesia cocktail, he hadn't gotten any exercise, so he was breathing harder than he'd like.

Twenty minutes later—nothing and nobody.

Satisfied that he wasn't being followed, Priest trotted south along the high-tide line to the Venice Pier and rested for another five minutes, trying to look normal, in case there were night-shift cops shooting the shit in the Venice Pier parking lot. He sauntered up the slope of the beach near the pylons, turned onto the pier, squeezed through the chained gate, and headed straight out to the end like any avid fisherman trying to get a jump on the day's fishing. Out of the pre-dawn gloaming, six faces were familiar enough to merit a nod. Priest stuck his pole over the south side of the pier, his line weighted but without hook or lure. He sat with his back against the concrete wall and drowsed until Yorben showed up two hours later, by which time Priest was chilled to the bone.

"The fuck?" Yorben said.

"I'll give you a hundred bucks to drive me to Westwood," Priest said.

"Where's your car?"

"Impound."

"DUI?"

"Suspicion of murder," Priest said. "I'll give you a hundred and twenty bucks if we pick up a coffee at the Cow's End on the way."

"You got me a whole shark and whatnot," Yorben said. "I'll

drive you to Texas if that's where you want to go, *gratis,* free of charge." He extended one of his plastic bottles of Chinese brandy.

Yorben's vehicle—he called it a "whip"—was a fourteen-year-old Toyota Tacoma that he'd spray painted the same color as the Golden Gate Bridge a decade ago. Over the years, it had faded to a blotchy, undefinable salmon-peach color. The bed of the truck was filled with fishing gear, boxes, bags, and furniture that people had dumped in alleys in the hope that someone would haul it away. Yorben made what he called "good cash money" restoring and fixing these discards, some of which he sold to upscale antique stores and some of which he sold to junk stores.

Priest directed Yorben toward Giselle and Nikki's apartments in the renovated mansion on the hill above UCLA in Westwood. The morning sun had risen far enough to warm Priest through the passenger window.

Priest asked Yorben to let him out in front of the building. "Park down the hill half a'ways. I won't be long."

Priest got out of the Tacoma and stretched, stiff from drowsing upright on the cold concrete of the pier. It was yet another beautiful Southern California morning. February. He would never understand those who grew tired of a perfect day every day. What did they think the heaven myth was all about? A couple of runners ran by him up the hill. Otherwise, the neighborhood was still in bed.

Priest heard the Tacoma's engine turn off and click. He approached the six stone steps leading up to the vestibule of Nikki's building and pressed Giselle's doorbell first. Even if Nikki were here, she might not be receiving guests. He caught himself wondering what his hair looked like. He smelled his breath. He was crushing on an escort, which meant that Priest should probably be kinder when it came to Dusty and her misguided love for Nikki Celeste.

No answer from Giselle. He tried Nikki's bell.

A woman's voice responded, "Hello?"

"It's Xavier Priestly," Priest said. "I'm a friend of Dusty Queen's."

"Fuck," the woman said. But the door buzzed. Priest entered the vestibule and climbed the stairs past Giselle's place on the second floor—*No Soliciting*—and up the next flight of stairs to Nikki's apartment. The door was ajar. He pushed it open and entered the apartment. "Hello?"

Everything looked exactly as it had the last time he'd been there.

Except for a gap on the wall where a painting was missing. "Hello?"

The wood of the door splintered a micro-second before Priest heard the gunshot. He hadn't pulled the door shut behind him, which probably saved his life, and he was out the door and bounding downstairs as fast as he could gallop, pressing his left shoulder to the wall of the stairwell, so the shooter couldn't get a clear shot from above. Three more shots whizzed and splintered around him as he passed Giselle's door, taking the stairs two and three at a time, hoping he wouldn't fall and break his ankle. Two more bullets cracked the tile floor in the foyer and ricocheted into the mailboxes. He leapt down the six stone steps, deciding to forego zig-zagging in favor of running as fast as he could in a straight line because—unless the shooter had a rifle—every foot of increased range lowered the already low chances of a lucky handgun shot putting him down.

To Priest's horror, Yorben stood before him in the street, his legs spread in the classic shooter's stance—the first time Priest had ever seen daylight through the big man's thighs— his battered, Ruger .357 with the duct-taped grip extended at shoulder level.

Aimed straight at Priest.

For one quick, shameful moment—a moment he would never confess to Yorben or anyone else—Priest thought, *Yorben is going to kill me!*

"Kiss it!" Yorben yelled.

Priest realized that he meant "kiss the ground." He threw himself down, and Yorben shot twice over him at the doorway to Nikki's building. Someone shot back three times. Priest noted the difference between the shooter's semi-automatic crack and Yorben's revolver, which sounded more like a cannon. Yorben's bullets smashed into the old mansion. Priest had no idea where the shooter's three rounds went. He hoped they weren't embedded in Yorben or some innocent bystander picking up the morning paper across the street.

"Truck," Yorben said.

Yorben was either a fool or the bravest man in the world, calmly walking backward, presenting himself as a target that seemed impossible to miss, eclipsing Priest like the Earth eclipsing the moon. When they reached the Tacoma, Yorben placed the engine block between himself and the shooter, his arms steadied on the hood, aiming his whacking big gun and chewing gum while Priest crouched beside the front tire.

"You okay?" Yorben asked.

"I'm might've shit myself," Priest said. "But otherwise, yeah."

Another ten seconds passed, Yorben displaying a fisherman's patience, his gun never wavering, his jaw opening and closing like an ancient buffalo chewing its cud.

"She's gone," Priest said.

"It's a girl?"

"I didn't get a good look," Priest admitted. "Did you?"

"Naw. Whoever it was stayed in the foyer. Maybe I shot 'em?"

"You think I should go look?"

"Jesus fuck no I don't think you should go look."

"Is that weapon registered?" Priest asked. "Are you allowed to own a firearm?"

"I can't have a gun?"

"Maybe you got a felony in your past?"

Yorben grunted.

"If that gun was ever off law enforcement radar, it won't be anymore," Priest said.

"Time to vamoose," Yorben said.

"You go. I gotta stay."

"You think that's smart? Because I don't."

"The shooter's long gone." Priest pointed at his bare feet. "I ran right out of my sliders. They're still in the house. I left all sorts of other forensic evidence: fingerprints, sweat, maybe a drop or two of urine . . ."

Yorben wedged himself behind the wheel of the Tacoma and started it up.

"You want my gun? Tell the cops you bought it on the Boardwalk for protection and whatnot?"

"Better you toss it off the pier." And then, "Wait. Yorben, I need you to get my bicycle—it's in my garage—and drop it off down the hill at the Sycamore tennis courts. See? Over there? . . . Not that over there, the other over there. Never mind, you can't see it if you don't know where to look. Google it. Can you do that within, say, an hour?"

"Anything else? Breakfast burrito from Tommy's?"

"Just the bicycle. And Yorben?"

"What now?"

"Thank you for saving my life. We're even for the shark."

"I dunno," Yorben said, jamming the truck into gear. "That was a big shark."

Priest poked his head into the foyer. He found one of his

sliders just inside the door; the other he saw on the first landing but decided he didn't need it just yet. He returned to sit on the curb across the street, his head swiveling as sirens approached, but no one else appeared on the street until after the police arrived, when it started to fill with frat boys and college students, some positioning themselves for selfies in front of the fracas, some bending forward from the waist to get their faces in the frame with the police helicopter circling above.

The uniforms put Priest into the back of a cruiser until Diodato and Vidal arrived, thirty minutes later.

"God in heaven," Diodato said when he saw Priest.

Priest declined to answer questions until his lawyer arrived, a completely reasonable legal dodge that bought him just shy of another hour.

20

This time, Baz and Priest sat on comfortable, ergonomic Herman Miller chairs, facing detectives Diodato and Vidal across an oval glass table in a conference room at Baz's office in Century City. The air-conditioned air smelled of lavender, primo coffee, fresh pastries from Milo and Olive, and competence. A view of Beverly Hills, the Hollywood Hills, the Hollywood sign, and off in the mid-morning distance, the skyscrapers of downtown Los Angeles. Diodato was on his third cup of coffee, and he still closed his eyes in ecstasy every time he took a sip.

Much better than a police interview room.

"You rode your bike?" Detective Rhonda Vidal asked, adjusting her glasses.

"Yes," Priest said.

"Your *bicycle?*" she asked again.

"Asked and answered," Baz said.

"A bicycle? Not a motorcycle. A ten-speed?" Vidal continued.

"Sixteen speed," Priest said.

"You wear a helmet?" Diodato asked.

"Safety first."

"So, yes?"

"Yes."

"And where would we find that helmet now?" Vidal asked.

"Clipped to the handlebars."

"Where would we find your bicycle now?"

"At the tennis courts, down the hill from where I got shot at. It's a silver Trek Dual Sport 3. Three years old. I hope nobody steals it."

"You rode a bicycle, at five in the morning, from Venice to Westwood, in cargo shorts, sliders, and a Jane's Addiction t-shirt?" Vidal asked.

"It's only six miles. Some mornings Dusty runs three times that far, and I ride along to keep her company. Also, I love Jane's Addiction."

Detective Vidal poked at her mobile. Priest assumed that she was arranging for some uniform back in Westwood to check the tennis courts for his bicycle.

"You left your bicycle where, exactly?"

"At the tennis courts down the hill."

"I'm looking for a specific location."

"In the bike racks," Priest said, hoping that there were bike racks at the tennis courts and, if so, that Yorben had put his bicycle in the racks. He hoped Vidal wouldn't ask him to be more specific than that.

"Where exactly are those bike racks?" Vidal asked.

"At the tennis courts," Priest said. "The Sycamore tennis courts."

"If it hasn't conveniently been stolen," Diodato said.

"It wouldn't be convenient for me," Priest said.

"In front of the tennis courts or behind the tennis courts?" Vidal asked.

"You're gonna have to explain to me the difference between the fronts and backs of tennis courts."

Vidal gritted her teeth and turned to Diodato. "You believe this shit?"

This was language Detective Vidal would not use if the interview were being recorded for later use in front of a jury. Which probably meant that Vidal didn't expect it to be played in front of a jury.

Which probably meant that Priest was mostly okay. Unless that was what Detective Vidal wanted him to think. Nuns were sneaky. Vidal might be working on a plan to nudge him into saying something that could put him in jail for a few days, where she didn't have to worry about him.

Diodato flashed Baz a look of regret. "No, I do not believe this shit."

"You forming any kind of theory?" Vidal asked Diodato.

"Am I still being questioned?" Priest asked. "Or are you just talking between yourselves?"

"Shut up, Priest," Baz said. "That's my legal advice to you."

"My theory," Diodato said, "is that Mr. Priestly was still looking for Nikki Celeste after we asked him not—"

"You did *not* ask my client to cease his search for Nikki Celeste," Baz said.

"We shouldn't have had to ask," Vidal said. For the first time, Priest heard a minor note of defensiveness in her voice.

"Mr. Priestly is the kind of person you have to be very direct with," Baz said.

"My theory," Diodato continued, "is that Priest decided to see for himself whether Nikki Celeste had returned to her apartment—"

"Correct," Priest said.

"—and that whoever drove Mr. Priestly . . ." Diodato

checked his notes. ". . . in either a pink, beige, orange, light green, light brown, or flesh-colored pick-up truck . . . exchanged gunshots with person or persons unknown, who was lying in wait for Mr. Priestly in Nikki Celeste's apartment."

Yorben would have to repaint the Tacoma. Knowing Yorben and his criminal family, it was already done, and in another color that they knew different witnesses would describe differently.

"Nobody drove me," Priest said. "I rode my bicycle. It's a silver Trek Dual Sport 3. Three years old."

"If Mr. Priestly's savior fired his or her weapon in self-defense, why abandon him?" Vidal asked Diodato. She was not buying Priest's bicycle gambit, but that didn't matter. All Priest needed was to deny Vidal and Diodato enough probable cause to take him into custody.

"Illegal weapon? Outstanding warrant? Parole? Some other such scurrilous shit," Diodato said.

"You did not see who shot at you?" Vidal asked Priest.

"I was running away as fast as I could. But when I first buzzed Nikki Celeste's apartment, a woman's voice said 'Fuck!' after I identified myself."

"I'm guessing you get that a lot," Vidal said.

"Heh-heh," Diodato said.

Baz made a noise that could have been construed as a kind of objection.

"Could you positively identify that voice as Nikki Celeste's?" Diodato asked.

"Nikki? You think it was Nikki?" Priest asked.

"I'm asking if *you* could identify the voice as Nikki Celeste's."

"I could not. It was just the one word."

"A word freighted with meaning," Detective Vidal said. "Could you identify the voice as the woman who attacked you in your garage?"

"I've never heard Blue Wig's voice," Priest said. "Are you suggesting that Nikki is Blue Wig?"

"Why are you lying about whoever drove you?" Vidal asked.

"Did Nikki Celeste drive you?" Diodato asked. "Did you find her?"

"I'm confused," Priest said. "One second you think Nikki Celeste is Blue Wig, the next you're asking if she saved me from Blue Wig."

"Priest is lying," Diodato said to Baz. "He's looking us right in the face and lying."

"Any more questions?" Baz asked.

"Did you see the person who returned fire on your behalf?" Vidal asked.

"Hint: it was probably the same person who drove you," Diodato said.

"I did not get a look at the person who returned fire. I was lying on the ground between the two of them and figured it would be best to stay there."

"Like an ostrich?"

"Exactly like an ostrich."

"So you never saw an orange pick-up truck?" Diodato asked.

"No."

"He's lying again," Diodato complained to Baz.

"The question isn't whether or not he's lying," Vidal said. "He's definitely lying. The question is whether he's lying about *everything*."

"I think he's telling the truth about there being a shooter in Nikki Celeste's apartment," Diodato said, "He's lying about the truck and the bicycle and whoever returned fire."

"Traditionally," Baz said, "you would try to find an inconsistency in my client's story and force *him* to explain it. So far, you have not succeeded in that endeavor."

"He's a really accomplished liar," Diodato said.

"All due respect, Detective, if my client was a really good liar, you'd never suspect that he was lying," Baz said.

"Here's the pertinent question," Vidal said. "Did you set up this sideshow to deflect suspicion from your friend, Dusty Queen, in the homicide of Parris Ferrer?"

"How would pretending to get shot at clear Dusty?" Priest asked.

"It sows confusion and doubt," Diodato said. "It forces us to waste resources and energy looking for links between the first attempt on your life, the disappearance of Nikki Celeste, the murder of Parris Ferrer, and the second attempt on your life. It might even obligate law enforcement to search for Nikki Celeste."

"In one way, you're giving me too much credit," Priest said, "and in another, you're not giving me nearly enough." With Baz's permission, Priest explained that the confusion-and-doubt plan, though convoluted and risky, wasn't without merit. "On the other hand," he added, "if I'd planned it, I would have come up with a better way of saving my own life than a mysterious savior showing up at the last minute."

"My client is too intelligent for that bad a plan," Baz said.

"Is he though?" Vidal asked.

"Apparently only one in two hundred thirty-four people is as sharp as Mr. Priestly," Diodato told Vidal.

"No matter what else people say about you, they say you're smart," Vidal told Priest. "So how's about you be smart?"

She wanted to make a deal: *Come clean about the orange truck, and we'll let Dusty Queen go.*

"What else do people say about me?" Priest asked, thus turning down the deal.

"If we accept the premise that somebody genuinely tried to

kill Mr. Priestly," Vidal said, "my question is, how would that person know Mr. Priestly was going to show up at Nikki Celeste's apartment this morning?"

Priest had been chewing on that one a lot himself.

"Who knew you intended to check out Nikki Celeste's apartment?" Diodato asked Priest.

"Nobody."

"Except the person who drove you," Diodato said.

"I rode my bicycle. It's a silver Trek—"

"Dual Sport 3. Three years old. Yeah, we got that," Diodato said.

"Then we're back to wondering how the shooter knew you'd be coming to check on Nikki Celeste," Vidal said.

Vidal and Diodato had a natural rhythm, like long-time partners. Priest wondered whether this case might get Diodato promoted to Robbery-Homicide. Or else ruin his career.

"I'm not positive the shooter did know I was coming," Priest said. "The voice on the intercom sounded surprised."

"A coincidence?" Vidal asked.

"Well, I texted Giselle Santa Domingo to ask if Nikki had come home," Priest said. "It's possible that Giselle texted Parris—Parris's associates don't do anything without checking with her first—before Parris invited me to come see her at the House of Pies. Blue Wig could have become privy to that sequence of events. Do you have Parris's phone, or did Blue Wig take it?"

Silence. They were not about to answer that question.

"If it was a coincidence," Priest continued, "then the shooter could have been one of the artists . . . or Blue Wig followed me on my bicycle."

"If she followed you on your bicycle, she'd have run you over and made it look like a hit and run," Vidal said. "That's what I'd like to do."

"He wasn't on his bicycle," Diodato said. "Somebody in an orange truck drove him."

"Detective Diodato is right," Vidal told Baz. "We keep circling back to the person who drove your client."

"I rode my bicycle," Priest said. "This whole driver-in-a-blue-truck pantomime is a non-starter."

"Fuck me," Diodato said.

"Excuse me?" Baz asked.

"Blue is the only color no one's come up with. So big ups on your client getting 'blue' into the official record and wasting even more of law enforcement's resources."

"Tell us who your savior was," Vidal said. "Who showed up just in time to save your life?"

"My client has answered the question multiple times," Baz said.

"We've asked the question multiple times," Diodato said. "He has not answered even once."

"In referring to the shooter, you keep saying 'she,'" Vidal said, "yet you say you didn't see the person who shot at you."

"You're right," Priest said. "I'm assuming the shooter was the same person who said 'Fuck' on the intercom and who jabbed me and Parris Ferrer with hypodermic needles."

"If it was the woman in the blue wig," Diodato said, "then she's changed her modus operandi by shooting at you with a gun. Which suggests that we're dealing with a whole new person."

Except that Blue Wig had also tried to kill Priest with her car—yet a third modus operandi. Either Blue Wig didn't have a single modus operandi or she was getting desperate.

"Point taken," Priest said. "I shouldn't jump to the conclusion that it's the same hitter."

Vidal received a text. She showed it to Diodato.

"Good news. Your bike wasn't stolen," Diodato said.

"Fortunate, considering that you left it unlocked. Maybe your friend in the coral-colored pick-up truck can swing by the Westwood Station and pick it up for you."

"What about my helmet?" Priest asked.

"Not with your bicycle," Vidal said. "I guess you finally ran out of luck."

Priest realized that, when he got home, he'd have to find some way to get rid of his helmet. Too bad. Priest really liked that helmet.

21

Venice Fishing Pier, four p.m. The sun throwing gold over the ocean behind him, Xavier Priestly leaned over the wooden railing near the warning sign about cancer. Yorben slouched low in his red-white-and-blue striped lawn chair, in his usual spot, ten feet farther along the pier.

"What're you even looking for?" Yorben said. "Looking ain't gonna help you catch goddamn nothing. Or you still looking for bullshit you can and cannot see?"

"Something like that."

"I'll tell you one thing can't be seen," Yorben said. "A perfectly good Ruger on the bottom of the ocean."

"I'll buy you another one," Priest said. "By which I mean, I'll give you the money to buy one, because I suspect that you don't purchase your firearms at Walmart. I'll pay to repaint your truck, too. What's that gonna set me back? Three gallons of latex and a brush?"

Yorben waved his arm toward the sky like a magician. "The shark covers all."

"I owe you, Yorben," Priest said, after making sure that

nobody was within eavesdropping distance. "Putting yourself between me and the shooter."

"That was fun," Yorben said. "Made me feel like a kid again and whatnot."

"Interesting childhood."

"It's like I got a new truck, too. A greeny-blue-teal-gray truck. With new plates. Dirty Princess approaching, nine o'clock."

Here came Dusty. Black jeans, black tactical boots, black leather jacket, black gloves, black military backpack, cradling her matte-black helmet.

"Within you is a sanctuary," she said.

"Inner peace knows no defeat," Priest responded. "Are you out on bail? Or did you escape?"

"Baz did that alchemy where she turns felonies into misdemeanors," Dusty said. She described how, technically, the knives the police found in her backpack didn't satisfy all the characteristics of a prohibited weapon as defined by the vague parameters of the California Criminal Code, and Dusty got off with a sentence of thirty days in jail—suspended—and a thousand-dollar fine.

"They keep your knives and whatnot?" Yorben asked.

"Yup."

"That's a shame."

Priest offered to cover the fine.

"Keep your thousand bucks," Dusty said. "Find Nikki."

Dusty asked whether Priest had a death wish, hanging out in broad daylight on the Venice Pier. Priest informed her that the pier was a quarter-mile long, which, if he needed more warning than that, he deserved to get killed.

"What are you gonna do? Jump in the ocean?"

"I got my guardian angel here," Priest said, jerking his thumb at Yorben.

"That was you, huh?" Dusty asked.

Yorben's eyes flicked to Priest. Getting no help, he simply shrugged.

Dusty nodded. "Dude!"

Yorben shrugged again, flattered. Priest brought Dusty up to speed. Both Nikki and Giselle's apartments appeared to have been abandoned. Possibly on Parris's instruction before she was killed, more likely because they'd found out Parris was murdered and wanted to get clear.

"Sorry your girlfriend is still missing," Yorben told Dusty.

Dusty nodded and exhaled.

"Any chance you stop being so mad at Priest for sending the kid back since somebody is still gunning for him?" Yorben asked. "Because, what else could he do?"

"Something," Dusty said. "What's the use of being so smart if you can't do the right thing by your own kid?"

"My work here is done," Yorben said, thinking he'd fixed the rupture between Priest and Dusty. Or maybe just for trying, because Dusty looked like Yorben might have given her something to think about.

"I've been thinking about something," Dusty said.

Priest really hoped that Yorben wouldn't bring up his theory that Nikki had ghosted Dusty because Dusty was too intense. Thankfully, Yorben concentrated on fishing and eavesdropping, his two primary superpowers.

"When I caught Nikki's stalker, Parris paid me off and sent me home," Dusty said.

"Makes sense," Priest said. "The job was done."

"That's just it," Dusty said. "Parris told me, 'Next time, finish the job.'"

"She wanted you to kill the guy?"

"I thought she was joking at the time," Dusty said. "Now I wonder if she wanted the guy . . . gone."

"Parris got what she wanted," Priest said.

"Not from me. I don't do that kind of thing," Dusty said. "Not for money, anyway."

"You think Parris found someone else to disappear the guy?"

"I do now."

"Blue Wig?" Priest asked.

"That's nuts, right?" Dusty said. "It sounds nuts."

"You know my motto," Priest said. "Just because I lack the imagination to think something up doesn't prove it didn't happen."

"That doesn't sound like you," Dusty said. "It's inspired."

"Probably because I stole it from Cody Fiso."

"Fiso is deeper than you give him credit for."

Priest didn't know whether Dusty was being sincere or just trying to hurt his feelings.

———

Having gotten all the forensic evidence they were going to get, the LAPD released Priest's matte-black 300. Dusty gave him a lift on the back of her Moto Guzzi to an impound yard near a dog hospital just off the 405, and then followed him back to his place.

"I expected seats pulled out and slashed open, the headliner slit, everything that could be pulled or yanked or jimmied," Dusty said, "including the tires."

"I'm not a drug mule, Dusty. I was the victim of an unprovoked assault."

"The assault was provoked, Priest. We just don't know by what."

When he opened his front door, there was a slip of paper on the floor. Dusty picked it up and read aloud. "*Michaela Crann:*

*Modesto Mem Cen. Rez, S.L.O. Bettina Subaric: Desert View H
Pahrump. Rez, Goodsprings, NV. PLZ EAT THIS."*

"It's from Fiso," Priest said. "People and the emergency
rooms they showed up to needing treatment for facial lacera-
tions."

Priest hurried to his computer. He called up the list of artists
he'd warned that Parris was re-selling their work. He knocked
on the monitor with a knuckle to show Dusty.

"Bettina Subaric," he said. "She got treated in Pahrump,
Nevada, and lives in Goodsprings. That's Blue Wig."

"How do you know?" Dusty said.

"Bettina Subaric is one of the artists Parris and Nikki ripped
off . . . Fuck me. Olive and Martin told me that, if this were a
movie script, the artists would be key to the plot. It looks like
they were right. It makes no sense."

"It makes a little sense," Dusty countered. "Blue Wig is
pissed at her art being ripped off. So she kidnaps Nikki—"

"Nikki wasn't kidnapped. She ran off with a client."

"We still don't know what happened to Nikki," Dusty said.
"Then, Blue Wig tries to kill you for looking for Nikki—"

"Blue Wig didn't know about Parris's art scheme until I
sent her an email."

"You don't know that . . . What's that noise mean? Are you
agreeing with me? Or hating me?"

"It doesn't add up," Priest said.

"Bettina Subaric lives in the desert." Dusty dug out her
mobile and started clicking. "Serial killers love the desert. If
we're going with the stereotypes."

"Archetypes."

"Oh, I wouldn't want to mix up my types of types," Dusty
said, scrolling through maps on her phone. "From where Blue
Wig attacked us, she could have avoided highways and gotten

herself to Pahrump using secondary roads. If she wasn't bleeding too bad."

"Same from Pahrump home to Goodsprings," Priest said.

"How'd you get Fiso to work for you?" Dusty asked.

"What's it matter?"

"Priest, how'd you get Fiso to extra-legally check out emergency rooms in two states?"

"He owed me a favor."

"Cody Fiso did *not* owe you a favor," Dusty said. "In fact, you still owe Fiso a favor for the jab-in-the-neck casino lead . . . Don't wave me off like I'm crazy! Did you agree to work for Fiso at Security Outcomes?"

"We're this close to catching Blue Wig, who tried to kill me, and tried to kill you, and you're fixating on how I got Fiso to help us?"

"You did something. What was it? . . . Don't look for a way to escape, just tell me."

"I gave him Charlie McGinn," Priest said.

Dusty blinked at Priest a couple of times, then made a whistling shape with her lips, but no sound came out. "You gave Fiso Charlie McGinn in return for such a basic favor?"

"Yes."

"Why?"

"I think trading Charlie McGinn for the identity of the person who tried to kill me is fair."

Dusty eyeballed Priest for a good ten seconds before she accepted, at least temporarily, that the subject of Charlie McGinn was closed. She showed Priest what she'd found on her phone: Bettina Subaric's webpage. "Artist and sculptor. She left out murderer."

"Historical fact: the evilest people in history are failed artists," Priest said. "Nero played the lyre. Hitler painted. Stalin wrote Romantic poetry. Charles Manson was a songwriter—"

"Could this be Blue Wig?" Dusty asked, turning her phone toward Priest. It displayed a photo of a young woman standing in front of one of her sculptures in a gallery in Palm Springs. The sculpture looked like a bronze industrial street sweeper's broom mounted on a cracked black knuckle on top of a golden doughnut.

"Yes," Priest said. "She has a thing for golden doughnuts."

"Whaddaya think her deal is?" Dusty asked. "She tosses in a free work of art every time she kills somebody?"

"It's her way of justifying her income," Priest said. "Smart."

"We'd better get out to Goodsprings and kill her."

"Okay, but only after we're a hundred percent sure. We can't kill people just because they're crappy doughnut artists."

Priest drove. Dusty rode shotgun. They hardly spoke until they reached the Ivanpah Solar Energy Array in the Mojave Desert, astride the boundary where California bled into Nevada. Ranks of mirrors focused sunlight onto towers.

"You think that's really a solar energy farm?" Priest asked.

"Don't you?"

"I've heard things."

"From who?" Dusty asked.

"Beck."

"Your Flat Earth tenant? What does he think it is?"

"Time travel," Priest said.

"Makes more sense than a solar energy farm," Dusty said.

"Hardly anything is ever only one thing."

"I'm not in the mood for metaphor-ing or philosophy-ing."

"I'm being literal," Priest said. "That solar energy farm marks the border between California and Nevada, which means you just transubstantiated from a law-abiding citizen into a criminal who contravened the terms of her suspended sentence: 'no leaving the state.'"

"You're welcome," Dusty said. "But the main reason I'm

helping you is to remove your only excuse for not fighting for your son. Twelve miles to the Goodsprings Road exit."

Ten minutes later, Terrible's Hotel and Casino loomed on their right. They exited and headed northwest into the desert, where Goodsprings Highway turned into a narrow two-lane macadam road. No vehicles came toward them. Priest couldn't see anyone in his rearview mirror, even though the road was straight and flat, bordered by shriveled mesquite and creosote bushes.

No birds.

No rabbits.

No people.

"You know what I love?" Priest asked. "The spare, harsh, Biblical aesthetic of the desert. The cleanliness. The purity."

"I don't like it either," Dusty said.

Ten minutes later, they passed two buildings: the Pioneer Saloon and the Goodsprings General Store.

"Welcome to the greater Goodsprings metropolitan area," Priest said.

After another ten minutes, Dusty said, "Next left."

"That's not a real road."

Priest turned onto the dirt road, and they wound up in the hills.

"Potosi Mountain," Dusty said, squinting at her phone. "Carole Lombard's plane crashed here in 1943."

"How'd she take it?"

"She died," Dusty said. "Turn right."

The track grew narrower, the car brushing mesquite. Over a rise and around a curve, they came to a gate with a rustic metal sign: *Bettina Subaric—Sculptor, Carver, Ceramics, Metalwork.*

"Nothing about murderer for hire," Priest said.

The driveway wound up through a cluster of trees, startlingly green after so much brown and gray. Big cottonwoods.

A tiny orchard. Quince, apricot, persimmon. Priest pulled up to a wooden house that might once have been red, with a couple of mobile homes from the sixties beyond it. To the left, a galvanized, barn-sized outbuilding with a sign on it: *Studio.* And again: *Bettina Subaric—Sculptor, Carver, Ceramics, Metalwork.*

"I don't see anybody," Priest said.

"You'd think living out here, alone, she'd, at least, have a dog."

Priest stopped the car equidistant between the house and studio. He turned off the engine. They listened to the engine click and cool. It was pleasant in the shade of these cottonwoods. The car's thermometer showed a balmy 72 degrees this high above the desert valley floor, where the temperature had registered in the low 90s.

"Wanna torch the place?" Dusty asked.

"Let's make sure it's Blue Wig before we burn her out," Priest said. "Ditto before killing her."

A woman wearing mustard-colored coveralls, blue Crocs, and a straw fedora exited the studio and stood, her hands on her hips, looking at them. She removed her hat and held it up to shade her eyes from the sun.

The bandages covering the left side of her face and neck flared white.

Dusty was up and out of the car, sprinting across the yard before Priest opened his door. Bettina Subaric managed to run maybe four steps toward her studio barn before Dusty launched herself like Spartacus and came down hard, driving her elbow into Bettina Subaric's back between her shoulder and neck. Priest heard her clavicle crack. Subaric screamed and collapsed.

Even if Priest's higher brain didn't remember Blue Wig, his heart and gut clenched. Subaric gaped as Priest pulled a pair of blue latex gloves from his crime scene backpack. He gave a second pair to Dusty, who flipped Subaric onto her back, not gently, and conducted a thorough and painful search for weapons.

Nothing. A blue knot the size of an orange rose along Subaric's collarbone.

"Oh, my God," she groaned.

Priest scanned what he could see of the property and the ridge beyond. The desert tended to be a place where neighbor watched out for neighbor, where people loved their guns and pined for a righteous excuse to use them. But there were no other structures in view. Bettina Subaric lived alone on this mountain flank. Priest heard only the wind in the grove of cottonwoods, the sound of sparrows, blackbirds, and jays.

"Why'd you try to murder my friend?" Dusty asked.

"No, no, no," Subaric said. "You're wrong." Her voice had a rasp to it.

"Now can I kill her?" Dusty asked Priest.

Subaric probably thought Dusty was playing hard ass to scare her into talking. Priest knew that Dusty wasn't playing anything. She was going to list recommendations, beginning with what she saw as the wisest course of action.

"How many people do you think saw us drive in here?" Priest asked. "I figure a dozen, maybe more, since turning off the highway. Plus, casino security cameras covering the exits to and from the highway."

"I've heard that, after three days in the desert, there's nothing left of a naked corpse except dust and coyote shit," Dusty suggested. "No body, no murder."

"What if I'm not a hundred percent positive she's Blue Wig?" Priest asked.

"Ha!" Dusty said, zip-tying Subaric's arms behind her, which caused a nauseating grating sound from her broken clavicle. Subaric barfed. Priest grunted in sympathy.

"Don't do that," Dusty told Priest, a warning that this was not the time to be soft-hearted and foolish. "Wheelbarrow."

"What?"

"Wheelbarrow," Dusty said, pointing.

Priest headed over to the side of the house and fetched the pale blue wheelbarrow.

"Ankles," Dusty said. Priest grabbed Subaric's ankles and held her over the wheelbarrow. Dusty dropped Subaric's shoulders from the height of about two feet, leaving Priest holding her feet. Her head thumped against the wheelbarrow, making a bongo sound. Priest groaned again.

"She jabbed a needle of poison into your neck," Dusty said. "She tried to crush you into a tree. She didn't give a shit that your twelve-year-old son was there. She tried to run me over. She killed Parris Ferrer. She got me arrested as a murder suspect. She shot at you and Yorben. That's just the shit we know about . . . Don't make *maybe-maybe-not* faces! We have no idea how many people she's killed. She's lucky to get a wheelbarrow. What she deserves is to be dragged through that stand of prickly pear."

Priest trailed as Dusty wheeled Subaric in front of the open roll-up garage door leading to her workshop. Full of metal and vices and half-completed sculptures, an oven, shelves, and flowers, the breezy barn made for a very pleasant environment.

"Find all her computers, devices, records, files, any of that stuff. Just load it into the car, we'll go through it later," Dusty said.

"Promise not to kill her while I'm robbing her," Priest said.

"I might ask a few questions," Dusty said.

"Do not torture her while I'm robbing her."

"You're not the boss of me."

"I kind of am . . ."

"You work for me," Dusty said. "That makes me the boss."

"I work for you on the missing person's case," Priest said. "I'm the boss on this attempted homicide case."

Priest turned to Subaric. Despite the grime and bandages, the fear and pain twisting her face, she was beautiful. "Please, just answer my friend's questions."

"I don't understand what's happening," Subaric said, her voice clouded with confusion and terror. "Why are you doing this to me?"

Subaric was either innocent—no—or a very fine actor.

"That is not the right approach," Priest cautioned. "It's the wrongest possible approach. You know exactly who I am. Who *we* are. And you know exactly why we're here. This little pageant you're putting on tells me that you're not as smart as you think you are. It tells Dusty that she should kill you."

Bettina Subaric fell silent. She was, at least, as smart as Priest thought she was.

He left the studio, crossed the driveway, and entered the cozy wooden bungalow. It looked to have been built in the 1920s. It smelled of eggs and toast. Breakfast. Priest collected a ThinkPad laptop from the kitchen table and a Hewlett-Packard desktop computer from the second bedroom where Subaric had set up her office. There was also a MacBook Pro, two iPads, a Kindle, and a Surface tablet. In her closet, he found three Transcend StoreJet external hard drives. He loaded it all into the trunk of his car, Subaric's eyes following his every move from the wheelbarrow.

The studio was a delightful workspace, especially considering that it was being used by a sociopathic murderer. Music played. Priest didn't recognize it. He found a fairly new, high-quality Naim music-streamer in a cabinet.

"K-Pop," Priest read aloud.

A railing extended along the ceiling's steel beam, from which hung an electric lift and trolley with snatch-blocks. Over to one side sat a six-sided orange machine of some kind, with three offset wheels on the front and an electrical power source at the side. Priest had no idea what it was, until he noticed the dozen straight, two-inch pipes stacked on one side and the half-dozen curved two-inch pipes stacked on the other. Subaric moved heavy stuff around with a power-assisted pallet-trolley and the smallest, cutest, propane-powered forklift Priest had ever seen. What looked like a kiln or furnace, also propane-powered, took up nearly an entire wall, its fume hood arching up, across, and out of the building.

Under a worktable, a canvas leaned.

Priest pulled it out and laid it face up on the table. He'd definitely seen it before: a golden pointillist doughnut encircling what was either a sheaf of wheat or a hank of hair. But just in case, he pulled up the photo he'd taken in Nikki's apartment.

Identical, except that the "Callie Vaughan" signature had been removed, inelegantly—perhaps even violently—with some solvent, leaving only canvas below.

Priest tucked the painting under his arm. There was no sign of a security system, which made little sense for a lonely sculptor out in the desert. But who knew what else this psycho got up to out here that she didn't want security cameras to see.

Priest dumped out a plastic bin of aluminum tailings and filled it with the electronics he'd lifted, then lugged it out to his trunk. If he stole much more, he'd have to hire a U-Haul.

"How we doing out here?" Priest asked Dusty. "She tell you if Parris hired her to kill me?"

"Nope."

"The problem is," Priest said, "if there's no murderous evidence on these computers, I don't see how we can prove it's her. I didn't even find a blue wig."

"We're not cops, Priest. We aren't bound by a preponderance of evidence or reasonable doubt. We have much more effective options than turning her over to the authorities for a fair trial."

"A trial?" Priest said. "Total waste of taxpayer money. And I did find this . . ." He indicated the doughnut painting. "This used to hang in Nikki's apartment. Except then, it was signed 'Callie Vaughan.'"

"Where's Nikki?" Dusty asked Subaric.

The way she asked made the hair on Priest's arms stand on end.

"Nobody gives a shit about Nikki," Bettina said.

For a moment, the façade fell, and it was suddenly obvious: Subaric was insane enough to defy Dusty Queen.

"You still having qualms?" Dusty asked Priest.

"I didn't find any syringes or drugs," Priest said. "But I haven't checked any of those mobile homes yet."

"We should do that," Dusty said. "Jab her in the neck with them and see what happens. Bury her under a bunch of cactus."

"It would be a tragic loss to the art world," Priest said.

"There's no call to insult my work," Subaric said.

"Your painting work?" Dusty asked. "Or your murder work?"

"I don't think we should kill her," Priest said.

"Why?"

"What if she knows where Nikki is?"

"I know exactly where Nikki is," Subaric said. "Kill me, and you'll never find her."

"She's lying," Dusty said.

"I'm ninety-nine point nine percent sure you're right," Priest said. "But on the small chance you aren't, we should turn her over to the cops. Let them figure it out."

Dusty sighed. Some very small kernel of her must have agreed with Priest. As for Subaric, she showed nothing. Fearless.

Priest hit his speed dial.

Dusty spat.

"Maybe don't splash your DNA all over the scene?" Priest said.

"What's it matter now?"

"You're in Nevada, Dusty. Breaking the conditions of your release. You were never here."

Baz answered her mobile.

"Hey, Baz. It's Priest. First, promise me you won't get mad . . ."

22

In the three and a half hours it took Diodato and Baz to arrive at Bettina Subaric's studio on the flanks of Mount Petosi in the high desert of Nevada, Dusty set out on foot for the ten-mile schlepp to Mountain Springs Trailhead, where Yorben Ybarra picked her up in his newly painted teal truck and drove her back to LA, no questions asked.

"You expect me to believe you did this alone?" Diodato asked Priest while they waited for local law enforcement—the Goodsprings Township Constable—to arrive from Sandy Valley.

"I'd appreciate that," Priest said.

Diodato pointed at Subaric and addressed his response to Baz, who sat sideways in the passenger seat of Diodato's car, her legs outside the door. "She provided a perfect description of Dusty Queen."

"Bettina Subaric is Blue Wig," Priest said. "She knows Dusty. She tried to kill me"—he almost said *three* times—"twice."

It had felt like a long wait for Diodato to arrive from Los Angeles. When he and Baz finally showed up, together, Subaric had very convincingly wept in gratitude and relief. Despite

Baz's arguments, Diodato handcuffed Priest, because Priest had confessed that he—and he alone—had assaulted Bettina Subaric and broken her collarbone. Diodato arrested Subaric on assault charges after Priest identified her as the person who had attacked him in his garage. Baz pointed out that it was ridiculous to arrest Priest for assaulting Subaric if Subaric insisted it was Dusty Queen who had broken her collarbone.

"Priest is not arrested," Diodato said. "He's detained."

"Does Diodato have the jurisdiction to detain me in Nevada?" Priest asked. Baz narrowed her eyes at him.

Diodato discovered ampules and needles in one of the mobile homes. After that, all Subaric said was, "I am invoking my Fifth Amendment right to remain silent. I want a lawyer."

"How'd you track her down?" Diodato asked Priest.

If Priest told Diodato the truth, that Blue Wig—Bettina Subaric—had tried to run him over in the Pacheco Pass, and that Dusty had responded by firing an illegal weapon using illegal ammunition, and that Priest had subsequently managed to uncover Blue Wig's secret identity by using a high-profile unsolved missing person's case to bribe Cody Fiso to extra-legally canvas emergency rooms, then Dusty would be sent to jail, Priest would lose his private investigator's license, Cody Fiso would face an ethics inquiry, and Priest would owe Cody Fiso even more, Charlie McGinn or no Charlie McGinn. And Priest felt confident that Bettina wouldn't admit the truth, that she'd hurt her face facing off with Dusty in the Pacheco Pass, because it would be as good as admitting that she was a killer.

"How did I track her down?" Priest repeated. "She has a webpage."

Priest leaned heavily into the art angle: the reverse image search, the painting that had once hung in Nikki Celeste's apartment and was now here.

"So, you came here," Diodato said, "and saw this woman . . . Was that a nod or a shrug?"

"Nod," Priest said.

"And you knew instantly that she was the woman in the blue wig who attacked you?"

"Correct," Priest said.

"She's a disgruntled artist who killed Parris Ferrer for stealing her art?"

"That's my theory," Priest said.

"Why would she want to kill you?" Diodato asked.

"Ah, well, that's a good question," Priest said. "Maybe because she's responsible for Nikki Celeste going missing and feared that my legendary, investigatory prowess would lead to her discovery?"

"What happened to her face?" Baz asked Priest. She was doing that thing where she pieced together the truth behind all the bullshit and lies that the world threw at her.

"Her face was like that when I got here," Priest said—also God's own truth.

"What happened to your face?" Diodato asked Subaric.

"Car accident last week," Subaric said.

Just then the Goodsprings Township Constable arrived from Sandy Valley.

When Detective Diodato held up his badge and approached the man, Baz beckoned Priest away from both cops and Subaric.

"Interesting that you and Bettina Subaric were both in car accidents last week."

"I declare privilege."

"Don't say it like a crooked ambassador declaring diplomatic immunity," Baz said. She poked Priest on his sore, recently dislocated shoulder with a stiff index finger. "Client-attorney privilege is not something you declare; it just exists."

The Goodsprings Township Constable listened to Diodato's

explanation of the multi-jurisdictional situation and instantly punted to the Clark County Sheriff's Department. The Clark County Sheriff's Department held no great love for California law enforcement in general, and even less for the LAPD, and when Detective Rhonda Vidal showed up from Los Angeles's vaunted Robbery-Homicide Division, it did not make the developing jurisdictional rub-and-tug any better. Priest watched as day turned to evening and the Nevada cops argued with the LA cop over who had the right and privilege to arrest him. It was Baz who somehow persuaded all present to acknowledge the possible multiple murderer in their midst.

The Clark County Sheriff's Department took Bettina Subaric, under guard, to the Southern Hills Hospital Emergency Room, while Priest ended up at the tiny Nevada Highway Patrol building just down the road in the town of Jean, behind Terrible's Casino. An hour later, he was moved to the Nevada Department of Public Safety complex in Las Vegas.

Under questioning by Clark County Sheriff's investigators and the watchful eyes of Diodato and Vidal, Priest pretended to sound contrite. "Everybody kept saying that the murder attempt on me was linked to a missing escort. I kept saying 'no.' I now accept that I might have been wrong."

Much discussion ensued.

The Clark County sheriff booked Priest for assaulting Subaric. Baz then persuaded the Clark County assistant district attorney not to lay those assault charges after law enforcement found syringes and needles—one-point-five-inch, twenty-one gauge, ultra-sharp, with a tri-beveled Luer Lock tip—matching the type used on Priest, and a cocktail of drugs that partly matched what the hospital had found in Priest's blood.

Propofol. Ketamine. Clonidine. Chloral hydrate.

Thank you, Baz. Priest was free to go home.

23

"Why are all the omelets named after people?" Diodato asked, his blunt finger hovering above the menu.

"The Sidewalk Café is attached to Small World Books," Baz said, "which explains the writers. I don't know about the singers and artists."

"Jack Kerouac makes a much better omelet than he did a writer," Priest said.

He drank his coffee and—while Diodato and Baz made flirty small talk—watched a hunched street performer named Nathan set up his piano directly across the Venice Boardwalk. Back in the day, Nathan had toured with the psychedelic band Iron Butterfly. When Priest was a kid, he was forbidden to go into the basement when his father's music—including Iron Butterfly—was blaring. At his father's trial, it came out that Oliver Priest planned his bank heists down there. Priest didn't care for Nathan's "In-A-Gadda-Da-Vida," but he loved the way Nathan played Rachmaninoff, as though the main objective was pure speed. He chased those notes so hard they sometimes combined into one massive, continuous chord, communing with the Music of the Spheres, reaching for Nirvana.

Glorious, Priest thought.

"Was this a bad idea?" Baz asked, twirling her finger around the table.

"I guess I don't see the point," Priest said, snapping back from his reverie.

Baz turned to Diodato. "Go ahead. Revoke his investigator's license."

"For what?" Priest asked. "Tracking down the person who tried to murder me?"

"For assaulting Bettina Subaric," Baz said.

"Oh, right. I most definitely did do that. *Mea culpa*."

"I don't believe for one second that you were the one who assaulted her," Diodato said. "When I find the truth, I will revoke your license."

"I'd like to remind both of you that we are not gathered here as lawyer, suspect, and law enforcement," Baz said.

"What are we here as?" Priest asked.

"Three hungry people eating food named after accomplished creatives."

"An overrated writer in my case," Priest said. "But a good omelet."

"Except that we aren't just three hungry people," Diodato said. He gestured toward Priest with his coffee cup, without spilling a drop. "I'd very much like to ask your lawyer out socially, but I can't. Why? Because as your lawyer, Baz holds herself to the highest ethical standards. Those ethics are why she and I are unable to embark upon any other kind of relationship until I'm done sifting through the ongoing, expanding corona of legal bullshit that swirls around you. If you keep multiplying the reasons that I can't make romantic overtures to Baz, I'll wreck your career."

Silently, Priest thought through his corona of legal bullshit: Parris's homicide, the assault on Bettina Subaric, the shooting at Nikki's place, Nikki and Giselle's disappearances . . .

"Fire me," he said to Baz.

"What?" she asked.

"Or I can fire you if that works better," Priest said. "You're fired."

"What?" Baz asked again.

"Now you are free to engage in romance with Detective Diodato."

"No, I'm not," Baz said.

"Why?"

"Because it's not just you," Baz said. "You'll be shocked to discover that there are other people in the world."

Dusty Queen.

If certain events surfaced—some of which Baz must already have smelled in the ether—Dusty would need Baz even more than Diodato knew.

"I appreciate the effort," Diodato told Priest. Very slightly mollified.

"Oh, c'mon! You two are actually waiting?" Priest asked. "Not just being discreet?"

"That's right," Diodato said.

"We're adults," Baz said.

"That's exactly what two discreet people would say," Priest said.

"If we could switch for a moment from three hungry people eating together," Diodato said, "I'd like to bring you up to speed on the investigation into your assault."

"The assault on me? Or by me?" Priest asked.

Diodato explained that a search of Bettina Subaric's house and studio had produced a modified stun gun that matched the kind of burn marks Priest had received, which still stung him every time he took a hot shower. However, there was no way to match the exact stun gun.

"I followed up on your theory that Bettina Subaric was involved in the disappearance of missing music producer Jack Stallion," Diodato said. "That she might have used her studio furnace to dispose of his remains. And yes, anything that can melt bronze and brass is capable of rendering human remains into fine ash. We also had the mountainside searched for mines and pits and caves where piles of ash and/or the missing cars of missing people might be buried. Both of which avenues of investigation were commended by my superiors, so thank you."

Elements within the LAPD and the Clark County Sheriff's department, Diodato informed Priest, were troubled by Priest stacking all of Subaric's computers and hard drives in the trunk of his car.

"I *moved* that stuff," Priest said. "I didn't *steal* it."

"Tampering with evidence," Baz said.

"Forensics found nothing probative on those drives," Diodato said.

"Maybe try cross-referencing people she's sold art to with people who wanted other people dead," Priest said. "Before she wipes all that info. Has she said anything the least bit incriminating?"

"Nope. Hollered for a lawyer. Won't talk to anyone else."

"Much smarter than you in that way," Baz said.

"What about the painting she stole from Nikki?"

"There's no proof it ever hung on Nikki Celeste's wall."

"I took a photo of it hanging there," Priest said.

"A) It was a close-up, lacking context. B) Your mystery savior in the truck could easily have taken that painting so that you could plant it—at your convenience—in Ms. Subaric's studio," Diodato said.

"Also," Baz said, seeing Priest's distress, "Bettina Subaric created a number of paintings on that theme."

"A hairy golden doughnut theme?"

"Yes. The point is, it's not possible to establish that the painting in her studio was the same painting that hung in Nikki Celeste's apartment."

"What about the removal of the signature?"

"She said she messed it up and was going to take another whack at it," Diodato said.

"Who's her lawyer?"

"You're hoping her lawyer can be connected to Parris Ferrer in some way?" Baz asked. "No such luck."

"Ms. Subaric accepted the public defender assigned to her by the court," Diodato said.

Contrary to common perception, public defenders were usually very solid. Subaric's defense was going to be robust and direct. Not to mention that a jury would see a public defender as an indicator of innocence.

"You think there's a chance she'll walk?"

"You should prepare yourself for that eventuality," Diodato said.

"Anything can happen during a trial. You know that," Baz said.

Out on the boardwalk, Dusty sauntered up to Nathan and stuffed a couple of bills into his tip jar.

"Will you tell me Nikki Celeste's real name?" Priest asked Diodato.

Diodato thought about it for a moment, then said, "Karen Pollari."

"Morning," Dusty said. She declined Baz's invitation to

jump the railing and sit with them. "Pow-Pow texted," she said to Priest. "He invited me to watch him box."

"Well, he didn't invite me."

"Well, I'm inviting you."

"Well, if the kid didn't invite me, it's because he doesn't want me to come."

"Well, what if I want you to come?"

"Well, where is it?"

"Vegas."

"The MGM Grand Garden Arena?"

"Community center in Durango."

"Tell the kid 'good luck' from me," Priest said.

"A few days in county jail would not do this guy any harm," Diodato said to Baz.

"Shoot him," Baz said. "We'll claim self-defense."

"Count me in," Dusty said.

"Fine," Priest said. "I'll watch the kid fight."

24

"Boxing venue in Vegas," Olive said, like she was standing in the Roman Colosseum.

"Super atmospheric," Martin said.

"It stinks," said Priest.

Priest, his sister, her husband, and Dusty sat on blue resin folding chairs on the floor of a cavernous gym at a sprawling community center with a pool, water slides, and a skatepark. The gym had been temporarily modified for the day's boxing matches, with a ring erected on the basketball/dodgeball/floor hockey/multi-purpose center line. Baz had suggested that Priest show Tarquin that he had a bigger and more supportive family than he thought, and Olive and Martin had immediately accepted Priest's invitation, thrilled that they too had a bigger family than they knew.

Olive took notes with a mechanical pencil. *Primal and barbaric,* she wrote in a Moleskine notebook.

Martin preferred to preserve his ideas by muttering into what looked to Priest like a Stasi recording device, consisting of a tiny microphone connected to a wire that disappeared into

Martin's baby blue chambray shirt with a brightly embroidered toucan on the pocket.

Families with children began to fill the risers on either side of the gym. More focused aficionados sat closer to the ring on interconnected folding chairs, which was where Dusty insisted they park themselves.

"Pow-Pow needs to see and hear us," she said.

"Hear us say what?" Priest asked.

"I'll provide you with good stuff to holler . . . Don't *huff*, Priest! Yelling is what parents do." Dusty knotted and un-knotted her fingers, pretending to speak in sign language, saying slowly and distinctly, "Parents . . . shout encouragement . . . to . . . their . . . offspring."

"Mostly Hispanic," Martin whispered into his recording device. "Over half the audience appears to be brown, another quarter paler, another quarter darker."

"When's our boy up?" Olive asked.

Priest was irritated and touched by Olive's use of *our*. He imagined parental hormones slopping around his brain to un-foreseen and confusing effect.

Olive sketched the ring and wrote *R-W-B* in her notebook, probably referring to the colors of the ropes.

"How would you describe that smell?" she asked Priest.

"Why would I ever do that," he replied, "ever in my life?"

"Testosterone, sweat, chewing gum, body spray, dirty gloves, and shoes," Dusty said.

Olive wrote *smell = goat boys*.

"Why didn't Baz come?" Dusty asked.

"She's morally opposed to boxing," Priest said.

They watched two fights between little kids wearing giant gloves and helmets. It looked like a pillow-fight between two respectful dwarfs with brittle bone disease. During the toddlers' fight the referee also acted as judge. But then four judges—three men and a woman—took their seats at collapsible lunchroom tables set up on each side of the ring. The last judge shared a table with an old man in a bolo, who nodded at a white kid in a wheelchair, who rolled up with a stopwatch around his neck and a hammer and bell in his lap. The referee was a young, very shiny brown man wearing a white short-sleeved shirt with a black bow tie and waiter's pants. His hair was dyed yellow. His ears were enormous. He mumbled his way through some announcements. Priest assumed that he was welcoming spectators to the card and promising top-notch entertainment, but the referee was difficult to understand, and nobody seemed to care much what he was saying. He enunciated only when he thanked the financial sponsors of the events: car dealerships, restaurants, a nursery, and—it being Vegas—a couple of casinos. One of those sponsors was Orange Air Conditioning and Ducts.

"No sign of Old Man Orange?" Dusty asked.

"Maybe the old man doesn't have time, given the demands of the cutthroat world of air conditioning and ducts," Priest said.

The referee announced the first bout in the ninety-pound category. Tarquin shuffled his feet near the red corner. Priest nudged his sister. "That's him. That's Tarquin."

"Like you have to tell me," Olive said. "Holy cramoly."

"Schnozzerola like that, boxing is a bold choice of sport," Martin said. "Should've been a swimmer with that built-in rudder."

In high school, Priest had competed as a runner and wrestler, and he'd played baseball. All three sports hurt his nose, and even in cross-country, he took more than a few elbows before he learned to duck and weave.

A man in his forties, wearing a navy-blue TITANIUM GYM tracksuit, separated the ropes so that Tarquin could climb into the ring. Tarquin wore blue shorts, a blue tank top, and black shoes. The tank top was gathered and duct-taped in the back to make it tighter across his chest. His helmet was decorated with a stylized burning skull. He'd affixed his go-to tough-guy scowl.

"Trainer is a military veteran," Martin muttered into his spy microphone.

"Just because he's missing a leg doesn't mean he's a veteran, Martin," Olive said.

Dusty whistled through her fingers so loudly that even the referee was startled. Tarquin looked over at her and nodded without changing his expression.

"Awesome game face," Dusty said.

"Should I shout that?" Priest asked.

"Do *not* do that."

Priest threw Tarquin a thumbs-up. Tarquin spat, which Priest hoped was a coincidence. Tarquin's opponent in the blue corner, a stringy Latino kid, wore a black shirt, long red shorts that hit him mid-shin, and orange shoes. When he smiled, which was constantly, multi-colored braces flashed, which up until now Priest had not known was a thing. The kid's helmet displayed the American flag, and he was accompanied by a Malaysian or Indonesian man whose nose had been mashed into his face so many times it looked like a squashed potato.

"Skull versus American flag. So far, our boy looks like the baddie," Martin said.

"Perhaps the usual semiotics are reversed in blood sports," Olive said.

"*Cobra Kai*," Dusty said. Priest looked to Olive and Martin for an explanation, but they shrugged. They had no idea what Dusty was talking about either.

"Yell '*Head moving! Eyes open!*'" Dusty told Priest. And when he grimaced at her, "Yell it. *Head moving! Eyes open!* Like that."

"Why?"

"It's called encouragement. Do it. *Head moving! Eyes open!* . . . Don't rub your forehead! It looks like you're worried. We gotta exude confidence."

Priest still hesitated.

Dusty yelled, "Head moving! Eyes open!"

Tarquin favored her with a smile just before his trainer stuck a mouthguard in his gob. Priest realized that, if he had done as Dusty suggested, *he* would have won that smile.

"What's the drill?" Olive asked.

"Junior class," Martin read from his phone. "Three rounds, each one minute in length, one minute rest between rounds."

The old-man timekeeper struck the bell with his hammer and said, through the PA system, "Out of the blue corner, representing Saints of the Cristero War Gym, give it up for Julian 'The Hispanic Panic' *Por-TI-llo!*"

Applause, whoops, and whistles from the risers.

"Are we, as gringos, allowed to clap for that?" Olive asked.

The Hispanic Panic bobbed and nodded at the audience, struck his chest with his glove, looked upward, and made the sign of the cross. The announcer hit the bell with his hammer and continued, "And his opponent, across the ring, in the red corner, representing Titanium Boxing Gym . . . TAR-quin *OH-range!*"

Tarquin received a muted response, and even that only after his trainer turned and glared at the other Titanium Gym boxers. Tarquin blew out his cheeks, probably because he wanted to be called Tarquin "Pow-Pow" Orange. Unlike The Hispanic Panic, Tarquin didn't acknowledge the crowd. Priest had no idea if that was cool or uncool.

"Yell 'Pow-Pow'!" Dusty advised Priest.

This time Priest took Dusty's advice, but he was drowned out by the announcer: "Seconds out. Round One."

"I don't think he heard you," Olive said.

The corner-men and coaches and trainers vacated the ring. The announcer rang the bell, and the fight began. Tarquin and The Hispanic Panic lunged toward each other and touched gloves with outstretched arms. Two head bobs later, Tarquin came after The Hispanic Panic, swinging his left arm like a baseball bat. Twenty seconds into the first round, Tarquin was pummeling The Hispanic Panic all over the ring. Tarquin yelled "Pow!" every time he threw a punch, whether he landed it or not.

"Cute," Olive said.

Martin made a high, whining, doubtful noise in the back of his throat.

Priest agreed with Martin.

"He's doing great, right?" Priest asked Dusty.

"He's feisty," Dusty said.

Tarquin hit the other boy three more times in the ribs.

"Pow! Pow! Pow!"

"It sure sounds like he's winning," Martin said.

"Tarquin's got a good right hand," Dusty said. "A good stiff high jab. Too bad the only time he lands a punch, it's that left hook."

"What's wrong with a left hook?"

"All Pow-Pow's weight is on his right heel when he throws it. Looks good, no power behind it. And when The Hispanic Panic realizes that, and Tarquin throws that left hook and recovers slowly, he'll plaster our boy."

The bell rang. The two boxers retreated to their respective corners. The Hispanic Panic's coach mimed a slow left hook that stopped just short of the Hispanic Panic's chin. He nodded, flashing his multi-colored braces in a huge smile, and opened his mouth for water. When the trainer squirted him in the eye, the Hispanic Panic laughed. In Tarquin's corner, the one-legged coach spoke to Tarquin. Priest hoped he was saying the same thing Dusty had told him about weight and recovery, the same thing The Hispanic Panic's coach had obviously just told him.

Tarquin didn't acknowledge his coach.

"It doesn't mean he isn't paying attention," Olive said. "You do it all the time. We think you're not listening, except it turns out you are."

The announcer rang the bell. Tarquin came out of his corner, aggressively jabbing with his right hand before throwing his specialty left hook. The Hispanic Panic ducked and came back with a left uppercut that looked like nothing. It caught Tarquin under the ribs, well above the high waist on his blue shorts.

"Boom," Dusty said.

"What boom? Nothing happened," Priest said.

Tarquin stepped back and jabbed a couple of times. The Hispanic Panic peeked at him from behind raised gloves, like he was waiting.

The bell rang.

Tarquin dropped to one knee, but he bounced up five seconds later, slapping his gloves together in irritation as he headed for his corner.

"Attaboy," Priest said.

"Fight's over," Dusty said.

"There's a round to go!"

"Fight's over."

In Tarquin's corner, when his trainer removed his mouthpiece, Tarquin said something and the trainer shrugged, pushing the mouthguard in while the kid was still yapping. The third round, nothing much happened. Tarquin tried not to throw his left hook at all, which left him jab-jab-jabbing. Then the bell rang, and it was over.

The Hispanic Panic's corner clapped him on the back and

squirted him with water. The referee gathered pieces of paper from all four judges, called the boys together, and raised The Hispanic Panic's arm in victory. He flashed his multicolored braces, bobbing up and down on his toes for joy.

Seeing Tarquin's face when the referee lifted the other guy's arm, Priest felt for the kid. Hearing the crowd's approval, he felt worse. And worse again when The Hispanic Panic reached out to bump gloves and Tarquin turned his back and left the ring. The Hispanic Panic turned and bowed to each of the judges, who nodded back at him. The alpha judge gave him a thumbs-up.

"He's only twelve," Olive said, patting Priest on the back.

Even kind, forgiving, pothead Olive thought Tarquin was kind of a dick.

But that didn't mean she intended to give up on him. When Tarquin emerged from the locker room wearing his camo duffle bag like a backpack, hoodie up, earbuds in, his mouth set like a clamp, Olive said, "I'm your father's big sister."

"Okay."

"You can call me either Aunt Olive, Aunt Ollie, Olive, or Ollie. Whatever floats your boat."

"Okay."

Dusty persuaded Tarquin to let Priest drive him home instead of going for lunch with the rest of the team in the team van. The lesser of two evils. Under the winter sun, a dry wind blew from the desert, and they shuffled in an awkward, discombobulated clump across the community center parking lot. Olive and Martin offered to treat everybody to lunch, but Tarquin said he could never eat after a fight. Priest hoped the kid was regretting his unsportsmanlike behavior following the loss, but more likely he was cogitating upon all the ways victory had been unfairly snatched from him.

"You mind if I tell you something, Pow-Pow?" Martin asked.

The nickname cheered the boy up for a few seconds. Cheered up, Tarquin looked like a different kid.

"Okay," he said.

"I don't know anything about boxing, but you got something I saw in nobody else there today. *Charisma*. You know that means?"

Tarquin looked like he didn't know whether he was supposed to respond, so Olive said, "Charisma is an inherent quality that draws the eye."

Martin made a motion like he was snatching a fly from just in front of his face.

"You pull focus," he said, releasing the fly into Tarquin's eyeball. "It's not something a person can learn. It's a gift from the cosmos. And you got that gift, Pow-Pow. You know how I know? Because I'm in show business. I'm a show business professional."

"Martin's a screenwriter," Priest said. "So is Olive."

"Okay."

"Kiss of death for a kid to be an actor," Martin said.

"Who said anything about being an actor?" Priest asked.

"Pow-Pow's got charisma to burn, he's got a look, he's got kinetics, energy, athleticism. He is fearless. It's not unreasonable to assume he might want to be an actor."

"Might as well jump off a bridge," Olive said.

"Might as well throw yourself off a bridge!" Martin agreed. "But in, say . . . What do you think, Olive?"

"Ten years?"

"In ten years—maybe eight if you got your head on straight—you want to maybe consider going the actor route, as an adult person, you come see your Aunt Olive and Uncle Martin."

"I don't want to be an actor," Tarquin said.

"Good," Olive said. "Might as well jump off a bridge."

"I'm saying if you feel different in eight or ten years."

"Pow-Pow is interested in stunt work," Dusty said.

"We still might be able to help with that," Olive said, apparently not remembering that Dusty had a decade of solid experience already.

"If we're not dead," Martin said, seizing Tarquin's hand and shaking it.

"What about college?" Priest asked.

Everyone ignored him. After Tarquin admitted he'd never seen *Raging Bull*, Martin offered to send Tarquin a list of boxing movies he should watch.

"Sayonara for now, Pow-Pow," Martin said.

"I look forward to seeing you fight again," Olive said. "Maybe a fight you win, next time, especially if you remember"—she checked her notes—"to put your weight on your back foot when you slang that left hook, then recover faster, hands up, chin down. I get all that right, Dusty?"

"I'm not familiar with *slanging*, Olive, but the context sold me."

"Wow," Tarquin said, watching as Martin and Olive drove off in their Tesla. "Any other massive wackjobs in your family?"

Your family.

"Pow-Pow know about your old man in prison?" Dusty asked Priest.

Tarquin laughed.

"Serious," Dusty said. "You remember that ugly briefcase? It was your grandfather's back before he got sent to prison."

It took Tarquin a second or two to remember that he had two grandfathers and Dusty was referring to the other one. The one he'd never met. The grandfather Priest had told him had "retired to a walled community in Oregon." For the first time all day, the boy turned and looked Priest directly in the eyes. "Your old man's in prison? For what?"

"Robbing banks, mostly."

"Pops says armed robbers are morons."

"Pops is right," Priest said, although he didn't much care for the kid stressing the modifier *armed*.

"What about your mother?" Tarquin asked. "She a bank robber, too?"

"She's on a sailboat somewhere in the South Pacific with her second husband," Priest said.

Tarquin looked at Dusty to see if that was also true. Dusty nodded.

"Ha!" Tarquin said.

Priest blipped the locks on the 300.

"This your actual car?" Tarquin asked.

"What's wrong with it?"

"It looks like a cartoon."

"Lemme sit in the back so Tarquin can direct you," Dusty said.

"The Jockey Club," Tarquin said, like it was the MGM Grand and Priest was a local Uber driver. Priest entered it into the GPS. The Jockey Club was on the Strip, wedged between the Cosmopolitan and the Bellagio. Twenty-three-minute drive.

"How long you live there?" Dusty asked.

"Me and Mom lived with Pops since COVID," Tarquin said. "I like it better than the condo where we lived before, but Mom didn't."

Priest envied how easily Dusty talked with the boy, even though Tarquin was in the front seat with Priest and she was in the back. They talked about boxing in a way that sounded like a foreign language to Priest. Dusty asked about training schedules and Tarquin's coach and the other kids in his boxing club. After a few minutes, Priest realized that Dusty was like a clever interrogator in an interview room, with Priest observing from behind the two-way mirror. She moved seamlessly from boxing into Tarquin's personal life. Without Tarquin even knowing, he let slip that he didn't have any real friends, that he wasn't very close to his boxing coach, that he didn't play any other sports. Aside from his grandfather, Tarquin was alone.

Dusty wondered aloud why Old Man Orange hadn't shown up today to watch his grandson box. Tarquin took the bait.

"Pops couldn't come. He had work. Most of the time, he's there. Front row. Pops knows a shit-ton about boxing. He boxed himself, back in the day."

"How about your Mom?" Dusty asked.

"She never boxed," Tarquin said, making a joke.

"Hilarious," Dusty said. "Was she okay with you boxing?"

"Why wouldn't she be okay with it?"

"In the letter, she wrote the two of you had a big argument. I figured boxing might be the thing you argued about. Unless it was smoking."

"Nope," Tarquin said, clamping his mouth shut.

Good effort, Dusty, but that was the end of that conversation. Except nobody told Dusty, because she pressed on.

"My mother went apeshit when I took up mixed martial arts," Dusty said. A total lie. Dusty had raised herself. Nobody had given a shit about her behavior or her choices.

Tarquin was quiet for a moment. "Mom liked that I got exercise, but she didn't like me getting punched in the head."

"Boxing is great exercise," Dusty said.

"Which part? Punching or getting punched in the head?" Priest asked.

"Hilarious," Dusty said. She told Tarquin that he and Priest shared the same lame sense of humor. What was she today? A family therapist?

"If he doesn't get it, he doesn't get it," Tarquin said. "And he doesn't get it."

"He gets it," Dusty said. "We took a self-defense class. Your old man took a few hits and got back up."

"Took hits because he wasn't any good at it?" Tarquin asked.

"Priest is pretty good at anything he puts his mind to," Dusty said. "The hard part is getting him to put his mind anywhere. You got a girlfriend?" She slipped that one in there like an ice-pick.

"I play the field."

Priest caught Dusty's eye in the mirror and beamed *Thank you* as hard as he could.

"Your mom ever watch you fight?" Dusty asked. She was playing Tarquin, switching topics, keeping him off balance. Another technique she'd learned from Priest.

"Nope," Tarquin said.

For the first time, Priest heard grief in Tarquin's voice.

Priest was being too hard on the kid because the more he heard about his son's life—the more he got to know him—the less Priest liked him. Tarquin Orange was boastful and conceited, vain, uninterested in things outside himself, not self-reflective in any way. He didn't read or watch movies. He liked watching clips on his phone. Video games. Probably a creepy, chronic-masturbating porn kid.

"I bet she'd've been proud," Priest said, "if she saw you today."

"You don't know," Tarquin said. "You don't know fuck all."

Priest wished The Hispanic Panic had punched Tarquin in the face. Busted that Priestly nose. It must have shown on Priest's face because he caught Dusty looking at him in the rearview mirror and very slightly shaking her head. But Priest was tired of people telling him how to deal with this little shit.

"You wanna know what I know?"

"Nope."

"You're a sore loser and a bad sport. You don't listen. You're disrespectful to your coach, the ref, the judges, and your opponent. That's probably why your teammates don't cheer for you. Maybe that's why you and your mother fought. Because you're a dick."

In the rearview mirror, Dusty clamped her eyes shut.

"Lemme out," Tarquin said.

"We're on a highway," Priest said. "It works for me, you getting run over by a truck, but the police wouldn't agree. I'll let you out on the Strip."

A few silent minutes later, Dusty leaned forward and tapped Tarquin on the shoulder with the Altoid tin. Tarquin took it and opened it. It was empty. He snapped the lid closed again and turned it over and over in his hands, tapped it on his bouncing knee.

"Thank you," he said.

Tarquin didn't care about the weed. He cared about the box it came in. His mother's box.

After a long silence, he said, "For your information, me and Mom didn't fight about boxing or smoking. We fought about Mom wanting to move out of the Jockey Club and get our own place. She didn't like me working for Pops."

"Doing what? Installing air conditioning ducts?" Priest asked.

"I delivered stuff."

"Like drugs or something?"

"Papers," Tarquin said.

"Your grandfather never heard of email?" Dusty said.

"Pops says emails aren't private. You might as well sky write messages as email them."

"Deliver to who?" Priest asked.

"Pops has a wide array of business associates," Tarquin said. He had to be aping his grandfather. No kid would talk like that.

"You skip school to do that? Mothers hate when you skip school."

"Nope. After school. An hour, maybe. Some of Pops's business associates would give me tips. Like, twenty bucks. Once I got a hundred bucks from a drunk guy. That's why I didn't want to move into our own place. I'd lose my job. Turn in here. Drop me off."

"I'm starving," Dusty said. "Let's get something to eat. You know someplace good?"

Tarquin glanced at Priest. Dusty pushed on Priest's back with her foot.

"I'm sorry I was shitty to you," Priest said. "I was upset you lost the fight. I wanted you to win. It takes guts to get into the ring in front of all those people. I knew your mother well enough to know that she'd have been impressed."

"What I wish is she'd a'seen me fight just once," Tarquin said. It was such an honest admission of vulnerability, such a capitulation, that Priest was taken aback.

The GPS informed them that they had arrived at their destination.

The Jockey Club consisted of two depressing ten-story wings, connected by the entrance lobby and jammed between taller, brighter, glistening steel and glass towers. It looked Soviet. Flat and gray and out of date, dwarfed by its neighbors. Even the desert sun couldn't reach the Jockey Club.

"We could eat at Planet Hollywood," Tarquin said. "Guest parking is on the third floor of the parking garage."

Priest parked as directed. He and Dusty followed Tarquin into the lobby of the Jockey Club. Oversized fake beams made the low ceiling feel even lower. Low orangey-colored furniture, probably intended to look golden. A dry fountain. Concrete stairs with wrought iron rails underneath a metal sculpture of a waist-high jockey surrounded by what might have been sun-flowers made from welded horseshoes. A mini-mart. The Jockey Club symbol—a horsehead chess piece facing left—was plas-tered everywhere. One tower called Ascot, the other Derby. Something about the place made Priest want to drink himself to death. No wonder Rachel had wanted to move out of there and into a place of their own.

"You want to drop off your stuff upstairs?" Dusty said. "It smells pretty janky."

"You can wait here." Tarquin pointed at a high-backed wooden bench.

"I'd like to say hello to your grandfather, if he's home," Priest said.

Tarquin looked doubtful.

Dusty smiled and said, "We'll tell him you got robbed in a close decision."

"We live in the Penthouse of Ascot," Tarquin said.

Nobody said a word on the short elevator ride up. Dusty wasn't wrong about the kid's gear stinking. Unless it was Tarquin himself, who hadn't showered after his bout. Olive got it right: *goat boy*. Tarquin led them down the hall and used a key card to enter the apartment. At least there was natural light up here. Windows.

"Pops?" Tarquin hollered. "You here? We got company."

Silence.

"He's not here," Tarquin said.

"Great view," Dusty said, walking toward the window.

"That's the Bellagio there. At night, the fountains light up. That there's the Strip."

"Like living in Paris," Priest said, gesturing toward the Eiffel Tower.

The kid looked blank.

"The Eiffel Tower. In Paris. France."

"Yeah, well, we got the original here and it's better," Tarquin said, tossing his bag into what Priest assumed was his room. Why would the kid want to live with Priest on the Venice Boardwalk, where his bedroom window looked out on an alley? Here, he had a fantastic view of the Vegas Strip. Fountains. The *real* Eiffel Tower. A neon hot air balloon. Bally's. Caesar's Palace. The Bellagio. At night, it had to look like the lit-up center of the universe.

On their way out, Priest noticed the sculpture beside the front door.

Bronze. Like an industrial street sweeper's broom mounted on a cracked black knuckle on top of a golden doughnut.

Priest said to Dusty, "Look at that."

Dusty grunted like she'd been struck. "What's her thing with doughnuts?"

Tarquin said, "Yeah. I think it's stupid, too, but Pops says it's an original work of art with deep hidden meanings."

"Pops got that right," said Priest.

25

Priest's first instinct was to cancel lunch with the kid and go hunting for Anthony Orange, but when he looked at Dusty, she jutted her chin at Tarquin. *First things first.*

So Priest ground through his Caesar salad and shrimp while Dusty did most of the talking, mostly about boxing. They left Tarquin in the Jockey Club lobby after awkwardly not shaking hands or hugging. At least Dusty got the kid to wave before the elevator doors closed.

Priest barely caught even that, because he was already dialing Anthony Orange. The old man barely got out "Hello" before Priest demanded that they meet. Somewhere remote, but not deserted.

Orange said, "Something to do with Tarquin? I don't presently have time. Just tell me now."

"It's only about Tarquin in the sense that you hired someone to kill his father," Priest said.

"The fuck? Don't say that shit on the phone!"

"You said, '*Just tell me now.*'"

"Where are you?" Orange asked.

"I'm in the lobby of your building. It's probably better that we don't meet at your place. Tarquin doesn't need to hear about how, right after his mother dies, his grandfather hires a psycho to kill his father. Or am I wrong that you don't want him to find out what an evil asshole you are?"

"Jesus, fuck! Stop talking that kinda shit on the phone, or I'll hang up."

"I'm so sorry," Priest said. "How can I be so rude? Threatening to expose the motherfucker who took a hit out on me?"

"Anybody's listening, I did not hire anyone to kill anybody," Orange said. "There's gotta be hundreds of other people who know this shithead better than me and want him dead more."

Orange hung up.

Priest considered his next step.

"You want to wait here until he comes home?" Dusty asked.

"You got a better idea?"

If she did, Priest never heard it because he immediately received a text message: *Tule Springs Fossil Beds National Monument. 1 hour.*

When they got there—Dusty driving because Priest was too angry—Fossil Beds National Monument turned out to be where the northernmost tip of Vegas ran headlong into the naked desert.

"Remote but not deserted," Dusty said. "Good call. Turn one way, you're looking at civilization, the other, you're on the moon. Next stop, Idaho."

"Old fucker maybe has some experience when it comes to murder showdowns."

"You gotta get a grip on yourself," Dusty said. "I don't mind taking drastic action, but not on an impulse."

"I'm good," Priest said. He felt the desert night approaching like winter.

"We got maybe an hour until sunset," Dusty said, reading his mind.

"This won't take long," Priest said.

"I'll take your word for it, because I'm not sure what this is yet."

The parking lot emptied out. Dusty and Priest waited at the far end, isolated from the few remaining cars, where asphalt gave way to dirt. Orange's Buick Regal pulled into the lot and floated toward them. Orange parked facing away from them, set up for a getaway. Dusty pulled up her jacket to show Priest that she had a gun tucked into the small of her back.

"If he's armed, I'll shoot him," she said. "After I do that, you hustle over and fire his gun off into the desert, using his dead hand on the grip and trigger so the prints and paraffin test indicate that he shot first. You wipe my prints off this gun, replace them with your own, and fire the gun again so that you test positive for paraffin while I get the hell out of here before anybody finds out I broke the terms of my probation to kill someone for you."

Dusty was still on probation for the weapons charge. She'd risked getting caught just to get Priest to Nevada to watch his shit of a son lose a boxing match.

"You mind jotting all that down for me, Dusty? That's a lot of steps, and I'd hate to get them out of order," Priest said.

"Joke all you want, but don't forget this geezer wants you dead."

Anthony Orange exited his car, looked around, straightened his tie, and unbuttoned his sports jacket to show the gun thrust into his belt.

"Looky there," Dusty said. "Now can I shoot him?"

"Only if he pulls it out of his pants," Priest said. Then, shouting at Orange, "I'm not armed."

"I am," Dusty shouted.

Orange put his hand on his gun.

"If you see my gun, it'll be the last thing you see," Dusty said.

"Because you'll shoot me?"

"Right between the eyes," Dusty said.

"What is this?" Priest asked. "Desert gothic? Nobody's gonna shoot anybody. This is a negotiation."

Orange moved his hand away from his gun and walked toward them. He stopped at the edge of the asphalt. "You come over here."

"Why?" Priest asked.

"These are six-hundred-dollar shoes," Orange said. "She's wearing army boots, and you're wearing . . . what're those, anyway? Surfer sandals?"

Priest shrugged. Dusty sighed. They stopped ten feet from Anthony Orange, the old man still on the asphalt, them on the dirt.

"Why'd you take a hit out on me?"

"I never did no such thing."

"If he denies it again," Priest told Dusty, "shoot him."

"Please deny it again," Dusty told Orange.

"Did you fuckin' amateurs think this through?" Orange asked. "What do you expect to happen here?"

"I want to know why," Priest said. "If you ask *Why what?* Dusty will shoot off your low-hanging old man balls."

Orange fluttered air through his lips and said, "Well, you know . . ."

"I don't know," Priest said.

"I love the kid. He's all I got left. I had to make sure you didn't take him from me. That's all. Nothing personal."

"It's one hundred percent personal," Priest said.

The old man laughed and shrugged. "Well, you got me there."

"Why would I get him? There's no way Rachel left him to me in her will."

"Rachel didn't leave a will," Orange said. "Just that letter in her safety deposit box."

"So you'd definitely get the kid."

"I couldn't risk you taking it to court. You die, I destroy the letter, there's nothing to link us. Everybody's happy."

"If I'd taken you to court for the boy, I'd have lost."

"You don't know that."

"I do know that. I work for a law firm. You've been in the kid's life since the day he was born. I haven't. His mother never even told me he existed. You're the only family that boy knows. No court would change that."

"I couldn't risk it. He's the only family I got left. The only part of Rachel that's still with me in this world," Orange said.

"So, you risk suborning murder?" Priest asked. "It doesn't make sense."

Orange raised and lowered his stiff arms, slapping his thighs. And just like that, it made perfect sense. Anthony Orange was afraid of losing Tarquin because the old man was more of a criminal than it appeared at first glance. Like Priest's father had said, *You're looking for somebody with easy access to contract killers.*

"He's an old-school crook," Priest said to Dusty. "He sees a problem; he solves it the simplest possible way."

"Ask him did he also have his daughter killed," Dusty said.

The old man stepped back like she'd pulled her gun. "The fuck you just say?"

"It's a fair question," Dusty said. "Your daughter had plans to move herself and your grandson out of your awesome crib into a place of their own. Obviously, that's some kind of murderous trigger for you."

Orange's eyes filled with tears. "I loved my daughter. I raised Rachel on my own since she was six years old."

Priest was unmoved.

These old racketeer types cried all the time. They were sentimental snakes drawing on a bottomless pit of self-pity, bursting into tears over how unfair life had been to them, what a cruel world they were forced to navigate by any means necessary: including extortion, blackmail, robbery, and taking out contracts to have people killed.

"Now what?" Orange asked.

"You buy out the hitter's contract. Pay her the full amount. Tell her to forget it."

"I heard she's in jail."

"Do it for my peace of mind," Priest said.

"Or what?"

"I sue for custody," Priest said. "Your income stream comes under intense scrutiny. Whatever it is you want to keep hidden gets revealed. You go to jail. Something like that."

"I call it off, you promise me Tarquin?"

"What don't you understand?" Priest asked. "He's already yours."

The sun was setting. Orange's long shadow stretched parallel to Priest and Dusty's, off into the desert. Soon their shadows would hit the terminator, the line between day and night, and meld with twilight.

Disappear.

"You want to shake on it?" Orange asked.

"No," Priest said. "Call off the hit or pay the price. We don't have to trust each other."

"Done," Orange said.

"One more thing," Priest said. "I don't get the link between you, Bettina Subaric, Parris Ferrer, and Nikki Celeste."

"I don't know the last name," Orange said. "I did some . . . accounting . . . for Parris Ferrer's Vegas operation."

Money-laundering.

"Parris recommended Blue Wig to you?"

"Ha," Orange said.

Meaning it had been the other way around. Parris wanted to vanish Nikki's stalker, and Old Man Orange had recommended Bettina Subaric.

"Is that all?" Orange asked.

"What about Nikki?" Dusty asked. "Where is she?"

"I don't know who she is," Orange says. "One of Parris's girls? Those girls come and go all the time. They either show up later or they don't."

The old man climbed back into his Buick and drove off toward the lights of Vegas.

"Cold," Dusty said.

"This is why I don't like the desert," Priest said. "I prefer the ocean. It mitigates temperature swings."

"I didn't mean the temperature."

Priest preceded Dusty toward the 300. He wanted a new car. The 300 didn't suit him anymore.

Dusty sat in the passenger seat like a sphinx, watching the desert slip by.

"What's going on?" Priest asked.

"Usually, you are my favorite person."

"But I'm not anymore? Because I didn't let you shoot Anthony Orange?"

Dusty said nothing.

"Think about it. The old man dies, it breaks Tarquin's heart," Priest said. "His grandfather is all he has left."

"There's one thing you got right," Dusty said.

26

Baz stood on Priest's roof deck, her back to the boardwalk, the beach, the pier, the ocean—all the good stuff—avoiding Priest's eyes, and instead watching a homeless guy pick through the recycling bins down on Speedway.

Baz sighed. "You left your son to be raised by the man who hired a contract killer to murder you?"

Priest wasn't sure he'd ever heard her so exasperated. "What do you think I should have done?"

"I don't know, Priest," she said, her voice tight. "Maybe tell Detective Diodato that the old man admitted that he took out a hit on you? Here's a revolutionary idea: let the police do their job."

"I handed Blue Wig over to law enforcement, and the next thing I know, my lawyer and the investigating detective are telling me she might walk."

"Along with Blue Wig, you handed the police a shitload of tainted and illegally obtained evidence. And you lied about Dusty being there."

"What about the needles and drugs?"

"You attacked Bettina Subaric without provocation and stole a bunch of her computer and audio equipment, all of which established enough reasonable doubt for Ms. Subaric's public defender to argue that you had the opportunity to plant said drugs and needles and a taser—and the painting—because you knew exactly what to plant. If they'd found a dead body on the premises, Bettina Subaric's lawyer could speculate that you put it there."

"Oh, c'mon! Why would I do that?" Priest asked.

"The same reason Dusty Queen assaulted Bettina Subaric."

"Dusty didn't attack Bettina Subaric," Priest reminded Baz.

"Nobody's buying that bullshit."

Baz never said things like "bullshit." Priest was in trouble.

"So why would Diodato believe me this time?" Priest asked.

"Maybe because you didn't touch the sculpture you found in Orange's apartment. Maybe Diodato could use that sculpture to connect the old man and Subaric. Maybe leverage them against each other. They both go to prison. You take over raising your son."

"Send Old Man Orange to prison?"

"He's a criminal, Priest. Yes."

"If I'm responsible for Orange going to prison, Tarquin will never forgive me, Baz," Priest said. "There'd be no coming back with the boy."

"So, that's it? You leave your kid to be raised by a criminal?"

"Exodus 14:14. *The Lord will fight for you; and you shall hold your peace.*"

"Do not Bible me just because I'm a woman of color," Baz said.

She headed down the ladder and toward Priest's front door.

Priest followed. "Orange won't be around forever," he said.

"That's your plan? Outwait the slow, inevitable march of mortality?"

"Would you prefer I ask Dusty to kill him for me?"

"That's not funny," Baz said.

"It's my only other option," Priest said.

Priest did not like the way Baz looked at him, with the same combination of pity and disgust she used with certain defendants she could not bring herself to defend.

On the street, blipping the lock on her BMW, Baz glanced again at the homeless guy pulling bottles. "I'm taking a few weeks off. I won't have any work for you for a while. If you decide to accept cases from other sources, I will understand and provide you very good references."

And then she drove away.

For his whole romantic life, Priest had been dumped by women who suddenly realized that he wasn't able to provide what they needed. They still liked him, but they were done making any of their well-being and happiness contingent upon his well-being and happiness.

Baz had just joined their ranks.

And she wasn't the only one.

Visiting his sister and Martin on the roof of their home in the Hollywood Hills, listening to a jazz combo run through their sound check at the Hollywood Bowl below, Priest ate pistachios and took another drubbing.

"Oh, honeybunch, of course, everybody hates you," Olive said. "You're leaving that vulnerable little boy in the care of a criminal."

"A man who suborns murder," Martin added. "Y'ever think the old man had Tarquin's mother killed?"

"A hit attempt, a death in the same family . . . there's probably a connection," Olive said.

"Laws of probability," said Martin.

Priest explained that he'd delved into Rachel's death, and

the driver of the car that struck and killed Rachel had also died in the crash. He'd had a blood alcohol level of 0.23.

"You doubted us when we said, 'Look at the artists,'" Martin said.

"The driver's death could have been unintended," Olive said.

"He chugs a bottle of vodka . . ."

". . . Dutch courage . . ."

". . . to blunt the import of what he's going to do . . ."

". . . which is to take his life and the life of another."

"Boom. Perfect crime," Martin said.

"This isn't a movie!" Priest protested.

"If you'd listened to us the first time . . ." Olive said, leaving the sentence hanging.

"If Orange wanted Rachel dead, he'd have used his underworld contacts to make it happen," Priest said. "Not a drunk in a Volvo."

"Guess who has underworld contacts?" Martin asked.

"Bad people," Olive said.

"Bad people like Dad, for example?" Priest said.

"No, not like Oliver," Martin said. "Actual murderous sonsabitches."

"Just thinking about that heartless old reptile hiring someone to kill his own grandson's biological father . . ." Olive said. "I hate him."

"The same biological father who is now allowing the man who hired a contract killer to raise his—meaning your—only son," Martin said.

"By the principles of transitive logic," Olive told Priest, "that makes you a reptile."

"Then, by the principles of transitive logic, I shouldn't be raising the boy either," Priest said.

"So far," Martin said, "the only good thing you have to say

about Anthony Orange is that he probably didn't murder his daughter."

"Orange loves the boy," Priest said, "and the boy loves him."

Olive grabbed his cheeks, pulled his forehead to hers—Priest could smell the weed on her breath—and said, "Honeybunch, you are fucking up."

"I'm sorry I didn't pay more attention when you suggested the artists," Priest said. "Okay?"

"You're being selfish. I understand that. Not being selfish is difficult for someone who's never been in love or had children."

"Not being selfish is hard for anyone who's never put someone else's life ahead of his own," Martin said.

"Maybe you forgot," Priest said, "but you don't have children either."

His sister turned pale.

"We have each other," Martin said, more to Olive than to Priest.

"We tried," Olive told Priest.

"You don't know if I've ever been in love or not," Priest said.

"Honeybunch, I have always loved you, and I know you love me back."

"You're my sister, of course I—"

"But I can't promise that, if you didn't love me, I'd love you back."

"Well, I do, so—"

"You don't have that."

"Have what?"

Olive looked to Martin for help.

"I'm not saying anything because I think this moment is between the two of you," Martin said.

"You don't require love to live," Olive said. "No man is an island. Except you."

"Now I'm an *island*?" Priest asked.

"You could wade to the mainland from it, but, yeah," Olive said.

"I do so want to be loved!" Priest said.

"I don't know if that's true or not," Olive said. "I think it isn't, but I don't know. What I do know is that you don't *require* love."

"What does that even mean?"

"You think it makes you strong," Olive said. "Maybe it does. But if so, it makes you strong in a way that is not good."

Priest wanted out of this conversation. "Listen to me. Anything I do, Tarquin ends up hating me."

"Don't change the subject," Olive said. "This is not about you."

"Olive, you and I were raised by a criminal. We turned out all right."

"Nope," his sister said, shaking her head.

Priest couldn't tell if she meant *No, they didn't turn out all right* or *No, they hadn't been raised by a criminal* or *Don't pull that debate shit on me.*

"If Rachel hadn't gotten killed, I'd probably never even have known about the boy. You know what? I wish I didn't know about him."

"You know who'd say that?" Olive asked.

"A reptile?" Priest asked.

"An island," Martin said.

Fuck.

"I'm going fishing," Priest said. And left.

———

Priest had never found the words or concepts to explain, even to himself, why he lost faith in the existence of God, except that the only thing he'd ever required to believe God existed was the certain knowledge that God loved him. But he had never felt the love of God. Not once. Even when pious little altar boy Xavier Priestly had loved God with all his fervent heart and promised the Holy Ghost that he'd pursue a Life in the Lord, God had not lived up to Priest's simple requirement.

Maybe Olive was right. Maybe that was when Priest had stopped requiring love. Because how could you expect people to provide something even God could not?

Psalm 27:10. *Though my father and my mother abandoned me, the LORD gathers me up.*

Except the LORD didn't gather him up.

"What are you muttering about over there?" Yorben asked.

"Talking to myself," Priest said.

"Wracking your brain about the kid?"

"He's repeating on me, yeah."

Yorben sucked on his plastic bottle of brandy, gazed up at the sky for inspiration, and belched. "What if you ease your way in? Take him to nice places? Buy him excellent shit. Video games? Michael Jordans? Kids love expensive sneakers. Take him on vacations!"

"Lure him slowly away from his grandfather?"

"Yeah. Emotionally and whatnot. Good plan."

"Buy his love?" Priest asked.

"Don't say it all disdainful. Buying shit to make people happy is the cornerstone of America," Yorben said. "For example, Christmas!"

Priest had no counter to Yorben's pragmatism, though he felt in his bones that, this time, Yorben's advice was not sound.

Then he felt the pier quiver beneath his feet.

"What the fuck?" Yorben said.

The last time Priest had felt anything like that had been

in March 2014, when a storm swell pummeled the pier with twenty-five-foot waves.

"Fee-fi-fo-fum," Yorben said. He jutted his chin toward Cody Fiso, who was striding along the Venice Pier toward them, people scattering in front of him like starlings off a train track. Priest felt each of Fiso's footfalls as a *Jurassic Park*-like tremor. Fiso was a storm front closing in fast. A hurricane crossed with an earthquake.

An angry hurricane and a pissed off earthquake.

Priest circled behind Yorben, intending to use him as a human shield, but Fiso picked Yorben up, lawn chair and all, like he was a baby in a car seat, and placed him gently to one side. Fiso seized Priest by his left wrist and his left ankle and, with the precise form of an Olympic hammer thrower, whirled Priest around twice before releasing him on an upward trajectory. Priest knew exactly what it was to be a starfish thrown back into the ocean by a child, like Ezekiel suspended between the arc of heaven and the fountains of the deep.

Jesus hanging from the cross.

Absalom hanging from the tree.

Priest surfaced and headed for the shore, swimming and wading. Up on the pier, people cheered for him. Surfers hooted as they shot past, flashing shaka signs, until Priest stood in knee-deep water, waves splashing up to the small of his back. A lifeguard with a chunk of his calf missing—his name was Alex—stood on the beach beside Fiso, holding his red torpedo buoy over his head. The top of the torpedo buoy almost reached Fiso's shoulders.

"You all right, Priest?" Alex-the-lifeguard asked.

"He's fine," Fiso said. "Look at him."

"Sir, I'm gonna need to hear it from him," Alex said.

Priest felt a burst of awe for the lifeguard's courage, standing up to an unhinged giant like Fiso.

"I'm fine, Alex," Priest said. "Except he owes me a pair of slides."

"What's that in your left hand?" Fiso asked.

"One slide isn't any use to me because, as you can see, I have two legs."

"You call those legs?"

"I'm gonna ask you both to please leave the beach," Alex said.

"Apparently, you're not allowed to jump off the pier," Fiso said.

"I didn't jump off the pier," Priest said.

"Then what did happen?" Alex asked Priest.

Fiso crossed his arms and waited for Priest's answer.

"I jumped off the pier," Priest said.

Alex shook his head and trudged through the sand toward the lifeguard station. Fiso, in the glare of daylight, looked like a Macy's Thanksgiving Day parade balloon. He literally blocked the sun.

"You coming ashore?" Fiso asked. "Or you gonna stand there all day?"

"I feel safer here," Priest said.

"You think standing in knee deep water will protect you from me?"

"It's not the water protecting me. It's your custom Nike Dunk Lows."

Fiso bent over to remove his sneakers. Priest waded ashore.

"Cup of coffee?" he asked.

"I don't drink coffee," Fiso said. "I'm a tea man, and you know it. You're offering me coffee, hoping I won't accept. But I accept."

Priest told Fiso to parallel park in front of his garage and walked home.

Standing on the roof deck of Priest's building, Fiso sipped a mug of PG Tips and watched a couple of retirees battle on the paddle-ball courts below. Priest looked at the stubbed-out remainders of roll-your-own cigarettes in a mason jar and wondered why Tarquin had chosen to smoke looking over the alleyway, instead of the boardwalk and ocean.

"I didn't know you smoked," Fiso said.

"I don't."

"Somebody does."

"The kid smokes."

"Your son? . . . Is that you nodding or shaking your head? How come you never mastered that basic human behavior? Two-year-olds know the difference between nodding and shaking their heads. Chimpanzees get it. Why can't you? Do you have any idea how hard it is for prepubescent kids who get addicted to quit later in life?"

"Look at you, shaking your head, Fiso. It doesn't mean no, does it? In this context, it conveys disgust or irritation or incredulity. Do two-year-olds and monkeys—"

"Chimpanzees."

"Fine. Would chimps understand why you threw me off the pier and what it is you want?"

"I'm here about the information I provided you, the emergency-room admissions in California and Nevada," Fiso said.

"I thought we agreed that that never happened."

"How did that information work out for you?"

"I was able to identify my attacker by cross-referencing the names you gave me with other information."

"And she is locked up where she can't jab you in the neck with a needle full of poison?" Fiso asked.

"Why are you talking like that? Are we being recorded?"

"You were to provide me . . ."

"Charlie McGinn," Priest said, "which I did. What's the problem?"

"The problem is I'm fighting an overwhelming urge to toss you off this roof."

"Don't Samoan rules of hospitality forbid killing your host?"

"Samoans aren't Arabs, Priest. Ask me how the Samoan culture deals with those who fail to keep their side of a bargain."

"I provided you Charlie McGinn's location."

"What you really promised me—what you sold me on— wasn't Charlie McGinn himself, was it, Priest? It was the acclaim and prestige of finding him."

"With attendant monetary rewards possibly reaching into the millions," Priest said. "You're welcome."

Fiso gritted his teeth, closed his eyes, and counted silently to six, by Priest's calculation. He found it a strange number until he realized that, when agitated, Fiso counted to ten faster than normal.

Fiso yanked a mobile from his back pocket, poked at it, and tossed it to Priest, which was when Priest discovered that it wasn't a phone but a full-sized tablet. He needed two hands to catch it. He swiped through a dozen photos of a man in his seventies, taken through an extreme telephoto lens that might have been mounted on a drone. The man wore the brown Carmelite scapular and white mantle of a monk, the hood thrown back over his shoulders, his head shaved except for an inch-wide ring of white hair interrupted where male pattern baldness left gaps at the front and back. An effect like racing stripes. The monk wore thick glasses. In one photo, he dug at something in the treads of his sandal.

Dog shit?

The miraculous visage of Christ?

Visible behind him was a wooden gate surmounted by a cross. In the distance, blue snow-topped mountains.

The old monk was, without a doubt, the former weapons designer and rock-star bassist Charlie McGinn, currently known as Brother Thomas.

"That's him," Priest said.

"Exactly where you said he'd be," Fiso said.

"So instead of throwing me off piers and roofs, call a news conference and announce that you did what nobody else could do. Not the FBI, not anyone. Go viral."

Fiso shook his head like an angry buffalo and exhaled. He did everything but paw the ground. "Priest, do you think you're better than me?"

"I am better than you. I found Charlie McGinn."

"Not superior to me as an investigator, Priest. I can accept that possibility. Better as a human being."

"What?"

"When you handed me that aluminum binder, you tempted me to sell my soul. That's demonic, Priest. It's evil. And you know it. You're the seminarian. You're trying to send me to hell."

"What's with always bringing up that I went to seminary?" Priest asked.

"Because your fall from grace is written all over you," Fiso said. "I'm a man of rectitude, and you're a lapsed seminarian, as proven by this binder bullshit."

"Jesus, Fiso. When did you get so dramatic?"

Fiso explained that the information in the aluminum binder indicated that Xavier Priestly had long ago stopped looking for Charlie McGinn and instead started looking for McGinn's rare 1936 Lancia Astura Pinan Cabriolet. Which had eventually led to a special windshield wiper order made to a vintage car dealer in Billings, Montana.

"Your binder says the car is in Switzerland," Fiso said, "but it's in Italy."

"I get from your tone that that's another huge betrayal," Priest said, "but it's the Roman Catholic way. A bishop takes it from a parish priest, an archbishop commandeers it, a cardinal confiscates it. Eventually, it's the Pope's."

"The Lancia was shipped to Italy *two years* ago," Fiso said.

"Still not a personal betrayal," Priest said.

"You've known Charlie McGinn's whereabouts for a minimum of two years, probably more, and yet you chose to sit on it. Why?"

"Charlie McGinn wasn't going anywhere."

"Correction. Brother Thomas wasn't going anywhere."

"Same guy."

"No! Not true. You gave me Brother Thomas. Either because you didn't care what I did with him or because you knew that I wouldn't do anything with him. Which was it?"

"I'm not following," Priest said.

"Brother Thomas is happy, Priest. He's away from the world, living a spiritual life. Completely fulfilled. To drag him back into the world he fled would be incredibly cruel. I think you knew I wouldn't do that. Morally speaking, you did not keep your side of the deal."

"That's why you threw me off the pier?" Priest asked.

Fiso heaved a sigh. Priest honestly couldn't tell whether it was the sigh that fluttered the flag over the paddle-ball courts, or an errant breeze.

"Let's call it the culmination of many slights and offenses," Fiso said, "but yeah, basically. If you knew I wouldn't take the temptation to sell my soul, if you knew I wasn't the kind of man who'd cash in on Charlie McGinn, then you straight-ahead ripped me off. Which is it? Were you looking to send me to

Hell? Or make a fool of me? Which is it that you think I am? Evil? Or stupid?"

Priest tried to remember what he'd been thinking the moment he'd opted to trade the aluminum binder for the information that led him to Blue Wig. His face went hot. Was that shame? For how he'd treated the unbearable Cody Fiso, of all people?

"I'm sorry," Priest said. "Lately I've started to think maybe I need someone to throw me off a pier every once in a while."

"How are you going to put this right?" Fiso asked.

"What's fair?"

"I give the Brother Thomas binder back to you," Fiso said, "and you bury it. Or burn it."

"That's it?"

"And you owe me three jobs."

"What three jobs?" Priest asked.

"Three jobs of my choosing, in the future, no statute of limitations."

"Like, whatever job you ask me to do, I have to do?"

"Yes. At your daily rate."

"Plus expenses," Priest said.

"Upon receipt of receipts," Fiso said. "I expect you to perform these three jobs to the best of your ability. No Priestly bullshit. Deal?"

"Define 'Priestly bullshit.'"

"We'll both know it when we see it. Deal?"

Priest looked at Fiso's extended hand and thought of the way he'd rejected Anthony Orange's when he promised to negate the hit on Priest.

He shook Fiso's hand—it was like shaking hands with a backhoe.

"One more thing," Fiso said.

"Shady," Priest said. "We already shook."

"I want to know your shazam moment."

"My what?" But Priest knew what Fiso wanted. Every investigator knew the shazam moment. The turning point when a precious cognitive leap leads inexorably to the solving of the puzzle.

"And don't tell me it was when you decided to look for the car instead of the man," Fiso said. He knew the difference between a run-of-the-mill investigatory notion and a shazam moment.

Back when Priest had confessed to old Father Clement that he was having doubts about his faith and his calling, Father Clement had quoted Cicero: *"Can earthly things seem important to him who is acquainted with the whole of eternity and the magnitude of the universe?"*

For Priest, the answer to Cicero's question had been a resounding *Yes*! But for rock-star weapons builder Charlie McGinn—navigating the world of debauchery and excess while also working on futuristic weapons of mass destruction—the answer to Cicero's question would have been a resounding *No*! Either the rock-star sex—or the I-Have-Become-Death-Destroyer-of-Worlds pressure—would have turned Charlie McGinn away from the material world and toward the Great Mystery.

Toward God.

And since Xavier Priestly and Charlie McGinn were demonstrably polar opposites in every way. It made sense that, when Xavier Priestly turned to the material world, Charlie McGinn fled it. Priest had gotten the hell out of seminary; Charlie McGinn got the hell out of the world. Abbeys, monasteries, seminaries: all were conceived as redoubts where the world is left behind, so that devout people—especially crazy, fanatical, beyond-brilliant people, like Charlie McGinn—could bake bread or herd cows or bang a drum and stare at the sun.

Shazam!

Priest could have started his search in India, Tibet, or Nepal, but since McGinn's rare and distinctive car had also disappeared, it was more likely McGinn had found his Shangri-La within driving distance, probably without crossing a border, which eliminated Mexico and Canada.

Thank you, Father Clement.

Thank you, Cicero.

"I can't go telling you all my secrets," Priest said.

"In that case, I want four jobs," Fiso said. He stood staring at Priest like Priest was an unsolved problem. "You should attend to whatever it is that's burdening you with guilt as soon as possible," he added. "Do what needs doing. You start thinking you deserve to be thrown off piers, you might be undergoing a serious emotional crisis."

"Thanks for the advice," Priest asked. "Anything else?"

"Yeah," Fiso said. "This way of making tea, where you pour boiling water into a mug and then dip a teabag in it? Unacceptable. They should have taught you that in seminary. Get yourself a proper tea pot. Try living like a grown-up, civilized human being."

———

Fiso was right about the tea. He was right about Priest leading Fiso deep into temptation using the millions of dollars and fame Fiso could have gotten from exposing Charlie McGinn. And it stood to reason that Fiso was also right that Priest had to go get his son back. But he knew he had to do it in a way that Tarquin would never discover.

Because the ocean had been warmer than Priest expected when Fiso threw him off the pier, and because he'd felt the smallest vibration of revelation while hanging between sky and sea, he decided to do some pondering while night swimming. He'd either drown or come up with a plan to get his Tarquin back.

It took approximately two hours before he shouted, "Shazzam!" and slogged his way—numb, hypothermic—across the sand and up into his apartment shower, where he stood in the steaming heat until the water ran cold.

Priest made himself a pot of coffee and sat at his computer.

It had been nine years since Rachel Orange's bogus cad of a fiancé—who might have been a fireman named Elton—broke three-year-old Tarquin Orange's arm. Anthony Orange had hired a contract killer to murder Priest on the chance that Priest might take his grandson after his daughter had died. What had the old crook done when somebody broke the boy's arm?

Priest went looking for Elton the Fireman, half-expecting to find the bastard murdered or missing. Did Old Man Orange get rid of anybody who threatened his way of life in any way?

First, Priest logged into Accurint to track Rachel's real-estate history. He found the condo she'd been paying half the mortgage on eight years ago. Anthony Orange had not only loaned Rachel her half of the down payment, but one of his companies—A.O. Investments—acted as the bank holding the mortgage. The other half of that mortgage had been paid by someone named James Alden Dean.

It made sense that someone named "James Dean" might choose to go by his middle name, and a little kid could easily have misremembered "Alden" as "Elton."

It took a couple of hours to run James Alden Dean through the usual battery of databases available to private investigators: LexisNexis, the Credit Bureau, Datalink, Equifax, Westlaw, IRB,

Tracers, TLO, and others. James Alden Dean wasn't a fireman. He was a prison guard. In Clark County, Nevada, the sheriff's department oversaw both law enforcement and prison guards. James Alden Dean was a cop. Did old Anthony Orange have the stones to take a hit out on a cop? Was he that crazy?

Priest combed through back issues of The Fraternal Order of Police bulletin, the police union's rag. He searched the LVMPD newsletter, and the LVMPD Foundation website, cobbling together the career trajectory of Officer James Alden Dean.

Three years as a guard in Corrections.

A year and a half at the Hoover Dam.

Back to Corrections, during which time he broke three-year-old Tarquin's arm.

Six years as a motorcycle cop in the Traffic Bureau.

Patrol officer in downtown Las Vegas.

Patrol officer in the area around Nellis Air Force Base.

All in all, an embarrassment of dead-end lateral moves, which indicated that James Alden Dean was probably the kind of cop who'd never found his place. Dean had either requested a lot of transfers, or his superior officers jumped at the first opportunity to pawn him off on other unsuspecting bosses.

According to a police-reform website, a Black Lives Matter website, and a leaked memo from the Internal Affairs Department, Dean was on more than one watchdog list of "problem cops" with a history of violence, substance abuse, domestic abuse, charges of racism and homophobia, and perjury.

Currently, Sergeant James Alden Dean was assigned to the airport.

How did this loser still have a job?

Easy: James Alden Dean came from a long line of cops, firefighters, and arson investigators. His father was a captain in the Organized Crime Bureau. His stepfather was a captain in Narcotics. His uncle worked as a deputy chief in Financial Crimes. There was an aunt in Criminal Intelligence, a sister at Information Technologies, a younger brother in the Investigative Services Division, a stepbrother in Gangs/Vice, and a cousin in Special Operations. And the capper: Dean's big brother was vice-president of the Las Vegas Police Protective Association, the police union. Sergeant James Alden Dean was the family fuck-up, but other cops—especially his family—protected him.

Dean's real-estate history showed that he had sold the condo he'd co-owned with Rachel Orange, neglected to pay the balanced owed to A.O. Investments, kept the entire amount of money from the sale, and used it as a down payment on a three-bedroom, 2,000-square-foot bungalow in the north of Las Vegas. A.O. Investments had taken Dean to court. Uncharacteristically, Orange had lost that suit.

Not only had James Alden Dean lied to Rachel about wanting to marry her, but he'd broken her three-year-old son's arm and then ripped off Rachel and her father. Orange had let it go, probably because Rachel begged him to, or because Orange knew he'd never win against such a well-connected bastard, or because the well-connected bastard had convincingly threatened Orange. Likely by threatening to harm Rachel and Tarquin.

Dean was currently in arrears on his latest mortgage. No big surprise in a town built on gambling debts.

The sun came up.

Priest walked down to the water's edge again as the sun rose behind him. He considered one of Dusty's favorite quotations from Sun Tzu: *"In all fighting, the direct method may be used for joining battle, but indirect methods will be needed in order to secure victory."*

Ephesians 5:15 popped into his head: *See therefore, brethren, how you walk circumspectly: not as unwise, But as wise: redeeming the time, because the days are evil.*

Then Romans 12:21 shouldered Ephesians out of the way: *Do not be overcome by evil, but overcome evil with good.*

Priest thought, *Fuck the Romans.* He headed back inside to get some sleep.

When he awoke, it was mid-afternoon. Priest ordered a Fun-Guy Pizza for pick-up at The Whaler, unwrapped a virgin burner, and called the Airport Bureau of the Las Vegas Metropolitan Police Department at Harry Reid International Airport, Terminal 1. He asked to speak with Sergeant Dean. Priest was transferred to Terminal 3, and from there to the Cargo Center, where a woman answered the phone. She identified herself as Officer Diaz. Priest asked her if he could please speak to Sergeant Dean.

"Sergeant Dean is currently unavailable," Officer Diaz said. "Can I help you?"

Priest identified himself as a source who had information about contraband liquor being flown into LAS under fake manifests and said he wouldn't speak to anyone but Sergeant Dean.

"Seriously?" Officer Diaz asked.

"Very seriously," Priest said. "A matter of life and death."

"How is mislabeled liquor a matter of life and death?" Officer Diaz asked. "Sir?"

Sergeant Dean was either not taken totally seriously by his subordinates, or they were accustomed to covering for him. Probably both.

"I'll only speak with Sergeant Dean," Priest said.

"If you leave me a number—"

"I'm not leaving a number!" Priest said.

"All right, sir, calm down. Sergeant Dean will be working the eleven-to-seven shift tonight. You can try him then."

"Eleven sharp?"

"I suggest you give Sergeant Dean time to, uh, get settled," Diaz said. "You'll have your best shot after midnight."

"Thank you."

"Thank you for being a good citizen," Diaz said. Just before she hung up Priest heard laughing in the background.

He found Yorben out on the pier, asked him for yet another favor, and then gave him a detailed list of what he needed.

"You promise me another shark?" Yorben asked.

"Hand on my heart," Priest said.

Priest had traded in his Chrysler 300 for a white, four-door, all-wheel-drive 2019 Volvo S60 T6. He'd bought it ironically, but on the drive back from CarMax to his place on the Venice Boardwalk, Priest had decided that the Volvo made him feel prosperous, sensible, and in touch with the adult world. Innocuous. Invisible. Perfect.

Sergeant Alden Dean was scheduled to be at work at eleven p.m. but was expected after midnight. Priest was in Vegas by nine p.m.. He ate a salad and drank iced tea at Denny's, for which he paid cash. By 9:45 p.m., he had parked the Volvo—fake plates—in a dark corner of the busy parking lot of the Stonehouse Bar and Grill. He yanked navy blue cargo pants over his board shorts, exchanged his baggy short-sleeved cowboy shirt for a skin-tight, long-sleeved gray waffle undershirt, and replaced his Keen sandals with Army-surplus combat boots. Over the thermal, he zipped on a tight black puffy vest. Dusty had taught him, over several dozen training sessions, *Don't give your opponent anything to grab.*

Priest pulled on a worn baby blue baseball cap emblazoned with *I Don't Have a Bucket List but My F*cket List is a Mile Long* in wacky orange letters. He tucked an eight-inch black steel tube into the thigh pocket of his cargo pants. When deployed, the expandable tactical baton telescoped to twenty-one inches.

"The twenty-six-incher generates more force," Dusty had told him during their first lesson with the baton. "But it's unwieldy indoors. Walls. Doorways. Furniture. Ceiling and light fixtures. These things all work for your opponent. For indoor work, give me the sixteen- or twenty-one-inch model every time."

Priest removed the rubber safety tip, because safety was not on his current list of priorities.

At 9:55 p.m., Priest stood on the sidewalk outside James Alden Dean's bungalow on a corner lot. Lots of pick-ups in neighboring driveways. Quiet neighborhood, but not so quiet that the neighbors would overhear a spirited conversation inside the house, as long as the doors were closed.

The blue light of televisions.

Dogs walked.

Doors locked.

Everyone home for the night.

James Alden Dean's house was a rancher with a double wooden front door. The lawn was well tended. There was a big plane tree in front of a picture window. Curtains drawn. The house was constructed of whitewashed brick, the surprisingly wide front walk made of slabs of amalgamate. Flecks within it glittered. Western motif shutters on each side of the windows. Two types of people kept their houses this neat: the house-proud, and alcoholics who didn't want any sign of their spiraling lives to register with the neighbors.

Ensuring that no one was on the street, no one peering at him from a picture window, Priest headed up the empty drive-way along the side of Dean's house. A separate yellow, vinyl-sided two-car garage was set back even with the backyard. Priest knew that Dean owned a three-year-old Tahoe, so either Dean had left early for work, or the Tahoe was in the garage or parked on the street. Light shone from a bathroom window onto the driveway.

Oil stains where Dean worked on cars or motorcycles.

A basketball hoop.

Moving farther up the driveway, Priest saw light spilling into the backyard from what was probably the kitchen.

There had been no indications online that James Alden Dean lived with anyone. He was not currently married. He'd been married once before moving in with Rachel Orange and her young son. Four years later, he'd married and divorced again. He was currently separated from a woman he'd married six months ago, but that didn't rule out a new live-in girlfriend. Or worse, a cop buddy tossed out by a soon-to-be ex-wife, staying with Dean temporarily. Priest hoped Dean didn't have a dog. Especially not the kind of dog a flailing alcoholic cop with manhood issues and a dead career might own: Alsatian, Pit, Doberman, Rottweiler.

Priest didn't have a dog because it would be irresponsible. Sure, he worked from home a lot, but he also left town without notice for days at a time. The big question for Priest was: should he wait for his life to change so that he could get a dog? Or should he get the dog to motivate him to change his life?

Did this cause-and-effect principle also apply to spouses?

If so, then instead of waiting to evolve into a man worth marrying, Priest should have married his ex, Tina, in an effort to transform himself into someone worth marrying, someone qualified to own a dog.

Or raise a child.

Priest force-breathed himself into the here and now. Into the moment. Into focusing on the task at hand. He took an accounting of his surroundings.

A postage-stamp pool.

A hot tub.

Cheap matchy-matchy lawn furniture.

A barbecue pit.

A picnic table, painted red.

He heard a window slide open to his left and halt with a bang. "Can I help you?"

Priest turned to see a flushed face looking down at him from the frosted window. Mid-forties. Tough. Pugnacious. Handsome, but showing signs of too much liquor and too many cigarettes. The kind of guy who masked his sins with quarts of cologne and mouthwash.

When Priest spoke, he affected a nasal voice, high above his normal register. "Hey, oh, yeah, sorry. I rang the doorbell, but nobody answered."

"I didn't hear the doorbell," the man said. "You ever hear of knocking? And maybe not sneaking around the side of the house if nobody answers?"

Dean thought Priest was canvassing the place for a robbery. He might be a crap cop, but he possessed rudimentary instincts.

"This is the part where you tell me you're delivering a package and it's really important I sign for it," Dean said. "Which might even be convincing if you were carrying a package or knew my name."

Priest met Dean's eyes. Fucker. Miserable bullying fucker. Breaker of children's arms. Fucking fucker.

"I do know your name if it's Mr. Dean," Priest said.

"*Sergeant* Dean. Of the Las Vegas Metropolitan Police Department. You start running now, maybe I won't get out there quick enough to shoot your ass."

"I'm glad I found you," Priest said.

"You got some kind of learning disability?" Dean asked.

This was the longest Priest had ever talked to someone through a bathroom window. The fan whirled behind Dean.

"I'm afraid you're sleeping with my wife," Priest said.

"What?"

"I don't blame you, even if you knew she was married."

"Jordana?"

"Far as I'm concerned, in these situations, it's never the fault of 'the other man' or 'the other woman,' right? It's not up to outsiders—like you—to preserve the sanctity of marriage. It's up to the man and woman in the marriage. You and me, we got no problem between us."

"Good to know, now fuck off," Dean said.

"Maybe Jordana didn't tell you she was married. Or she said we were separated or divorced. Whatever, I figure you got the right to know that she's lying to you. People owe each other basic transparency. And the fact is, she and I are still enjoying conjugal relations. Maybe she told you otherwise, but it's something you should know. Also, I have an STD, currently in remission, but again, something you should be aware of."

"You have two seconds to fuck off," Dean said.

Priest made a calming gesture with his hands. He wanted to show Dean that he was sensitive to the private nature of the conversation, but he also wanted to be a little too loud. He wanted to be grating. He infused his tone with grievance and accusation. If James Alden Dean was the kind of man Priest thought he was, Dean would be jarred, disgusted, and furious that he was a sharing a woman with a man like the weirdo standing out on his driveway at ten o'clock at night, wearing a hat that said *I Don't Have a Bucket List but My F*cket List is a Mile Long.*

"Something else you should know is she's got photos," Priest said.

"What?"

"Maybe that's your thing. Fine. But if it isn't, you need to know she's got some pretty graphic footage of you in action. With audio. You being a peace officer, maybe there's some kind of rules of conduct or some shit?"

"Come around to the back door," Dean said, his face disappearing from the window.

Priest rolled his shoulders and let himself through a chain-link gate into the backyard. He stepped around the barbecue pit and walked up three steps, onto the back porch, heading for the sliding door into the kitchen. It was already open. He was reaching for his expandable baton when the world exploded in a flash of blue and silver.

Priest's knees buckled. His face was heading for the deck when something caught him by the vest and yanked him inside through the sliding doors. He was thrown to the floor, the side of his head bouncing off the kitchen tiles. The sliding door crashed shut and vibrated in the frame.

He had long ago realized that his best defensive move when being crushed in a physical confrontation was to go down fast and hard and stay down. Hit the ground like you meant it. Feign semi-consciousness, because absolute unconsciousness seldom happened in real life, and when it did it, it was hardly ever instantaneous. Keep your eyes half-opened and unfocused. Don't let them track or focus. Groan. Gurgle. Buy time to think.

But he didn't need to fake any of that. He'd collapsed on his right side, couldn't see straight, and was making guttural noises he'd never heard before. A sharp pain lanced through his head. Had he been shot? Some people survived a shot in the head. For a while.

A dark shape inches from his nose.

Two shapes.

Priest let his left leg quiver, as though he was twitching or having a small seizure. He allowed himself to focus for one hot moment.

The dark shapes were a pair of big, shiny cop shoes. Really big. Like size fourteen.

Jesus. Yet another big man. Not Fiso tall or Yorben fat, but bigger than Priest.

The pain in his head consolidated just above the bridge of his nose.

He hadn't been shot. He'd been struck with something solid. Maybe a Maglite or a truncheon. The brim of his F*CKET cap might have saved his life, but it was gone now. He felt blood trickling and pulled his chin into his chest so that it wouldn't flow into his eyes. Dean was a cop. He might have struck Priest with the butt of his service weapon. If so, Dean would still be holding the gun. Priest extended his right hand toward the expandable baton in his pocket.

It wasn't there.

He twitched and groaned again.

Running out of time.

He felt the baton against his thigh, in the lower pocket.

Priest pulled in his knees like he'd been stabbed in the stomach and thought, *Turn me over, turn me over . . .*

Dean kicked Priest in the back, near his kidney. It took every ounce of Priest's willpower not to betray that he was mostly conscious.

He found the grip of the baton.

Please, God, make him turn me over.

He groaned something that sounded like a man trying to form words, a man who was hurt, but not so bad you might as well finish him off and bury him beneath the house.

Prithee, Lord, hear my lament! Maketh the fucker turneth me upon my back . . .

Dean seized Priest's shoulder and flipped him over.

Priest used the rotation of his body and a flick of his wrist to extend the tactical baton. His eyes wouldn't focus, but he saw something blurry looming over him, and he put everything he had into one big swing.

The baton struck Dean's neck immediately beneath the ear.

Dean hollered and—*Yes, that's a gun in his hand*—swung his weapon at Priest's body mass. Priest rolled to his feet and struck the wrist holding the gun, as hard as he could, remembering Dusty: *Never let your opponent step inside the arc of the baton.*

The gun went off just before it fell to the floor. Searing pain in his calf. Priest resisted the temptation to follow the gun with his eyes.

Forget the gun. Pay attention!

Dean's right wrist hung useless at his side. Priest struck again, aiming for Dean's throat, no longer worried about killing the man. Priest had blood in his eyes, and he was drunk-ass wobbly from the blow to his forehead. He could barely stand, much less maintain the balance he needed for a fight to the death. Dean loomed in his police uniform. If Priest had been smart, if he'd checked out Dean's physical stature before forming this plan, he'd have come up with a better plan, a plan that included a cattle prod or flame-thrower or sawed-off shotgun, instead of the majorette's baton.

Dean swung a fist at Priest. Priest evaded the punch, more by luck than design. Dean lunged for his gun, on the floor, near the refrigerator.

Mistake.

Priest struck Dean on the right ankle. He didn't have enough strength or leverage to break any bones, but it still hurt like hell. Priest struck Dean's Achilles tendon with a backhand cut. Dean shouted in pain and did what he should have done in the first place: he stepped inside the baton's range, seized Priest's throat, and tried to crush Priest's larynx with his thumbs.

Luckily for Priest, Dean was rapidly losing the use of his left leg. Priest slipped the baton over the bend of Dean's right elbow—*Thank you, Dusty, for making me practice this move a thousand times*—reached under with his left hand, seized the baton, and pulled his knees to his chest, using all his weight to yank the baton down. Both his feet left the ground, like he was a kid on a jungle gym.

Dean started screaming even before his wrist snapped.

He threw his left fist at Priest, and Priest sliced the baton straight into the knuckles. Dean's hand split like Priest had wielded a machete. Priest drew back the baton and struck Dean in the face. Without the rubber safety tip, the baton opened Dean's cheek like a calzone. Priest reversed and used the butt of the baton like a knife, stabbing Dean twice in the eye and then slashing down on the bridge of his nose.

Just like that, the big man was done.

Dean wasn't even able to twist his body to fall onto his back. His face hit the floor with a sound like a dropped meat pie. If Dean hadn't been breathing like a bellows, Priest might have thought he was dead. Priest stepped back, wiping blood out of his face with his sleeve.

Dean rolled onto his side and hunched over his broken wrist and split fist, his nose gushing blood. He looked at Priest through his one good eye. "Keep your fucking wife."

Priest lost his temper.

He struck Dean three more times with the baton: top of the head, left shoulder, right knee. Dean shouted and whimpered, trying with all his failing limbs to scuttle back into the corner of the kitchen, leaving a smear of blood across the kitchen floor.

Priest found his F*CKET cap and pulled it on. He picked up Dean's service revolver and aimed it at Dean until he smelled urine. In order to prevent himself from pulling the trigger, Priest counted his breaths, striving for calm.

Shoot the fucker!
Inhale for five . . .
Shoot the fucker!

. . . hold for seven . . .

Shoot the fucker.

. . . exhale for nine.

Do not shoot the fucker.

"You're not really sleeping with my wife," Priest said. "I'm not married. That was a ruse. A stupid ruse, too. I figured that's why you hit me. Turns out you're an idiot."

"What do you want?" Dean asked.

At least that's what Priest thought Dean said. It's what he would have said in Dean's place, but Dean's cheek flapped blood with every word, so it sounded like a child clapping.

Child . . .

Priest thought of this huge, piss-drenched bully wrenching a toddler's arm so hard it broke his wrist. He'd probably hit Rachel, too. Lovely, single-mother, silver-boots-wearing Rachel.

Five in . . . Shoot the fucker . . . hold for seven . . . out for nine . . . Don't shoot the fucker.

"You're going through everything you've ever done, wondering what brought you to this point," Priest said. "It's a long list. Assaults. Racist bullshit. Maybe you got some scam going at the airport that's gone bad. And then there's those gambling debts. Take my advice: you can't keep pushing those off forever. Vegas is a tough town."

Dean stared at him through his one eye.

"Surprise!" Priest said. "It's none of those things."

He glanced down at his burning calf. The bullet had creased his leg. Painful, but nothing serious. Still, there'd been a gunshot. A neighbor might have called the cops. It might have felt like an hour ago, but it had been only a minute, maybe a minute and a half, since the firearm discharged. The LVMPD's average response time for priority calls in this area averaged six minutes. This wouldn't be a priority. Priest had time.

Almost all the blood on the kitchen floor was Dean's, gushing from his mouth, nose, and hand. But still, some would have trickled from the bullet wound in Priest's leg. A little more from the gash in his forehead above his nose, dripping off his chin. As a licensed legal investigator, Priest's DNA was in the national registry. If they matched it, then they'd have him, and he'd be fucked. So Priest used his foot to push Dean's blood over toward where Priest had been standing when the bullet grazed his calf. Where he'd been on the ground after Dean hit him in the forehead with the butt of his gun. If he spread around enough of Dean's blood, the forensics people wouldn't be able to find a sample of Priest's blood large enough to analyze. Suddenly, he didn't feel any shame at all about shattering Dean's teeth, flaying his lips and gums, busting his nose.

Priest wondered if he was completely in his right mind.

"What it is, is very simple," Priest said. "You sold a condo and kept all the money. You ripped off a man and his daughter. Recently, the daughter died. Are you with me?"

Dean tried to nod. It was more of a head-waggle. Priest had shredded the muscles between Dean's ear and his collarbone. Waggling was the best the man could manage. His head lolled against the refrigerator. But he was conscious. Listening. Priest needed Dean to remember everything he said, or all of this would be nothing more than personal revenge. Which he was okay with, too.

"Pay the man what you owe," Priest said, placing the tip of the baton in Dean's good eye and pushing. Dean sobbed.

Priest left the way he'd come in.

He hurried back to the Stonehouse parking lot, trying not to limp, trying to look like a neighborhood guy on his way to a neighborhood bar. He removed his bloody outer clothing and tossed it into the bar's dumpster. He used baby wipes to clean the blood off his face, Super Glue and a butterfly bandage to close the gash in his forehead. He drove to the southern edge of Las Vegas and stopped at a McDonald's, where he removed the magazine from Dean's service revolver and dropped the bullets into a storm drain.

He tossed the extractor spring out the window at the 15/215 interchange.

The barrel at West Cactus Avenue.

The trigger bar assembly at West Starr Avenue.

The slide behind the Blue Hawk Tavern.

The locking block off Blue Diamond Road.

The magazine assembly in a junkyard at the dead end of Wigwam Avenue.

The frame at the Lion Habitat Ranch.

By the time he passed Seven Magic Mountains, he was free of the gun and on his way home. The baton he kept until he got back to Venice. He limped down to the jetty and tossed it off the end of the rocks. Someday, somebody might find it on the beach, rusty and sand-pitted, but it wouldn't open smoothly and would probably end its days propping open a window or stored beneath the bed, waiting for intruders who would never come.

27

The cut on Priest's forehead where James Alden Dean had struck him was not as bad as Priest had feared, but it was still an attention-getter. An angry red welt more than an inch long sat above Priest's swollen nose and black eyes. Mottled bruises on his throat—unmistakably fingers—told enough of a story that Priest covered them with a neck brace. When his Flat-Earth tenant, Beck, asked what happened, Priest told him that a giant, crazed Samoan berserker had thrown him off the Venice Pier.

"Everybody's talking about that," Beck said. "You've had one hell of a winter."

Priest disinfected the seeping gouge the bullet had left in his calf, wrapped it in gauze, and wore long pants on the rare occasions he left his apartment. He began to wonder whether the hypothermia he'd acquired during his night swim had affected his decision-making process. And how long would he have to wait to discover if his convoluted plan to get Tarquin would work?

He decided to assail his rising doubts, get off his ass, and find Nikki Celeste.

When Diodato had coughed up Nikki's real name—Karen

Pollari—Priest knew that, if she hadn't been killed and buried in a shallow grave by Subaric or a demented stalker, or been spirited off to the United Arab Emirates or Singapore or Russia by an oligarch, he'd be able to track her down.

After all, he was the guy who'd found Charlie McGinn.

Priest assumed that Nikki was still alive, and that the ne'er-do-well cokehead Tedeschi brother had been cut off from the money faucet by his more conventional brother. Priest also figured that Giselle had either known how to make contact with Nikki the whole time or, even more likely, was the person Nikki called to ask whether Parris was mad at her, only to find out that Parris had been murdered. That would explain why Giselle and Nikki had moved out of their Parris Ferrer-owned apartments, likely then dissolving their escort identities and regrouping to figure out what to do next.

In a better world, Nikki would have come running back to Dusty. But it had been three weeks now, and Dusty hadn't even received a text message, which probably meant either that Nikki Celeste a.k.a. Callie Vaughan a.k.a. Karen Pollari didn't love Dusty, or that Yorben was right and Nikki was afraid of Dusty.

Dusty deserved to know the truth. And Priest was the one to find it out for her.

He couldn't find any information online about "Karen Pollari," but he found a Karin Pollarhi and a Karyn Polari. Karyn Polari was dead. Karin Pollarhi lived in a senior facility in Wadesboro, South Carolina.

Priest cracked open a new burner and, posing as a researcher for the PBS family-tree program *Finding Your Roots*, called South Carolinian Karin Pollarhi. South Carolinian Karin Pollarhi informed Priest that she had distant family in Spokane, Washington. Did that qualify her to appear on the show?

Priest found a number for Maxwell and Kelsey Pollarhi in

Moses Lake, Washington, a hundred miles west of Spokane. An agricultural center in sheep-and-cattle country, Moses Lake had recently enjoyed a surge in manufacturing and technology, led by a major producer of polysilicon and the world's largest maker of carbon fiber.

A woman answered, dragging on a cigarette before she said, "Hello." Priest surmised that she was one of those people who preferred smoke to air, with the grating voice to prove it.

"Hello, my name is Jules Trunk from the Biliary Atresia Foundation. Am I speaking to Karen Pollarhi?"

"What's this about?"

Good. Kelsey Pollarhi knew Karen Pollarhi, or else she would simply have said "wrong number" or hung up. And if Karen Pollarhi was the name of a dead child that Nikki Celeste had stolen as a backup identity, the response would have been more emotional.

"I promise I'm not after money," Priest said. "Would it be possible to speak with Karen?"

"If you're not looking for money, what do you want?"

"It's medically confidential. Do you mind if I ask your relationship to Karen Pollarhi?"

"I'm her mother."

"Could you please confirm the spelling of her full name?"

"C-A-R-I-N . . . G-L-O-R-I-A . . . P-O-L-L-A-R-H-I."

"Thank you, Ms. Pollarhi. I'm reaching out to your daughter on behalf of a toddler suffering from biliary atresia."

"What's that?"

"Biliary atresia is a disease of the very young, Ms. Pollarhi. Infants. Heart-breaking. The bile ducts inside the liver are blocked. When surgery fails, the child will most certainly die unless he or she is provided with what's called a living liver transplant. We believe your daughter is a good match for—"

"Wouldn't Carin have to be dead for that?"

"Oh, no, Mrs. Pollarhi, she'd only have to provide a lobe of her liver. Not the whole thing. The lobe grows back. That's why it's called a living liver—"

"Well, Carin's not here."

"That is so unfortunate because this two-year-old boy, who is currently at death's door, would be able to enjoy a full, active life if we can only find a donor—"

"Well, I'm sorry for the little boy, but I don't know where Carin is."

"There is often a finder's fee involved, Mrs. Pollarhi, provided by the family, if the match is successful."

"How much?"

"It depends upon the means of the family, but it's usually a few thousand dollars. The largest I've seen is twenty-five thousand dollars, but that family was very wealthy."

Kelsey Pollarhi stayed on the line, trying to figure out a way to ask if Priest's imaginary two-year-old biliary atresia victim came from money. Luckily, imaginary people had lots of money.

"The family has means," Priest said, "but I can't say much more than that. You understand."

"I guess."

"Can I ask if you've seen your daughter lately?"

"No."

Priest resisted asking whether she meant *No, you may not ask* or *No, I have not seen her.*

"Carin filled out a donor card," Priest said. "In Los Angeles, California. Do you think she might still be there?"

"Yes, last I heard, that's where she's based. Carin travels a lot for her job."

"Her job?"

"She works for an art gallery, finding new talent."

"That's very helpful. Do you, by any chance, know which gallery?"

"How did you get to us?"

"This is the number your daughter provided on the donor card."

"Well, why would Carin go and do that?"

"Sometimes busy people whose lives change a lot put down their parents' number."

"Ha!" she said. Priest heard her drag on a cigarette. Heard a TV playing in the background. That didn't happen much anymore. People tended to pause the TV. Someone else was watching TV. Someone else who wasn't waiting for her to finish her call.

"If I leave you my name and number, then perhaps you could have Carin call us? That might be enough to justify, at least, a portion of the finder's fee if Carin becomes a donor."

"She sent me a photo of herself a couple of days ago."

"Oh, excellent. From where?"

"I don't know. Just her face. It's not like there's the Eiffel Tower behind her or the Grand Canyon."

Priest thought of Tarquin boasting that Vegas had the real Eiffel Tower and Paris was a copycat. He thought of estranged children and what happens to them.

"Can you give me the number she sent it from?"

"It's blocked."

"Oh."

"Carin's a very private person."

"You did your best. Ms. Pollarhi. Thank you very much."

"Well, you're welcome for nothing, I guess."

"Could you possibly send me the photo? We don't have a picture on file for Carin, and we like to keep our records current."

"Would that kind of thing apply to the finder's fee?"

"Of course."

Priest made sure he'd successfully downloaded the photo on his burner before he said goodbye to chain-smoking Kelsey Pollarhi in Moses Lake, Washington.

Definitely Nikki Celeste. A selfie. At night. Outside. Nikki looked tired. Prettier than Priest remembered. Raising one hand in a wave. Putting on a brave smile for her mother. The background behind Nikki told him nothing, even after Priest used his photo-editing program to pull a more detailed image from the shadows. A wooden wall. Rustic. A barn? A roadhouse? A fence? A trapper's cabin in Canada?

Priest ran the selfie through his EXIF program and found that Nikki had set her phone not to display the metadata. But she hadn't told it not to record the metadata. And because Nikki didn't know that the metadata existed, she hadn't stripped it from the photo she sent her mother. Within a few minutes, Priest knew what kind of phone Nikki had used to take the photo; the white balance, ISO, aperture, and shutter speed; and the time the photo was taken: 11:02 pm, three days before. The temperature: 73 degrees Fahrenheit. In February. If Nikki had taken the selfie outside, it could be California. And—jackpot—accurate to within six feet, give or take, the GPS coordinates where Nikki Celeste had taken the photo and texted: *Hi, Mom, I'm all right!*

28

The next day, Priest took the Volvo for a mid-morning drive from where he lived—at 33.9850° N, 118.4695° W—to 34° 26.878052' N, 119° 14.578857' W.

Priest removed his neck brace. Up Pacific Coast Highway through Santa Monica and Pacific Palisades, past Topanga, surfers bobbing patiently in the chuck. He cruised through Malibu and past Point Mugu Air Station, where weapons designer Charlie McGinn hadn't shown up to work all those decades ago. Through Oxnard onto the 101 past Ventura, right onto California 33 North to Ojai. Priest knew where he was going; he'd once babysat a paranoid witness at the Lake Casitas Mobile Home Estates in Oak View during a corporate embezzlement trial. Ojai was tucked into a valley in the Topatopa Mountains, a town of boutique hotels and inns, farm-to-table restaurants, and wineries. A haven for artists and magic crystal lovers. Priest and his ex, Tina, had escaped to Ojai two or three times during the most promising part of their relationship, when it seemed that it might be going somewhere. They'd stayed in the Ojai Rancho Inn and sampled wine in tasting rooms up and down

Ventura Avenue. They'd gone horseback riding and hiking. They'd made love on a blanket in a secluded area of the Old Creek Ranch.

If you needed to hide out, Ojai wasn't the worst place in the world.

34° 26.878052' N, 119° 14.578857' W turned out to be a hilltop overlooking Ojai's main drag. Atop the hill was a charming inn, a dozen guest rooms and a handful of cottages. A waterfall. A highly acclaimed kitchen featuring a Los Angeles chef who was recovering from methamphetamine addiction. A rustic wing against which a woman might take a reassuring selfie to send her mother. There was a terrace where guests sat and ate and drank and looked at the town spread out below. Nikki and Giselle were eating lunch under a eucalyptus tree.

Priest joined them. "Is there fresh coffee in that pot?" he asked. "Or should I order another?"

Nikki rose to her feet, knocking her chair over backward. Scared. Giselle leaned back and folded her arms, not at all scared.

"Are you alone?" Nikki asked.

"What happened to you?" Giselle asked.

"I'm alone," Priest said.

"Did you walk into a propeller?" Giselle asked.

"Where's Dusty?" Nikki asked.

"I don't know," Priest said.

"You two always know where the other is," Nikki said.

"How'd you find us?" Giselle asked.

"I'm a brilliant investigator," Priest said.

"Why isn't Dusty with you?" Nikki asked.

"We're having a disagreement," Priest said.

"That explains the strangle-marks on his neck," Giselle told Nikki. "Dusty tried to strangle him."

"If Dusty tried to strangle me," Priest said, "I'd be strangled.

Aren't you going to ask how Dusty is doing? How worried and broken-hearted she might be since you abandoned her?"

"Nik has a lot of intense feelings for Dusty," Giselle said. "Unfortunately, fear is one of them."

"Why?" Priest asked.

"It's obvious," Nikki said.

"It's the opposite of obvious," Priest said. "It's obscure."

Priest felt a thrill when Giselle laughed. What was wrong with him? He could barely look away from her, leaning back in her chair, foot on the table, like Wyatt Earp cheating at poker.

"Dusty killed Parris," Nikki said, "so that we could be together."

"Even if Dusty was dumb-in-love enough to murder for you, which she isn't—"

"She most definitely is," Giselle said.

"—she did not kill Parris," Priest said.

"You don't know," Nikki said. "The woman's psycho. You think you know her? You don't."

"A professional hitter out of Vegas is currently being held on suspicion of killing Parris Ferrer," Priest said.

"She put my stalker in a coma," Nikki said. "Within a day of being released from hospital, he disappeared. Who do you think did that?"

"Parris hired someone to make that happen," Priest said. "The same person who turned around and killed her. And tried to kill me."

Nikki turned to Giselle. Giselle shrugged.

Priest entered a text into his phone, showed it to Nikki, showed it to Giselle, and read it aloud. "Found Nikki—big eyes emoji."

"We can read. Thank you," Giselle said. "I speak three languages."

Priest continued to read aloud as he texted, "Home . . . in . . . two . . . hours. Roadrunner emoji." And then to Nikki, "Let's hit the road."

"No, wait, I have to think—"

"Two hours from here to Venice," Priest said, "whatever time you need to tell Dusty you're okay, do whatever you two do—apparently not have sex—two hours later, I have you back here in time for drinks before dinner with Giselle. Unless you decide to stay with Dusty, who you love passionately with all your heart."

"Fuck off," Nikki said.

"Bring Giselle if you want," Priest said. "My Volvo has surprisingly roomy rear seating."

"Volvo?" Giselle said. "I'll be fine here."

"I'm not going just because you say Dusty didn't kill Parris," Nikki said. "I need to see proof."

"Jesus, Nik," Giselle said. "He's not lying."

"The next thing I'm going to do is text Dusty your location," Priest told Nikki. "She'll be here on her bike in an hour and twenty minutes max."

"Go get 'er done," Giselle told Nikki.

At the Volvo, before Priest and Nikki left, Giselle touched the mark on Priest's forehead. "How's the other guy look?" Priest almost confessed everything through a swell of hazy lust.

Driving through Malibu, Nikki said, "Giselle likes you. She thinks you're smart. She gets turned on by smart. She'd totally do you on her own time."

"Would I have to clear that with her new pimp? Or is she looking to quit the escort business, too?"

Nikki didn't speak again until they pulled up into his garage. "What if Dusty isn't here?"

"She's here."

And she was, standing in Priest's living room.

"What a shithole," Nikki said.

"Location, location, location," Priest said. He grabbed a beer from the fridge. "I'm heading up onto the roof to watch the sun set."

———

Priest sat on his roof in a lime-green lounge chair that weighed a ton, which he liked because he didn't have to worry about it blowing away, even when El Niño rolled in from the Pacific or the Santa Anas tumbled down the canyons from the high desert. Priest nursed his beer, listening to the clattering of palm tree fonds in the breeze, wondering if Dusty and Nikki were still downstairs or if they had left, either separately or together.

Then Dusty appeared, standing at the foot of the lounge chair, her arms crossed.

"Thank you," Dusty said.

"Are you and Nikki back together?"

"Yup."

"Is Nikki leaving the life?"

"We're on schedule for that."

"Nikki thought you killed Parris," Priest said. "She thought you disappeared Nikki's stalker. You'd think she'd have more faith in you."

"Hey," Dusty said, "even you pictured me in that blue wig. I'm sorry you hate her so much."

"Oh, c'mon! I found her for you. Would I do that if I hated her?"

"Of course, you would."

"Because I'm a pro?" Priest asked.

"Because you care about *me*," Dusty said, "as much as you care about anything or anybody."

Dusty was still angry about Tarquin.

"Do you want to know Nikki's real name?" Priest asked.

"No."

"Don't you think it's weird that I know it and you don't?"

"I can live with it," Dusty said.

"You'll laugh," Priest said. "It's a normal name spelled really stupid."

But Dusty didn't want to play.

Priest said, "It just seems like, with Parris gone, this would be an ideal time for Nikki to hang up her stilettos."

"Giselle wants to move into management," Dusty said. "She asked Nikki to give her another six months before leaving. Giselle's already contacted some of Parris's other clients."

"When you say 'clients' do you mean 'customers'?"

"I mean four other working girls and two boys. Do you have any other questions?"

Priest did, but he already knew the answers to those questions, and they weren't going to help close this rift with Dusty.

"My turn," Dusty said. "Is it true that Cody Fiso strangled you before he threw you off the Venice Pier?"

"Yup." Priest pointed at his forehead. "A wave smacked me into a pylon. I cut my head on some mussels."

"That cut isn't from a mussel. What did you do to piss Fiso off?"

Priest told her about Fiso and Charlie McGinn and Brother Thomas.

"Cody Fiso threw you off the Venice Pier because he didn't want to become a legend if it meant ruining Charlie McGinn's new life as a monk?"

"You think Fiso did it out of principle," Priest said. "But Cody Fiso is all about how things look. How would it *look* for

Fiso to find Charlie McGinn and then expose him to the world he left behind? Bad. That's all he cares about. His image."

Dusty shook her head. She thought Cody Fiso was not a venal giant. She thought Fiso had decided to allow Charlie McGinn to keep his secret and live anonymously in his hermit-hut in the mountains out of kindness and human empathy.

People were blind when it came to other people.

"Thank you for finding Nikki," Dusty said. "I'd appreciate it if you sent me an invoice."

"I'm not going to do that."

"I'd appreciate it if you did."

Dusty left. Priest called after her, "Well, I'm still your friend if you aren't mine. And now I feel like I'm back in high school."

He had no idea if she heard him. He hoped not.

———

The next morning, Priest got a text from Baz, asking him to meet her down at the chess table between the paddle-ball courts. She was down there already, eating from a giant bag of kettle-corn.

The news wasn't good. The Clark County district attorney had not found enough evidence to bring charges against Bettina Subaric for the attack on Priest or any other person or persons.

"You knew it was going to go this way," Priest said.

"Looking at it as a defense lawyer," Baz said, "I couldn't imagine a prosecutor thick enough to think he or she could win in trial."

"How long before the Clark County sheriff issues an arrest warrant for me and/or Dusty?"

"Against her lawyer's advice, Bettina Subaric has declined to press assault and battery, trespassing, or theft charges," Baz said.

"Why?" Priest asked.

"Ms. Subaric said the two of you obviously had major emotional problems. She suggested you stop spending time with each other and consult a mental health professional."

Old Man Orange must have paid Bettina off. She wanted to sever all ties, to let it all fade away, like none of it had ever happened.

"Well, Dusty and I aren't spending much time together, that's for sure," Priest said. "The good news is that now you can see Detective Diodato socially."

"Next time you need a lawyer, you call someone else," Baz said.

————

February turned to March.

It had been two weeks since Priest had seen Dusty or Baz. The only people he'd spoken more than four words to were Yorben on the fishing pier, Nathan playing his piano for tips across from the Sidewalk Café, Flat-Earth Beck, and Olive, on the phone.

His father had called from prison, but Priest was in the shower and the rules didn't allow him to call back.

The wound on Priest's forehead still looked red, but it had stopped oozing. The strangulation marks on his throat had faded, so he would soon be able to remove the neck brace when he went out in public. Priest surfed and paddle-boarded and found himself wishing that Cody Fiso would call in one of his four obligatory cases.

Ten o'clock in the morning on a Tuesday, Priest received a call from Ms. Jacinto at the California Department of Social Services. Ms. Jacinto worked for the Foster Caregiver Policy and Support Unit. She wanted to know if she was speaking to Xavier

Priestly of 1903½ Ocean Front Walk, Venice, California, and, if so, was he related to Tarquin Xavier Orange?

"Yes."

"What is your relationship to Tarquin, Mr. Priestly?"

"I'm his father," Priest said. "Biological father. I only found out about him—"

Ms. Jacinto didn't care how or when Priest discovered he had a son. Tarquin's current legal guardian, his grandfather, Mr. Anthony Orange, had been arrested early this morning and placed in custody awaiting booking and arraignment. Ms. Jacinto only cared about whether or not Priest was willing to take in Tarquin Xavier Orange, at least temporarily.

"Yes. Do I need to come and get him?"

"Definitely not," Ms. Jacinto said.

She asked whether Priest would take Tarquin under the auspices of "Formal Kinship Care" or "Informal Kinship Care."

"What's the difference?" Priest asked.

"A state subsidy," Ms. Jacinto said.

"I'll take him for free," Priest said. "Why can't I come and get him?"

"Policy," Ms. Jacinto said. "First, we have to establish that you are willing. Then we establish that you are able."

Priest gave her Baz's email, so that Ms. Jacinto, the Department of Social Services, the Foster Caregiver and Policy Support Unit, and the Kinship Support Services Program could all copy Baz on all further communications.

"When will he get here?" Priest said.

"If everything goes smoothly, anytime between now and the end of forever," Ms. Jacinto said. "We will be in touch. Goodbye."

"Wait, Ms. Jacinto? Can you tell me why Tarquin's grandfather was arrested?"

"I have no idea," she said. "Goodbye."

Priest called Baz on her personal cellphone. When she didn't pick up, he texted that he knew that she wanted him to get a new lawyer, but he hadn't got around to it yet and something urgent had come up concerning Tarquin.

Baz called him back immediately. "What happened?"

"Tarquin's grandfather got arrested, the boy needs a place to stay, and Child Services called me."

"What did you say?"

"Oh, c'mon! Do you have to ask?"

"Yes," Baz said. "Sadly, I have to ask. That's why I'm asking. What did you say?"

"I told them I'd take him and nobody has to give me money," Priest said.

"Well, good."

"They said I can't just go get him."

"No."

"What happens next seems really complicated."

"Priest, what do you *want* to happen next?"

"I want his grandfather to be imprisoned so that Tarquin can come and live with me. I want to be his official guardian. Or adopt him? Whatever. So what happens next to make that happen?"

"Let me look into the situation with his grandfather," Baz said. "I'll get back to you."

Priest cleaned up the apartment, stocked the refrigerator, bought a bigger television, and waited.

29

Priest didn't leave his house the entire next day. When he finally left to pick up a burrito from El Tarasco for dinner, he left word with Beck that he'd be back in ten minutes, in case social workers showed up.

When he got back, he found Dusty leaning on his garage door.

"You want half a burrito?" Priest asked.

Dusty followed Priest into his kitchen. She stood, hands on her hips. Priest wasn't sure he'd ever seen Dusty place her hands on her hips outside of checking for a gun or taser or throwing star.

"I talked to Baz," Dusty said. "She's looking into how you get Tarquin on a permanent basis."

"Yeah. Old Man Orange got arrested. I don't know why."

"It's quite a story. You don't know?"

"I assume he got caught doing something nefarious?"

"It's possible Baz thinks that. More likely she's deluding herself. But I think I have a pretty good idea what happened. So, I'm going to ask you again. Do you know why Old Man Orange was arrested? . . . Is that supposed to be a shrug? Human beings shrug with two shoulders, not one."

"I've only heard from Child Services and Baz. Neither of them have told me anything."

"Priest," Dusty said, "why didn't you come to me? . . . Honest to God, you one-shoulder-shrug at me one more time and I will twist that shoulder out of its socket. Answer me one question, no bullshit."

"Okay."

"How'd you get that scar between your eyes?"

Priest touched the wound. If he'd gone and got stitches the night Dean hit him, it would have healed up cleaner and not so angry red. But because he'd used Super Glue, it might be permanent, like the mark of Cain, proclaiming his guilt to the world.

"A Vegas cop slammed the butt of his Smith & Wesson into my head," Priest said.

Dusty turned her back on Priest. Turned around to face him, then repeated the move. She literally did not know what to do with herself.

"Give me money," she said.

"How much?"

"Enough for client privilege."

"Shouldn't *you* be the one giving *me* money?" Priest asked.

"No. You're officially hiring me as your private security consultant."

"Why?"

"Client privilege," Dusty said.

"Why bother?" Priest asked. "You don't mind lying to police or perjuring yourself on the stand. You don't have to claim any kind of privilege."

Dusty snapped her fingers. Priest gave her twenty bucks.

"If law enforcement were to get a warrant to trace your

mobile location on the night James Alden Dean was assaulted," Dusty asked, "what would they find?"

"James Alden Dean?" Priest said. "The old-time Hollywood idol who died when he crashed his Porsche?"

"Priest, we got privilege covered. Just tell me the truth."

"My mobile was with my friend Yorben Ybarra, who was fishing at Salmon Creek, north of San Simeon."

"Will Yorben testify that you and he were together?"

"If anyone asks him, yeah."

"Fishing?"

"That's right."

"For what?" Dusty asked.

"Steelhead."

"Catch anything?"

"Yes," Priest said. "Steelhead."

"You got any in your freezer as proof?"

"Nope."

"Why? Have you already eaten it all?"

"No. It was a catch-and-release trip," Priest said.

"You have a fishing license?"

Priest went to his junk drawer and found his license. A couple of receipts came with it. Both from the night in question.

Gas from Morro Bay.

Paid in cash.

Two meals, two coffees, from the McDonald's drive-through in Cambria.

Paid in cash.

Dusty nodded, satisfied. "Can you think of any way or reason for the Vegas police to tie you to an assault on James Alden Dean?"

"I'd have said no, but here you are, hawking all over me, so somehow *you* found a connection."

"Baz said Old Man Orange was arrested after he sent some guys to beat up James Alden Dean."

"*Some* guys? How many?"

"Don't puff up your chest."

"Multiple assailants? Dean must have fought like a lion."

"Baz discovered that, while Dean was being treated in the emergency room, in pain and under the influence of medication, in the presence of several members of his family—most of whom work in law enforcement—James Alden Dean threatened to kill Anthony Orange."

"For sending how many guys to rough him up?"

"Officer Dean's big brother is a captain in the Organized Crime Bureau. It turns out that Anthony Orange is known to the police. Real-estate fraud. Insurance fraud. Money laundering."

"Old time Vegas crook. A dying breed," Priest said.

"Anthony Orange has gotten himself out of trouble a couple of times by snitching," Dusty said. "The Vegas cops knew exactly where to look to pop him on multiple charges."

"Huh," Priest said. "Dean's family decided on a lawful approach, instead of letting Dean kill the old man?"

"It happens," Dusty said. "Even in a family of cops who should know better."

"Did Officer Dean say why Anthony Orange had him attacked by several very tough guys who really knew how to handle themselves?" Priest asked.

"Dean says that Anthony Orange is under the mistaken impression that Dean owes him money from the sale of a condo eight years ago."

"What does Orange say?"

"He denies sending anyone to rough Dean up but admitted that Dean owes him money from the sale of that condo."

"Did my name come up?"

"Nope."

"Then everything is fine."

"Unless Alden James Dean sees your face," Dusty said.

"No worries. I did the hat gambit."

Dusty waited for more, until she realized he wasn't kidding. "What the hell is the hat gambit?"

"It's a well-known psychological ploy," Priest said. "Wear a distinctive hat, nobody remembers your face."

"Where'd you hear that?"

"From my father," Priest said.

"Your father?"

"Yes," Priest said. "Why do you say it like that?"

"Because your father is locked up in prison for the rest of his life."

"I'm pretty sure my father didn't choose a hat as distinctive as mine."

"You can never go back to Vegas," Dusty said.

"Okay."

"If you do, you have to wear lifts, get a nose job, and grow a mustache."

"You're underestimating the hat gambit."

"I don't know how you won that fight."

"I was well trained," Priest said. "I follow instructions well."

"I mean, what made you think you could pull something off like that without me?"

"I had no choice. You weren't speaking to me."

"That was my mistake," Dusty conceded. "Your mistake was not telling me your stupid plan and letting me commit the necessary violence. Your other mistake was not letting me know that you had every intention of rising to the occasion when it came to Tarquin, even if it was in a super stupid way."

"I'm not proud of how long it took me to come to that decision," Priest said. "Anything else?"

"Yeah," Dusty said. "How did you know that James Alden Dean wouldn't just kill the old man?"

"I didn't," Priest said.

Dusty reached out her hand to shake Priest's. When Priest took it, her grasp felt like a tiny, iron vice-grip. "All choice is made in the mind," she said.

"All acceptance is made by the soul," Priest responded.

"I've been a good influence on you," Dusty said. "A necessary counterbalance to all that seminary bullshit."

30

Tarquin appeared at Priest's door the next morning, a surly big-nosed boy sandwiched between two middle-aged women. The taller was Mia, from the Southern Nevada Children's Advocacy Center. She wore a CELEBRATE BLACK HISTORY T-shirt. The shorter was Adrienne, who worked for the Los Angeles County Department of Children and Family Services. She wore bright orange Hoka sneakers and a blue cardigan cut like a sports jacket. Tarquin wore his backpack and carried a knotted black garbage bag stuffed with clothes. Mia said that Tarquin and Priest would be permitted to enter Anthony Orange's apartment in the Jockey Club to fetch the rest of Tarquin's belongings as soon as Vegas law enforcement gave the okay.

Priest figured that he'd have to wear a wig and false moustache on that day.

"Will my Pops be there?" Tarquin asked.

"That depends on whether or not the judge grants him bail," Adrienne said.

Mia and Adrienne tornadoed around Priest's place, the

strangest combination of warmth and tough talk Priest had ever come across.

"This floor is all you?" Adrienne asked.

"Yes," Priest said. "I own the entire building."

"You live alone?" Mia asked.

"I got a tenant on the ground floor who has a room at the back and rents out bicycles and scooters to tourists at the front. His rent mostly covers the mortgage. There's a roof deck. And there's that long balcony there that looks down on the courtyard."

"I've seen worse," Mia said.

"Oh, there's worse," said Adrienne.

Adrienne and Mia laughed and slapped air toward each other. Priest and Tarquin exchanged quick glances; neither had a clue what the two social workers found so funny.

Adrienne and Mia took turns asking questions and poking around the apartment and checking things off on their battered government-issue tablets. Tarquin slumped on the couch. Priest leaned forward, propped on his elbows at the kitchen table, trying not to jiggle his legs. Priest was worried that, when Tarquin showed up, they hadn't hugged. They hadn't shaken hands or bumped fists. Nothing. Adrienne and Mia must have noticed, but Priest reminded himself that he had seen worse parent/child dynamics in the course of his investigations. As social workers working the sharp bloody point of the stick, surely Adrienne and Mia must have seen unimaginably worse.

"Me or you?" Adrienne asked Mia, standing midway between Priest and Tarquin.

"It's your city," Mia said, "go ahead and tell them the hows and whats of their new lives."

Adrienne informed Priest and Tarquin that she'd be checking in on them often. Maybe every day. Maybe several times a day. She was not required to give any warning.

"You get that?" Mia asked. "No advance warning. Day or night."

"I'm an insomniac," Adrienne said. "And you know what they say?"

"Misery loves company," Mia said.

"Especially in the middle of the night!"

Another inside social-work joke, because they laughed again and slapped the air toward each other.

"This situation here is contingent upon forthcoming character references," Adrienne told Priest, twirling her finger around and pointing at the floor.

Olive and Martin would provide good references. So would Baz. If only for the good of the boy. He knew a couple of other clients and lawyers, including an assistant D.A. who thought well of him. Cody Fiso would give a good reference, though it would count as a favor. People respected Fiso on a cellular level. People were idiots.

"You got a stable income, Mr. Priestly?" Mia asked.

"I'm a freelance legal investigator," Priest said. "If it helps, I can take a salaried position with a law firm or a security company."

"Helps what?" Tarquin asked.

"Ooh, private eye!" Adrienne said.

"You know they hate to be called that," Mia said.

"A saddlery position helps what?" Tarquin asked again.

"If you have to stay here with me longer," Priest said. "Just in case. Long term."

"No way," Tarquin said.

"You're welcome," Priest said. "In fact, I like you being here. Think of it as a second home."

Too far! Priest's stomach clenched when Tarquin announced that he'd rather be a *foster* kid than live with Priest. He'd rather be in an *orphanage*. If they left him here, he'd run away before the end of the day. He said that Priest liked to watch him take showers.

"Oh, c'mon!" Priest said.

Apparently, Adrienne and Mia had been here before. Maybe every day. They told Tarquin that, if this didn't work out, he'd get his wish and go into the foster system.

"See if you like that better," Mia said, dry as a Santa Ana.

"Pops said you legally got to do a test," Tarquin said. "In case he isn't my biological father?"

"That's in the works," Mia said. "But a smart boy like you gots to know, every time he looks in the mirror, that there's no doubt this man sitting here is your daddy. A daddy who wants you. That's a beautiful thing."

"It's bullshit," Tarquin said.

"I'd like to see Tarquin registered in school as soon as possible," Adrienne said.

"School?" Tarquin asked. "What the fuck? Pops said he'd be out in a couple days."

"I pre-registered Tarquin at the Magnet over on Pacific," Priest said. "Seven-minute walk door to door. I timed it. They expect him Monday."

"Anyone tries to make me go to school, I'm outta here."

Mia and Adrienne provided Priest a list of improvements he was expected to make immediately, including a lock on the medicine cabinet in Priest's bathroom and a lock on the cabinet where he kept his liquor.

"Piece of advice? Know exactly how many cans of beer you got in the fridge."

Tarquin needed a closet. A wardrobe would do as long as it got bolted to the wall so an earthquake didn't crush the boy. A desk with a light where Tarquin could study. Parental controls on the internet. An inspector would come by to make sure that the tenant downstairs wasn't storing any chemicals detrimental to a child. Mr. Priestly might want to give his tenant fair warning.

"There's more," Mia said.

Garbage can with a lid under the kitchen sink. Smoke detectors. Sprinklers. The roof deck had to be brought up to safety code. Until then, the access hatch was to be kept locked.

The two social workers moved toward the front door, nodding and shrugging at each other, coming to the mutual, unspoken conclusion that they were comfortable—at least temporarily—leaving Tarquin with Priest. As they exited the apartment, Mia beckoned Priest to join them on the other side of the door, then down the stairs to Speedway, leaving Tarquin alone up in the apartment.

"I was present at Tarquin's last meeting with his grandfather before Mr. Orange was taken into custody," Mia said, "and I gotta advise you, you got a steep hill to climb with the boy."

"Okay."

"Mr. Orange told the child to remember that you never wanted him and that he always did."

"I only let Tarquin go back to his grandfather because that's what he said he wanted."

"Trust me, Mr. Priestly," Adrienne said, "kids know what they want about half the time. And they're usually wrong."

"They're wrong about the other half the time, too," Mia said from inside the car.

"You got to climb that hill every minute of every day, even if you think he's not noticing," Adrienne said. "You gotta make young Tarquin up there feel like you wanted him the second you found out he existed. Even if that's not strictly true, which is a question I am not asking you."

After the social workers drove away, Priest climbed the stairs up to the apartment thinking, *Fuck that old man*. Then he remembered that Anthony Orange wanted the boy so much that he'd hired a contract killer to keep him. Right or wrong, that showed commitment. Priest half-expected Tarquin to have bolted, but there he was, sitting in the same spot, looking miserable, picking at the piping on the couch cushion. They were alone for the first time since they'd waited for Dusty to find them in the coffee shop after Blue Wig tried to crush Priest to death against a tree. Someone on the paddle-ball courts below hollered, "Out!"

"Where am I supposed to smoke if I can't go on the roof? Like, that balcony?"

"I'm sorry about your grandfather," Priest said.

"It's not your fault," Tarquin said. "Fuckin' cops. He did some so-called friends a favor, and when he wouldn't rat out those friends, the cops arrested him."

Priest hoped Tarquin would eventually discern the unpleasant truth that his grandfather was a shifty old crook, *without* discerning that Priest was the one who put his grandfather, the only person Tarquin loved, in prison.

"They'll never get Pops," Tarquin said. "They say he's gonna get ten years, but Pops has slick lawyers. He'll get out on bail, and I'll go back and live with him at the Jockey Club. Fuck your magnets."

"Were you there when they arrested him?"

Tarquin's pugnacity abandoned him. Priest could see it in the boy's face. Cops cuffing Orange. Orange telling Tarquin it was fine, don't worry, they'd be back together in no time. Mia or one of her associates either there already or called the minute cops realized there was a minor on the premises with no place to go, except for a recently discovered biological father in another city, another state.

"Where do I smoke if I can't go on the roof?"

Priest decided to get all the bad stuff out of the way at once, like pulling off a Band-Aid or yanking a tooth. He'd take Officer Harb's advice to say "no" to the boy. To let him know that somebody cared.

No more smoking. Not tobacco. Not weed.

"Fuck that," Tarquin said.

From his wallet, Priest extracted the titanium card with the geometric shapes that Olive had given him, extending it to Tarquin.

"What's this shit?" Tarquin asked.

"It makes it easier to quit," Priest said.

"How?" Tarquin asked.

"It has electro-magnetic vibrations. Ask your Aunt Olive next time you see her."

"Don't call that crazy lady my aunt. We aren't family. Pops is the only family I got, and I'm the only family he's got," Tarquin said.

But he took the card. Then he stomped into the guest room—*his* room—slammed the door, and locked it, which meant he wouldn't be running away today.

Seventy-two long, miserable, tense, contentious hours later, after Tarquin's first day at the Magnet School, Baz appeared with the official DNA test that proved that Tarquin Xavier Orange was the biological son of Xavier Priestly. Priest felt something uncoil in his guts. He'd been afraid, on some level, that there'd been a mistake. That Tarquin wasn't his. He didn't feel relief, exactly. He felt . . . not pride. Not achievement. Vindication? Gratification? Something new? Priest had no idea what he felt. Something new, he supposed.

Tarquin advised Baz to fuck the test. He didn't believe it. Baz went through it with the boy, line by line, talking about the *locus column* and *alleles* and a *combined paternity index* of over 500,000, which translated into a probability of paternity of 99.9998%

"That's not a hundred percent," Tarquin said.

"Legally, it is," Baz said.

"I'm not changing my name," Tarquin said, heading for the door.

"Where are you going?" Priest asked. "In case Adrienne shows up?"

"To see if Yorben caught a shark," Tarquin said.

He slammed the door on the way out.

"Going great, huh?" Baz asked.

"He's still here. I haven't choked him in his sleep. We've survived two snap investigations from Child Services. So, yeah, going great. He seemed determined to make you say there's no real proof that I'm his father."

"Or," Baz said, "he was trying to make me say that it is absolutely 100% true that you're his father."

Baz was looking at him with compassion instead of disdain, so Priest asked, "What's going on?"

"Dusty says you're responsible for getting the old man put in jail," Baz said. "And getting Tarquin here with you."

"Whatever Dusty told you is just her own private theory."

"She didn't say how," Baz said. "You want to tell me what you did?"

"C'mon, Baz . . ."

"I'm not stupid, Priest," Baz said. "The only fulcrum I can find where you might have applied pressure is the assault on the cop. I thought Dusty did that. She promised me it wasn't her. Was it you?"

"It wasn't Dusty. Everyone always wants to blame Dusty, but it wasn't her."

"I'm having trouble seeing you as someone capable of such violence," Baz said.

"Maybe the situation escalated beyond my control."

"Violence does that."

"I couldn't figure any other way to get Anthony Orange out of the picture without Tarquin ending up hating my guts," Priest said. "Maybe even more than he does already. If that's possible."

"Priest, if you'd come at Tarquin straight on, he'd know how much you wanted him. Now, as far as he's concerned, he's a responsibility you didn't want but took on out of a sense of duty."

"That's completely what he is," Priest said. "It's the truth."

"For something you didn't want, you chased Tarquin down diabolically hard."

Baz offered to check with her firm, to convince them to bring Priest in-house as an investigator so he'd get employee benefits, which would make him look even more appealing to Child Services when Baz started the process to make him Tarquin's permanent legal guardian.

"I might have to take you up on that," Priest said. "Thank you, Baz. Thank you."

"The reason I couldn't look you in the face for a while was because I couldn't stand the thought of you not stepping up to do right by your boy."

"Maybe it was you who forced me to do the right thing, Baz," Priest said. "What you think matters to me."

"Don't put that on me. And the next time I goad you to do the right thing, maybe you could do it in a way that isn't one hundred percent completely wrong?"

Baz left. Ten minutes later, Adrienne from Child Services was at the door.

"Spot check!" she announced and pushed past Priest into

the apartment, sniffing for trouble, looking for deficits, flops, fiascos. "Where's Tarquin?"

"Out on the pier."

"Let's go," she said.

To Priest's relief, Tarquin was standing near Yorben, staring down at the surfers. Not smoking. Olive's titanium card jutted from between his teeth. Dusty had given him a chain so that he could wear it around his neck, dog-tag style. Adrienne waved at Tarquin. He gave her the finger.

"Okay," Adrienne said, patting Priest on the back. "Goin' good."

"Is it?" Priest asked.

"Honey, I'd love to give you a pep talk, but I do not have the energy." She pointed at Tarquin. "He's the luckiest kid I've seen today. You, I'm not so sure."

31

"Why we gotta get up so early?" Tarquin asked.

Over the past three weeks, Priest had found it best to answer Tarquin's questions in earnest, even when they were insulting, facetious, sarcastic, passive aggressive, or rhetorical.

"Visiting hours commence at 8:30 am," Priest said. "The later you get there, the longer you gotta wait, and maybe you don't get in . . . Don't roll your eyes. It's a long way to go to wait in a shitty place for nothing."

"I don't see why I even gotta go."

Inmate Oliver Priestly, recently moved from his longtime home in FCI Sheridan in Oregon to United States Penitentiary - Lompoc, had asked to meet his grandson in person.

"Your grandfather got moved to a closer prison up in Lompoc. He really wants to meet you."

Tarquin chewed on his titanium talisman. "I got two grand-fathers, and they're both in jail."

"One's in jail," Priest said. "The other's in federal prison."

"Big difference."

"There is a big difference," Priest said.

He didn't bother telling Tarquin that jail could be worse than prison. As the charges against him piled up, Anthony Orange had been denied bail. If the wrong people found out that the old man had snitched "from time to time," it could go really wrong for him. Every time Priest felt a twinge of guilt about that, Dusty reminded him that the old man had tried to have him murdered.

"You want me to go, I'll go," Tarquin said.

Things had microscopically improved between Priest and Tarquin, or maybe Priest had just adapted to having the miserable little shit around the house. If Tarquin smoked, he did it when Priest wasn't looking. But his clothes didn't stink of cigarettes, so maybe he'd actually quit. Tarquin had made, at least, one friend in school, a stocky clenched-jaw kind of kid called Kicker with wild sunburned hair. Priest had no idea why the kid was called Kicker, and when he asked, Kicker shrugged and said he'd always been called Kicker. Flat-Earth Beck knew most of the kids who hung around the beach, skate park, and pier, and he told Priest that Kicker was "good people." Tarquin made fun of the way Kicker dressed in hoodies zipped to the chin, blue board shorts, dark knee socks pulled to his knees, and camouflage Vans, but Kicker took no offense. Kicker surfed and got Tarquin into surfing. Everyone knew Kicker, probably because, unlike most groms, he wore a neon green wetsuit.

"No shark is gonna mistake my ass for a delicious seal meal," Kicker said.

Priest figured Kicker's single mom, Ann, who seemed to have about six waitressing jobs, had bought Kicker the wetsuit on clearance, and Kicker was the kind of boy who turned lemons into lemonade. Or neon green limes, in this case.

Tarquin asked Priest to buy him a wetsuit, the first thing he'd asked for since moving in. When Priest and Dusty took

Tarquin shopping, he'd agonized between the cool black wet-suits most surfers wore and Kicker's green wetsuit.

"Color is kind of Kicker's thing," Tarquin said.

When Dusty kicked him in the ankle, Priest realized that Tarquin was waiting for him to weigh in, probably so Tarquin could do the opposite of what Priest advised, but still, it was something.

"Green is Kicker's thing," Priest said. "If you want colorful, make it a different color." Priest pointed at a black suit with orange shoulders. To his surprise, Tarquin agreed.

On the road at five a.m., Tarquin slept all the way to the McDonald's in Lompoc, where Priest woke the kid up.

"We got time to grab a quick breakfast."

As they ate, Tarquin complained about the clothes he had to wear to visit prison: black jeans, white long-sleeve, button-up shirt, laced shoes, socks.

"They got strict rules in prison, even for visitors," Priest said. "No T-shirts, no open-toe shoes. No tight clothing. And you gotta wear a bra."

"You think you're so funny, but you're not," Tarquin said.

Tarquin showed no emotion between McDonald's and the penitentiary. They parked, the boy squinting at the buildings.

"Maybe leave your titanium card in the car," Priest said.

"What if I don't want to?"

The fact that Tarquin asked it as a question rather than simply refusing was an example of the kind of microscopic im-provement Priest had noticed in their interactions.

"Up to you, but they might confiscate it."

"What's that?"

"They'll take it away from you. They might even keep it."

Tarquin grunted and stuffed the card in the glove box. He remained silent at each checkpoint. He looked back at Priest after going through a metal detector, probably wondering whether Priest was going to say "I told you so" about the titanium card, which stopped Priest from saying "I told you so." Questioned about his name and age, checked against a list, less and less oxygen in the air at each oppressive security check, Tarquin answered the detention officers' questions as briefly as he could with zero attitude. It was nearly ten by the time they sat down in a big room full of plastic tables and folding chairs. There must have been a hundred people around them. Kids. Noise. Crying. Upset. Joy. Intense sexual frustration. Rejection, imprecations, arguments, strained smiles, big laughs, hoots and hollers, grievous disappointments and broken hearts.

"Here he comes," Priest said, jerking his chin toward his father, who was being escorted across the room by a guard.

Oliver Priestly had spent the last decade in various prisons, with decades left to serve, and every day showed. He looked like a fit seventy, which was fine, except that he was sixty. He had all his hair, but it was white at the temples and black on top, which made it look like a toupee. Even hunched, Oliver Priestly stood two inches taller than his son. He wore prison-issue brown glasses, plastic frames, fastened around his neck by a red and orange work-boot shoelace. Priest felt the familiar tightening in his throat. His father. Dad. The criminal. The inmate. The convict.

"You're only allowed to touch at the beginning of the visit and at the end," Priest warned Tarquin as Oliver Priestly approached.

"I gotta touch him?" Tarquin asked.

"Just shake his hand."

"X," his father said. "Nice to see you in person."

"Dad," Priest said.

Trying to set an example for Tarquin, Priest hugged his

father, which he hadn't done since he was a child. Once in there, he almost forgot to let go.

"Thank you," his father said. "Introduce us."

"Tarquin Xavier Orange, this is your grandfather, Oliver Robert Priestly."

"You're gonna say me 'n him got the same nose," Tarquin said. *Him* meaning Priest. The boy still didn't know what to call Priest or how to refer to him. Even to Kicker. Even to Dusty. Yorben told Priest that Tarquin referred to him as "Mr. Priestly" in a snotty tone.

"As you can see from my handsome face," Oliver Priestly said, "X got that nose from his mother's side of the family. Difference is, on you it works."

For that, he was rewarded. Tarquin stuck out his hand to shake.

Oliver took it. "Nice to meet you. What do you go by? Tarquin? Tarq?"

"Whatever."

"Where'd your mother come up with that name? Tarquin?"

"From a vampire in a book she liked," Tarquin said.

"Tarquin Blackwood?" Oliver said, sitting down. "*The Vampire Chronicles*. Some of the other characters call him Quinn . . . Don't make a face at me, X. I teach convicts to read. They like vampires. They identify."

"My mother called me Quinn," Tarquin said, his voice strained. "But only her."

"Got it." Oliver looked at Priest to make sure that he got it, too. Tarquin was grief-stricken. His whole life disrupted. Priest should most definitely *not* call the boy Quinn. Point taken. Thanks, Dad.

"You can call me Oliver," Oliver told Tarquin. "Or by my inmate number. It's got eleven digits, so people inside shorten it to Goose."

If Oliver was trying to distract Tarquin from thinking about Rachel, it worked.

"Goose?" Tarquin asked.

"There's a lot of zeroes in my number . . . You don't get it? Zeroes? Goose Eggs? So, 'Goose'?"

Priest had no idea whether this was true or if Oliver had made it up on the spot.

"Not to mention, I got a big 'O' at the beginning of my real name. Oliver. Some people call me Zero. Some people shorten it down to Zee. A Canadian called me Zed and that kinda stuck up in Oregon."

"So, you're a bank robber?" Tarquin asked.

"Retired," Oliver said. "What do you do for a living?"

Priest couldn't believe that Tarquin smiled.

It went like that for half an hour, Tarquin trying not to like this new grandfather out of loyalty to the other one, but torn because like most fatherless boys, he ached for a substitute, and he still hadn't accepted Priest as anything more than a babysitter. Priest brought Oliver up to date on a couple cases, told him about giving Charlie McGinn to Cody Fiso and Cody Fiso giving Charlie back. Oliver talked about tutoring inmates in auto mechanics, helping them to get their GEDs. When Tarquin went to get something to drink from the vending machines, Oliver asked, "You two having a tough time?"

"Basically, we're roommates who don't like each other," Priest said.

"What's the main stumbling block?"

"His grandfather—the other one—told Tarquin that I didn't really want him," Priest said.

"Did you?"

"Did I what?"

"Really want him?" his father asked.

"What's it matter? There isn't anyone else to take him in."

Priest's father nodded. "Am I right to assume that the other grandfather is the same fucker who hired a contract killer to murder you?" his father asked.

"Tarquin has only two grandfathers, Dad. So yeah. The other one. Who isn't you. Who wanted me dead to make sure Tarquin would stay with him. Tarquin doesn't know that, by the way, and I see no reason to tell him."

"The boy deserves to know what kind of man his grandfather really is."

"Trust me, for Tarquin, taking a hit out on me would only prove Orange loved him," Priest said.

"What did you do to get the boy?" his father asked.

"What?"

"You ended up with the boy. How did you manage that?"

"Nothing to do with me. The old man got arrested. Money laundering. Insurance fraud. Receiving stolen goods. I'm the kid's only living relative."

"A natural unfolding of the Buddhist universe, right?" his father said. "Except you aren't Buddhist. So, I gotta ask you again. What did you do?"

What Priest had done was drive to Vegas, nearly get himself killed and nearly killed someone else, and—not to put too fine a point on it—risked getting the old man killed, too.

"Nothing," Priest said.

"Okay, you don't want to tell me. Only fair, right? I kept secrets from you for years. I'm reaping what I sowed. But take my advice, X. Let Tarquin know what you did. Let him know you went above and beyond to bring him into your home and make it his home."

Priest leaned forward and whispered, "Dad, what I did will end up putting his grandfather, the only person in the world that he loves, in prison for, at least, ten years, where he'll probably get killed as a snitch."

"Jesus. Really?" Oliver said. "Fuck me! Do not tell him that. It's better he doesn't know . . . Don't dead-eye me like that. People got a right to change their point of view when they get more facts. You're a very difficult person. That's where the kid gets it, if you're wondering."

"I never thought I'd be getting parental insights from you," Priest said.

Oliver Priestly waggled his head back and forth as though Priest had made a good point in a political discussion. "What you and Tarquin gotta do," he said, "is bond."

"How?" Priest asked. "Play catch in the backyard?"

"Scoff all you want, X, but find something the two of you can do together."

"Like you and me? Except we never did anything together."

"I'm one of those guys who's gonna be way better as a grandfather than a father," Oliver said.

"Setting a pretty low bar." Priest looked up as Tarquin banged on the vending machine. A nearby guard told him to cut it out. "Tarquin and I have exactly zero converging interests."

"I can help. Follow my lead."

"Follow your lead? Where?"

"Trust me," his father said. "And you're welcome in advance."

When Tarquin came back, Oliver Priestly leaned forward and indicated that Priest and Tarquin should lean forward, too. When Priest hung back, Oliver said, "If you make me pull on your ear, they'll end our visit." Priest leaned forward.

"I don't think I'm getting out of here soon, son," Oliver told Priest. He'd never called Priest "son" before. And "not getting out of here soon" was a staggering understatement.

"You gotta think positively, Dad," Priest said, trying to follow his father's lead. "Visualize and crystallize the future you desire."

"What?" his father said.

"Don't give up, is what I'm saying."

"I'm just facing facts," his father said. "So, I'm gonna tell you something. Consider it insurance. In case I die in here."

"Like, get shivved?" Tarquin whispered.

Oliver touched his nose and pointed at Tarquin. He said a string of nonsense words and numbers. He insisted that Priest remember the letters and that Tarquin remember the numbers, then made them repeat their parts to him and each other until he was satisfied that they had it memorized.

"Don't tell anybody," Oliver said. "Don't write anything down. And whatever happens, don't forget. Promise."

Tarquin promised first. Oliver looked at Priest.

"Right. Okay. I promise," Priest said. "You gonna tell us what it means?"

"Gotta go," Oliver said, standing up and waving at a guard. "Catch you next time."

And he walked off.

"What the fuck?" Tarquin asked.

"I haven't got a clue," Priest said.

Halfway home, Tarquin said, "Hey, X?"

The first time Tarquin had ever called him by a name.

"Yeah?" Priest asked.

"I got a theory."

"About what?"

"About all that stuff Zed said."

Tarquin had decided to call his grandfather *Zed* and Priest *X*. They were an end-of-the-alphabet family.

"Let's hear it," Priest said.

"It's code."

"What kind of code? For what?"

"His treasure," Tarquin said, touching his nose in a perfect imitation of Priest's father.

"Who told you about the treasure?" Priest asked.

"Dusty," Tarquin said. "Zed gave you and me each half the code to find his treasure."

"Why?"

"Because you and me are Zed's only heirs," Tarquin said. "That's a big deal, being direct descendants. We're his blood."

As promised, Priest's bank-robber father had given Priest and Tarquin some common ground, a goal they could share and pursue together. Later, buying a copy of one of *The Vampire Chronicles* at Small World Books, Priest realized that his father had done more than provide a father-and-son objective for Priest and Tarquin. Oliver had provided a father-and-son objective for himself and Priest.

X and Zed were working together to persuade Tarquin Orange to be a Priestly.

32

May—a super-premium Southern California month, warmer than winter, sunnier than June Gloom.

Priest slumped over the side of the Venice Fishing Pier, gazing into the blue-green depths, and muttered Psalm 8:9 under his breath: "*The birds of the air, and the fishes of the sea, that pass through the paths of the sea.*"

"Bible magic again?" Yorben asked. "Looking for what you cannot see?"

Priest glanced to his left, his eye drawn by a bright flash of neon orange as Tarquin caught a wave south of the pier. Neon-green Kicker yelled profane encouragement.

"Here comes the Dirty Princess and whatnot," Yorben said.

"What do you mean, 'and whatnot'?" Priest asked.

"She's not alone."

"That'll be Nikki," Priest said without looking. "One day very soon, Nikki will leave the escort business, and Dusty will finally have the true love she's longed for her whole life."

"You suck at sarcasm," Yorben said. "That sounded like you meant it."

"A guy can say something and mean it but still know he's wrong," Priest said.

But it wasn't Nikki with Dusty. It was Baz.

And with Baz was Bettina Subaric.

Baz gestured for Priest to join them farther out along the pier, ten yards from Yorben.

"If you don't want Yorben to hear," Priest said, "we gotta go another five yards. He's got ears like a bat."

Baz moved another five yards, and they followed.

"You remember Bettina," Dusty said, like this was a champagne reception.

"Apparently, better than you do," Priest said. "I can hardly wait to hear what's going on here."

"Ms. Subaric has asked me to represent her in a certain matter," Baz said. "But I need to talk to you about it."

Usually, Baz had no problem turning down clients she didn't want to represent.

"She get popped for killing somebody new?" Priest asked. "Maybe this time in an orange wig?"

"I kind of need you to agree to work for me," Bettina said, "before we get into further specifics."

"I wouldn't be working for you. I'd be working for your lawyer," Priest said.

"This is going to take *forever*," Bettina told Baz.

"Does Baz know further specifics?" Priest asked.

"Baz knows—" Subaric said.

"No, no, no," Baz said. "My friends call me Baz. You call me Ms. Amerson."

"Ms. Amerson knows the general specifics," Bettina said, apparently taking no offense. "Not the specific further specifics."

"What the hell?" Priest said to Dusty.

"No comment, until I hear something worth commenting on," Dusty said, looking at Baz.

"There are compelling reasons why I'm considering taking Ms. Subaric on as a client," Baz said. "Ms. Subaric? Do we have your attention?"

Bettina was staring at Yorben.

"How could anyone miss a target that big?" Bettina asked.

Baz did the math and glared daggers at Priest. She turned to look out to sea. She needed Priest to understand that, if everybody agreed not to speak the unspoken, Baz might not feel compelled to tell Detective Diodato that Yorben Ybarra was the mystery man in the multi-colored mystery truck who returned fire when Blue Wig tried to kill Priest, an extraneous detail that sometimes kept Detective Diodato awake in the middle of the night, which Baz knew because Baz was currently spending the middle of most nights with Diodato.

"What do you think?" Priest asked Dusty.

"I still don't know anything worth commenting on," Dusty said.

"Yeah, but you still think something," Priest said.

"I think either take her on as a client," Dusty said, "or kill her."

"Prickly," Bettina said.

"Why would you accept a contract killer as a client?" Priest asked Baz.

"Never indicted. So, legally . . ." Baz said.

"She jabbed a needle in my neck. She tried to shoot me. She killed Parris Ferrer. She tried to run me over in front of my kid."

"What?" Baz asked. "What?"

"Forget I mentioned that last one," Priest said.

But Baz did the math again. She figured out what had happened in the Pacheco Pass and did not like it. This time, she glared at Dusty, who shrugged, confirming that she'd been part of that, too.

"Any other little surprises?" Baz asked.

"Maybe we could all agree that I'm a former contract killer?" Bettina said. "Out of the business? Move on from there?"

"Pro bono bit of lawyerly advice," Baz said. "Never say anything that stupid, out loud, again."

"People change jobs, Priest," Dusty said.

"Like Nikki?" Priest said. "How's that going?"

"Prickly," Dusty said.

"Bettina has recently moved full-time into her art career," Baz said.

"I guess now that law enforcement is on to you, your former gig as a contract killer is no longer viable?" Priest said.

"That's true," Bettina said. "But I was also recently featured on the most popular true-crime podcast on the planet."

"As a result, works of art that Ms. Subaric used to sell for a thousand dollars now go for a hundred thousand," Baz said. "After the Netflix show, those prices will skyrocket again. Possibly into seven figures. Quick warning: if you buy up that art now, you could expose yourselves to charges of insider trading. And yes, thanks to NFTs, that is now a thing."

"A Netflix show?" Dusty asked.

"Working title: *Killer Artist*," Baz said.

Priest thought of the sculpture beside the door in Anthony Orange's empty condo at The Jockey Club in Vegas. There was Tarquin's college tuition, if Priest had any luck steering Tarquin toward college. And if Dusty could go pick it up, since Priest had to avoid Vegas for the next decade or so.

"Crime pays in mysterious ways," Priest said.

"What Ms. Subaric is suggesting to me, in terms of representation," Baz said, "is worthy of our consideration."

"I can't help but notice you are being crazy careful in your word choice," Priest said.

"Her case will require the full-time attention of an investigator. I'm not saying it will make up for things she may or may not have done in the past, but if we are all able to set aside personal animosity, this case could have far-reaching effects that could benefit a lot of people."

"Would it help," Bettina asked, "if I promised you that, if I ever killed anyone—which I'm neither confirming nor denying—they genuinely deserved it?"

"*I* didn't deserve it," Priest said.

"I didn't kill you," Subaric said.

"If we decided to take her out, how would we do it?" Priest asked Dusty.

"Normally, I'd suggest you let me kill her right now."

"Normally?" Baz said.

"*Now* now?" Priest asked. "Here and now?"

"Yup," Dusty said. "I shoot her. Plant Yorben's backpack gun on her dead body. You give a sworn statement that I shot her in self-defense."

"Hello?" Baz said.

"Right," Dusty said. "Baz would never agree to cover up a cold-blooded execution, even for her friends."

"Even when the executionee is a maniacal psychopath who deserves executing?" Priest asked.

Dusty shook her head.

Priest was beginning to suspect that Dusty trusted Baz's contention, that perhaps they should take on Subaric as a client for reasons thus far unexplained. If Priest were still a religious man, he'd ask God for a sign. But he'd left all that hooey behind thirteen years ago, at around the same time he had fathered a son. Nowadays, Xavier Priestly was a man with his feet set firmly in the physical world. There were no signs from God.

Priest heard a familiar yelp and turned to see Tarquin spinning through the air, surfboard leash coiling like a whip.

"If you listen to Bettina's story," Baz said, "you might find that you want to be a part of her case."

Tarquin surfaced. Kicker pointed at him and laughed. Tarquin swore at Kicker. Kicker swore back. Tarquin waded ashore and shoved Kicker. Kicker shoved him back. Tarquin punched Kicker in the face, then looked confused when Kicker didn't fall down or retreat, and even more confused when Kicker, lip split and bleeding, yanked Tarquin off his feet and deeper into the surf. Tarquin punched Kicker again, but the tide was literally turning. Priest remembered stories of beavers pulling wolves into ponds and drowning them.

Who'd bet on the beaver against a wolf?

Kicker would, that's who.

"You might find that it's the most important thing you could do with your time and energy right now," Baz said. "Priest?"

Tarquin and Kicker grappled in chest-deep water. Tarquin's flailing efforts to slug Kicker began to look like *I'm drowning!* Kicker ducked under a wave, and a second later, Tarquin disappeared, dragged under the foam. Beaver was well on the way to defeating wolf. People up on the pier—gawkers, both tourist and local—stared into the water, wondering how many boys would resurface. Other surfers took notice and hooted. Alex the lifeguard appeared, craning his neck.

Kicker surfaced and spat blood. One arm remained submerged. With the other, he jiggled his teeth to see if any were loose. Only after that did he pull Tarquin to the surface by the collar of his wetsuit.

Tarquin coughed and retched. He'd had his ass handed to

him. Kicker shook him and spoke into his ear, then pushed Tarquin toward the shore. Gasping, Tarquin extended his middle finger to Kicker, and then to all those on the beach and pier who'd watched, turning three hundred sixty degrees to encompass the whole world, including his father, in a full fuck-the-universe circle.

"No can do, Baz," Priest said. "I recommend Cody Fiso."

"I do not know what to make of a world in which Xavier Priestly recommends Cody Fiso for anything, anywhere, at any time," Baz said. "Why him?"

"Fiso will help keep you out of the gray areas. Which sounds to me like the whole area."

"I'm pretty sure Baz meant 'Why no can do' for you," Dusty said. Following Priest's gaze, she looked out at Tarquin, on the beach, rejecting the whole goddamn universe.

"I gotta prioritize something else," Priest said. "I got a stupid treasure that needs finding."

ACKNOWLEDGMENTS

Thank you for reading this book—I know you have a lot of other things to do, so I don't take your time and energy for granted.

I count myself fortunate to live smack-dab in the thick of Venice, California, where I've seen a version of every character in this book drinking coffee at the Cow's End, sauntering along the boardwalk, practicing movie fights on the sand, fishing from the pier, surfing, busking, conspiring, cycling, paddle-balling, lifting, skating, declaiming, dancing, drumming—who's to say they don't do exactly what I imagine them doing when I'm not watching?

I thank my friends who encourage me to keep typing. I refuse to provide full names, because what we do together is unforgiveable: mostly drink coffee and mock perfectly decent people. Andrew, Christopher, Karyn, Josh 2.0, Karine, Michael, Peter, Dan, David, other Josh, Ryan, Roy, Steve, Chris, other David, Alyson, Alison, and Babs. Let's get together more often.

Many thanks to my first readers: Eve Attermann, Scot Morison, Stephen Nathan, Dave Thomas, and Rainn Wilson. (I'm afraid you will have to read the book again to see if I paid attention to you.)

Thank you, Jeanne Newman: lawyer, friend, therapist/angel/miracle-worker/spiritual adviser/ninja bodyguard/alchemist, and antianxiety faith healer.

Thanks to my bigshot LA TV agent at WME—Rick Rosen—who helps me carve out time and energy for writing books when it'd be better for him if I put those efforts into creating a long-running TV show.

Thanks to my book agent at WME, Eve Atterman. Eve's other clients are super cool, with amazing curb appeal, and I'm . . . me. Eve has to explain everything to me at least twice.

Tara Hahto talked to me about boxing.

Michael Green and Rainn Wilson talked to me about spirituality.

David Shore is my favorite edifying contrarian.

Thank you to my friend of many decades, Jack Hodgins: brilliant novelist, mentor, teacher, and role model.

Thank you to my editor, Jason Kirk. When I was in my midthirties, I got glasses, which meant that, for the first time, I was able to drive at night in the rain without risking my life and the lives of others. Working with Jason is like that.

Thank you, everybody at Blackstone Publishing: Rick Bleiweiss, Francie Crawford, Windy Goodloe (dibs on that name for a character), Tatiana Radujkovic, and Josie Woodbridge.

My family has been providing me with material my whole life, whether they like it or not. And no matter what their actual surnames are, I refer to them all as Hansons: the Castro Valley Hansons, the Vancouver Island Hansons, the Pacific Northwest Hansons, the Ontario Hansons, the Sonoma Valley Hansons, amongst others.

A special shout-out to my late father, Hartwick Paul Hanson, who died before this book was finished. When I told Dad the story, he said, "I like Vegas." I will miss that fun, funny, optimistic old man.

And then there's my nuclear family. Sons, Hartwick and Joe—to whom I dedicate this book—and daughter-in-law Mikaela (mother to Harvey and Otis and a much-needed mental health professional in the family).

And always and forever, thank you to Brigitte. Without Brigitte, nothing works, but, beyond the pragmatics, she remains my main source of joy even if she's always showing me ridiculous stretches or trying to get me to drink green muck.